CAVE DIVER

Jake Avila is a full-time writer with a BA in Writing and Information Technology. He has a background in freelance journalism writing on politics, culture, technology, and sport, and taught secondary English for ten years. In 2019, he won the Adventure Writer's Competition Clive Cussler Grandmaster Award for *Cave Diver* and then went on to win the Wilbur Smith Adventure Writing Prize for the same book in 2020.

CAVE DIVER

Jake Avila

ZAFFRE

First published in the UK in 2021 by
ZAFFRE
An imprint of Bonnier Books UK
4th Floor, Victoria House
Bloomsbury Square, London WC1B 4DA
Owned by Bonnier Books
Sveavägen 56, Stockholm, Sweden

A CIP catalogue record for this book is
available from the British Library.

ISBN: 978–1–83877–536–0

Also available as an ebook and in audio

1 3 5 7 9 10 8 6 4 2

Typeset by IDSUK (Data Connection) Ltd
Printed and bound in Great Britain by Clays Ltd, Elcograf S.p.A.

Zaffre is an imprint of Bonnier Books UK
www.bonnierbooks.co.uk

For my wife, Cathy.
For everything.

Prologue

Carving a long white furrow, the Australian patrol boat prowled her designated section of the great river: a thirty-mile stretch below Ambunti. Despite the oppressive glare and hammer-like heat, her bare-chested, sunburned lookouts were on full alert, scanning the dense, riverine forest lining the banks through powerful Zeiss binoculars. The war had ended six months ago, but there were still plenty of Japanese soldiers who preferred to rot in the jungle rather than face the shame of surrender. *Operation Housekeeping* was the reluctant Allied response. No one wanted to get killed rounding up fanatics but, as colonial overlords, the Australians had a responsibility to protect the locals from theft, murder or worse. Keeping our cannibals from being eaten, or so the joke went.

Just two days ago, the patrol boat had surprised a ragged band of Japanese crossing a shallow creek mouth. The skipper blasted the horn three times and, over the tannoy, ordered them to drop their weapons. The skeletal-looking men raised rusting rifles in a weak show of defiance and began screaming '*banzai.*' If they wanted to die, HMAS *Bowen* was happy to oblige. Her 20 mm Oerlikon cannons unleashed a withering burst that shook the boat to her keel. The heavy shells blew the screaming men into conveniently sized pieces for the ever-present crocs, who were enthusiastically cleaning up before the cordite smoke cleared.

The skipper, a twenty-five-year-old accountant from Melbourne, flinched as an engorged mosquito punctured the tanned skin of his forearm. It zipped away before he could swat it. The little bastard was probably teeming with malaria or dengue fever – one of the many hazards in this voracious country which would swallow you whole at the slightest opportunity and not even bother to belch. At least in the navy you only had to deal with it from the relative safety of a thirty-tonne patrol boat. Not like those poor sods in the infantry.

Suddenly, a lookout on the bow screamed, 'Hard aport . . . object dead ahead!'

Floating debris was a constant hazard on the Sepik. Mostly it was great clumps of vegetation uprooted from the riverbanks by floods, which could easily foul a prop. But, occasionally, it was a hardwood log washed down from the great forests of the mountainous interior. One of these could rip the boat open in an instant. The skipper flung the helm over without question.

Avoiding the object by half a length, the skipper slowed the boat. Something about it had caught his eye. About four yards long, grey in colour, it was too uniformly shaped to be anything but man-made. In a wide churn of coffee-coloured foam they came about alongside the object. The mate struggled to snag it with the gaff. Finally, he located a tear in the upper surface and hauled it to the gunwale.

Closer inspection revealed it to be a battered aluminium cylinder, tapered at one end. A thick coating of slime and finger-like tendrils of weed growing on the bottom suggested it had been in the river for some time. A long-range fuel tank?

2

Perhaps a parachute supply canister? A panel on the top was loose, hanging on by just one rivet.

'Better look inside, Smithy,' the skipper ordered. 'You never know, it might be full of grog!'

'Keep an eye on the bloody crocs then,' the sailor muttered under his breath. While his mates held on to his legs, he leaned out over the murky water and swung the panel out of the way. With a gasp, he reeled back as a wave of hot, putrid air punched him in the face. 'Stone me sideways, that bloody reeks!'

The cylinder had become a casket for a human body. Baked under the tropical sun, the skin of the corpse was a dark mummified parchment stretched tightly over protruding bones. Big white teeth grinned malevolently. Only the blond hair told them that he had been white.

'Thinking of inviting him on board?' some wag commented.

The crew laughed uneasily. A European corpse had rights, even in this godforsaken place. But they were a day from Wewak, and in this heat the boat would stink for a month.

'Bring him around to the stern,' said the skipper. 'See if you can find some identification.'

He held the boat steady in the current, as the men manoeuvred the cylinder around to the transom step.

The luckless Smithy tried not to breathe, as he gingerly searched the tattered remains for dog tags.

'Skip, you'd better take a look at this.'

The skipper stared in wonder at the silver objects. One was an Iron Cross with 'M. H. 1941' engraved on the back. The other was the unmistakable grinning death's head badge of the Waffen SS. It didn't make sense: German forces hadn't been

3

seen in Papua New Guinea since 1914, when Australian troops invaded the Kaiser's colony at the outbreak of World War I.

The skipper sought the bosun's advice. At thirty-one, he was the oldest man on board, and the only one who had encountered German troops while serving in the Mediterranean. The thickset man scrutinised the items intensely. Turning the medal over, he gave a low whistle.

'It's not an Iron Cross, Skip, it's a silver Knight's Cross with oak leaf cluster. They didn't hand out too many of these.'

An extensive and unpleasant search revealed nothing else about M. H. There were no weapons, dog tags or a wallet, just a pair of huge size fifteen jackboots complete with femur and foot bones. Someone suggested the cylinder was a float from a seaplane. It seemed plausible; there were Japanese characters on one of the panels.

'Skip,' whined Smithy, 'for the love of God, can we let him go now?'

The sun beat down as the skipper weighed his options. Whoever this SS hotshot was, he was long dead, just like his boss back in the rubble of Berlin. As for what he'd been doing in this hellhole, the evidence suggested he had been an adviser to the Japs and, sure as shit, he didn't deserve a funeral. The skipper nodded to himself. Yep, he'd hand the medals over to the adjutant in Wewak, along with his report. Let the navy figure out what, if anything, should be done. Meanwhile, his boys needed clear air and the cold ale awaiting them back at base.

'Let him go, Smithy. Let the river have him.'

Chapter 1

Cowaramup Bombie, Margaret River,
Western Australia, present day

Whipped by howling gales across the lonely wastes of the inter-continental fetch, the massive winter swell bore down on the rugged coast still hidden in the darkness. A crimson band in the eastern sky heralded dawn, soon to crest the hills overlooking Gracetown where street lights twinkled insignificantly. Come daybreak, a handful of international big wave surfers and film crews would ride out from its protected bay on jet skis to greet these monstrous waves as they struck a submerged platform of limestone the size of an aircraft carrier. But for now, there was just one figure in the gloom.

Powering through the water on his custom big wave, stand-up paddleboard, Rob Nash maintained the robotic cadence that had propelled him from his home in Margaret River, twenty kilometres to the south. Long of limb and 1.93 metres tall, Nash was a formidable physical specimen, with years of surfing, swimming and sailing hard-wired into his DNA. A renowned waterman in the Western Australian aquatic fraternity, his cave-diving exploits had propelled him into wider public consciousness, yet the last two years had hardened him in such a way that even those who knew him best had to look twice. A diet of obsessive, big wave surfing and open sea paddling had excised every gram of fat from his frame. His once open, boyishly handsome face was now a gaunt mask. Tendons stood out on his muscled arms like steel cords, and the clinical resolve which had underpinned his success in the life-or-death stakes of cave diving had devolved into the psychological equivalent of a white-knuckle joyride. Deep down, Rob Nash was looking for the release of death, but the sea had stubbornly refused to give it to him.

He scanned the Cow break with intense green eyes, hungry for the narcotic release of extreme danger. Three hundred metres ahead, a huge set was building. Suddenly, the leading waves broke through into an oblique shaft of sunlight. On their towering crests, the spindrift blown back in streaming arcs by the offshore wind looked like a high-altitude blizzard, wreaking havoc on a distant mountain range.

Taking up station in the deep channel beside the break, Nash calculated the period – the time taken for each wave crest to traverse a given point. As each breaking wave detonated, it sent shock waves through the air, followed by the pungent odour of kelpy brine, as trillions of airborne water droplets fell in a cold mist. Its chill cleared his mind. By jettisoning the debris, everything was reduced to cause and effect, now and forever, in this moment . . .

Nash flexed his powerful shoulders, digging the blade of his paddle into the water, bracing himself on bent knees to transfer force to momentum, as the next set began to form. Entering the break zone, he calibrated his run for the last and most ominous-looking wave. Knowledge, experience and instinct guided him, as he turned and built up the speed of the SUP to match that of the gigantic black wall towering above him.

The wave was reaching amplitude – critical mass. Now, timing was everything. Too slow, and he risked a late take-off with a sickening drop, perhaps getting caught by the crest and sucked over the falls. Too fast, and he would lose precious velocity gained by a steeper angle of descent and be run down by a fifteen-metre-high wall of white water. Either would lead to a horrifying hold-down and the certain loss of his board in shark-infested waters. The stakes were high . . . way too high. But for Nash, losing himself in the moment meant exactly this.

Some part of him began to hum, as the irresistible energy of the wave took command. A cavernous stomach-churning lurch marked the point of no return. The SUP hung in the air at the very crest, and then, like an elevator cable snapping, plunged down the near-vertical face. Feet splayed like a boxer, Nash braced against the wind buffeting under the nose, angling his body to offset the forces trying to bury him in the trough three storeys below. With a vicious thud, the bottom of the SUP reconnected. Nash transferred his weight to his back leg to dig in his rail for a bottom turn. Simultaneously, he leaned back hard on the paddle, using it as an extended rudder to carve purchase in the face towering above him. Finessing the torque through heightened nerve endings, he made the turn as sharply as he dared. Water contrails hissed off the embedded rail. In a heady rush of elation, he flattened out his trim.

Now, it was about using his wiles to outrun a wave with forces approaching six tonnes per square metre. Off his right shoulder, he could feel the maw of the beast, gnashing its foamy jaws as he skipped along at more than forty kilometres an hour. Like a sardine surfing the bow wave of a blue whale, he was insignificant. And in that moment of total commitment and connection, the man known as Rob Nash and all his worldly problems ceased to exist.

He surfed three more giants before the first jet-ski team arrived. As he cut across its bow, its stunned driver and tow surfer stared at him in disbelief.

A SUP all the way out here? Man, this guy is fucking insane!

Nash made it back to the Margaret River mouth by 10.30, caught a long blue peeler into the river, and fifteen minutes later was paddling up to his home on the riverbank.

Once a 1960s brick box, his architect brother-in-law's design had extended it to maximise the river views, best enjoyed from a large, cantilevered deck, which sat among a canopy of mature peppermint gum trees. He hadn't spoken to Jonathan in months – not since the edition of *The World Tonight* which had hastened Nash's descent into the abyss.

After sluicing himself and the board under the outdoor shower, Nash made his way up the boat ramp to the expansive basement under the house.

Here, the concrete floor was thick with dead gum leaves, blown in on the prevailing westerlies. They crunched underfoot as Nash replaced the SUP on its rack. Threading his way through the rows of underwater equipment – tanks, scooters, sleds, light arrays and a portable decompression chamber – he was all too conscious that this gear gathering dust, once so integral to his identity, now made him feel like a fraud. Despite all the emblazoned sponsors' logos, it had the aura of a self-indulgent hobby, long forgotten. He wasn't yet at the point of being able to make a decision on selling it. He wasn't at the point of being able to decide on anything.

At the top of the stairs, he paused before opening the living room door. It was his practice to inhale deeply here and, for a brief moment, open an olfactory portal to the past. But Natalie's smell had faded. Recently he'd moved most of her things to the spare bedroom. He wasn't trying to forget, far from it. But every knick-knack, every book, every article of clothing generated myriad associations, and the memories kept flooding in and drowning him. One day he would work out what to keep.

In the kitchen, he threw oats, salt, raisins and water into a saucepan and flicked on the gas. After nine hours on the board, Nash was both dehydrated and ravenous, and he downed a litre of water and three bananas while he stirred. He was spooning the steaming porridge into a bowl when there was an all too familiar brusque triple knock on the front door.

'Unbelievable,' he muttered. Wasn't she supposed to be coming tomorrow?

Padding across the jarrah floorboards, Nash went to let his sister in.

Only it wasn't Jacquie on the doorstep.

Nash's eyes widened in alarm as a heavily made-up woman thrust a long black microphone at him. Behind her were a burly cameraman and another man in a black T-shirt. It was not the local news mob, but a city outfit.

'Rob Nash? Tracey Burnshore from *Tonight*. Can you explain to our viewers why you left your wife to die?'

Nash couldn't slam the door because she was already half inside. Over her shoulder, the eye of the camera bored accusingly into him.

'Get out of the way,' he told her. 'I'm closing the door.'

'Why won't you answer our questions, Rob? People want to know your side of the story.'

'I said, get out.'

'Rob, was it really an accident?'

Nash leaned his weight against the door until she was forced back onto the veranda and had to retract the microphone for fear of having it cut in half. He crouched down on his haunches as she began authoritatively pounding on the door.

'What about Natalie's family? Don't you think they deserve some answers?'

It was the third such ambush in as many months. Ever since *The World Tonight* had gone to air, the tabloid press had been stalking him. He'd hoped the inquest, which had exonerated him from legal culpability, would have put an end to it. No chance. There was nothing more newsworthy than a high-profile fall from grace, and in a small-population state like Western Australia, they were determined to milk it for all it was worth.

Burning with shame, he listened through the door as they wound up the segment.

'Natalie Nash . . . drowned in suspicious circumstances . . . suggestions of foul play for financial gain . . . problems in the marriage.'

The reporter reeled off the collapse of their sponsorship deals and reiterated a breathless call for justice – at the very least, a civil case. Finally, they packed up, got back in their van and drove off. Nash realised he was shaking.

A few moments later, another vehicle pulled up. Heart pounding, he peered out through a crack in the blinds. This time it was Jacquie, and he opened the door before she got to it.

'You look bloody terrible,' she said. 'Were you out there all night again?' Scrutinising him with eyes uncannily like his own, she took his hand and saw how badly it was shaking. 'Oh God, don't tell me. That van – was it the press again?'

He pulled her inside and quickly shut the door.

'Oh, Rob, the bastards.' She hugged him tightly for a long moment. Then she looked around the room. 'Christ, what a mess! I hope you didn't let them see this?'

He managed a smile. Classic Jac, one minute picking you up off the floor, the next kicking your ass. His little sister was irrepressible, a twenty-nine-year-old live wire who ran a highly successful boutique travel company. From deserted islands in Indonesia to shady hotels in Marrakesh, she had carved out an original niche in a crowded online market.

She smiled back at Nash with perfect white teeth. Sassy and vivacious, Jac was an attractive woman with no shortage of admirers, but she had never been able to put up with a man for long, the standard complaint being that they slowed her down. Her self-confessed major weakness was idolising her big brother. And Nash's apparent indifference to the demise of his illustrious career was driving her crazy. She'd been bombarding him with books and DVDs on post-traumatic stress syndrome, trying to tee up shrinks, offering him work as a travel guide for her air safaris . . . anything to get him up and firing again.

11

Today, he was relieved to see she was carrying nothing but her handbag.

Jacquie began picking up his discarded clothes and throwing them in a pile.

'For God's sake, Rob –' she scrunched up her button nose – 'this towel stinks. When did you last do the washing?'

'I don't know,' he told her truthfully.

She looked at him closely. 'Have you seen the front of the house recently?'

Before he could stop her, she'd pulled open the blinds.

'Don't –' he began.

'Fuck them,' she snapped. 'You've done nothing wrong. Stop behaving like a criminal.'

'Jac . . .'

'Look,' she told him. 'The grass is waist-high. It's a firebomb waiting to go off. You want the council over, too?'

'I've got to eat,' he said, shutting the blinds again. 'Do you want a cup of tea? There might be some milk.'

As he wolfed down the porridge, Jacquie expended more of her pent-up energy loading the dishwasher. Then, she made them both a cup of strong tea and sat down opposite him.

'I know you never want to talk, Rob. But don't you think you should? How long can you go on like this?'

He took another spoonful.

'OK, so I'll talk. Did you ring the bank? What's happening with the mortgage?'

Jacquie followed his gaze to the letter stand by the phone. It was overflowing with unopened letters, many of which bore the Bankwest logo. Her voice trailed off in frustration.

Nash tried to say something and gave up. Since Natalie's death, he had become increasingly inarticulate, as if the synapses that enabled conversation had been cauterised or withered away.

The clock on the kitchen wall was ticking off the seconds in an interminably slow motion. A great lethargy came over him. The ocean paddle had done its job. All he wanted now was to crash and forget. Why hadn't Jacquie just come tomorrow as arranged? Inadvertently, he let out a loud yawn.

It was if he'd slapped her. Jacquie's tanned cheeks flushed white.

'You think it's easy coming over here, knowing you can't stand the sight of me? Wondering every day if you've managed to let the ocean kill you? Well, it bloody well isn't!' She was so angry she was shaking.

'Jac . . .' He was hopelessly inadequate in the face of her emotion.

'Have you thought about how Mum and Dad will feel when you vanish?' she interrupted him.

'Look, I appreciate that you're worried about me –'

'Worried?' she exploded. 'Rob, we're fucking *terrified* for you! It's been a year now and as far as I can tell you've shut everyone out – friends, family, work . . . the whole bloody world. You haven't been on an expedition since the accident. Hell, you haven't been outside of Margaret River in six months!'

'Look,' he said firmly, 'I am just trying to figure things out.'

Jacquie gave a shrill laugh. 'And how long is that going to take? Face facts, you're *broke*, Rob. The bank's about to take everything and you're just sitting here in a pile of smelly laundry. For God's sake, brother!' Her eyes flashed with contempt. 'You used to follow your dreams and make them happen. Now you're a shadow. A zombie. I can't stand watching it anymore. It's like both of you died in that cave.'

Her words thumped home like the well-aimed jabs they were. And because it was unbearable, he found himself lashing out blindly.

'Why won't you say her name, Jac?'

Her stare was incredulous. 'You mean, Natalie?'

'Yes,' he snapped. 'Natalie. *My wife.* The woman that everyone in this family seems so bloody keen to forget. Well, I can't. And I won't.'

Jacquie's eyes widened. 'Rob, I loved Nat like my own sister . . . Mum and Dad loved her, too.' She reached out and gripped his hands. 'You know that. What's going on?'

Self-pity threatened to erupt out of him, and Nash fought hard to smother it.

'Jac, I know you want me back the way I was,' he said unsteadily. 'But I'm not that person anymore. Can you understand that?'

She bit her lip. 'Of course, I understand. And we've been waiting for you to heal in your own way, but it's not happening. You're stuck, and we can't just stand by and watch you fade away.'

'It's gone too far,' he admitted. 'But you have to let me live my own life. OK? Hey, come on, please don't cry, Jac.'

Jacquie was an intense soul, but the raw pain of her sobs as they hugged was unusual.

'Is something wrong, Jac?'

'I'm worried for you. For Mum and Dad. I don't know how it's all going to work out.'

'What do you mean?'

Nash pulled back to stare at her thoughtfully. He knew her business empire was at that fragile point of equilibrium, where it would either soar or crash. And then there were his parents. He knew they'd invested heavily in the project, and they weren't getting any younger.

'Nothing. It's nothing.' She managed a smile. 'I just love you so much. Please get some help and sort things out. If not for yourself, then do it for me. *Please*.'

He let her out of the front door and watched her stride determinedly up the path. Then she stopped and turned around with a laugh.

'I just remembered why I came over. Uncle Frank is trying to get on to you.'

'Uncle' Frank Douglas was an old navy comrade of their father's they'd known since childhood. Something of a rough diamond, he'd lived most of his adult life in Papua New Guinea, flying choppers. Nash had got him a contract five years ago on a major expedition in PNG with the Global Geographic channel, and they had worked on several projects until Natalie's death.

'What does he want?' Nash was fond of the old roustabout, but he wasn't in the mood to talk to anyone.

Jacquie rolled her eyes. 'If you won't answer the phone, then at least check your messages. He's driving me nuts. Wants to talk to you about some cave. It's all in an email.'

After watching Jacquie drive away, Nash went back inside and made himself a strong black coffee. Then he divided up the mail into three big piles and forced himself to look through it. Most of it was bills, final demands for electricity, gas, rates . . . some of them were dated six months before. With a guilty start, he realised they must have been paid by Jacquie or his parents. Then there were the letters from old friends, trying not to sound hurt at being cut off and offering support. There was plenty of hate mail, too. The most succinct simply read: 'Fucking coward, hope you burn in Hell for what you did to that girl'. Finally, he got to the bank statements. The facts were stark. His credit cards had just been cancelled with total debts of 25,000 dollars. His 300,000 dollar mortgage was five months in arrears. The most recent letter from the bank was threatening foreclosure if he didn't immediately make arrangements.

It was one hell of a comedown. For the last decade, Nash had shot documentaries with several cable channels and published three books. Until the accident, it had all been on an upward trajectory, and he'd been poised to rake in serious money. But, with his name trashed, the projects and the dollars had all dried up.

With a hollow feeling in his chest, he considered his options. He could sell the house, clear his debts, and walk out with a couple of hundred K in his pocket. But that felt cheap, like losing Natalie and his life all over again, so the question remained: what was he going to do?

Remembering Uncle Frank's email, he plugged in the laptop. His screen saver was a shot of Natalie, taken on their wedding day after the guests had gone home. She was sitting on the deck, slightly tipsy, one tanned leg up, arms around her knee, just looking at him. The nakedness of her joy had always confronted him, even when she was alive. Some part of him couldn't quite believe that he could have had that effect on someone.

The enormity of her loss threatened to derail him, and he opened the mail browser to escape her gaze. There were hundreds of emails. He found Douglas's and opened it.

SUBJECT: *You won't believe this!*

Rob,

Mate, do you <u>ever</u> check your phone? A TV outfit wants to shoot a major doco in a cave you're <u>very</u> familiar with. Still hush-hush, but they've got the funding, chopper, boat, but they need a pro to lead the penetration! Your gear, your call, all expenses paid and a healthy fee to be negotiated!

Could be just what you need.
Get in touch ASAP!

Frank

Nash was struck by a word that Natalie sometimes used: kismet. Surely Douglas had to be talking about the Kaiserin Grotto?

Opening Google Earth, Nash clicked on the red place-mark pinpointing its location in the foothills of the Star Mountains, Papua New Guinea. Five years ago, he had mapped over three kilometres of submerged caves down to depths of 185 metres, before diminishing funds halted proceedings. He recalled soaring on his underwater scooter through a lost gallery of

17

hauntingly beautiful calcite columns, towering like organ pipes in some vast cathedral. A product of ten metres of annual rainfall, the underground river ran on and on . . .

Nash sat back in his chair. Expeditions like this easily ran into the millions and took years to set up. By any measure, this was an incredible opportunity.

A familiar spark of energy flickered within him. The sensation was a precursor to that irresistible moment when the compulsion to seek and discover burst into a bright and implacable flame. A flame which could only be quenched by nothing less than all-out commitment to the pursuit and realisation of the goal.

Abruptly the spark sputtered and went out. Confused, Nash found himself staring blankly at the screen.

Chapter 2

Leaving her lover sprawled in bed like a fallen colossus, Sura Suyanto wrapped herself in a silk sarong and padded across the mahogany floorboards to her 350-year-old Javan desk. Taking a seat, she opened the well-thumbed dossier. Although she had practised her pitch for weeks and committed to memory every detail of her momentous two-year quest, even a shuddering orgasm had not helped her sleep. It was hardly surprising. The man she was going to see was a dangerous and unpredictable foe, the second most powerful man in Indonesia. He was also her father and would spot any inconsistency in the story she was about to tell, so once again she prepared to tell it the best way she could.

Methodically, she ran through the maps, ledgers and historical documents, cross-referencing facts with scripted and memorised anecdotes, using skills she had picked up at Cambridge University and refined through ten years of top-flight investigative journalism. Only when the flowerpecker birds in the moon orchid grove outside her window trilled the coming of dawn, did she reach for the rosewood presentation box with her father's carved initials embossed in pure gold.

Its contents had cost her a quarter of a million US dollars, and one awful night in Sydney with an obese collector of militaria.

But this was a fraction of its potential value and well worth the sacrifice. Opening the box, Sura felt the same tingle of anticipation all over again. Dazzling against black velvet padding, the grinning death's head badge and Knight's Cross in pure silver gleamed as brightly as the day they'd been minted in 1941.

'My lucky charms,' she murmured, unnecessarily repolishing their faces with a fold of silken fabric. 'Bring me good fortune, won't you?'

There was a murmur from the bed, and Sura quietly closed the lid. Best to let Jaap sleep. When she needed to be focused and calm, he tended to provoke the exact opposite.

Inside the cavernous wet room, enormous jade tiles ran floor to ceiling, gold-plated tapware gleamed, and a bespoke porcelain bath emerged like a white lotus flower from the floor. Conspicuous consumption was intrinsic to the Suyanto dynasty. No matter how humble the object, it must dazzle and amaze. Not that this bothered Sura. The problem was it all belonged to him.

She punched in the shower code for her preferred temperature and flow and began washing in fine sandalwood soap. Her mother's genetics – another astute purchase by her father – had blessed her with long legs, a waist Jaap could easily span with his hands, and full, pear-shaped breasts. Keeping that body looking fantastic was part of her job, and she ran thirty-five kilometres a week on top of doing free weights and Pilates. Sura Suyanto was twenty-eight, but she looked eighteen. Her symmetrical features and plump Cupid lips made her popular with her fifty-five-million-strong Indostar News audience, and something about her huge, widely spaced brown eyes created an impression of naivety, which inspired men to fancy they could realise their will in them.

How very wrong they were.

Jaap was sitting up in bed when she returned. The gigantic Afrikaner could have been carved from a block of white marble. A chiselled study in muscle, everything about him was over-sized, except his intellect.

He asked how she was feeling while staring hungrily at her crotch.

'I'm a little nervous.' She slipped in to a demure grey *kebaya*, the kind her father approved of her wearing when she wasn't on camera. 'He can be unpredictable.'

'Ah, once he sees what you've brought him, he'll be putty in your hands.'

Jaap had never met her father, and if she had anything to do with it, he never would. Sura was dabbing perfume behind her ears when he grabbed her from behind. He was more than twice her weight, and his biceps were bigger than her thighs.

'I want you,' he said fiercely, his short beard tickling her neck. As her feet left the floor, she could feel him pressed against her back like an iron bar. 'How about a quickie for good luck?'

'Idiot, put me down!' The hurt in his china-blue eyes reminded her of how immature he could be. 'Wait for me here, and whatever you do, do *not* go outside. Do you hear me?'

'Ja.' He frowned. 'I heard you the first time.'

Outside on the driveway, her father's chief of security, Angka, waited impassive as a toad in a luxury Mercedes AMG. The driver was a soldier in civilian clothes. Behind them, another black Mercedes contained a heavily armed detachment of

21

bodyguards. The drive took a few minutes. The general owned significant chunks of Kebayoran Baru and Menteng and preferred to keep his children close by. Tommy, his only son, lived in the biggest house next door, while Sura and her two older sisters, now both married, lived further along the road.

They drove beside an imposing white wall for a kilometre before arriving at a fortified gatehouse. Sura straightened her shoulders as the sentry approached the car. Dealings with her father were never easy.

Steel security gates silently swung open, and the AMG purred up a long driveway through extensive manicured gardens. With dawn painting the sky, scores of shabbily dressed men were already out pruning, sweeping and hosing. The driver negotiated an elaborate turning circle with a leaping bronze tiger fountain at its centre, and pulled up beside a flight of white marble steps that swept up to the house – if you could call it that, for Wijaya Suyanto's residence was the third biggest in Indonesia, and its three storeys and 2000 square metres of decadent baroque opulence were testament to her father's pervasive influence over four decades of corruption.

Angka stiffly held the car door open for Sura. Ignoring him, she got out of the car and made her way up the stairs to the vestibule where the skins of sixteen Balinese tigers carpeted the floor. Their heads mounted on the walls seemed to gape in surprise that extinction was the price of such excess. Reaching the inner courtyard, with its genuine Florentine marble fountains, she turned left and made her way to the inner sanctum, a soundproof room her father rarely left, and her mother was not permitted to enter. Sometimes, Sura wondered how the great man had ever found the time to breed.

As usual, he was working. The office was dominated by a huge photograph of her father standing arm in arm with the former president, Suharto, founder of the Golkar party, the leadership of which he aspired. As ever, her father was immaculate: jet-black hair combed to perfection across his box-like head, crisp tan uniform replete with campaign and medal ribbons, and a large solid gold badge that proclaimed his name to the world. *Wijaya* meant 'victorious', and her father had made it his life's business to live up to it.

'Ah, there you are,' he said. 'What was so important that I had to reschedule my briefing?'

Feeling light-headed, Sura stepped up to his massive desk.

'Father, I have something for you.'

When she passed him the display box, she realised her hands were shaking. The general ran his finger over his golden initials and raised a shrewd eyebrow.

'It's not even my birthday, Sura. What *are* you up to?'

'Please just open it, Father.'

She held her breath as he beheld what lay inside.

'Oh, these are absolutely splendid,' he said. 'Genuine first-rate examples. A Knight's Cross and *Totenkopf* insignia in silver? This must have cost you a fortune.'

'Look at the reverse, Father. The initials.'

A rare moment of surprise transformed his usually blank features.

'M. H!' he exclaimed. 'No, I don't believe it!'

23

Jumping to his feet, he went to the glass cabinet housing the most precious items of his extensive militaria collection: a *Pour le Mérite* awarded to an ace in Richthofen's circus; a Victoria Cross from the horrors of the Somme. His most valuable item was a cutlass owned by Lord Nelson, valued at over half a million dollars. Sometimes, Sura thought her father's obsession was driven by a compulsive need to vicariously possess the bravery of men. Despite his own medals and awards, the Bintang Sakti, Indonesia's highest military award for valour, had eluded him in his fighting years.

'Here we are.'

He reached in and retrieved an evil-looking dagger with a bulbous black handle. By far the most battered item in his collection, it was indisputably his favourite, for he had sourced it himself as a young lieutenant, when policing the border of Indonesia's brand-new colonial possession. How a wizened old Papuan came to be walking around the jungle with an SS dagger in 1971 had been a family talking point ever since.

'M. H.' Her father read aloud the familiar initials on the oiled blade. He looked at her with a sparkle in his brown eyes. 'Well, well. Have you solved the mystery, my clever girl?'

Her heart skipped a pathetic beat. All her life she had thirsted for his approval as dry earth does rain. Suddenly she felt like a giddy schoolgirl.

Having set the lure, she needed to keep these rare and unruly emotions in check, if she were to reel him in. If years of negotiating General Wijaya Suyanto's affections had taught her anything, it was that they were transient and insubstantial. She

24

must never let herself forget that he was as hard as Javan teak, deadlier than a pit viper.

'It was a hunch, Father. Do you recall that find of Nazi weaponry in the upper Sepik last year?'

'Of course. It was in all the papers.'

She explained how it had inspired her to search thousands of American and Australian military records, looking for a link to the dagger – and, hopefully, an explanation.

'Sura, I checked already.'

'Yes, Father, but you were looking at the war years, 1939 to 1945.'

She recounted finding the report on a deceased SS officer, filed by an Australian patrol boat in 1946; how the trail had led her to a clerk who had pocketed the artefacts and taken them back to Australia, where they stayed in a drawer for years, until he died. From here, they were sold by his son to a wealthy militaria collector, who had only reluctantly surrendered them to her for an astronomical sum.

Her father's canny eyes glowed. 'And you went to all this trouble for *me*?'

She held his gaze. 'I did it to make you happy. But in the process I have discovered something so incredible, and so valuable, that I could not share it with anyone but you.'

From her bag she placed a dossier on the desk and extracted a grainy photo.

'This is the *I-403*, a 120-metre-long Japanese *Sentoku* submarine, which left Kure Naval Base more than seventy years ago for the Nazi port of Lorient. It was carrying a large consignment of gold and raw opium, payment for German uranium oxide which was to be its return cargo. With it the Japanese planned to construct a so-called dirty bomb.'

Her father studied the picture. 'I recall they found the wreck in the Atlantic some years ago, but at two miles down were unable to salvage her.'

'That was actually the *I-52*, a cargo submarine.' Sura said this delicately, as her father hated being contradicted. 'As defeat loomed, the desperate Japanese launched several of these *Yanagi*, or trade missions, using every submarine type capable of the range. Only one ever made it. The rest were presumed sunk.'

'But what's this got to do with M. H?'

She pressed on quickly. 'The *I-403* sailed on the twentieth of April 1945. Two weeks later, her mission ended because Hitler killed himself. But she never returned to port, nor was she reported sunk.' Spreading out a map of the South China Sea, Sura pointed to an island on the southern tip of the Philippines. 'A US coast watcher on Jolo Island spotted her on the surface, early morning on the fifth of May, bearing south-east.'

'*Away* from Japan?'

'It's the last confirmed sighting.'

Her father raised his eyebrows. 'Doesn't sound very Japanese. They would have fought to the last man, woman and child, had Hirohito not conceded after Nagasaki.'

'You are right, Father. But it wasn't only Japanese personnel on board. The gold was escorted by a detachment of elite Nazi troops, none other than the Leibstandarte SS Adolf Hitler, stationed at the German Embassy in Tokyo.' She placed a black and white photograph on the desk. 'And this was their commander, SS Standartenführer *Martin Heider*.'

Her father hissed between his teeth. 'M. H.'

Heider was classically handsome, his face dominated by a straight blade of a nose, a powerful square jaw, and well-defined lips. He might have been attractive, but for his eyes, which were frighteningly devoid of emotion.

'You've found him, Sura!' The general's quick eyes latched on to hers, then widened. 'You think *he* stole the gold?'

She nodded eagerly. 'With a king's ransom there for the taking, why would Heider and his men willingly surrender, only to be executed for war crimes?' She placed her finger on the map and began tracing a line. 'Assuming they commandeered the submarine, they would have headed east to dodge the US invasion fleet. Across the Celebes Sea, past Halmahera Island, along the northern coastline of New Guinea . . . looking for somewhere to hide.' She tapped her finger on the mouth of the Sepik River. 'Somewhere no one would ever think of looking for them.'

'And you think they took it all the way upriver to Papua?' He looked doubtful. 'You said the submarine was 120 metres long.'

'Where else could you hide something that big? This report states the body of Martin Heider was found in a seaplane float. And a *Sentoku* submarine carried three in a waterproof hangar!'

He nodded slowly, wanting, yet not quite able, to believe. 'But surely after all these years it would have been found?'

'You know what that country is like upriver, Father. You could hide twenty submarines up there and no one would ever know.'

She saw distaste in the set of his mouth. General Suyanto had loathed his years in Papua – the jungle, the insects and, most of all, the people, who were primitive savages.

'The Sepik is vast,' he agreed. 'Do you have a specific location in mind, my darling?'

Sura spread out the topographical map upon which she had marked known German weapons finds, including the village where Wijaya had traded the old man for the dagger. Taking a pencil, she drew a circle around each of the four crosses.

'These locations are less than seventy kilometres apart. Notice how every valley or tributary stems from the Hoosenbeck Gorge? Like branches from the same tree, the survivors fanned out looking for escape routes.'

'My God, Sura, I think you're right.'

'Of greater interest is the Ford Mission.' She pointed to its location. 'Construction began in the late 1940s, and unlike similar organisations it is self-funded and has sister hospitals across the world. When I researched the founders, I discovered nothing. They seem to have no past, no explanation for their incredible resources.'

General Suyanto looked thoughtfully at the gleaming Knight's Cross in his hand, then back to her.

'An incredible story, Sura. But if you are right . . . How much gold was the submarine carrying?'

'Four metric tonnes, Father.'

There was a loaded silence. General Wijaya Suyanto was one of Indonesia's richest men, a billionaire, but the idea of 280 million US dollars' worth of unclaimed gold and opium just sitting there for the taking was having the tantalising effect she had anticipated. To her surprise, he suddenly embraced her tightly.

'You are *truly* my daughter. You have steel in you . . . like me.'

28

When he pulled away, eyes bright with emotion, she guessed it was as much grief for her brother, who would never amount to much, as it was pride in her achievement.

Seizing the moment, she launched into her case for leading the recovery.

'We can do it under the guise of a documentary film. The Hoosenbeck Cave is world renowned and largely unexplored – no one would suspect a thing! Let me be a part of this, Father, let me see it through, you know I have experience in the field. Please, I beg you.'

His face went blank, and she knew she had crossed a line. Picking up the dossier, he deftly tucked it under his arm.

'This will need careful handling. That region of Papua is controlled by Kopassus special forces who will do anything to jeopardise my career. I need to gather intelligence, starting with the Ford Mission. It is quite likely that the answers we seek are there.'

Sura nodded slowly. *We.* It wasn't much – a tiny shred. But it was still an opening all the same.

Chapter 3

Using the distinctive forked peak of Mount Mosapua as a marker, Doctor Paul Ford smoothly banked the twin-engine Beechcraft King to line up on a swathe of mown grass on the plateau below. It had been a good flight from Jayapura, without the usual roller coaster turbulence, first dropping off a heavily pregnant mother with complications, then picking up surgical supplies and a few staples like his favourite Macallan Scotch. Nothing beat an icy tumbler after a long day in clinic.

Looking down on the cluster of buildings surrounding the long white roof of the hospital, the mission appeared as an island in a sea of endless green. In a very real sense, it was. To the east lay the Papua New Guinea border and the stultifying heat and swamps of the Sepik flood plain, while to the north and west, impenetrable jungle stretched for hundreds of square kilometres. To the south, lowland rainforest ran for some fifty kilometres, before colliding with the stone feet of the Jayawijaya Mountains. The snow-capped 4000-metre peaks loomed above the horizon like some vast *trompe l'œil*. In these humid tropics, it was a dramatic juxtaposition he never stopped marvelling at. There were no roads or railways. The closest river was ten kilometres away. The only direct route to the mission was by air.

Paul Ford revelled in the extreme remoteness. The mission hospital was a sanctuary from the madness of the chaotic world outside. Serving the needs of the local people – delivering their babies, stitching their wounds and splinting their bones – had been his father's vision of atonement, and it had become his, too. But it was more than that. The vocation nourished his sense of self-worth, sustained him spiritually and intellectually. It had helped him bear the loss of his wife to cancer twenty years before, and the fact they had had no children.

Dropping to 200 metres, Ford looked for the usual gaggle of kids winding their way home from school, but the paths to the village were empty. Nor was there any sign of Jackson, who was in the midst of harvesting the coffee rows alongside the runway. The sight of an unfamiliar, small olive-green plane parked next to the hangar made Ford pause. They were not expecting visitors. Then the obvious explanation struck in a rush of elation: Mia had returned early!

Dr Mia Carter was the child he'd never had. The talented young American had come for a vocational year and stayed for two, winning the community over with her dedication and generosity of spirit. She'd brought new methods, professional stimulation and friendship, and when she'd returned to the States three years ago, it had damn near broken his heart. But after the wilds of Papua, she had found Connecticut tame, and was now set to return on a five-year contract with a view to a permanent position.

Trying to contain his excitement, Ford corrected a mild yaw, and lightly dropped the King's three tonnes to kiss the close-cropped kikuyu turf. Whistling cheerfully, he taxied up to the hangar door and switched off. Normally, Avis would guide him inside with a set of battered wheel chocks and a gap-toothed smile. No doubt the cheerful young mechanic was up at the house, celebrating.

Extending the King's retractable stairs, Ford was in such a hurry he almost forgot his precious Macallan. Just this week he had been putting together a transition timetable for Mia to take over the running of the hospital, and to learn how to fly. Of course, she would have doubts, but she was more than capable. Ford clattered his way down the bouncy steps and almost tripped.

Calm down, you old fool, he told himself, *and for God's sake whatever you do, don't overwhelm the poor girl.*

It was really quite selfish, the way he was mapping out her future. As well as wanting the mission to be in safe hands, Ford's secret hope was to grow old in Mia Carter's company.

A loud electrical sound coming from inside the hangar made him pause. Was it that faulty generator again? Ford went in through the side door. For a moment he stared in incomprehension at the buzzing frenzy of flies. Then he realised the seething black form was a human body in a pool of blood.

Dear God, Avis!

The Macallan shattered on the concrete. Dropping down beside the spread-eagled young man, Ford waved away the flies. Even as he felt for a pulse, he knew it was pointless. A large-calibre bullet had punched a hole the size of a fist through the back of Avis's blue overalls. The poor boy had been dead for at least an hour.

Violence was a way of life in Papua. From inter-tribal squabbles over pigs and territory, to accusations of witchcraft or adultery, people tended to take the law into their own hands. But the mission had always been a safe zone where rival villages refrained from conflict. Over the years they had quietly patched up members of the OPM – the Free Papua Movement – and treated Indonesian soldiers for snakebites, gunshots and malaria, when rapid evacuation to Jayapura was not an option.

So, who had done this?

The olive-green plane . . .

A stab of fear lanced through him and Ford was tempted to immediately wing it back to Ambunti to fetch the police. He dismissed the thought as unworthy. The mission staff were more than employees – they were family – and they needed help now.

He was halfway out of the hangar door when he heard a whirring sound and his world exploded.

'Wake up, Doctor Ford. Wake up.'

Ford could taste blood. A bucket of tepid water hit him full in the face. Throbbing pain split his skull when he opened his eyes. He was now in his office. It had been ransacked, every drawer opened and flung to the ground, documents and files scattered recklessly. He discovered his hands were secured with plastic cable ties to the arms of his office chair. Before him stood two Indonesian men wearing jungle fatigues and combat boots. He wondered if they were Kopassus – Indonesian special forces – but they usually flew by chopper . . .

'Who are you?' Ford asked. 'What do you want?'

The shorter man sat on the edge of the desk. He had a bland, genial face with hard eyes.

'We have much to discuss.'

'Yes, we do. This is a hospital. What have you done with my staff? I have patients that need attending to.'

Ford caught a whiff of clove cigarettes as the man exhaled. Then he punched Ford full in the face – a short, bunched right, followed by a left – which left him on the edge of passing out again. It was a vicious, controlled application of violence. Ford gasped and spat out a mouthful of fresh blood.

'You will listen, all right?'

Between Ford's feet, he could see broken vials of morphine on the floor, which meant they had got into the wall safe behind him. Obviously, the drugs and several thousand US dollars had not been enough to satisfy them. Then, he thought of what else the safe had contained.

It was in the second Indonesian's hand: a gold and silver embossed Luger, engraved with the initials M. H. With a sickening start, it occurred to Ford that the thing his family had always dreaded was probably happening right now.

'Doctor Ford, we know you are a very rich man. Your air ambulance cost more than four million dollars.' The man's brown eyes were cold.

Ford forced a dry laugh. 'We're a church-based organisation. We run on donations.'

'Oh? We know these donations represent only a fraction of the money your family has spent over the years, equipping this mission and others like it around the world. What is the true source of this income, Doctor Ford?'

'I would need my accountant to–'

A stiff jab to the sternum sucked the wind out of his lungs.

'Stop wasting time, all right? There are no trusts. No endowments. We know the source of your wealth is gold, Doctor Ford. *Japanese gold*. So, let me make it easy for you. Where is the submarine located?'

Oxygen fizzled out of Ford's bloodstream.

They know.

Hearing this stranger exposing their dark secret – a secret kept safe for more than seventy years – was appalling. The ramifications cascaded through his mind. The hospitals would close. He would end up in jail. And then there was the shame, the irreparable damage to their legacy. As the Indonesian's almond eyes bored into his, Ford fought to keep his expression calm. No matter what happened, they must never find it. Never. And the chances of them doing so were next to none – as long as he kept his mouth shut.

Perhaps sensing this new-found resolve, his interrogator barked, 'Send her in.'

For one, long, terrible moment, Ford thought they had Mia, and his heart almost burst, so powerfully did it beat. When the taller man dragged in Millie, relief flooded through his body, and was just as quickly extinguished by shame. Dear Millie had been there from the very beginning. She was his sister. The mother he'd never had. Goodness personified.

Millie had been savagely beaten. Predictably, she shed no tears, just stood there in quiet dignity, with a bloody nose and a livid-looking contusion on her cheek. Seeing the ruined morphine on the floor, she dropped her head.

'So sorry, Doctor Paul. They kill patients if I don't tell them combination.'

'It doesn't matter, Millie,' he replied gently.

The stocky man drew a lethal-looking commando dagger with a serrated underblade and roughly shoved the old woman's head onto the desk. Using the tip of the blade, he scooped a bleeding divot from her right cheek. The brutality was incomprehensible.

'What the hell are you doing, man?' Ford roared, struggling against his bonds. 'Leave her alone, you bloody swine!'

The man chuckled. 'You care for the old monkey?' Pulling Millie's right ear taut, he cut it off in one savage motion and tossed the severed ear into Ford's lap, where it lay like a desiccated mollusc, weeping blood. 'Now I take the other.' He wrenched her head back the other way. 'Then we cut off her nose, all right?'

'Stop!' protested Ford. 'For God's sake . . .'

With knife poised, the man waited.

'There is gold in the vault . . . under the hospital.'

Ford led them outside to the hospital entrance, where Old Max, his faithful ridgeback, was splayed at the foot of stairs, shot between the eyes. A nurse lay flat on her back. An exit wound had inflicted such terrible damage that Ford only recognised it was Frances by her lurid red nail polish. From inside the ward they heard moaning and crying. Ford identified Mrs Vuata, who was close to term, begging for assistance. Millie briefly met his eyes. Did she know, he wondered, about their dirty secret?

Leading them around the side of the building, Ford stopped by a nondescript timber door built into the brick foundations.

'There is a key in my pocket.'

The stocky man delivered two hefty kicks and the bolt gave way to reveal a storeroom stuffed with non-perishable supplies.

'Behind the cupboard.'

It was mounted on hinges and the stocky man eagerly flung it open to reveal a heavy steel door with a combination dial. Ford recited the password without being asked. '15061945' was the date his parents had reached the nearby village after escaping the submarine.

It took the stocky man two attempts to work the dial correctly. With a clunk, the heavy steel door swung open. Inside, the vault was pitch-black. Giving Ford a suspicious look, he pushed him ahead.

'You first.'

When Ford turned on the light, the Indonesian man scowled.

'Is this a joke?'

Aside from a large timber wine rack full of dusty bottles, the vault appeared to be empty.

'Look under the rack.'

The Indonesian grunted as he pulled out a flat, nondescript box made of dark timber. Prying open the lid, he let out a soft hiss. The gold ingots were the size of chocolate bars. Covetously, he picked one up and held it to the light, where it gleamed seductively.

'You see,' he told the other man, tracing his fingertip over the finely embossed surface. 'The Chrysanthemum Seal of Japan.'

Ford cleared his throat. 'You're holding a kilogram of gold bullion worth 40,000 US dollars. There are ten bars in the box. I'm afraid that's all that's left. Please take it and go.'

He held his breath and prayed. It was a tiny percentage of the cargo the submarine had brought upriver in 1945, and although there were still tonnes on board, nobody would ever be able to retrieve it from the bottomless depths of the Hoosenbeck Cavern.

The stocky man sighed and got to his feet.

'You have fifteen patients alive upstairs. And I will execute them one by one until you give me the *exact* location of the submarine.'

With a sinking heart, Ford knew it was over.

'Third brandy box, on the right. There is a map.'

Chapter 4

Margaret River, Western Australia, present day

Making love underwater, her skin is slippery as slick rubber. Weightless, effortless, nerve endings sing. He can feel Natalie is close, lifts and lunges, consumed with her pleasure. Above him she grips his shoulders, starts to shudder. They roll over, and he drives even harder. Her hair floats like a shroud and he can't see her face, but he can feel the torrent of bubbles as she comes. He can't stop pounding. Even when he feels her fingers scrabbling at his throat, her ribcage collapsing under his hands.

Dear God, he wants to stop, but he can't. The awful, relentless, pounding, pounding . . .

Breathe, why don't you, Nat?

BREATHE!

Nash opened the door a crack to learn that the source of the relentless pounding was Frank Douglas hammering on his front door.

'Robbie!' His eyes were wide. 'Had to come and see you. This deal is big, my friend. *Huge.* Hey, did you just get out of bed?'

Blinking in the early morning sunlight, Nash reluctantly opened the door. The dream had jangled his senses. Was this part of the nightmare?

In a fawn leisure suit and tan loafers, Frank Douglas looked like a time traveller from the 1970s. Even more incongruous was the shiny new black briefcase he was holding.

'Frank . . . you came all this way?'

'You left me no choice, laddie. Time and tide wait for no one.'

Douglas flashed a too-perfect smile. Years ago, a shard of aluminium from an exploding helicopter rotor had removed most of his teeth and half his nose. The resultant stitch work had given him a porcine aspect that hadn't improved with age.

He looked Nash critically up and down. 'You look like an escapee from the Burma Railway – all skin and bone. Get some duds on and I'll take you down to the surf club for a fry-up before we get down to business.'

'Slow down, Frank. What about a cup of tea?'

'OK, OK, but have you got coffee?'

Nash got the machine going while Douglas expanded on the merits of his AirAsia flight crew.

'Nothing's too much trouble, service with a smile, and there's nothing more sexy than small and demure, am I right?'

Handing him a long black, Nash realised Douglas must now be about seventy. Although the tropical tan made him appear hale, there was a hint of jaundice in the whites of his eyes, which were a similar colour to his nicotine-stained fingers. There was also a hint of desperation. It was a six-hour flight from Port Moresby, and Nash wasn't looking forward to telling Douglas he wasn't interested in the expedition.

Back in the living room, Douglas saw the picture of Natalie on the laptop, which Nash had forgotten to switch off.

'Mate, I'm sorry,' he mumbled.

If they'd spoken at the funeral, Nash couldn't remember. He closed the laptop. Every time someone brought up Natalie's loss it was like tearing the scab off the wound.

Douglas reached for his cigarettes, then hesitated.

'You can smoke on the deck.'

Nash opened the bi-fold doors. As Douglas went past him, an odour of Scotch trailed in his wake. Placing his shiny briefcase on the outdoor table, he extracted a cigarette from the packet with his too-white false teeth. Seeing Nash was drinking peppermint tea, he smiled.

'Still the health nut, eh? You're as bad as your dad and mum. How are they, by the way?'

'Keeping busy.'

'With the . . . what do you call it?'

'Wildlife sanctuary.'

Nash's parents were long-term volunteers, repairing fences, trapping feral animals, planting trees, although age was restricting their physical contributions. Nash thought better of asking Douglas if he planned to see them while he was here. Over the years they had drifted apart.

Douglas lit his cigarette with a gold lighter and blew out a nervy stream of smoke.

'Who'd've thought Peter Perfect would end up a hippie?'

Nash saw no point in dignifying the comment with a reply. In his narrow expat microcosm, Frank Douglas was so out of touch he couldn't fathom that he was the anachronism. But there was no denying the man was an incredible pilot. Nash would never forget that sudden storm in the Star Mountains where Douglas, in near zero visibility and a seventy kph crosswind, had somehow found his way out of a dead-end valley, then landed safely in a hewn-out jungle clearing the size of a postage stamp. No question, his skills had saved their lives that day.

Nash decided to just get it over with.

'Uncle Frank, I'm sorry you came all this way, but I'm not interested.'

Douglas looked bewildered.

'It's nothing personal, Frank. It's me. I'm not . . . ready.'

Although it was the truth, saying it out loud was somehow shameful, and suddenly Nash felt secretly furious with Douglas for arriving unannounced.

'Christ, laddie, I know you've been smashed by all this.' Douglas stubbed out his cigarette. 'But you've got to take the bull by the horns, get right back on board and ride that fucker for all he's worth.'

Nash stared into space. Douglas meant well. Didn't they all? But grief was like navigating an alien world, and the old pilot was starting to suck up all the available oxygen.

'OK, OK, let's hear it, then.'

It seemed the fastest way to get him out of there.

'That's the spirit.' Douglas gave him a wink. Self-importantly opening his briefcase, he took out a document and placed it in front of Nash with a flourish. 'This is a confidentiality deed. You need to sign it first.'

'You're kidding me?'

Douglas coloured slightly. 'You're not signing your life away, mate, you're just agreeing not to disclose any aspect of the proposal being offered to you.'

The official-looking deed had been drafted by a law firm in Jakarta, on behalf of a production company called Shangri-La. Nash frowned at this; Indonesians were not welcome in PNG, although that could explain why they were prepared to sign a pariah like him to the team. He scanned the legalese with a rising sense of scorn. The following offer would be one-time only, the details of which he was not to reveal from this moment on in perpetuity, on pain of litigation, and they weren't even naming the cave, just referring to it as the 'nominated location'.

What a joke.

Nash scrawled his name and pushed it back across the table. 'This better be good, Frank.'

Douglas grinned broadly. 'Robbie, it's the Hoosenbeck.'

A shudder ran through Nash.

The Hoosenbeck?

The Southern Hemisphere's holy grail of cave diving was a so-called 'bottomless lake' inside a vast cavern at the end of a sheer-sided river gorge, discovered by a Dutch speleological team in the late 1960s. Their weighted ropes had not hit bottom, and no one knew how deep it was, or how far it extended. The fact it was situated five or so kilometres inside Indonesian Papua, a 'paradise lost' of inaccessible rainforests and impenetrable mountains, where a vicious guerrilla war had raged for decades, had prevented any chance of further exploration.

Nash breathed out slowly. 'Frank, you're talking about my boyhood dream.'

'I know, laddie.'

Douglas handed him a stunningly detailed aerial photo of the three-gorge Hoosenbeck system, a deep and narrow cut in the flanks of the Jayawijaya mountain range. Nash devoured the image with his eyes. Once liberated from its cave, the snowmelt-driven Hoosenbeck River ran fast and strong for twenty kilometres until it fed into the Sepik's headwaters. All that rock-boring power had fuelled Nash's suspicion that this system was linked to the Kaiserin, a mere ten kilometres across the border. On their last expedition, he had been tantalised by the possibility of making the connection below ground.

From his magic suitcase, Douglas presented Nash with a contract. The fee almost made his eyes pop out of his head.

'You can write about the expedition afterwards –' Douglas tapped a threatening non-disclosure clause – 'but not before. They want the scoop, you see?' He handed Nash a pen.

The signature field seemed to swim before his eyes as Nash placed pen against paper. Then a vision of last night's dream returned, of Natalie's broken ribs, and his racing pulse slowed.

'I need to think, Frank.'

Douglas shook his head in exasperation. 'About what? This is all you've ever talked about. Remember our last trip to Lanzarote? Soon as you conquered that five-kilometre lava tunnel, we cracked the porto, and you started raving about the Hoosenbeck all over again.'

'I know. It just doesn't . . . feel right.'

'Robbie, mate, you gotta see reason.' Douglas stabbed the contract with his yellow forefinger. 'It's pay dirt, the big time. Are you telling me you can't use the money?'

Douglas was breathing heavily now. Although he'd notched up decades flying the most dangerous skies on earth, PNG was flooded with young western pilots desperate for commercial hours and the school maverick was being left on the ground. And while the diving expeditions had got him out of penury, Nash knew the truth was he couldn't afford to come home.

A throbbing pain erupted inside Nash's skull. Cornered by Douglas's need, he felt trapped within his own home, simultaneously aware that its shelter was fleeting, that soon all its memories of Natalie would be gone, repossessed by the bank, and he couldn't do anything about it because inside him there was fucking nothing left.

Nash got up unsteadily. 'I need you to go, Frank.'

'Aw, come on, Robbie. Let's talk it through.'

'I said *go*!' Nash erupted. 'What, are you fucking deaf, too?'

Watching Douglas leave, stiff and hunched, part of Nash wanted to call him back to apologise. He hadn't wanted to send a wrecking ball through a lifelong relationship, but the old guy was never going to understand.

Needing to clear his head, Nash went down to the river and waded in. With no destination in mind, he swam upriver, the brackish high tide giving way to fresh water. Here the river was shallow, in summer often retreating to pools. He swam on, losing himself in the river's gentle flow. Gliding over tangles of paperbark limbs, pygmy perch scattered while schools of minnows, confident in their diminutive scale, darted around him, picking off dislodged food particles. A marron waved a claw and thought better of it. Hauling himself onto a rock, Nash listened to the wind rustling through the tall karri on the ridge. Sometimes, he and Natalie had come up here for picnics. If you went far enough, and were prepared to wade through the rocky sections, you could lose the tourist kayaks, leave it all behind.

When he got back to the house it was dusk. Jacquie's VW was in the drive and he felt sick with guilt. Frank would have turned up at her place in a mess.

She was sitting on the deck in a fleecy jacket, arms wrapped around herself even though it wasn't cold.

'Where were you?' she asked without looking at him. 'I've been sitting here for hours.'

'In the river . . . I don't know.' She must have seen the bills on the table. And having spoken to Frank, she would know what he had just turned down. Clearing his throat, he said, 'Look, Jac, I'm going to get my shit together. I just need a bit more time.'

She nodded without conviction. 'The thing is, it's not just about you anymore.'

'What do you mean?'

'I've been diagnosed with cancer.' She turned to face him, and her eyes were dull with pain. 'It's ovarian.'

'*What?*' He stared at her in disbelief. 'Isn't that . . .?'

'Rare?' Jacquie breathed out slowly. 'I thought it was gluten intolerance. Lucky the specialist bothered to check. Rob, it's stage three.'

The horror struck him like a rogue wave on a rocky jump-off. His sister was the healthiest person he'd ever known. It was family lore that she had never missed a day of school. She'd completed her first Rottnest Island swim aged fourteen, beating every girl under eighteen. She'd captained her school at netball, despite being the shortest girl in her year. Her enthusiasm and drive were legendary. She was bulletproof. More importantly, she was the engine, the heart of the family. In short, she was irreplaceable.

He pulled her to him. They held each other and sobbed. When the first rush of grief had passed, Jacquie explained chemo would begin next week. They needed to shrink the tumours down and hopefully she would be operable within a few months. She said her chances were fair, which didn't sound promising to Nash, but he was in that strange limbo of trying to put a brave face on things, without diminishing their import.

'It's Mum and Dad I'm most worried about,' Jacquie said. 'This is going to hit them hard.' She looked up at him. 'Will you come over there with me tomorrow, Rob?'

Instantly he agreed to pick her up in the morning. When she was ready to head home, he gave her another bear hug by the door, and found himself unable to let go. It was as if he was holding the history of his life in his hands, and he began crying at the thought of losing her, too.

'I love you so much, sis,' he breathed at last. 'Is there anything else I can do to help?'

'Yes!' She thumped her balled fists against his powerful chest. 'Yes, there bloody well is. Get on with being who you were meant to be.' Freeing herself from his embrace, she laughed. 'Oh shit, now I'm crying again – I've got a Zoom meeting at seven.' She gave him a kiss and yelped at his bristles. 'And make sure you shave tomorrow morning. Look human for Mum and Dad, OK? They haven't seen you in ages.'

As her tail lights disappeared down the road, he bit his lip.

Not Jacquie.

How on earth was it fair that fate might take her before him? It was a travesty. Like this dirty, stinking house.

Standing in the chaos, Nash saw it clearly for the first time. Jacquie's bombshell had blown away the emotional miasma. His sister was sick, she needed his help. So did his mum and dad.

Ringing Douglas's number, Nash hoped he was not too late. The old pilot was half-drunk.

'Robbie, I'm sorry, kid, I shouldn't have sprung it on you like that.'

'Frank, it's OK. I'm sorry, too. Look . . . I am interested. Can I buy you dinner?'

They met in an almost deserted airport hotel bar. Douglas had cold-showered and only a slight unsteadiness revealed his intoxication. He made no mention of Nash's change of heart, just handed him the contract.

Nash scanned it briefly before signing on the spot.

Douglas was thrilled. It might be Shangri-La's scoop, he kept saying, but Nash was going to get all the glory *and* write the book.

'Oh, and don't forget 250 grand, laddie.' Insisting on cracking a bottle of expensive champagne, Douglas raised his flute high. 'Well, here's to the mighty Hoosenbeck. And the man who's going to plumb her virgin depths!'

Taking a token sip, Nash felt no emotion beyond a steely sense of duty, which was to cover his dread at the magnitude of what lay ahead. Never had he felt so ill-prepared for an expedition. All he could do was trust his experience would provide when the time came.

'So, when are we going, Frank?' He pushed away his plate of trout half eaten.

'Three weeks.' Douglas wiped his mouth on a napkin. 'There's a ship leaving Fremantle on Wednesday. A container for your gear is coming tomorrow. You'll need to book a flight to Moresby. Get your shots up to date. Now, we'd better figure out your inventory before my gate is called.'

As they tallied up the lengthy gear list, Nash was suddenly curious.

'Tell me, Frank, how on earth did you wangle this?'

Douglas gave him a lopsided grin. 'After the Indonesians couldn't get on to you, they came a-knocking on bended knee. For two hundred grand I agreed to get your signature, but only if they signed me on as pilot!' He patted Nash's forearm with a trembling hand. 'The team's back in business, Robbie my lad. Now, how about buying me one for the road?'

Chapter 5

Kebayoran Baru, Jakarta, Indonesia,
one month previously

'For you, my darling, a token of my appreciation.'

Sura stared in utter disbelief at the gleaming gold bar, for the chrysanthemum seal and Japanese logographs were unmistakable.

'You found it *already*?' She forced herself to smile through the turmoil raging within. One pathetic bar . . . How would she fund a new life with that?

Wijaya sat back in his chair, looking satisfied. 'I'm afraid there was only a small cache at the mission, but thanks to you we now have the location of the submarine and an estimated two metric tonnes of gold bullion.'

Sura breathed again. 'How wonderful! Where?'

'Under our friend Martin Heider's command, the *I-403* was indeed sailed up the Sepik and Hoosenbeck rivers, before being hidden inside a huge cave at the end of the Hoosenbeck Gorge. The founder of the Ford Mission removed approximately half the gold before it sank in the 1950s.'

Sura's head was spinning. 'And they *stayed* up there? What on earth happened, Father?'

Wijaya pulled a face. 'I'm afraid by that stage Doctor Paul Ford was unable to provide more detailed explanations.' He pushed a box of assorted papers and journals across the desk. 'I thought you might be able to find out more in his grandfather's diaries. I've had them translated, they're quite fascinating.'

Sura was privately furious at the needless loss of precious information. Her father's goons were expert in violence and little else.

Wijaya got to his feet. 'I have already actioned a plan to locate the submarine and retrieve the gold. It will involve deep-water salvage inside an unexplored cave system.'

Sura sat up hopefully and he patted her head as one would an eager pet.

'Believe me, I am grateful for your acumen, darling. Who would ever have believed it? Hundreds of millions, just sitting there in the jungle. With that money, we will be able to build significant ties in the region. You know how difficult it is for me there.'

She nodded politely. Kopassus was one of his constant grievances, and they had the western sector of Indonesian Papua sewn up like a fiefdom. To combat their influence, her father had to bribe the émigré landholders who now controlled significant interests in timber and mining.

'Which is why I am going to send the recovery expedition in via the back door,' he continued.

At this she frowned. 'Papua New Guinea?'

'PNG's defence minister, Sir Julius Michaels, has agreed to a covert mission. In return for half the proceeds, he will provide both right of passage and a crew to sail my ship up the Sepik.' Wijaya smiled merrily. 'We will extract the gold and opium right under the noses of Kopassus.'

Half the proceeds? Sura was reeling, stunned and appalled by the thought of an inconsequential politician pocketing a fortune that was rightfully hers.

'But, Father,' she blurted out, 'I had hoped for a legitimate share of the enterprise!'

His eyes narrowed to two cold slits. 'You forget your place, Sura. This is not some grubby personal windfall. Sir Julius will use his share to buy his way to the prime minister's office, and when I am president, the money we will make from mining contracts in PNG will make two metric tonnes of gold pale into insignificance.'

She had thought Paris would make a nice base. A large ivy-covered house in the Avenue Montaigne, ski trips to the Alps by private helicopter, endless European sojourns – the freedom to enjoy great wealth, not just be surrounded by it like a pretty bird in a gilded cage. Above all, what she craved was the freedom to pursue her own life, to break free of Wijaya's relentless march to power; and now, yet again, he was taking it all away from her.

He stood there, looking down at her while she fought to get her disappointment under control.

'My best man, Goki, will lead the expedition. However, given the extreme nature of this remote cave, we are contracting an expert Australian cave diver and his associate. Of course, they will know nothing of our true purpose and will be terminated once their usefulness is at an end.' He put his finger under her chin and raised it until he could look into her eyes. 'Which is why I need you. Your film cover story is the perfect lure. Can I count on you to help me, my darling?'

Taking his hand, she kissed it fervently.

'Thank you, Father. Forgive my impulsiveness. I am always honoured and grateful to serve you.'

* * *

Being the truthful account of Dr Jürgen Fürth (George Ford), Wednesday, 30th May 1945

My execution is certain if this is found. Yet the overriding emotion is a stubborn desire to record events, because the world must know of this crime and I do not believe I will return home to tell of it. Three days ago, SS Standartenführer Martin Heider and his Leiberstandarte honour guard seized the giant Japanese submarine I-403 conveying us back to Europe.

Had we known of their plot, we would have alerted the Japanese. Unfortunately, their code of Bushido was their undoing. It was beyond Captain Nishigori's comprehension that a member of the officer class could act so despicably, which is why he failed to disarm Heider and his brutes when the news came in that the Fatherland had surrendered. The SS struck in the middle of the day when the submarine was running deep, and most of the crew were asleep. To ensure they were not overwhelmed by weight of numbers, the cowardly SS closed the main crew compartment and threw in smoke canisters. More than a hundred sailors suffocated. The SS then seized the officers and engineers.

We didn't think the SS were capable of operating this vessel. The I-403 is like an underwater town, with multiple decks, weapons, stores and seaplanes, and can sail all the way to Europe without refuelling. We also thought it impossible that any of the surviving Japanese could be persuaded to help. However, the translator, Hideko, proved traitorous and convinced two engineers to join the conspiracy.

Thus far, Heider has refused to tell us what his plans are. Ambassador Hartmann tells us that there are 4000 kilos of gold aboard, payment for German war technology, and he believes Heider is planning to steal it. The question is, where can he possibly go? It seems we are doomed. If he finds a haven, Heider will kill us to protect his gold, or the Americans will blow us out of the water.

* * *

Sura Suyanto hated it when Jaap Boerman stared at her with his mouth open, for it made him look like a big, stupid schoolboy.

'You're flying to Jayapura tonight?' he groaned. 'But why?'

Putting down the diary entry, she sighed into the mirror on her dresser.

'My father's insatiable greed for power leaves me with no alternative. I'm meeting a high-level contact in Kopassus to arrange a secret alliance. It will be a complex and delicate negotiation which must be handled face to face.'

'But surely Kopassus is under his command?'

'I've explained this to you before. Our defence force is like a corporation – different arms compete for available resources. My father may be CEO, but Kopassus is a rival department, and believe me, they hate each other.'

'But Jayapura is a shithole.' He spread his big hands in consternation. 'At least let me come and protect you.'

'Negative. I will be quite safe, and you would stand out like a white elephant.'

Boerman's reflection was sullen. 'I don't like it. We should stay together.'

Sura irritably checked her lipstick and mascara. Boerman's possessiveness was setting her teeth on edge. She picked up her ivory comb and ran it through her glossy black hair.

'I don't like it either, but unless you prefer a world where you have to hide in my house, you must grow up.'

Boerman capitulated and sat down on the bed. 'When will you be back?'

'Tomorrow.'

There was a brief silence as he digested this.

'How do you know you can trust this contact?'

Sura smiled knowingly. 'We are old friends, and no, Jaap, I am not attracted to him. She went over and he pressed his face against the naked skin of her belly. His beard tickled and she felt his tongue creep out. With a groan he slid his hand up her inner thigh. Gently she pushed it away. 'I'm trying to set us up for life, don't you understand that? It's the only way we can ever be free.'

He broke into an uncertain smile. 'Do you really mean that?'

Sura kissed the top of his head.

'Stop feeling sorry for yourself and get me my *kebaya*. The delivery van leaves in ten minutes and I must be inside it.'

From an unmarked Kopassus Learjet 45XR, Sura observed the stunning night-time brilliance of Jakarta give way to a jagged black line as they crossed the coast on a westerly heading. Her four-hour flight bisected the very heart of the strong Indonesian archipelago. To the north lay the massive bulk of Borneo, and the jagged four-pronged island of Sulawesi. To the south, the necklace of islands beginning with Java, passing through Bali and Timor, and ending with Trangan. Her flight path crossed three conjoined seas: the Java, Flores, and finally the wide Banda, where on its far eastern shore, the lurking presence of Papua would have been completely invisible if it hadn't been for a few coastal hamlets and the rich gas field of Bintuni Bay. Indeed, the last hour of the flight across the Papuan land mass was over a black nothingness as inhospitable as any ocean. It was disconcerting that a flight back to the Stone Age took just four hours. And as the Learjet descended, the modest glow of Papua's capital, Jayapura, seemed to mock distant Javanese aspirations of control – a reminder to Sura that their occupation would always be tenuous and hard-fought.

The driver of the shiny black van opened the door for her, his chiselled face expressionless.

'You were not followed, Mba Suyanto.' She'd always liked that about Kopassus men. Well trained.

He weaved his way skilfully through mid-evening traffic to the Swiss-Belhotel and its discreet undercover parking. Then he escorted her to a top-floor suite. Rapping three times on the door, he was gone before it opened.

'Sura, how wonderful to see you again.'

The well-dressed man standing before her was fifty, fit and compact, and his roving brown eyes missed nothing. Well, she had chosen her most revealing *kebaya*.

'Kapten Alatas.' She received his kiss and inhaled his woody cologne. 'It's been too long.'

He led her into the suite – luxurious by Jayapurian standards – and indicated she sit on the soft leather couch. The air conditioning was blissful, and she allowed herself a contented sigh.

'Mojito?'

His enquiring eyebrow was loaded with charm. Had it really been fifteen years since he'd taken her virginity at one of her father's parties? She remembered him leading her through the gardens at Kebayoran Baru with a magnum of Bollinger. She'd got tipsy, and then he'd seduced her atop a marble pedestal in the Florentine grotto, within earshot of the courtyard balcony. While it had never happened again, the secret tryst had forged a bond between them. He'd given her some juicy leads over the years, and she had provided him with mostly harmless information on her father's machinations at *Tentara Nasional Indonesia* or TNI – the headquarters of the Indonesian National Armed Forces.

Alatas stood at the bar and stirred the drinks vigorously with a swizzle stick.

'When are you going back to the Indostar news desk? I miss seeing you every night.'

'I'm on a six-month sabbatical. After seven straight years, I needed a break.'

'Seven years? I don't believe it. You haven't aged a bit.' The smooth operator ensured their fingers touched when he passed her the chilled glass. 'So, what's this about, Sura? Why come all this way in the middle of the night to see little old me? Not that I'm unhappy about it, of course.'

She batted her eyelashes seductively. Little was not a word you associated with this man. The low rank of kapten was nominal, designed to keep him under the radar. But those in the know were aware that Alatas was the second most powerful man in Kopassus, and that his boss, Major General Suparman Herianto, aka 'Superman' to his followers, was one of her father's chief rivals for the leadership of Golkar.

'You know that I've always struggled to get along with my father. He's always been so busy with matters of state.'

Alatas raised his glass in a sardonic toast. 'A true nationalist.'

Sura bared her teeth. 'A ruthless, self-aggrandising plutocrat who treats his daughter like a chattel.'

The sudden edge in her voice made him uncomfortable and he pursed his neat lips.

'I imagine it was difficult growing up in such a milieu.'

'Are you becoming a politician, too, Alatas?'

He laughed. 'Oh, please.'

Sura crossed her legs and let the sarong ride a little further up her thigh.

'What would you say if I told you my father was planning to swindle over 200 million US dollars from Kopassus territory with the help of a foreign power?'

'I'd say you were telling fibs.' His eyes were glued to her legs. 'We don't have that kind of money, and he wouldn't dare.'

Reaching into her bag, she pulled out the Ford diary translation and put it on the table.

'What if I told you that as well as embarrassing him, half of it could be yours in the next three weeks?'

'I'd say, tell me what you're offering.'

Later, grinding her pussy into his face, she reflected on the aphrodisiacal nature of power. With a hundred million dollars – and the potential scalp of the second most powerful man in Indonesia – lending fervour to his lust, Alatas was as horny as a man half his age. It was easy for men, though. They could dream and scheme, and if they were strong-willed and wealthy enough, achieve their ambitions. For a woman in her country, though, power and wealth could only be enjoyed vicariously, which is why she was prepared to risk it all to escape.

Chapter 6

Nullarbor Plain, Western Australia

The nondescript dirt track was just one of hundreds running off the Eyre Highway between Caiguna and Eucla, but Nash would never forget it. Shifting down a gear, he nursed the Land Cruiser over a battered stock grid, the victim of too many road trains, and took a long, slow breath. It had taken fourteen hours of hard driving to get here from Margaret River, and aside from fuel and coffee at Esperance, he hadn't stopped.

At least there had been plenty to think about. Shangri-La Productions were paying him a quarter of a million to lead the penetration, plus expenses and hire of his equipment, and he got to keep the rights to his own photography, which meant a glossy book down the track. It seemed too good to be true for an estimated one month's work, but Nash had a 150,000 Australian dollar advance payment propping up his sagging mortgage account to prove it. Jacquie was ecstatic for him; she said it was the best medicine she could have hoped for and was making the chemo easier to bear.

He felt uneasy concealing the Hoosenbeck from his family, though. As far as they were concerned, he was heading back to the Kaiserin Grotto to pick up where he'd left off. According to Douglas, the Indonesian subterfuge was about avoiding trouble with OPM – the Free Papua movement – and their sympathisers in PNG. Nash was sympathetic to their cause, but not enough – he had to admit – to pull out.

Staring out at the wide Nullarbor landscape, it seemed inconceivable that he would be exchanging it for tropical jungle in just two weeks. His equipment was already on a container ship headed for Port Moresby, but there was something important he needed to do here first.

The sun was low in the western sky when Nash passed the familiar outcrop of limestone rocks. A corrugated iron gate peppered with bullet holes appeared, and he felt his trepidation harden into something more. Had it really been a year since that dreadful day? The track descended into a depression dotted with saltbush and bluebush scrub. He was relieved to see there were no other vehicles present. Pulling up by a rough, barbed wire fence strung with ominous 'keep out' signs, he cut the engine. A glint of bright blue water marked the entrance pool.

Life and death. Once they'd been abstract concepts, one taken for granted, the other deferred. This place, the Octopus, had taught him they were cold, hard reality.

The cave got its name from its profile, which resembled an upside-down funnel with several arms radiating from its base. It lay ten kilometres south of the vast chambers of Cocklebiddy Cave, and many suspected a connection to that system lay hidden somewhere within the rockfall at the end of the longest tentacle.

The light was fading fast. Too late to set up camp. He would sleep in the car tonight and get started early the next morning.

Watching star belts wheel across an impossibly clear sky, Nash remembered their last moments together, and the aftermath. Like a worn tape, the sequence of events had been replayed in his mind so many times that he could dredge up every scene, dissect its beats, evaluate its import.

Hindsight. If only he'd listened. If only he'd read the signs.

He found himself fast-forwarding to the funeral. It had been a suitably bleak day. Riven with pain, he'd agreed Natalie should be buried in her home town of Melbourne. Natalie's father, Brendan, had tried to be gracious and managed it for the most part. At the wake, Nash had found himself drunkenly apologising and tried to give him back the wedding money they'd used to help fund the renovations on the house, but they were both broken men whose gestures of goodwill could offer no consolation to each other. Natalie's architect brother, Jonathan, on the other hand, had refused to even look at him.

Some months later, he had turned up unannounced in Margaret River. Letting him in, Nash felt ashamed. The beautiful house Jonathan had designed was a mess – bottles, dishes, rubbish piling up in the bins.

'Doing it tough, are you?' Jonathan said, looking around.

In the months since Natalie's accident, Nash had lost weight and the stress lines on his forehead had deepened into angry cracks.

'I don't want sympathy. I don't deserve it.'

'No, you don't,' Jonathan told him evenly. 'That's why I'm here. We're going to bring a civil suit against you for negligence, hopefully manslaughter.'

Nash stared at him for several seconds. 'Brendan? I thought . . .'

Jonathan shook his head. 'It's nothing to do with Dad. Bec and I have decided it's the right thing to do.'

Jonathan's wife was a crown prosecutor, a hyper-efficient legal bloodhound whom even Natalie had struggled to like. Nash found himself laughing shrilly.

'You want the house, Jonathan? Mate, take it – take everything!'

Jonathan leaned forward, his dark eyes radiating malice. 'I don't want the house. I want *you*. I want everyone to know what a fucked-up piece of selfish shit you are. I want your name to become synonymous with cowardice and incompetence. The Rob Nash brand is going to turn sponsors off so fast, you'll forget you ever had a phone number!'

There had been no suit because there didn't need to be. With Jonathan and Bec's assistance, *The World Tonight* had produced a one-hour special entitled 'Maverick of the Deep'. Every rival Nash had ever had was trotted out to cast aspersions, every error he had ever made was ruthlessly dissected. They made his career look like a sequence of lucky breaks and double-crosses. The breathless voice-over and sinister soundtrack even had him believing it.

The next morning, Nash mechanically geared up under a dark sky. A front had moved in during the early hours and dumped a rare drenching of rain. He'd had a tormented night, twisting and turning in the back of the Land Cruiser. At some point, he'd decided that he didn't want to dive today, but the feeling was uncomfortably close to fear, and now he had to prove that it wasn't.

Nash checked the rebreather. The size of a large backpack, the closed-circuit device had revolutionised cave diving by recycling the gases a diver breathed. Gone were the days of lugging multiple cylinders around for use at different depths. The rebreather contained bottles of oxygen and trimix – a combination of nitrogen, oxygen and helium – their percentages varied with depth by computer to offset the pernicious side effects of gas under pressure. Exhalations were run through a scrubbing agent to remove carbon dioxide. Nash also strapped on a small side-mounted trimix tank, which he would switch to when it was time to penetrate the squeeze.

In the middle of the saucer-shaped entrance pool lay the jagged mouth of the Octopus. While swimming down to it, a sense of foreboding came over him, as if a vestigial element of Natalie's spirit waited here in anguish.

He should have come sooner. Paid his respects.

Free-falling the ten-metre-wide tube was like skydiving through an empty grain silo. Normally, he relished the feeling. Now, he found himself thinking how strangely devoid of life this place was. There were no fish, no crustaceans, just occasional finger-like curtains of bacteria on the rocks.

He reached the halocline – the boundary where fresh water floated on top of salty water – marked by a brownish line on the rocks. On a clear day, the tonality of the water shifted from gin clear to a brilliant blue, so alive and electric, as if the very molecules were charged with neon. The phenomenon was responsible for the formation of the Nullarbor caves. When seepage from rainfall hit the salt-water table, it supercharged the attack on the limestone. Thus, the caves quietly continued to grow, calving off blocks which could have been cut from a quarry.

At the bottom, Nash swam quickly down the main arm. The rectangular passage was about the size of a railway tunnel, but it seemed smaller and meaner than he remembered. The water on his exposed skin was cold. The rain had created turbidity, restricting visibility to five or six metres, despite his high-intensity dive lights.

After 100 metres, he reached the rockfall which had closed the arm. There was the stack of limestone blocks they had shifted to uncover the passage in the side wall. Just inside was the little six-litre tank he had abandoned to drag Natalie to the surface. No one had dived here since. This was unusual. Nash felt as if he was intruding on a grave. Or a crime scene.

Steeling himself, he entered the mouth of the passage. At this juncture it was treacherously roomy – about the internal dimensions of a small car. However, the tempting aperture curving out of sight would soon narrow dramatically. In preparation for this, he removed the rebreather and switched to his smaller open-circuit trimix tank.

After the whisper quiet of the rebreather, the regulator was astonishingly loud and its cloud of trimix bubbles distracting. Positioning the tank in front of him, Nash pushed it into the narrow passage which soon became a squeeze, about the circumference of a kitchen waste bin. He shimmied forwards, using his elbows and knees for leverage. The ceiling scraped the top of his protective helmet. Dislodged particles, swept ahead of him by the unseen current, shone ghostly in the lights.

It was only a few body lengths, but it seemed to take forever to reach the vertical dog-leg where Natalie had become wedged. He had not meant to tarry here – his destination was a huge chamber he'd discovered, which he planned to chart and name in her honour. But now, a visceral sense of the terror Natalie must have felt, trapped and alone in that confined and dreadful space, overcame him, and he saw his plan for what it really was: a misguided attempt at closure. In the bright lights, he could see the abrasions her rebreather had left on the soft limestone roof . . . even the faint scratches made by her scrabbling fingernails. The post-mortem report recorded she had lost them.

And the baby.

Neither of them had known Nat was six weeks pregnant.

Nash managed to remove the regulator and vent his meagre breakfast into the cold water. The paroxysm triggered a psychological reflex. All at once he was hyperconscious of the rock around him. The knowledge of all that mass pressing down upon him – that he couldn't just turn around and flee – became an intolerable concept.

Nash began shunting backwards. Then his weight belt snagged on a projection. On a normal day, this was easily rectified by reversing direction and trying again. But now he believed the cave was hungry for another victim, that it was out to swallow him alive, and he simply could not countenance surrendering even a single centimetre to it.

The most dangerous hazard in any underwater cave is the human mind. Nash had seen divers with regulator failure freak out and drown in terror, despite having a spare buckled to their chest. Although training and experience mitigated the risk, they were not fail-safe, because you could never foresee every contingency. But not in a million years would Rob Nash ever have conceived of something like this happening to him. Everybody said there was antifreeze in his veins.

In a rising, ugly panic, Nash fought to free himself. His helmet slammed repeatedly on the rock above. Then he lost his grip on the tank. It slid deeper into the passage sloping away from the dog-leg.

Lunging after it, he grabbed hold of the valve. The movement freed the snag. But now the surface seemed so much further away . . .

Oblivious to everything but the need to escape, Nash wriggled backwards out of the squeeze in a frenzy of fear. Even the relative expanse of the passage mouth failed to calm him. Panic shut down his peripheral vision. He was physically unable to strap on the rebreather, so he clutched it to his chest and finned madly back down the long passage. His thighs were on fire, threatening to cramp. The arm of the Octopus had doubled in length and, in the turbid water, Nash believed he was being sucked backwards. His gear was trying to kill him, too! Dragging gas through the mouthpiece was like sucking mud through a straw. His throat was burning: were the oxygen sensors faulty, or had the computer failed? He wanted to scream, to rip off the suffocating equipment and smash his way through the rocks to the air above.

Some distant part of him observing his plight wondered whether Natalie was watching on, too. Perhaps she wanted him to stay down there with her and their unborn child forever?

At the main shaft, Nash stared longingly at the disc of bright blue above. He required a five-minute decompression, but with a glance back down the dark tunnel, he made his decision.

No way was he staying a second longer. Inflating his buoyancy control vest, he shot to the surface like a wayward cork – screaming an exhalation to save exploding his lungs with a pulmonary barotrauma.

On hands and knees, he crawled out of the pool, so terrorised that he didn't even feel safe by the water's edge. Hanging on to a barbed wire fence, he sobbed Natalie's name, begged for her forgiveness.

The cold south wind was indifferent.

Chapter 7

In the interests of future authentication, I should briefly establish my personal circumstances. I am the personal physician of Ambassador Erwin Hartmann. Privately wealthy, he took me to Japan with him in 1943 to treat his hypertension. There is not much to say about me. Boring and middle class, connections in high places kept me out of uniform and the only thing that will make me interesting to you is the love of my life.

Of course, I am referring to Ilse Hufnagl. You will have heard of her because she is the most innovative film-maker the world has ever seen. It is a tragic disgrace that her talent has been debased for propaganda. She was the Führer's favourite until her big mouth got the better of her. We met while she was in Tokyo, filming more Axis lies. I still don't know what she sees in me. I am a humble doctor, but she tells me I am the only man she has ever been able to truly rely on.

So much for bona fides. Since the mutiny we have been confined to the crew's quarters, which absolutely stink because it has taken us two terrible days to carry all the bodies to the torpedo room and fire them into the sea. I also had to carry the bodies of Captain Nishigori, and his officers, who Heider personally executed with Nishigori's own katana sword so as to maximise their humiliation.

You will know of Heider. He is the blond-haired blue-eyed Über-mensch of Nazi propaganda and a true monster. Even though he is exempt from combat, Ilse said he got special permission to participate in mass executions in Poland. That would be his style. I loathe the way he looks at her.

* * *

Kebayoran Baru, Jakarta, Indonesia

It took Sura several moments to realise it was Jaap snoring and not the savage dogs of her father's military police. Another nightmare. This time they had come for her during a news bulletin and dragged her away to the cells under Menteng. Since hatching the plan with Alatas, such dreams had plagued her. And seeing her father during the interminable planning meetings over the past six weeks had been fraught; every raised eyebrow and disapproving sniff set her on edge. She was a consummate liar, but he had always been able to see right through her.

Rolling over, she straddled Jaap, who opened his eyes in surprise.

'This is our last morning under his roof.' She ground herself against him. 'Make it count.'

She was stepping out of the shower when the intercom bleeped. Angka's heavyset face filled the screen.

'He wants to see you now.'

A shiver passed through her.

'This early in the day? I wonder why.'

Angka had no time for rhetorical questions and hung up.

'I told you this was too dangerous.' Jaap paced up and down as she hurriedly got dressed. 'Let's just go to the fucking airport. Get on a plane to South Africa. We've got more than enough money to start a new life there.'

'Don't be stupid. We'd be intercepted before we got out of the car park.'

'Then we'll go to the docks –'

'Stop being an idiot!' she exploded. 'And keep packing.'

She wanted to say, *in case I don't come back*, but the last thing she needed was meaningless heroics from Jaap. What he failed to understand was that her father was a vast malignancy, and no part of the Javan organism was immune to his influence.

When she knocked on her father's open door, his gaze was so cold she went numb.

He pushed his leather chair backwards. Woodenly she came forward to kiss the backs of his hands, but he pulled them away. Kneeling, she placed her head in his lap in the ritualised gesture of filial apology. He pulled her upright.

'Once again I find out that you have not been honest with me.'

She thought her heart might burst when he placed surveillance photos on the desk. She was so scared it took several moments for her to work out that the naked figures in the photos were her and Jaap, having sex in the spa at the Singapore Hyatt a week before. Thinking themselves anonymous on the

75

tenth floor, they had not closed the curtains in the living room or shut the bathroom door.

Almost delirious with relief, she closed her eyes.

'I thought he was your cameraman. Now I discover you are his whore.' Spots of white were flaring in Wijaya's cheeks.

Although the images were pornographic, Sura knew her father was no prude. He was probably more furious that Jaap was white.

'Father, he has converted.'

His savage slap made her ears ring. 'Stupid slut! Golkar is a party of respectability and I will soon become its leader. Did it ever cross your mind what would happen if this reached the tabloids? Our Suyanto name would be dragged through the mud! How could you be so reckless? Never forget you're a *celebrity*.'

Sura felt a surge of icy hate. That had been *his* choice, not hers.

'I've a strong mind to replace you with Tommy on our little project,' he mused. 'Say what you like about him, at least he can be trusted.'

Sura felt sick. Was he really going to entrust her prize to that spoilt brat? Her younger brother had spent his life fooling around with sports cars and whores. Where she worked slavishly for success, Tommy had it laid out before him. Even when she won her scholarship to Cambridge, on merit, Wijaya's reaction had been one of benign amusement. And then, when she chose journalism as a career, he had hijacked it by buying up half the Indostar Network to ensure favourable coverage, a move that had contaminated her professional integrity forever.

'I'm so sorry, Father. It was stupid and selfish of me. I promise it will never happen again. You know I have only ever worked for your success.'

Wijaya made a steeple with his fingers and nodded slowly. 'Well, perhaps bringing Tommy up to speed now might be challenging.' He reached for a glass of water on the table and took a measured sip. 'So, you fly to Jayapura today. Is everything prepared?'

Sura exhaled slowly. The wily old jackal had been bluffing all along.

'Yes, Father. The ship will leave Port Moresby tomorrow with the salvage equipment and the Australians aboard. It should reach the Sepik next week.'

He glanced at the laptop on his desk. 'What exactly are your concerns with the cave diver?'

'Mr Nash hasn't worked for some time, and there are questions concerning his mental state after the accident last year which killed his wife. He may not be reliable.'

He stared at her shrewdly. 'Is this a pitch to keep Mr Boerman on?'

'As well as being a first-rate cameraman, who has worked with me for years, Jaap is also a certified commercial diver. To replace him at this late stage would be risky, but of course –' she dropped her eyes – 'it is entirely your decision.'

'Very well. But you will not embarrass me again, is that clear? A ship is a small place.'

'Absolutely, Father.'

Wijaya put his hand under her chin and looked into her eyes.

'Promise me now that you will respect and obey Goki's commands. The expedition will be dangerous, and I cannot afford to lose you.'

He almost sounded sincere. Sura kissed the back of his hand.

'I swear it, Father. This means as much to me as it does to you.' Kissing him again, she rose to her feet. '*Salam*. I will make you proud of me. You'll see.'

General Suyanto watched her go before picking up the topmost photo on the desk. Unwittingly, the agent had captured the impulsive ferocity Sura worked so hard to conceal. Suyanto sighed. His beautiful daughter had inherited his drive, and she had an almost frightening intelligence, but she was also headstrong and vicious. Tommy had numerous childhood scars to prove it. After almost losing him to a swimming pool incident, they had never left him alone with Sura again.

A bamboo side panel slid open and Goki stepped out, resplendent in his uniform with its chest full of medals, including the prized golden star of the Bintang Sakti. The squat commando had served General Suyanto for more than two decades. From wet work sorting out the fanatics in Aceh, to covert intelligence gathering in Timor, he was a lethal and efficient operator, and Suyanto had absolute faith in his abilities.

'What do you think? Speak freely.'

Goki blinked slowly. 'She'll be a handful, sir. Especially with her muscle man, but it's nothing I can't manage.'

'Are you sure you don't want backup? You'll be a long way from help.'

The commando shrugged. 'Do you really need another loose end, sir? It would mean more cleaning up when this thing is done.'

'I suppose you're right,' Suyanto conceded.

There were preparations underway for the disappearance of the Indonesian contingent – compensations with no-fault damage waivers for grieving relatives to sign. No doubt, Sir Julius was making equivalent arrangements in Port Moresby. With two tonnes of gold at stake, it was vital no one was left alive to tell the tale.

'You will need to watch her very carefully, Goki. She's devilishly clever.'

'A chip off the old block, sir.' Goki gave a rare grin.

'And very precious to me. So, when you dispose of Boerman, make sure she can't do anything stupid. Understood? I want her brought back in one piece.'

The commando fired off a smart salute, about-faced and departed.

One by one, General Suyanto fed the photos into the paper shredder by his desk. For a time, celebrity had given his wayward daughter fulfilment in life; in fact, they had been getting on – so much so that he'd even believed her gift of the submarine was genuine, until her greedy outburst.

Paris? *Good God, Sura, what were you thinking?* Those real estate brochures in her email cache were a reminder she wasn't thinking straight. Clearly, the liberal views she'd picked up at that infuriating English university continued to contaminate her priorities.

Suyanto consigned the last image to oblivion and sighed.

'When this little adventure is over, my girl, you will knuckle down, or I'll have you married to a man strong enough to handle you. Either that, or committed.'

Chapter 8

Nash was taking refuge in the terminal's air-conditioned office when the glass doors swung open and Frank Douglas strode in on a wave of hot air.

'Robbie, lad, great to see you!'

'Likewise.'

They shook hands awkwardly, laughed, then gave each other a hug.

Feeling how skinny the other man was, Nash stepped back and observed him critically. Douglas's faded khaki dungarees, cinched up tight by an army belt, were comically baggy, and the disturbing yellow cast about his skin and eyes was much more pronounced than it had been three weeks ago in Margaret River.

'Hey, are you feeling OK, Frank?'

'Had a touch of malaria last week, but I'm good to go. How about you, kiddo? Ready to rock and roll?'

Nash forced a grin he didn't feel. 'You bet.'

He should have been jumping out of his skin with excitement, but the debacle in the Octopus was weighing on his mind. Had the panic attack been a one-off, or was it something more insidious? Added to the pressure was that, for the first time in his professional life, Nash was being paid for his services, as opposed to creating and selling a product, and with his doubts unresolved he felt uncomfortably like a fraud.

Douglas jabbed a gnarled thumb at the exit. 'Come on, then, we'd better fetch your container before it goes missing.'

Outside, the midday heat struck like a moving wall. The concrete and steel of the long wharves were shimmering in a blinding glare, and Nash had to screw up his eyes despite the sunglasses he was wearing. A handful of docked freighters, mostly from Australia and New Zealand, were being relieved of their shipping containers. The sluggish harbour beneath their hulls was a milky coffee, awash with multicoloured plastic bags which billowed like jellyfish. A stink of anaerobic mud and fuel oil thickened the foetid atmosphere.

A fluoro-jacketed port official in a dented hard hat ushered them into a white car whose interior was as cold as a fridge and drove them through rows of stacked containers. Nash was relieved to see his insulated white container in the shade of a huge canopy, as per instructions. A mobile crane was standing by.

'Wait a minute,' said Douglas, as the crane edged forwards. 'Open it up.'

The official stabbed his clipboard with a chubby finger. 'Inspection was done a week ago. You please sign here.'

Douglas shook his head. 'We're not signing anything until we look inside.'

The official indicated the impressive fence on the perimeter. 'You see that razor wire? It's the tallest in PNG.'

'It's not out there I'm worried about,' said Douglas flatly.

Fortunately, everything was as Nash had left it in Perth: twelve steel scuba tanks stacked along the left-hand side and a compressor to fill them. He and the cameraman he was yet to meet would be using rebreathers. Packed in rubber-coated racks were colour-coded gas tanks of helium, nitrogen and oxygen. Two underwater scooters took up the rear wall, beside a great mound of plastic storage boxes containing everything from a defibrillator to writing slates. An emergency decompression chamber completed the inventory.

Nash signed the chit. The container was then loaded onto a battered-looking truck, under the watchful eye of Douglas. In sweaty fatigues, he looked like a reproving drill instructor.

Nash smiled. 'Still winning friends, Frank?'

'Mate, if it's not bolted down, you'll never see it again – it's a bloody national disgrace.'

At the main gate, they transferred to Douglas's ancient red Land Rover, and followed the truck out of the cargo terminal into the city.

Moresby hadn't changed. The overwhelming impression was one of neglectful decay. Litter lay in drifts. Bus stop seats had all their planks removed. A modern children's playground lay smashed in vandalised ruins. Men wearing shorts and singlets and carrying plastic bags seemed to wander aimlessly. There were few women about, and none were unattended. Shabby unarmed security guards in faded fluoro vests could be seen on every street corner, yet what they were guarding was unclear. Businesses and residences hid behind ubiquitous razor wire. After dark, Moresby got uglier. Endemic poverty, corruption and unemployment fed a culture of gangland – *raskol* – violence. Locals carried machetes for self-defence, while the homes of expats resembled maximum security prisons. Moresby was routinely ranked first on the list of the world's worst cities. Little wonder that refugees dumped here by the Australian government had declined the invitation of citizenship.

Nash had assumed they would embark from Jayapura, the capital of Indonesian Papua, for it was much closer to the mouth of the Sepik. But with seven eighths of the river in PNG, a dual-national approach had been organised with the Papua New Guinea Defence Force (PNGDF). How Shangri-La Productions had been able to organise this so quickly was another mystery.

Douglas's air conditioner was just moving hot air, so Nash wound down his window to let the breeze dry the sweat on his face. The container truck turned north on the Napa Napa road, and Douglas explained the ship was moored at the dockyards to keep a low profile.

'Is this all really necessary, Frank?'

'Oh, it's necessary. You wouldn't believe the bullshit around here, Robbie. I bought a load of bulk diesel, and when this officious prick saw an Indo address on the docket . . . Well, it was like I'd done a deal with the Devil. Ratbag even rang the ministry. I mean, sure, the Indos get a little heavy-handed at times, but they do a way better job of running things over there.'

'Down the barrel of a gun?' Nash laughed derisively. 'Come off it, Frank.'

Douglas swerved to avoid a massive pothole. 'Don't be so bloody politically correct. You know what it's like here.'

Nash knew all right. Papua was ethnically Melanesian and clearly distinct from Asia; quolls and tree kangaroos roamed its forests, not tigers and monkeys. Whatever the socio-economic problems plaguing PNG, he was sure heavy-handed colonialism in Papua was not the solution. The origins of the province were mired in controversy, too. After the Dutch vacated in 1969, the Indonesians had seized the western half of the island and rigged a referendum to shut up the UN and swindle more than ninety-nine per cent of the indigenous population out of a vote. Despised and persecuted, they were becoming a minority, dispossessed of territory for resources, with just minimal resistance from the Free Papua movement known as Organisasi Papua Merdeka (OPM). Of course, it was pointless arguing this with Frank Douglas, whose old-school politics were as unshakeable as his belief that Vietnam had been a just war.

The dramatic sound of Wagner's 'Ride of the Valkyries' abruptly filled the car and Douglas snatched up his mobile.

'Hello? Yep. I've got him. And the gear. Yep, uh huh, uh huh . . . *What?*' He braked violently and Nash held on to the handgrip as they slithered and swayed back down to walking pace. Taking his hand off the wheel, Douglas savagely changed gear, oblivious to the horns of the irate drivers behind. 'So, what am I supposed to do now – peel potatoes? Yeah, well, how do you think I feel? Uh-huh. Well, I'd expect nothing less, Sura. Yep. Understood. See you in a week.'

He slammed the phone back into the centre console and swore loudly.

'Something wrong?'

'Sura's got herself another pilot, fuck you very much.'

'What?'

'Apparently, the network has insisted on one of their own.'

'Shit, can they do that?' Nash was genuinely worried because flying out here demanded the best.

'It's in the contract.' Douglas exhaled moodily. 'And I'm now the highest paid gofer in television history.'

Usually, it was Nash who was the mover and shaker, and he felt bad. 'Sorry, Uncle Frank.'

'Nah, I'll live.'

Nash glanced knowingly at the old pilot. 'And how do you think you'll go being Sura's assistant?'

'The woman's a control freak!' Douglas promptly took the bait. 'I swear to God if I hear her say "do we understand each other?" one more time, I'm going to follow you into that cave myself.'

Nash chuckled. 'It's the military pedigree. Leave nothing to chance and assume everyone is an idiot.'

'Well, you know me and military discipline.' Douglas grinned. 'Maybe my expertise in that department will loosen the ramrod up her arse.'

The general's daughter was clearly used to getting her way. In recent emails, Sura had informed Nash that they would only begin detailed planning when her team joined the ship on the lower reaches of the Sepik. She had not addressed his request for the credentials of her dive crew, and Nash was consoling himself with the fact he could veto anything suboptimal, as per his contract.

They cleared a security checkpoint and drove down a long, straight road flanked by scrubby coastal forest. The dockyard was located on a baking isthmus, expanded by several million tonnes of earth and rocks to stabilise it against the northern wash of Fairfax Harbour. Inexplicably, the smooth bitumen road turned to gravel with the gates in sight. Douglas dropped back, cursing, as the truck ahead kicked up clouds of dust and flying stones. They passed rows of dilapidated storage sheds, various tanks, and rust-streaked infrastructure, until at last they came to a large concrete dry dock – currently flooded – in which a long grey vessel was moored.

'There she is,' said Douglas. 'Isn't she a beauty? Ex-Aussie, cutting-edge, before we flogged her to the Indo navy.'

It was an old patrol boat. But her sleek lines were compromised by a rough-looking helicopter pad welded onto the stern, and an incongruous-looking yellow crane in place of a deck gun. The ship looked deserted and run-down.

'Was that back in the sixties, Frank? I thought you said the PNG navy were taking us upriver?'

'Navy?' Douglas guffawed. 'Give me a break. The Papua New Guinea Defence Force has four shitty patrol boats, three of which don't work on any given day because someone's either spent the petrol money or stolen the spare parts.'

Nash was speechless. The idea of venturing into the *raskol*-infested interior of PNG – not to mention crossing into the Papuan war zone without armed protection – was something he would never have agreed to.

Douglas slapped him cheerfully on the knee. 'Just messing with you, kid. A PNGDF crew is running the boat, and a squad of commandos will join us on the Sepik.' His lopsided grin faded. 'I'd rather do without the locals riding shotgun, but unfortunately their government wouldn't agree to private contractors.'

It sounded entirely reasonable to Nash. Ever since getting shafted by a bunch of South African mercenaries on an expedition to Lake Otjikoto in Namibia, he'd had an acute distrust of them. The bastards had left his team stranded without protection, while they drove the vehicles up to Angola to sell them.

Douglas pulled up behind the truck. 'You go meet Captain Ahab while I make sure this container doesn't end up back in Moresby. Oh, and don't mention the Hoosenbeck. All they know is we're going up the Sepik to shoot a doco. OK? The Suyantos were insistent.'

Nash stared at him.

'Mate, it's PNG.' Douglas tapped his mutilated nose. 'Can't be too careful.'

Nash got out, grumbling.

It's a cave, for Christs sake.

Secrets were toxic on expeditions; add the pressure cooker environment of a boat, and things could become explosive very quickly.

Standing on the dock, he ran a critical eye over the ship. The helicopter deck was a shambles of rusty steel joists and perforated steel plating, shoddily welded together and several degrees out of true. Nash wondered how it would affect her balance, for patrol boats tended to roll like a bathtub in the lightest of swells, and to reach the Sepik they had to negotiate the shallow Torres Strait, notorious for its big, wind-driven seas, then traverse the stormy northern coastline of PNG. The state of the superstructure was also appalling. Beneath hastily applied grey paintwork, patches of bubbling rust were erupting like pus from an infected cut. The ship looked ready for the scrapyard, which is where he figured Sura's production company had found her.

'You must be Mr Nash.' A powerfully built man in khaki was standing at the head of the gangway. 'Lieutenant Michael Kaboro, PNGDF. Please, come aboard.'

Everything about Kaboro was smooth and polished. Nash thought him about forty-five, although with that bald head, it would not have surprised him if he were ten years out either way.

'Has your ship got a name, Lieutenant?' he asked as Kaboro's huge hand swallowed his.

'Her Indonesian designation is *Nusa Kambangan*.' It seemed a bad omen, for the so-called 'Execution Island' had become infamous after some young Australian drug smugglers were stood before an Indonesian firing squad. Kaboro smiled to put him at ease. 'Don't worry, we're using her original name of *Albany*. It's less of a mouthful, too.'

Once inside the ship, Nash was hit by a pervasive odour of diesel oil and fish sauce with a hint of septic. The *Albany*'s paintwork was scuffed to bare metal in high traffic zones, and the red linoleum floor was chipping off in large flakes. Screws were missing in door frames and exposed wiring was evident in light fittings. Kaboro, however, was upbeat.

'She's a first-class boat,' he rumbled proudly, as they stood on the bridge. 'Fremantle class, built 1981. Original displacement 220 tonnes, forty-one metres long, twin diesels making 3000 horsepower.'

Nash ran a finger along the rusty frame of the windshield.

'How will she stand shipping a swell?'

'We brought her over from Java, no problem. Don't worry, Mr Nash, we'll take care of you.'

He led Nash below to a junior officers' cabin which contained a bunk bed, a battered aluminium wardrobe, and a small desk and chair – all bolted down. There was no air conditioning, not even a porthole. An old fan in a dangerously corroded cage tried to stir the hot air. The bottom bunk had already been claimed, with a grubby green kitbag spilling cartons of cigarettes. Three cases of beer were shoved underneath.

Remembering Douglas's sleep-murdering apnoea, Nash figured it was probably too late to amend the contract, and shoved his rucksack on the top bunk.

'Excellent,' said Kaboro. 'Now to your equipment.'

Down in the forward hold, Nash was relieved that the steel hull looked solid. Kaboro supervised the unloading of the dive gear. He seemed a capable leader, staying patient with the irascible Douglas, who insisted on manning the crane, and lowering material before they were ready, and ensuring that everything was securely stowed by three young servicemen who were exceedingly polite.

When they were finished, Kaboro wiped his scalp with a handkerchief.

'Come on, I'll introduce you to Saworno.'

The tiny Javanese ex-navy engineer was busy greasing a bearing on the starboard engine. Nash figured he was in his mid-sixties. Behind thick round glasses, his eyes were good-humoured.

'Saworno worked on this ship for years until they were both mothballed,' explained Kaboro, with a straight face. 'There's no better spare part in the inventory.'

Beaming at the joke, the engineer revealed snaggled yellow teeth.

'These engines are like my wife.' He patted one of the 16-cylinder behemoths. 'They go like the crappers.'

Later, as the sun sank quickly in the tropical sky, Nash shared a few ice-cold South Pacific lagers with Douglas and Kaboro, while Saworno stuck with iced tea. Dinner was a spicy Fairfax Harbour fish masala, whipped up by the ship's cook, Ensign Faiwalati, during which Kaboro and Saworno exchanged sea stories and amusing anecdotes on the ineptitude of their respective armed forces.

'Rest assured, Mr Nash,' Kaboro added, 'our Long-Range Reconnaissance group are solid men who train with your Aussie SAS. A squad will join us on the lower Sepik.'

'Do you expect trouble?'

'Not specifically, but the Sepik provinces are remote, and we need to be prepared, wouldn't you agree, Mr Douglas?'

'If you say so, sport.'

Douglas did not bother looking up from his phone. He seemed withdrawn, probably still stung by the news of the other pilot. Nash had been enjoying himself too much to worry about it. For the first time since the accident, he felt anonymous. Free. With a guilty start, he realised he hadn't thought about Natalie or Jacqueline all afternoon.

'Well, here's to the Hoosenbeck.' Nash was fuzzily expansive after his fifth beer, and raised his bottle in a toast. 'May she prove as exciting as we think she is.'

He felt foolish when Douglas gave him a long stare. Kaboro diplomatically suggested they turn in for an early start on the ebb tide.

Chapter 9

Port Moresby Harbour, Papua New Guinea

After rounding the depth marker on Natera Reef, Kaboro opened the throttles. Now the *Albany* revealed her pedigree. Sitting back on her haunches, she dug her twin screws into the blue tropical water and was soon planing at twenty-two knots, thudding across the small swells with ease.

'Don't want to push too hard with the extra weight on the stern!' Kaboro shouted conversationally from his position at the helm.

Nash was drinking coffee in the captain's chair against the aft bulkhead. Beside him was the chart table, in front, the VHF radio. A magical sea breeze poured in through the open windows, as Saworno's diesels hummed reassuringly. Exhaust was vented below the waterline and a long, smoky wake billowed in the sparkling sea behind them. Up on the bow, Kaboro's sailors were revelling bare-chested in the cooling spray.

Observing Nash examining the gauges, Kaboro said, 'Know your way around a ship, Mr Nash?'

'A little. My father was navy.'

'Oh, what rank?'

'First Lieutenant. Navigation officer.'

In fact, Nash's first memory was of his father's long brown legs encased in white knee-length socks. Peter Nash had been absent for much of Nash's early childhood. When his father came home on leave, it was faintly disturbing to find a bearded stranger in his mother's bed. In the all too brief weeks that followed, his father had behaved like a fun-loving big brother, taking him fishing and sailing, teaching him and Jacquie to surf. He never pushed too hard because they were all getting to know one another again. Then, just as they began to crave his paternal guidance, off he would go again. It got Nash thinking: When Natalie died there had been two major expeditions to Alaska and Switzerland in the pipeline. What might their child's first memory have been? Would he have even been there to share it?

'I'm sorry,' he said to Kaboro. 'Did you say something?'

'You weren't tempted to follow in your father's footsteps?'

'I thought about becoming a clearance diver, but the rules and regulations put me off.'

Kaboro's face softened. 'You sound like my son.'

'What's his name?'

'Toby.' Kaboro pulled out his wallet and showed Nash a picture of a powerfully built young man with a high forehead and startlingly bright eyes. 'He's run a little wild, but he's going to join up and complete a degree programme as part of officer training. One day I hope to see him in command of a vessel like this one.'

Saworno came up and joined them. 'Everything AOK,' he beamed, the wind ruffling his thin grey beard. 'The alarm sensor on the high-pressure leak-off tank is behaving itself.' He inhaled a few draughts of air and pretended to shiver. 'It's too cold up here.'

'Saworno's thermostat is stuck on high,' grinned Kaboro. 'How does your wife cope in Jakarta?'

'No air con in bedroom.' Saworno winked. 'Wife sleep in living room.'

Kaboro gave Nash a turn at the helm, and the pleasure of focused concentration helped clear his head. Taking the swells head on, lightly bracing for the shocks, and adjusting when things went wrong. No point dwelling or looking back. It was a good metaphor for life.

'Did your father teach you navigation, Mr Nash?'

'A little.'

Kaboro indicated the chart table. 'Why don't you give me an estimate on how long it will take us to reach the mouth of the Sepik.'

Relinquishing the helm, Nash bent over the map of Papua New Guinea, and with ruler and brass dividers, guesstimated a likely course and distance.

'What's our range, Lieutenant?'

'At this speed? 1600 nautical miles, give or take.'

Nash nodded. 'If we were able to maintain this speed, I'd say three days. But I figure you need suitable anchorages to get some sleep.' He examined the coastline for bays and protective islands. 'Say, five days?'

Kaboro laughed, but not unkindly. 'Saworno and I will take shifts in the captain's cabin behind us. My men know how to read a compass and steer. As for your estimate, I make it three to three and half days, *if* the weather holds.'

On the second night, a squall off west New Britain whipped up three-metre seas, cutting their speed to eight knots. The *Albany* gave good account of herself, but the weight on her stern made her wallow in the deeper troughs. Kaboro remained welded to the helm, staring out through the beating rain and the foaming combers to ensure they didn't broach from an unexpected broadside. It was miserable pitching around inside the little ship, and only Douglas avoided seasickness by scoffing meclizine, which added a green hue to his hepatic tint, giving him the waxy appearance of a three-day-old corpse.

With the rough weather, Nash's nagging self-doubt returned, and he quizzed Douglas about whether there was to be an advance party – the possibility of flying gear up to the Hoosenbeck so that he might be able to grab a few exploratory dives before the pressure of shooting began.

'Robbie, all I can tell you is how many cans of tomato soup there are in the galley. Sura is calling the shots and when it comes to information, she's tighter than a nun.'

'But, Frank, these kinds of dives usually take months to plan. I have to calculate staging, supplies, recovery periods, risk factors, and I don't even know who I'm going to be diving with.' Nash shook his head. 'To be honest, I'm over the information vacuum. Why can't they bloody well provide me with some details?'

Douglas massaged his temples. 'Robbie, this is PNG. Half the bloody population is in a *raskol* gang, and the less people who know your business the better.'

'Are you saying I can't be *trusted* with the facts?' Nash could feel heat rising in his cheeks.

'Well, you did tell Kaboro where we're headed.' Douglas smiled to soften the sting. 'Look, I know you're stressed. But just try to go with the flow. If you don't like the look of anything, you just tell them no. I'll back you up.'

When they came in range of mobile networks near Madang, Nash called Jacquie, who happened to be at their parents' house. On her second round of chemo, she was coping with the nausea well enough to still be chasing work.

'Only another few rounds to go,' she said cheerfully. 'Then I'll worry about surgery.'

'You're bulletproof,' he told her. 'It's going to be fine.'

'You sound flat.' Jacquie always read his moods. 'What's up?'

'I'm fine,' he lied. 'Raring to go.'

'You won't do anything too risky, will you, Rob? You're a long way from help up there.'

He was about to give her some stick about it being all her bloody fault if he did, but he sensed she was more fragile than she was letting on.

'Don't worry, Jac. Remember, you're talking to the second biggest control freak in the universe.' He grinned at her familiar groan. 'Love you, sis.'

He was going to ring off, but then his father wanted to talk. This was unusual, for Peter was partially deaf and struggled on the phone.

'Son, a word about Frank,' Peter said in his quiet voice. 'He means well, but he can be a bit . . . flaky.'

Nash found his father's ambivalence towards his old naval buddy intriguing. Sure, he was rough around the edges, but hadn't Douglas always looked out for him? For example, the selection trials at his cricket-mad junior school. Nash was an athlete but struggled with ball sports. After a week of Uncle Frank's tough love – a hail of bouncers and yorkers – he'd managed not to embarrass himself and even ended up playing for the second XI.

'Dad, you gave me the same advice five years ago, remember?'

'True, but that time you were running the show, and there were twenty other people looking out for you. All I'm saying is don't be too reliant on him. Watch your back. If you don't like the look of something, use your instincts and get the hell out of there. Understood?'

'Yeah, sure, Dad. I'll do that. Love you.'

It struck Nash that he had always taken his parents' support for granted, a birthright for the golden boy. Recalling their farewell at the airport – his father's frailty, his mother's sadness, Jacquie's strained optimism – he realised they must have felt like that every time he'd embarked on a major dive.

It was dawn on the fourth day when they reached Broken Water Bay in the Bismarck Sea. Dense, white mist obliterated the river mouth, ten kilometres distant, but the Sepik's brooding presence was evident in the brown water beneath their keel. Kaboro slowed the boat to ten knots and warned his men to look out for trees and other detritus.

The rising sun began clearing the mist, revealing a well-defined river mouth, a kilometre and a half wide, fringed by a low jungle of mangroves on each side. Kaboro handed Nash the binoculars.

'There is no delta,' he explained. 'The river flows fast, and the sea floor drops steeply.' He indicated a chart showing they were travelling over a vast submarine canyon, bisecting the narrow continental shelf, a feature which swallowed the endless sediments washing down from the mountainous interior. 'There is a shallower bar one nautical mile upstream,' Kaboro added. 'But it won't be a problem for us – even this late in the dry season.'

As the river narrowed, the gnarled mangrove sentinels guarding the coast gave way to vast swampy flood plains of impenetrable sago forest. Even at this early hour, it was stiflingly humid. Only the raised riverbank levees and the occasional low hill studded in small trees resembled anything like terra firma.

Frank Douglas joined them as they passed a settlement of thatched huts perched precariously on rickety timber legs. A lone naked man in a hollowed-out wooden canoe watched impassively from the shallows. Wisps of steam rose from the river's surface and hung primordially about him like ghostly streamers.

'It's like going back in time,' marvelled Nash.

'Yeah, the Stone Age.' Douglas spat over the side.

'Half these people have mobile phones, Mr Douglas,' chided Kaboro.

'How many are stolen?'

Nash grimaced. 'Sorry, Lieutenant, he's always a bit of a dickhead in the morning – aren't you, Frank?'

Minutes passed in silence, and then the thatched rooftops of another settlement came into view. Nash realised it was the same village seen from a different perspective. The river was a coiled maze of deep meanders, radical U-shaped bends, some of which over time would erode to become ox-bow lakes adjacent to the main channel. It was how the Sepik ran for 1100 kilometres, when the mountains from which it sprang were just one third that distance from the sea.

'Just how far is it navigable?' he asked Kaboro.

The lieutenant tapped a long finger on the chart. 'Large vessels have officially been recorded as far as the May river junction, which is 756 kilometres upriver. However, in wetter years the river rises by as much as eight metres. It is conceivable you could travel much further then.'

Chapter 10

Angoram, East Sepik Province, Papua New Guinea

The shanty town sweltering in the heat was a mixture of traditional thatched huts and rough corrugated iron shacks. A solid concrete wharf was the only reminder that this had once been the administrative hub of German New Guinea, and for fifty years after that a key Australian outpost.

Kaboro posted two armed sailors on the dock to keep the growing crowd of curious men and women at bay. Dressed in shabby Western clothes, their cheeks were stuffed with betel nut – a mildly stimulating berry– and the concrete was soon covered with the fresh red pulp they spat out. Nash was keen to go ashore and stretch his legs, but Douglas indicated a group of young men, sporting spiked haircuts and sunglasses, in possession of the only vehicle – a surprisingly late model Toyota Hilux.

'See those jokers over there? Soon as you're round the corner, they'll empty your pockets and cut your head off.'

'*Raskols*?'

Nash was surprised. They didn't fit the stereotype of bush-variety bandits wielding home-made shotguns.

An enthusiastic honking presaged the arrival of an old troop carrier with faded police markings. A nervy-looking constable navigated carefully through the throng. Sitting beside him was a thickset army NCO. When the vehicle had come to a halt, he jumped out to release a squad of soldiers from the rear. Five sweaty men unfolded themselves and a mountain of kit. Their M16A2 assault rifles looked suitably dangerous.

The NCO shouldered his way through the villagers and climbed up the ladder to meet Kaboro. With his massive neck and shoulders, he looked like undiscovered rugby talent. Stamping his boot down, he fired off a stiff salute.

'Sergeant Singkepe, Long-Range Reconnaissance Group.'

Kaboro looked back along the road and frowned. 'You were supposed to be escorting a fuel delivery for my ship, Sergeant.'

Singkepe's dense monobrow twitched. 'The tanker is bogged down two kilometres away. We need help to free it, sir.'

'And you left it *unguarded*?'

A tight-lipped Kaboro turned to the rail and whistled loudly.

'*Skius! Skius!*' he called out to the crowd. '*Nem bilong mi emi Lieutenant Kaboro. Nidim diesel. Plis helpin me. Tenkyu tumas.*'

Pidgin was PNG's default lingua franca, a polyglot language developed in the nineteenth century to deal with the fact there was no common language. The crowd stared impassively, and Kaboro directed his next words to the source of their reluctance – the young men by the 4WD.

'*Koan, nogatt be a lesbaga!*'

Douglas chuckled. 'Lazy buggers – yeah, you got that right.'

The leader of the young men, a brutal-looking fellow with a jagged scar across his forehead, stepped forward insolently.

'*Hamas you baim, captain?*'

Kaboro mused briefly before announcing, '150.'

The young man grinned as if this was a fine joke. Eventually they settled on 300.

'And that is what is wrong with this fucking country.' Douglas shook his head as the soldiers climbed back into the Land Cruiser and headed down the road after the Hilux. Within twenty minutes, they returned with an orange AWD fuel tanker. None of the vehicles was muddy and no one looked as if they had been exerting themselves. If Kaboro was angry at being diddled, he gave no sign of it, and got on with checking the quantity and quality of the fuel. Meanwhile, Singkepe and his troops exchanged pleasantries with the young men and shared cigarettes around.

'What did I fucking tell you?' snorted Douglas. 'That little scam was hatched on the way in.'

Most Westerners found wantokism – PNG's elaborate social system of allegiances – difficult to rationalise. When villages were marooned islands in the jungle, and your neighbours were out to eat your brains for lunch, it was vital for social cohesion; a man was defined not by what he owned, but by how much he gave away. In a twenty-first-century context it had led to endemic corruption. Money earmarked for roads, hospitals and police cars tended to vanish without trace. While it was a form of wealth redistribution, often those most in need missed out.

By mid-afternoon, the steel superstructure of the *Albany* shimmered like a barbecue hotplate, and in the near 100 per cent humidity, distractions like reading a book were impossible as pages became sodden and fell apart. Douglas took shelter under a small fan in the galley and nursed a tepid beer, while Kaboro cleaned out the captain's cabin in preparation for the Indonesians.

It was far too hot for exercise, but after four days cooped up on the boat Nash was stir-crazy. Out on the helicopter pad, he stripped off his sodden shirt. Acknowledging Singkepe's crack about mad dogs and white men with an ironic salute, Nash proceeded to skip, star jump, squat and run on the spot – anything he could do without pressing flesh to metal – until he could barely see for the rivulets of sweat. A group of locals enthusiastically cheered and clapped every set.

A cool down in the crocodile-infested river was out of the question, so Nash utilised the washing-up bucket to haul up loads of lukewarm water to sluice off.

Suddenly, a loud roar filled the sky as a chopper appeared low and fast over the village. The sleek gold Bell 505 Jet Ranger flared just once before it touched down on the pad Nash had just hastily evacuated. As the pilot decreased power, the *Albany*'s stern settled lower in the river.

A tiny woman alighted before the rotor stopped spinning. Indifferent to the prop wash, she moved with a lithe and confident elegance. Her body-hugging jumpsuit was made of some technological fabric which accentuated her figure, and a small pink headscarf, which was more of a headband, contained her shoulder-length black hair. Waving over Kaboro's sailors, she had them unload her Victorinox bags, which would not have looked out of place in a first-class lounge. The remainder of the load – several heavy-duty plastic crates – were stacked by the edge of the pad. The woman twirled an elegant finger skywards at the pilot – a darkly handsome Indonesian version of Maverick in *Top Gun* – and, with a flash of gold Aviators and white teeth, he took off, winging it back in the direction from which they had come.

Douglas welcomed her and then introduced Nash.

'Mr Nash.' Her eyes ran over his dripping wet body. 'I've been bingeing your films. Impressive.'

The sing-song Javanese accent made it hard to determine whether this was as insincere as it sounded. Nash responded with a vague compliment about her documentary work. Privately, he hadn't thought that much of what he'd found on YouTube. A lightweight series called *Wild Indonesia,* which totally glossed over the fact her country was burning every shred of habitat for palm oil.

Sura looked over the top of her Gucci sunglasses with a faint smile on her face.

'Still, I imagine the Hoosenbeck will be a challenge, even for you.'

'Indeed, it will. Which is why we need to begin planning ASAP. I'd like to start with a full inventory of your resources, proposed timeline . . . oh, and of course a script –'

She cut him off to snap at one of the crew sitting on a suitcase.

'*Get off dispela kago!*'

'You can speak pidgin?' Nash was impressed.

'My father was once stationed in Papua.' Her lip curled. 'They're like children here, you have to watch them all the time. Speaking of which . . . Ah, there you are, Lieutenant Kaboro. I'm glad you could make it.'

Ignoring the sarcasm, Kaboro formally welcomed Sura aboard. He was then subjected to what seemed to be an unnecessary interrogation about his organisation and refuelling.

'That will be all for now.' Sura dismissed him. 'I must get my luggage out of the sun.'

'I will supervise the men.' Kaboro moved forward.

'Absolutely not.' She shooed him away. 'I will see to it myself.'

Douglas spat as they watched her round up the sailors. 'Friendly, ain't she?'

'Indonesians think we're no better than pigs.' Kaboro's voice was flat. 'Small wonder the Papuans fight.'

Nash knew the PNG government was scared of antagonising its powerful neighbour while struggling with a growing sense of Melanesian solidarity across the South Pacific.

'Do you have any contacts in Papua, Lieutenant?'

Kaboro shook his head. 'Despite our proximity, it might as well be the far side of the Moon.' He lifted his cap to mop his brow. 'The Indonesians have locked up Papua to exploit its resources, and those who get in the way are disposed of. The world knows this – it just doesn't care.'

For the next two hours, the chopper ferried in cargo at its maximum lift capacity of 900 kilos. Kaboro's sweating men lugged it below. Suyanto's hectoring instructions bordered on racist bullying, but the fact the sailors treated it as a joke decided Nash against calling it out. Sura then got in a fight with Douglas about failing to procure the brand of iced tea she had mandated, then made Kaboro radio through an order to Jayapura for three cartons.

With the tropical sun dropping quickly on the western horizon, Nash joined Douglas for a beer on the stern. The old pilot was sucking down cigarette smoke as if it was too precious to waste.

'You all right there, Frank?'

'After a day like today, I can't wait to retire.'

'I thought you liked them small and demure?' Nash guffawed at Douglas's black expression.

'Yeah, go ahead and laugh.' Douglas flicked his bottle cap over the side. 'But I'm going to buy myself an old shack somewhere in far north Queensland and just fish. No bloody mobile, no bloody computer, no bloody razor wire . . . just me, a rod and a decent boat to fetch more beer.'

'Sounds good, Uncle Frank.'

Nash didn't begrudge the man one cent of the fee he had earned for signing him. Beyond endless stories of his colourful life, Douglas had little, and on his last visit, Nash had been shocked by his run-down apartment in Moresby. Although a Royal Australian Navy pension went a long way in Third World PNG, Douglas had a long list of failed business ventures, most notably a seaplane joy-flight operation written off by a cyclone where, naturally, he'd been uninsured.

They heard the distant *whup whup whup* of the chopper. Its final delivery was the Indonesian team, and Douglas lobbed his empty over the side before Nash could stop him.

'Let's welcome the rest of our happy campers.'

From the quarterdeck, one of Kaboro's men directed a spotlight onto the pad. With beacons flashing red, green and white, the Jet Ranger touched down, turbine whining like a banshee. The front-seat passenger was clearly gigantic: all knees and elbows filling the cockpit. Sensibly, he waited for the rotor to stop before egressing, for, even bent double, he would have been decapitated.

The big man crossed the pad, lugging rigid film equipment cases in each hand. Dressed in a T-shirt and jeans, his massive arms were covered in an eclectic array of tattoos. On his right bicep was a yin-yang symbol the size of a dinner plate. Below this, lines of Sanskrit trailed down to his wrist. On his left arm was a shield with a dagger, which appeared to be a regimental badge. He was about 30, with a heavyset face, softened slightly by shoulder-length blond hair and a short beard.

'Jaap Boerman,' he announced, towering over them.

Nash gave him a friendly smile. 'G'day, Jaap, you must be the camera operator. Maybe we can share a beer once you've settled in? We've a ton of stuff to get through.'

Boerman pointedly ignored him.

'Where's Sura?' he asked Douglas.

'Captain's quarters. Upstairs.' Thinking Boerman had mistaken Nash for crew, Douglas attempted to introduce him.

'I know who he is.' With measured contempt, Boerman looked Nash up and down. 'The legendary Robert Nash. I hear you're quite the hero, except when it comes to the ladies, hey?'

The wide grin magnified the inference of cowardice, and Nash was struck by a loathing so visceral that he unconsciously balled his right fist. Only a sense that Boerman was eagerly waiting for a punch prevented him from throwing it.

'I suggest you take that back,' said Douglas tightly.

'Or you'll do what?' Boerman sneered.

Further comment was interrupted by the dashing helicopter pilot.

'Ricki Hartono.' He gave them each a brisk handshake.

There was another man with him, who'd escaped notice in the back of the chopper. Mid-forties, stocky with a bullet-like head, he was dressed in a green T-shirt and camouflage pants and stank of clove cigarettes.

'Goki is our producer,' said Hartono. 'He doesn't speak English.'

'*Selamat malam*,' he said, with dead eyes and hands in pockets.

Shaken, but still trying to stay friendly, Nash offered to help them unload. Boerman cut him dead.

'We're sensitive about our gear. I'm sure you understand.'

'Suit yourself.'

'It's raining arseholes today,' Douglas commented when they reached the opposite end of the ship. 'That Goki gives me the creeps, too.'

Nash was churning in a way he hadn't since Jonathan had come for his pound of flesh. It didn't make any sense; if they didn't value his services, why pay him so much to be here?

'Frank, what just happened back there?'

'He's testing you out, trying to rattle your cage. Don't take it too personally, Robbie.'

'Frank, you know he meant Natalie.'

Douglas nodded slowly. 'Blokes like that thrive on finding your weakness, so don't give him anything.'

Nash wished Douglas's old-school counsel provided more comfort. He was a professional diver, not a brawler, and cave diving required trust. How was he supposed to take on the Hoosenbeck with a fuckwit like that?

'Hey, how about a nightcap?' Douglas lit up a cigarette. 'I've got some decent Scotch in the old kitbag. Let's take the edge off.'

'Thanks, Frank, but I'll pass. Goodnight.'

Back against the rail, Nash stared long at the waning crescent moon. He could hear the leathery flapping of foraging fruit bats, thousands of insects shrilling unseen. The jungle was getting on with the unceasing business of survival, which amplified the sense he was out of his depth and didn't belong. For a moment he flirted with the idea of telling Shangri-La where they could stick it in the morning. But then, getting his gear home would consume a sizeable chunk of the advance, which was the only thing letting his sister worry about herself for a change, Douglas wouldn't get his fishing shack, and he would be right back where he started.

'No way,' Nash muttered.

Because if he was brutally honest with himself, Boerman's crude jibe had found a weak spot. The Octopus was an aberration that needed to be excised. He needed to prove to himself that he still had what it took.

Chapter 11

Saturday, *June 2ⁿᵈ, 1945*

We are on a huge river. I'm sure of this as there is no longer any ocean swell and mosquitoes have begun to appear, even in this airless hell. Hartmann thinks it must be New Guinea. We travel on the surface at night and sit on the bottom by day. Last night, we hit something heavy and I heard it grind along the hull. The temperature is so hot, we are all suffering. Hartmann is very sick again; he can't seem to hold anything down.

Sunday, *June 3ʳᵈ, 1945*

My worst fears are realised. Ilse has been taken from me. We both knew it was coming but I believe my heart is broken. The smirk on Unterscharführer Müller's face tells me all I need to know. Can you bear it, my darling?

Thursday, June 7ᵗʰ, 1945

The day has ended in tragedy. When they told us to go on deck, I shook hands with Hartmann because we believed it was the hour of our execution. Outside the stars were shining, and Hartmann and I just stood there sucking in the precious air. A spotlight illuminated the dark water ahead. There were crocodiles by the hundreds and huge insects everywhere. The submarine moved very slowly. The guards let us walk up and down the deck. After twenty minutes they told us to return below. I couldn't believe we were going to live. Then Hartmann suddenly turned on Heider. As an upper-class Prussian of the old school, he expressed most eloquently what he thought of him. His last words were: 'You are a disgusting coward without honour.' Heider shot him through the forehead. I think Hartmann just couldn't bear going back below. He was a brave man.

* * *

The modest captain's cabin was jam-packed with luggage and equipment cases. Astride one of these, Boerman was stripping down his pride and joy, an original M60 machine gun from the Vietnam War, which he had acquired in Ho Chi Minh City after seeing *Rambo*.

'Nash seemed to think I'm his boy. Who does he fucking think he is?'

In a white T-shirt and black lacy underwear, Sura was lying on top of the single bed, studying her tablet.

'If the Hoosenbeck Cavern is as deep as they say it is, we'll need his services.'

Boerman frowned as he ran a wire brush through the flash suppressor.

'Nash has the thousand-yard stare – I saw it in the Legion – and I'm telling you, under pressure he'll turn to jelly. We don't need him *or* Douglas. The sooner we're rid of them, the better.'

Engrossed in the Ford diary entries, Sura was only half listening.

'You'll get your fun. Until then, keep your hands to yourself.'

'Do you really mean it, liefie?' he cooed, reaching over to cup her taut right buttock. Its nutmeg firmness made him want to sink his teeth into it.

She shifted irritably. 'Go back to your cabin. Goki will be wondering where you are.'

As far as Jaap was concerned, Goki could go to fucking Hell, but Sura had sworn him to be on his best behaviour.

'Just a quickie, *liefie*. I swear I'm going out of my mind here.'

It was a question, not a statement. Big Jaap Boerman was scared of no man, yet he lived in constant fear of losing Sura Suyanto. How a grifter like him had got so lucky never ceased to amaze him. Before Sura, there was the banal brutality of a childhood in the slums of Jo'burg, petty – then violent – crime, several stints in jail, followed by five years with the French Foreign Legion in Algeria. It was a good outlet for his talents, but he'd been dishonourably discharged for beating up an officer. There followed a stint diving Nigerian oil rigs as a welder, until an overbearing foreman made him shatter the man's skull with his bare fists. Evading justice, he made his way back down the African continent, washing up on the shark cage diving boats running out of Gansbaai.

'The answer is no.' She pushed away his hand. 'Now hurry up and hide that weapon.'

'Which one?'

At last he was rewarded with a hearty chuckle.

Ja, this is the gutsy Sura I know.

The first time he'd laid eyes on her, she was calmly staring down a six-metre great white with its snout stuck in the aluminium bars of her shark cage. The massive fish was shaking

113

it to pieces. He'd dived in, busted it on the nose, then hauled Sura and her terrified cameraman out of there. The man had refused to go back in the water, so Sura had handed Boerman the camera. That night, she came to his dingy lodgings, made him feel something for the first time in his life. Now, Jaap Boerman could not imagine life without her.

'Look here.' She sat up, excited. 'My father has sent new images of the Hoosenbeck.'

SUBJECT: *Your holiday in Jayapura.*

Thought these might help with the documentary.

Ayah.

The high-resolution shots were taken from an Indonesian EADS CASA C-295 at 1500 metres. The detail was far superior to the satellite photos, and they greedily pored over key features of the terrain. The three crooked arms of the gorge had been formed by many millennia of snowmelt through a sheer escarpment more than a kilometre high. At some point in the distant past, the river and waterfall that had sculpted the gorge had vanished atop the escarpment down a vertical shaft, which appeared in the photo as a ragged black slot.

'Unbelievable,' Boerman breathed. 'It just swallows the river.'

'A geological path of least resistance,' Sura mused. 'The subterranean river has carved out the giant cavern and the lake within.'

'The perfect hiding spot for a submarine.'

'But surely the Dutch should have found signs of a vessel that large?' With her jet-black fringe low over her eyes, Sura scrolled downstream, peering intently at the twists and turns of the gorge, where deep shadows masked possible hidden caverns. 'The diary entries are infuriatingly vague on the last days of the *I-403*'s voyage.'

Boerman slid the M60 under the bed and stood up to go.

'It's there, *liefie*. And I know you will find it.'

'Thank you, Jaap.'

Sura rarely used his name, especially not affectionately, and the familiarity hurt more than the ball of Libyan shrapnel working its way out of his left trapezius. Their relationship only existed behind closed doors, and Boerman's conversion to the faith, which he'd done for her, had changed nothing. As a *bule* – a white man – he had never been accepted. He was just the muscle who got to screw the goddess when no one who mattered was looking.

Godver doem dit.

'Jaap.'

Seeing that sultry look in her eyes fired his blood and he could barely get his pants down quick enough.

'No, no,' she chided when he reached for her. 'Let me.'

Gratefully he surrendered to her skilful ministrations and was almost ready to blow, when suddenly, there was a rap at the door.

'*Apa yang terjadi disana?*'

Boerman gave a piteous moan. 'Fucking Goki.'

'One minute!' Sura called out, before whispering to Jaap saucily, 'Your day just got better.'

With a wink she plunged her mouth down to receive him.

Goki's eyes were flat discs when Sura opened the door.

'When I knock, I expect your door to open.'

Sura crossed her arms. 'Oh, really?'

Boerman was not quite ready to fight, but he mustered a growl.

'We are all adults here. Why don't you mind your own business?'

The commando stepped inside and closed the door, filling the cabin with his clove stink and menace.

'Already you risk our security, Sura. Do you think these troopers are blind to your charms? Do you think they cannot hear, or *smell*, what you are up to?' His nose crinkled with distaste. 'This is a delicate operation involving two countries. It requires discipline and tact, all right?'

'Would that be the same discipline which cost us our source?' retorted Sura.

'You are a stupid and spoilt child.'

'And you forget yourself.' Sura flushed angrily. 'My father will hear of this.'

'Indeed, he will.' Goki's voice was silken. 'Do not forget your father put me in charge to safeguard his interests. From now on, you *will* conduct yourself professionally and modestly.' He turned to stare at Boerman, 'And you will keep that dick in your pants, or I'll cut it off and use it to shut your big mouth. That scene tonight with Nash was not only pathetic – you risked our mission before it has even started.'

Boerman was itching to go for Goki's throat, but Sura blocked his path.

'You've made your point, Sergeant. Please go.'

Goki gave Boerman a final dark look.

'I'll see you in two minutes.'

When he stalked away, the hilt of a commando knife protruded above his belt and Boerman knew it was a message.

'I want to be there when you take him apart.' Sura's low voice trembled with hate. 'Do you hear me?'

'Ja, I hear you, *liefie*.'

In the blocky commando, Boerman recognised a natural born killer, and a cool-headed one at that. Taking Goki down would require precision, with no room for error. But he would make him beg for death.

Chapter 12

Jayapura, Papua, Indonesia

In the unstable wake of the recent tropical storm, the Garuda 737-800 shuddered as it skimmed the lake 60 metres below. Doctor Mia Carter planted her feet on the floor and took a deep breath. She was not a nervous flyer, but Sentani International Airport was located in a natural depression, which meant a gut-churning approach to a steeply sloping runway.

They bounced once, twice, before the tyres bit with a slight side-skid. The comforting roar of reverse thrust confirmed they were safely down. Trundling along the taxiway, steam from the recent downpour rose like smoke, enveloping the windows in a sheen of condensation. Excited to be back, Mia pressed her face to the Plexiglas, hoping to spot Paul's plane among a gaggle of light aircraft beside the terminal.

It was strange she hadn't heard from him. While it often took him a week to respond to emails – he seemed to treat the computer like an old fashioned letter box – she had not received any response to her holiday snaps. And she hadn't spoken to him on the phone since leaving the US almost three months ago. Not that she'd dwelled on it during her long lazy holiday in Cambodia and Thailand, because that was precious time for doing absolutely nothing but recharging her batteries after three intense years without a break in the ER. But then she hadn't been able to get through to him from her hotel in Jakarta yesterday, either.

Retrieving her bag from the overhead locker, Mia told herself not to worry. The mission's satellite connection went down every few weeks, and Paul always noted times and dates down in his meticulous old-school longhand which put her scrawl to shame. He would be there.

There was a clunk as the stewardess opened the cabin door, and then the pungent waft of the tropics washing inside suddenly made her decision to return real.

At the Kantor Immigrasi, the squat official checked her passport and visa details with great care, flicking sceptical eyes up to study her face several times. This had been her experience last time. Averse to negative journalism, the Indonesian authorities were suspicious of Western tourists, and controlled their movements by way of travel permits.

'Jayawijaya?' he asked, pointing at her stated destination.

'Yes, the Ford Mission. I have a working visa.'

He picked up the phone and spoke in Indonesian too rapid to follow. Then a tall Indonesian military officer appeared from a doorway behind the desk and asked her to follow him.

'*Apakah ada yang sala?*' she asked. *Is anything wrong?*

In a small interview room, he meticulously searched her belongings. Mia stayed calm. It was probably a new protocol – nothing to do with her or the mission. While Christianity was discouraged in Papua, the long-running self-funded hospital was tolerated. Paul had explained that, provided they maintained a strictly apolitical stance on Papuan autonomy, their future was assured.

Zipping up Mia's medical bag, the officer seemed curious rather than threatening.

'So, you're a doctor?'

'Yes. And I very much enjoy working in your country.'

Up at the mission it was easy to forget the oppression. Its remoteness from mining and logging operations which the OPM targeted – and the Trans-Papua Highway, built to service them – was one of the reasons she loved being there. It was, she told friends, like Shangri-La, the lost world she had loved imagining in James Hilton's novel *Lost Horizon*.

The officer surprised her by politely opening the door.

'You are free to go. Have a nice stay.'

The arrivals hall was deserted, and Mia's optimism deflated. Where was he? Finding a payphone, she tried the mission. Again, the number rang out, and once again she checked with the operator, who said the line was not out of order. Mia frowned. Perhaps Paul *had* got the dates wrong? Maybe his plane had had an issue? But why, then, hadn't he left a message? Trying not to worry, she made her way to the airline desks and approached a representative from one of the small air charter firms she knew made deliveries to the mission.

'Hello, I need to get up to the Ford Mission. I can pay for a private charter if necessary.'

The young man smiled apologetically. 'All flights to the western Jayawijaya region are cancelled until further notice.'

'Even medical services?'

He nodded.

'But why?'

Glancing around, he lowered his voice. 'I believe it is military operations.'

Mia frowned. The mission was wholly dependent on air. Medical supplies would be running low – and what about emergencies?

'How long has this been going on?'

'I'm not sure. Maybe a few weeks.'

She thought of Paul, Millie, Avis and the nursing team cut off up there, in God only knew what kind of danger.

'Can I help you with anything else, madam?'

'No, thank you.'

She needed somewhere private to regroup, and caught a taxi to the closest hotel – a sterile resort with a large diamond-shaped pool, full of Indonesian tourists and businessmen. There were no indigenous staff apart from some men sweeping the paths. Remembering that Paul shared medical supplies with the hospital at Oksibil, a town on the other side of the mountains, Mia found the number and gave them a call.

'We've been trying to reach them,' grunted Roger Grant, the gruff Australian resident. 'Last time we spoke, Paul was going to fly me over some antibiotics, but he never turned up. When I couldn't raise them for a week or so, I flew in. A bloody attack helicopter sent me packing before I could land.'

'When was this, Roger?'

'About a month ago.'

'But they told me the region had only been closed for three weeks. Oh my God.' Her mind raced. 'Do you think they're all right?'

He was silent for a moment. 'Paul and the hospital are well regarded. I can't imagine they'd do him any harm – on the other hand, the army seem to have their blood up about something. But I've never known them to close down a province for this long.'

'Isn't there someone we can call?'

He gave a dry laugh. 'A waste of time, Doctor Carter. The more you ask, the less you'll get. If it were me, I'd go home, or find somewhere comfortable and wait until Paul calls. Manila's a one-hour direct flight. There's not much to do in Jayapura, if you catch my drift.'

Giving him her email, she begged him to keep her updated.

'No problem. Take care.'

Hanging up, Mia lay back on the bed and reflected on his veiled warning. She was under surveillance, which meant no talking things over with her mom and dad, who would only worry themselves sick anyway. But going home or relaxing by a pool in Manila?

Not a chance.

Mia opened a map of greater New Guinea on her laptop. The world's second largest island looked uncannily like its most famed inhabitant, the bird of paradise. And just above where the tail met the body, was the mouth of the Sepik. The great river had intrigued her since her first flight with Paul, when he had pointed out its sluggish brown coils from 20,000 feet. It crossed the PNG border not twenty miles from the site of the mission, and there was a well-used trail through the forest, which she had trekked with Avis, Mark and Jacinta over three wonderful days.

If she couldn't fly in, why not take a boat, and walk?

Mia stared out of the window at the listless palms by the pool. It was extremely dangerous travelling alone, and unattached women were fair game. Re-entering Papua on the sly was also highly irregular, and might see her arrested and deported. But what was at stake here? Paul Ford was not only offering to teach her how to run a fifteen-bed hospital and community clinic; he was putting his faith in her ability to lead a vital service for years to come. Was she really going to turn her back on all those wonderful people who were already depending on her?

Chapter 13

Sepik River, Papua New Guinea

Out on the bow, Sura, Hartono, Goki and Boerman were making obeisance on their knees. Presumably facing in the direction of Mecca, they were enveloped in a dense pre-dawn mist which made for an ethereal scene. Nash was surprised to see no sign of Saworno, for the devout engineer had been out there every other morning.

Douglas appeared with a mug of black coffee and spat into the invisible river.

'Kaboro won't get underway until this bloody mist clears.' He gave Nash a speculative look. 'Feeling any better?'

Nash could have mentioned Frank's insufferable snoring, which was even worse than mulling over bruised pride when it came to sleep, but instead he grinned.

'Don't let the bastards wear you down.'

'That's the spirit.' Douglas punched him on the shoulder. 'Let's get some breakfast before they stop wailing and eat all the eggs.'

It wasn't until 0900 that the *Albany* finally cast off. The locals waved farewell enthusiastically, and it seemed to Nash that they could have happily stood there all day. How different life was here from the insane juggle back home. He and Natalie had worked like maniacs during their time; now those rare moments of simply being together were the precious things. If only they had known.

At a steady 20 knots, they moved up the wide river. Pockets of rainforest thickened as the swampy sago plains gave way to the foothills of the still-distant mountains. Flattened down thickets of kunai grass served as pathways for local villagers who stopped to gawk at the sight of the helicopter mated to the ship like some lascivious dragonfly. Although little rough water was expected, Hartono had lashed it down with heavy-duty ratchet straps and covered the engine intakes with PVC covers to protect them from the tropical weather. He was wiping the chopper's Plexiglas when Nash approached.

'Morning, Ricki, how is Saworno? I didn't see him this morning.'

'He's working.'

The pilot's eyes were unreadable through dark Ray-Bans, but his tone suggested Nash should mind his own business.

Beneath the crane on the bow, Sergeant Singkepe was putting his bare-chested squad through a callisthenics routine. Jaap Boerman joined in the star jumps and burpees, and the deck reverberated alarmingly under his huge boots. It seemed to Nash he was trying to put them to shame. Boerman's massive oak-like physique was gym-honed, and despite the fact the soldiers were all in excellent condition, they looked like schoolboys in comparison.

Sura Suyanto was spectating from the bridge. Wearing a light tropical shirt cinched in with an army belt, she was smiling, but there was no warmth in it. Nash gave her a wave and went up to the bridge to approach her about the film, but when he got up there, she had retired to her cabin and the disagreeable Goki was leaning against her door.

Oh well, thought Nash. *It can wait.*

The morning wore on, the heat intensified, and the plucky *Albany* ploughed steadily through the chocolate river water, her deep wake stirring up the lotus in the shallows. The grassy riverbanks were topped with stately palm trees and looked as inviting as a tourist brochure, apart from the huge crocodiles sunning themselves below, mouths fiendishly agape. An egret stalking the margins stabbed the water and speared a large catfish, tossing it in the air to line up the long spines for a manageable swallow. Nash dozed restlessly in the shade until the clanging of Faiwalati's saucepan signalled lunch.

When he got to the mess, the Indonesians were already tucking into a coconut fish curry. Goki and Sura sat at one bench, Boerman and Hartono at the other. No one made a move to give Nash room. In fact, only Sura made eye contact when he said hello.

Nash nodded as he took a plate.

'I was thinking we could run through storyboards today. What do you say?'

'I think that can wait until we're on location.' She tried softening the rejection with a small smile, then, when Nash didn't concede, impatiently flicked the bangle on her wrist. 'Oh, relax, Mr Nash. Why not enjoy the cruise and save your energy for when we get up there?'

Nash was baffled. Every director he'd ever worked with was totally *obsessed* with shooting schedules and logistics. And even if Sura was usually the talent, she must be aware of the importance of planning.

'With respect, once we get to the cave, I'll be so focused on the technical aspects of the diving, there won't be time. We should begin planning now. It's a safety issue as well.'

'Didn't you hear the lady, Nash?' Boerman glowered from the next bench. 'Let us eat in peace, man.'

'An uncharted cave is a serious proposition at the best of times, and we're talking about the Hoosenbeck.'

When Boerman scoffed at this, Nash decided it was time to meet the big Afrikaner head-on.

'How much deep diving experience do you actually have, by the way?'

Boerman pushed his empty bowl aside and crossed his brawny arms. 'Three years on the Niger Two rig operating at depths of 275 metres.' He gave Hartono a knowing wink.

'With a diving bell?' Nash helped himself to a sago pancake.

'*Ja*, of course,' Boerman snorted. 'It's the middle of the fucking ocean.'

Nash took a bite of pancake and chewed slowly. 'Let me guess. Five days coming up nice and slowly, chilling out with pretzels and beer while you're watching porn?' He laughed scornfully. 'For God's sake, man, you might as well be latched on to your mamma's teat. We're going to a place where the only thing between you and certain oblivion is *my* experience. So, why don't you pull your head in and listen for a change?'

Boerman crashed a massive fist on the table. 'Damn it, Nash, I don't need your fucking approval. I have over 200 dives on trimix.'

'As a matter of fact, you do.' Nash calmly took another bite. 'As it states very clearly in my contract.'

'Enough!' Sura threw down her napkin and stood up. 'Mr Nash, you are right. There is much to consider, and I promise to consult with you later today. Now, if you will excuse me, I will go and prepare.'

Nash watched her leave with an ugly feeling in his chest. Something wasn't right. Something wasn't right at all. The remaining men were silent, and he was instantly struck by the feeling they were hiding something. Perhaps they sensed this, because they immediately got up and left without further comment.

Nash was too worked up to eat any more. He wanted some answers.

The engineer was hunched over a valve on the left engine.

'Saworno!' yelled Nash fruitlessly over the din.

Hesitantly, he stepped inside. The thick oily atmosphere was hotter than a sauna and stuck to the back of his throat. Reaching out, he tapped Saworno on the shoulder. The little man flinched. On seeing Nash, he registered surprise, but his expression was guarded, and he took some persuading to leave the noisy compartment.

'All good,' was his reply when Nash asked him why he was no longer coming up to eat, pray and socialise. 'Me look after engines. Mind business. Then go home. All OK.'

Nash's eyes narrowed. 'Did they *tell* you to stay down here?'

Saworno looked down at his oily hands.

'Come on, Saworno. Has something happened? Why are they so unfriendly?'

'Please, Mr Nash, I don't know.'

The poor man looked so put upon that Nash felt guilty.

'If you're sure. But if you need any help . . . you come and find me, OK?'

Douglas was dismissive when Nash shared his reservations.

'It's just a cultural thing, Robbie. Javanese like Sura will try to out-polite you. They'll smile and call you by your correct title even when they're hating your guts. Whereas Goki's from Makasar – I can tell by his accent. He's much more rough and ready.'

'That doesn't explain bullying Saworno, does it?'

Douglas shrugged. 'It's a stratified society. Saworno's lower class – they don't like him hobnobbing with us when he's supposed to be working. You'll get used to it.' He grinned. 'They're already treating us like the help.'

Nash stared at him doubtfully. 'Frank, who first approached you about the expedition?'

'A guy from Shangri-La productions. Arif, I think it was. I got a call and then he flew in to negotiate.' Douglas frowned. 'Hey, you're not getting cold feet, are you?'

'No. But they're too sloppy, Frank. And I'm having a hard time believing it's just cultural.'

Douglas scratched his grizzled cheek thoughtfully. 'Fair enough. But it sounds like you put a grenade under them today. Let's give them time to respond before you go in half-cocked.'

In the early evening, when the worst of the heat had dissipated, Nash was sprawled on the top bunk in a pair of shorts when there was a knock on his door. It was Sura, freshly showered, in a pink T-shirt, denim shorts and sandals. She was carrying a tablet and two bottles of iced tea.

'I'm so sorry for what happened earlier, Mr Nash.' Her eyes met his. 'We've all been so tense getting here, but it wasn't fair on you and I apologise. If you feel up to it, could we have that meeting now?'

'Be glad to.' Rolling off his bunk, he landed lightly on his feet and took the proffered drink. 'But why don't you call me Rob?'

'OK.' She smiled prettily. 'Rob it is.'

They went to the mess, where there was space to spread out. Sura began by showing him recent photos of the Hoosenbeck Gorge on her tablet, and Nash was captivated by the detail, especially the disappearing river at the top of the escarpment.

'Have you seen anything like this before?'

He shook his head. 'Rivers in limestone country often flow underground when a sinkhole collapses, but a 1000 metre subterranean drop? It's mind-boggling.' Nash paused to stare at the image again. 'There must be untold marvels inside that cliff face, a whole network of dry and wet caves to explore.' Looking up, he nodded thoughtfully. 'The forces involved suggest the cave lake may well be an incredible depth.'

'How deep?' Her brown eyes were intense.

'Well, easily one to two hundred metres, quite possibly more.'

'And you can go that deep?'

'Deeper, given the right equipment and resources.'

'What motivates you to do it, Rob?'

Hand beneath her chin, she stared up at him expectantly. Although it was probably Javanese flattery, it was a question he never tired of answering.

'I suppose I'm fascinated by hidden worlds. People talk about the ocean as *inner space*, but for me, an underwater cave is the ultimate expression of it. Not only is it knowing you are the first human being to have ever set foot in a place, it's the fact you are completely dependent on your planning, equipment and training, which makes it intensely satisfying, sometimes even . . . spiritual . . . to discover what is there.'

'But cut off beneath the surface in such dark and cruel places?' She shuddered. 'I think it would freak me out.'

Feeling the spectre of Natalie rising, Nash drained his iced tea, and wiped the condensation from his hands.

'So, how long is this film to be, then, Sura?'

'Oh, I think a one-hour feature – possibly ninety minutes if we get enough footage.'

'And the angle?'

Sura tapped her cute little nose. 'Excite viewers with an unexplored marvel of nature right on our doorstep. Oh, and scare them a little, too.'

It was the standard approach, and an effective one.

'OK.' He nodded. 'The challenge with filming underwater caves is giving viewers context, otherwise they don't appreciate what they're looking at – or the stakes involved – thus, infographics will be essential. I have a small laser mapping tool that we can use to collect data.' Nash let Sura finish jotting this down as he considered his next point. 'An important thing to remember is at least half the story happens *above* water. There's a wealth of interesting stuff on the origins of the cave, its geology, early exploration, and then you need to impress upon people the challenges of just getting to the Hoosenbeck.

Location shots on the boat, from the helicopter, insights from the local people, will all help with that.'

Sura looked up from her tablet and smiled. 'It's so good to get your advice, Rob. Normally I just read scripts and present.'

Given their massive budget, it seemed strange they hadn't bothered to bring a professional director or writer along, but he nodded politely.

'Of course, the story will be shaped by how far we penetrate, and what we discover. I'm optimistic we're going to get some amazing footage. But in an uncharted cave like the Hoosenbeck, our expectations need to fall within the limits of our equipment and experience.'

Sura looked up from her tablet. 'You're talking about Jaap, aren't you?'

'I'm afraid he's out of his depth.'

'He means well, Rob. And he's very brave and strong.'

'Unfortunately, that means little in an underwater cave. Caution born of experience and training, and a comprehensive understanding of physiology and psychology, are what keep you alive.'

Looking pensive, she twirled her empty bottle around.

'You *do* need a second camera, though, don't you?'

'Yes. Jaap will be essential for establishing shots, ferrying gear, and setting up lights for key scenes, but he needs to understand I'm not interested in having a chest-beating competition every time I make a decision.'

'I quite understand.' She blinked slowly before focusing on him. 'Don't worry, Rob, I shall make Jaap clear about his role.'

'And Goki?' Here he watched her carefully. 'Where does he fit in to all of this?'

'Goki?' She seemed puzzled. 'Our producer is a man of few words, but he writes the cheques, so we have to work with him as best we can.'

The answer was defensive, and Nash got the feeling he'd pushed her far enough for one night.

'Fair enough.' He flipped open a pad and picked up the pen. 'Shall we begin?'

They worked for two hours until Nash was reasonably satisfied that they had a basic plan for the penetration, but he still couldn't reconcile Sura's lack of preparation. Beyond taking a whole bunch of footage and stringing a story together later, he figured they'd had no plan whatsoever.

'Your problem is you think the rest of the world cares about details as much as you do,' Douglas advised over a beer afterwards. 'Don't overthink it.' He gave a low chuckle. 'Tell me, do you think Sura prefers it on top with big ol' Boerman? Because she sure as hell wears the pants.'

Chapter 14

Mia clutched her bags as the border settlement loomed into view. It had been a tense forty minute journey from Jayapura; the young Indonesian driver seemed hell-bent on pushing his decrepit minivan to the limit on the many hairpin bends, and although there was no tail to speak of, she was unable to shake the feeling of being watched.

They squealed to a halt at the border post complex, and Mia stepped out into simmering midday heat. Thankfully, it was busy; a large crowd of day trippers from PNG were eagerly buying up Indonesian goods at a road market – mostly cheap plastics – and Mia gratefully merged with the garrulous throng. Her long blond hair was hidden by a green bandana, a large pair of sunglasses and a wide-brimmed straw hat covered most of her face. Baggy grey hiking pants, heavy boots and a long khaki shirt helped disguise her figure.

Approaching the Kantor Immigrasi, her pulse was elevated, and her mouth bone-dry.

Calm down, she told herself. *Even if they suspect where you're going, they cant stop you.*

When it was her turn, a bored-looking officer merely glanced at her passport and waved her through without even checking his computer screen. Feeling slightly stupid, she walked on wobbly knees across a no-man's-land of mown grass to the Papua New Guinea checkpoint. Here a group of customs agents with brightly coloured bird of paradise shoulder patches waited beside a battered plastic table.

A plump man with a shock of frizzy white hair took her passport and scanned the details of her brand-new tourist visa. Fortunately, the clerk at the PNG embassy in Jayapura had accepted a hundred-dollar bribe to expedite it, saving her a week-long wait.

'What is the nature of your business in PNG?' The agent's eyes were fixed on her chest as he spoke.

'I'm going to visit Wewak,' she replied. 'And take a cruise on the Sepik.'

'A woman travelling alone is very dangerous.' The man wet his lips as the other two agents placed everything from her bags on the table, including her underwear. He made a great show of pointing out that her tourist visa was single entry. 'Wouldn't a repeat be prudent?'

Mia paid a small sum for the unnecessary stamp, to be quickly on her way.

'Have a nice trip.' He flashed an expensive gold-toothed smile.

Such corruption had shocked her when she first came to Papua, but Paul had put it in perspective in his inimitable way.

'My dear Mia, you earn more in half an hour than most people here do in a month. Why not embrace it as a harmless visitor tax?'

Remembering his common-sense approach to life, she smiled. Paul had made her a better doctor in so many ways. As she'd tried to explain to her mom and dad, both general practitioners in Connecticut, it went beyond diagnosis and treatment.

Paul's patients loved him because he really listened and cared about them beyond the duration of their appointments, and it was a major contributor to their health outcomes.

Mia made her way through the customs building to a car park framed by thick palm trees. An assortment of dilapidated cars and utes, known locally as PMVs – public motor vehicles – were waiting to ferry people to the coastal town of Vanimo, an hour away.

She rejected more modern air-conditioned 4WDs because of the way their drivers stared at her, and found a dilapidated van with several women and children already on board. The elderly driver quoted fifteen kina, a little under five US dollars. After stowing her large bag in the cargo bay, she climbed in and found two empty seats in the middle.

A little boy sitting in front of her turned around to peer shyly with big brown eyes. He was a cutie, with a shock of wiry red-brown hair and big round cheeks.

Mia raised one eyebrow. '*Husat nem bilong yu?*'

He giggled, and his mother, resplendent in a bright yellow T-shirt, turned around with a big smile.

'*Dispela nem, Joseph.*'

'*Joseph, namba wan!*'

Mia offered him a high five, which he smacked with delight.

The boy's mother introduced herself as Mandy. Impressed with Mia's pidgin, she offered her a banana.

'*Tenku tumas.*'

In truth, Pidgin was easy to learn, although its limited vocabulary could be frustrating when trying to explain complex conditions to patients. Paul had taught her how to use metaphors and analogies. Her favourite was for rheumatoid arthritis: *Bun paia bilong yu pait bodi*. 'Bone fire is your body fighting itself.' The next challenge was to persuade them it was no one else's fault!

It was a relief to get underway, for the humidity and redolent stench of durian fruit inside the cargo bay was suffocating. From her open window, Mia stared out at the vista unfolding. On her left sparkling blue water lapped at deserted idyllic palm-fringed sandy beaches, bisected by rocky headlands topped in lush tropical jungle, while on her right was a mysterious bulwark of green, the edge of a great forest that had once stretched almost unbroken for 1000 kilometres to the southern shore of the island. Now logging, mostly from Malaysian interests, was steadily reducing the great forests to a patchwork.

Nonetheless, the contrast with chilly, congested and completely tamed Connecticut was profound. New Guinea was a steamy, fecund world where physical geography still dominated, where people were more alive. You could see it in their body language and open expressions, their take-it-or-leave it approach to structured time. Mia knew her attraction to this place was partly a grass-is-greener paean to Rousseau's noble savage, that desire to get back to nature, which so many burned-out Westerners pined for at some point in their holidays. But reality here was often brutal and cruel. At least as a doctor, she had a valid reason to stay.

The van slowed suddenly for a crude roadblock comprised of a single palm trunk and two rusty oil drums. It was manned by a handful of men in rough patched uniforms. Parked on the verge was their battered-looking truck.

It seemed an odd place for a checkpoint.

'*Soldia?*' Mia asked.

Mandy pulled her son in tightly.

'*Nogut soldia.*'

A grim-looking man with a thick beard and a shell necklace approached the driver's window.

'*Halo, bos.*' The old driver nodded obsequiously.

Mia slipped down in her seat as the bearded man scanned them with ganja-clouded eyes. His wide flat nose and flared nostrils enhanced his aggressive appearance.

'*Westap bilong yu taksi pemit?*' he demanded.

The driver handed over his taxi licence and the bearded man made a show of examining it.

'*Pemit nogut,*' he announced. '*Olgeta offim. Dispela oda.*'

Nobody on the van made a move to comply. The driver protested his licence was current and offered ten kina, then twenty, and finally thirty. The bearded man flatly rejected this, and his men muttered as their knuckles grew white on machete handles. Mia hastily tapped Mandy on the shoulder and passed her two fifty-kina notes.

'*Plis givim draiva.*'

Mandy leaned forward to slip it to the driver, who quickly thrust it through the window. Clearly this was the kind of bribe the men were after, but with their blood up, would they accept it? Tense seconds passed before the leader shrugged and waved at his men.

'*Orait. Koan, hariap!*'

All smiles, the men lifted the barrier and let them proceed. Everyone began to chat again inside the van.

It was a reminder of how quickly moods changed here.

At Vanimo, Mia went straight to the airport and bought a ticket for the furthest destination possible up the Sepik that week – the small village of Timbunke, some 300 kilometres distant. It wasn't anywhere near the border, but she knew small tourist cruise ships called in, and there were always fishermen with motorised canoes.

It was stinking hot in the crowded Cessna Caravan. Wedged in between a young Italian nun and an old woman carrying a live chicken, Mia undid her bandana and opened the top of her shirt. The roar of the single prop made conversation impossible, and she fell into a stupor. In fact, she did not wake until they were bumping across Timbunke's grass airstrip.

'Are you all right?' the nun asked when at last the engine shut down. 'You were calling out in your sleep.'

'It must have been a dream,' Mia apologised. 'I've come a long way.'

Outside, a large group of men was waiting to meet the plane. The nun turned to Mia with concerned grey eyes.

'There is no hotel in town. Where will you stay?'

Mia gratefully accepted Sister Sofia's invitation to stay the night at the Catholic mission where she worked.

Kevin, the middle-aged Australian mission manager who picked them up, was less welcoming, and muttered something about tourists. After heaving Mia's luggage into the back of the old green Land Rover, he drove them down a muddy track. Children playing in flanking palm groves waved cheerfully and Sister Sofia waved back.

'So innocent, so sweet,' she sighed, making Mia wonder if she was hankering for children of her own.

'I caught that one in the petrol store last week,' muttered Kevin, nodding at a tall boy in tight shorts. 'If he's innocent, then I'm a bloody saint.'

A compound of corrugated iron buildings surrounded by razor wire fencing came into view. In contrast to the leafy open grandeur of the Ford Mission, it looked depressingly under siege.

'Can't be too careful around here,' Kevin said, pulling up in front of high steel gates festooned with more razor wire. 'There's a reason temptation's in the Lord's Prayer.'

'And forgiveness, Kevin,' said Sofia gently. 'Don't forget that.'

While Kevin unlocked the gates, she explained the mission's purpose was both educational – running a local primary school – and pastoral, working to strengthen the community. There were eight nuns in residence, all local women except Sofia, and the mother superior, Agnes, who was Kevin's sister.

She was on the veranda, snipping basil from a pot, when they pulled up beside the main building. An austere-looking woman with short grey hair, her blue eyes were clear and kind, and straightaway, Mia felt that she could trust her.

A few of the other nuns came out to welcome them, and they sat down to hot sweet tea and oat cake. Mia had begun explaining that she was heading upriver to Papua when Kevin cut in loudly.

'But you can't just wander around sightseeing on your own. It's asking for bloody trouble.'

'I appreciate your concern, Kevin, but I'm not a tourist.'

When she explained her purpose and destination, Agnes' eyes lit up.

'The Ford Mission?' Placing a calloused hand over Mia's, she looked around the table. 'It's one of the oldest surviving church

141

organisations in Papua. Oh, bless you, Doctor Carter. Of course, we'll do all we can to help a fellow traveller.'

The epithet made Mia feel only mildly embarrassed. Most white people here were missionaries, and shared faith was a common assumption.

Agnes looked at her brother. 'We have a boat, don't we, Kevin?'

'But it's more than 300 kilometres to the border.' Wilting under her stare, Kevin thought for a moment. 'There are no cruise boats due for a couple of days. I suppose I could run you up to Pagwi – it's about seventy kilometres upriver.'

Agnes nodded enthusiastically. 'There's a hospital there, and we're good friends with Jean-Bernard, the director. I'll give him a call. They might be able to fly you to one of the villages near the border.'

A surge of relief widened Mia's smile. 'Oh, that would be wonderful! Thank you so much. I could find my own way from there.'

'Not without an escort,' Kevin told her sternly.

Agnes patted Mia's hand. 'I'm sure Jean-Bernard will be able to help with that, too.'

After a rustic dinner of sweet potato and chicken stew, Mia helped the nuns wash up. Everything at the mission was simple, clean and spartan, and in no time it was back in its proper place. Most of the nuns left for bed, as they liked to start early to beat the heat. Mia was curious about the challenges of long-term commitment, and asked Agnes to share her experiences.

142

Agnes explained that they had been there for a little over ten years, trying to address the endemic poverty and domestic violence by educating the children, and of course, building the Kingdom of God.

'Sometimes it's thankless,' she admitted, 'but in your darkest moments just a single act of kindness can make sense of it all.' Closing her eyes for a moment, she opened them again and smiled. 'I expect that sounds like a missionary cliché!'

'No, not at all.'

Mia was hugely impressed by Agnes' and the nuns' work ethic, but the evangelical subtext had always bothered her. Was it really a free service if you were looking for souls in return?

'Well, I had better make that call.'

While Agnes went to the office, Sofia came in with a pot of sleepy herb tea.

'You have someone?' She was looking shyly at the slim platinum ring on Mia's finger.

Mia thought of Brad, the oncologist she had dated for the past couple of years. A handsome, successful and driven man, inevitably his priorities had become alien to hers.

'No,' she smiled. 'I'm far too busy for a husband.'

Sofia's eyes sparkled. 'That's what I told my papa.'

'You don't feel you're missing out?'

Sofia looked at her thoughtfully. 'Do you?'

There were times Mia wondered. Security, comfort – and most of all children – were appealing, but at 35 she still didn't feel ready. Perhaps her anxiety at the state of the world was a conceit rather than a reason. Brad had certainly thought so.

'Jean-Bernard is still on the ward,' Agnes reported when she returned, 'but his wife is expecting you tomorrow morning. It will take a few hours to get up there.'

The screen door banged and Kevin came in, scratching mosquito bites on his sun-bleached freckled arms.

'I've fuelled the tinnie. We'll head off by eight, if it's OK with you.'

Mia was given a small bedroom inside the main building. Getting undressed, she admired the beautiful Melanesian patterns adorning the stand of a hand-carved crucifix. A humble cot with ironed sheets was calling and, sliding gratefully inside, she slept a wonderful dreamless sleep.

They said a communal prayer for her safe travels over breakfast, and after seeing the old tinnie on the trailer, Mia figured she might need it. The aluminium boat was comically small for such a long trip, and she hoped gruff Kevin would not regret his kindness. He introduced her to Keso, a shy older man with two missing front teeth, who was travelling with them.

Clasping her hands, he said, 'God bleth.'

They drove down to the closest launching point, an earthen ramp a few hundred metres from the wharf upon which a dozen or so men were fishing. On the still river, tendrils of mist drifted across its surface. A few canoes drifted in the distance. After reversing the trailer in, Kevin sat behind the wheel, not trusting the vehicle's handbrake on the slippery mud. Mia helped Keso by unwinding the winch while he steadied the boat in knee-deep water. Then Kevin went and parked at the top of the ramp, spending several minutes attaching chains to the trailer and its wheels.

'Righto,' he said cheerfully, plonking a battered Akubra hat on his head. 'Let's be off, then.'

Mia was first in the boat, followed by Kevin, then Keso, who pushed them out into deeper water, before hopping in barefoot.

After yanking the pull cord a few times, Kevin got the outboard firing, and they motored out into the river. They were level with the wharf when the engine abruptly coughed and died. Kevin frowned and checked the settings. He tried the pull cord several times, to no avail.

'I don't understand it,' he said, red-faced with exertion and perhaps embarrassment. Grabbing hold of one of the twenty-five-litre fuel tanks, he gave it a shake, and then did the same to the other. 'Sweet Mary, Jesus and Joseph. The little cunt has stolen my fuel again!'

Mia might have laughed but for Keso's mortified expression.

'There'll be another bloody hole in the wire,' Kevin fumed as he fitted one oar to the rowlock, 'and I'll have to drive back to the mission.' Gauging the distance back to the Land Rover, he grunted. 'Damn it, it'll be faster walking.' Fitting the other oar, he rowed them over to the mossy steps leading down from the wharf. Retrieving the fuel cans, he got out. 'Keso, you stay here with Mia. Don't go anywhere, understand? I'll be back in half an hour.'

Keso gave Mia an apologetic grin. They sat in companionable silence for several minutes. Mia was staring at the cluster of thatched huts across the river, thinking how beautiful they were, when suddenly she felt water soaking through her shoes. Looking down, she cried out in alarm.

'We're sinking!'

Oblivious with his feet up on the seat, Keso was stunned.

'*Mas be plagim.*'

While he searched for the bung, she retrieved her bags from the rising water and put them on the steps. Then she hopped out, too. The water was now several centimetres deep and the bottoms of her trouser legs were wet.

'*Bos, bot sinkim!*' cried Keso, grabbing the oars. '*Mi pul long!*'

Nodding, Mia undid the tatty rope, which would surely break. It was twenty metres to the nearest bank, and Keso began rowing like mad to try and save the sinking boat. Mia glanced into the water and decided there was no point staying down here with the crocodiles. Picking up her bags, she squelched up the steps.

Chapter 15

'We're coming up on Timbunke,' Kaboro announced, reducing power to negotiate a sweeping bend in the river. A picturesque village framed by several huge figs and stands of ancient palm trees came into view. Long, traditional reed houses were set on lush green lawns which ran down to a substantial wharf. A few dugout canoes were out fishing. Seeing the *Albany,* their occupants began to wave excitedly.

'It's a tourist trap,' Douglas explained, as men, women and children ran down to the shore and jumped into their canoes. 'Cruise ships stop by for carvings and trinkets.'

Kaboro proceeded carefully up the middle channel as a small fleet of hawkers paddled enthusiastically out to intercept them. Holding up carved wooden masks, sculptures and shields, they flashed lurid betel smiles while calling on them to stop. The *Albany* slowly drew level with the large and pitted concrete wharf where a group was gathered.

'Something's going on over there.' Kaboro handed Nash his binoculars. 'Could you please take a look?'

Under magnification, Nash saw a Westerner in a wide-brimmed hat waving frantically. Then he did a double take.

'It's a woman.'

It became clear she was struggling to keep a number of aggressive men at bay. One was holding a knife. Another was grabbing at her bag while she was distracted.

'Kaboro, she's in big trouble!'

The lieutenant slowed immediately and sounded three blasts on the ship's horn as he changed course. However, it was clear getting the *Albany* to the wharf amid a flotilla of jostling canoes was not going to be easy.

Kaboro called out to Sergeant Singkepe, who was on the quarterdeck.

'Be ready to fire a burst over their heads. We will have to take her aboard.'

Drawn by the commotion, Sura appeared from her cabin next door, with Goki in tow.

'What is going on, Lieutenant?'

As Kaboro explained his intention, Sura's frown grew.

'But our contract expressly prohibits the picking up of passengers.'

Nash stared at her. Was this the same woman he'd discussed shooting with last night.

'Surely you're not serious? This is an emergency.'

'Lieutenant, I must insist that you follow your orders to the letter.'

Kaboro seemed paralysed by indecision, but after a few seconds he astonished Nash by veering away and increasing power. In a panic, the tall woman broke free and ran along the edge of the wharf, waving and yelling. Two men ran after her and began dragging her back. Struggling, she lashed out. The smaller man fell over, clutching her bag.

'What are you doing?' Douglas called, as Nash exited the bridge. 'Robbie!'

Ripping off his shirt, Nash clambered over the safety rail on the port side quarterdeck. It was a five-metre drop to the river and, in the interests of getting to the woman as fast as possible, he dived as flat as he dared, striking the water in a great *whump* of spray.

The river was warm and tasted like mud. On breaking the surface, he cut loose for the wharf in a powerful freestyle. The ship's horn reverberated, signalling man overboard. Nash could feel the current pulling him sideways. The thought of what might be lurking in the murk lent extra speed to his stroke, and he quickly covered the forty metres to a long flight of slimy concrete steps, taking them two at a time.

On the wharf, the situation had deteriorated. Fearful of being deprived of their prize by the approaching ship, three men were aggressively pulling the woman back and forth like a rag doll.

'*Baim kago*! *Baim kago*!' shouted a skinny man in jeans, trying to tear away her bags. A big strong guy in ragged shorts was enthusiastically thrusting himself against her, while the third circled with a knife.

'*Plis*!' the desperate woman implored the onlookers as she struggled to fight them off. '*Helpim mi*!'

Her cries merely encouraged the onlookers to goad on her assailants instead.

'*Hariup*!' they roared. '*Goan, fuck her*!'

The man in ragged shorts grabbed at the woman's breasts. In the ensuing struggle, he took hold of her shirt, and in one savage motion tore it off. A lustful thrall fell over the men, the prelude to an all-out attack.

'*Let her go!*'

Nash's enraged roar stopped everyone in their tracks. Barging a path through the crowd, he yanked the woman free.

'Back off!' he snarled at the men. 'Go home, now!'

Nash knew it was only his size – and the element of surprise – holding these men at bay. With his back to the river, he desperately wanted to know how close the *Albany* was to the wharf, but to look away for even for a second would show weakness.

The big man in the ragged shorts fronted up.

'*Yu wanem, faka tu?*' he jeered, thrusting his hips forwards lasciviously.

The men laughed, and the release of tension had an immediate and undesirable effect. A new opponent – this one a scarred, heavyset man with a bushy black beard – rushed forward, swinging a long-handled club at Nash's head.

Nash did not try to block the swing, because it would have broken his arm. Instead, he caught the club high before it could descend – an almighty slap which stung like hell. Ripping the weapon free, Nash raised it over his own head.

'Come on!' he bellowed in genuine rage. 'You gutless pricks!'

The bearded man stepped back in alarm as Nash swung the club in menacing arcs. His third swing caught the guy with the knife on the shoulder. Shrieking, he dropped the weapon. Suddenly, a deafening blast from the *Albany*'s siren split the air and a volley of gunshots whizzed overhead. The crowd broke and ran. The skinny man took off with the woman's luggage. Weighed down, he had only made a few strides before Nash took his feet out from under him with a one-armed swing. With a shout of pain, the man hobbled away empty-handed.

The *Albany*'s big diesels seemed to growl in defiance as Kaboro switched to maximum reverse thrust, just metres from the wharf. The river boiled. Two sailors clutching hawsers jumped ashore to secure her.

'Thank you,' the woman shivered.

Nash was instantly struck by her eyes – a hypnotic shade of electric blue which reminded him of something he could not put his finger on.

'You're welcome.' He handed her the smaller of her bags and she held it protectively against her chest. The *Albany*'s fenders squealed under the shock of 235 tonnes nudging the concrete. Nash hoisted her backpack over his shoulder as the sailors finished roping ship to wharf. 'Come on, let's get out of here.'

For a moment she hesitated, looked around. Then, with a shrug of her shoulders, she followed him aboard.

Mindful of the hungry stares of the crew, he took her directly to his cabin to change, waiting outside in the passageway. She soon reappeared in a dark blue cotton shirt and white shorts. She was about his age, with rosy tanned skin which seemed to radiate vitality. Her pointed chin had a small dimple in the middle, and above sculpted lips her nose was straight, but for a small bump on the bridge. Her face was framed by thick and lustrous blond hair.

'I'm Mia.' She held out her hand. 'Mia Carter. Thank you again.' Her accent was American.

'Rob Nash. Glad to help.'

When they shook hands, he flinched.

'Oh, you're hurt! Let me take a look.' Her slim fingers gently probed the bones and tendons of his hand. 'It's badly bruised,' she said, 'not broken. But you need to ice that.'

151

'What about you?' he said. 'Are you OK?'

'Me? I'm fine. A bit scared.' She smiled. 'Well, terrified actually. God, when I thought you weren't going to stop . . .'

'We weren't.'

Digesting this, she hesitated. 'Look, I'm trying to get upriver, but my ride is having problems with his boat. Are you guys going far?'

He nodded. 'Across the border.'

Her amazing eyes widened. 'That's where I'm going!'

Nash realised the *Albany* was still tied up at the wharf.

'Let's head upstairs,' he told her. 'We can argue about it with the people in charge.'

At the foot of the stairs they encountered Douglas.

'Jesus, Robbie, you could have been cut to pieces by that mob.'

'Mia, this is Frank. You'll have to get used to his manners.'

'Glad you're in one piece, darling.' Douglas perfunctorily shook her hand. 'But a word to the wise – don't ever do that again.' Glancing up the stairwell, he made a face. 'They're not too happy up there, Robbie.'

'You think I give a shit?'

Both quarterdeck and bridge were crowded with the Indonesian contingent, Lieutenant Kaboro, and Sergeant Singkepe, who was cradling a light machine gun. Nash gave him a nod.

'Thanks for watching my back.'

'Playing the hero, hey, Nash?' Boerman sneered. 'Better late than never, I suppose.'

'Everybody, this is Mia Carter.'

While Kaboro and Singkepe said hello, the rest stared in stony-faced silence.

'Thank you so much for stopping.' Mia proceeded smoothly in the vacuum. 'I don't know what I would have done if you hadn't.'

Sura's slim eyebrows formed two sceptical arches. 'Well, you didn't give us much of an option, did you? What are you doing out here anyway?'

'My ride went back to the mission for petrol. Then our boat started to sink.' Mia pointed to the riverbank, where a half-submerged tinnie was visible among the reeds. 'Poor Keso must have run when the shooting started.'

Sura frowned. 'You're staying *here*?'

'Just passing through.' Mia glanced hopefully at Nash, who cleared his throat.

'Mia could use a ride upriver.'

At once Sura replied coolly, 'Totally impossible. This is a private expedition. When your friends from the mission return, you must go with them.'

Douglas shook his head. 'Half that bloody village will be on the warpath by now.' He turned to Mia. 'Look, where exactly do you need to go?'

'Just across the border. The Ford Hospital Mission – I'm a doctor.'

At this, Sura turned strangely pale. 'Why didn't you fly direct from Jayapura?'

The light in Mia's blue eyes dimmed. 'The airspace up there is closed until further notice. I have a current visa, but the Indonesian authorities won't tell me what's going on. I'm very worried about my friends.'

Sura had heard enough.

'Doctor Carter, this vessel is owned by an Indonesian company, and if my government has closed the area, surely you understand we cannot take you there?'

Nash decided he had heard enough, too.

'Look, Sura, I don't know what the problem is, but leaving Mia here is clearly not an option. So, either we give her a ride, or I'm getting off, too.'

'Fuck off, Nash,' interjected Boerman indignantly. 'You can't *bleddy* –'

'Mr Boerman!' snapped Kaboro. 'Watch your language on my bridge.'

Immediately Singkepe came to attention with a stamp of his right boot.

In the silence that followed, Mia stared thoughtfully at the lieutenant.

'This vessel is flying a PNG flag. Are you in command, sir?'

Kaboro's body language suggested he wished otherwise.

'So long as we remain in PNG waters, yes.'

'Then consider this a formal request from an American citizen. Will you please take me away from this village? I think my life is in danger.' Mia looked pointedly over at Sura. 'Hopefully, that should have no impact on Indonesian foreign affairs.'

At that moment, Nash happened to be looking at Goki. Almost imperceptibly, the man shook his head at Sura, who looked fit to implode. Who was really in charge here?

Kaboro gathered himself and stood a little straighter.

'With respect, Ms Suyanto, although this vessel belongs to your organisation, under powers invested in me by the government of

154

Papua New Guinea, and in accordance with the rules of maritime law, it is my decision as commanding officer that we will take Dr Carter as far as the Indonesian border, but no further.'

'Thank you so much.' Mia smiled in relief. 'I'm incredibly grateful. If I could ask just one more favour, Lieutenant, can you please get a message to Kevin? Otherwise they might worry at the mission.'

'Very well.'

Sura's oval face was a mask of disapproval.

'You will hear more about this, Lieutenant.'

'Of that I have no doubt,' Kaboro replied wearily. Turning to Nash and Douglas, he said, 'Will you please escort Doctor Carter to your cabin? You gentlemen will have to bunk with the crew for a while.'

With that, he leaned out of the port-side window and ordered his men to cast off.

'I seem to have caused one hell of a fuss,' Mia said once they were below. 'What on earth is their problem?'

'We're still trying to figure that out,' replied Nash, as a shuddering *Albany* began to move off.

Mia's eyes filled with curiosity. 'What are you guys doing here, then?'

Douglas flashed a warning look, but Nash merely shrugged.

'We're shooting a documentary.'

'For Indonesian TV? Are you cameramen or something?'

'I'm a diver. Frank's a pilot.'

'You don't say?' She smiled at them. 'I wouldn't have thought there'd be much to see in the muddy old Sepik.'

'The plan is to explore a cave.'

'I'll get my gear out,' announced Douglas stiffly.

Without looking back, he descended the ladder. Mia made a face at Nash.

'Sorry, I didn't mean to pry.'

'It's nothing. What's the story with your hospital?'

A look of concern came over her and she lowered her voice. 'They haven't been in contact for weeks. I didn't want to say anything upstairs, but the Indonesian military is behind it. They're the only ones with the power to shut everything down like this.'

Nash felt a stab of worry for her. 'You sure it's safe going in there on your own?'

'I'm having my doubts,' she admitted, 'but once we get to the border it's not far, and I know some of the local people. They'll take care of me.'

As she explained her connection to the hospital, Nash found himself increasingly drawn to her. She reminded him of Natalie in her total commitment to the things she believed in.

Returning to the cabin, Nash switched on the fan and collected up his belongings.

'Well, if you need anything, it won't take long to find me.'

'Thank you, Rob.'

Her eyes held his for a moment longer than expected, and then he remembered where he'd seen that electric blue colour before. The Nullarbor halocline. Nash was processing the fact that he was attracted to Mia Carter when Natalie's ghost crashed like a boulder into the pit of his stomach. His pillow fell to the deck. And when Mia handed it back, her fingertips brushing his felt like sweet little knives.

Chapter 16

(Date unknown – Saturday, June 9th, 1945?)

I have learned from Unterscharführer Müller (whose boils I am treating) that we are now five hundred kilometres up the Sepik River in Papua New Guinea. Heider now travels by day because there is so much debris in the water. Today we heard distant planes. God, how I prayed for them to find us, but none came near.

I have been put to work helping the SS camouflage the submarine. The work is terrible, and my hands are a mess. We cut vegetation and branches from the riverbanks and ferry them to the submarine by dinghy. Crocodiles are a constant threat. The sun beats down mercilessly on the steel decks and the submarine is like an oven. No one can handle it below deck during the day, which is why I caught my first sight of Ilse. She was on the conning tower with a parasol, looking pale and withdrawn. Not once would she meet my eye. It has upset me tremendously. Heider barks orders and scans the swampy forest on both sides of the river for natives, whom he shoots with either the heavy machine gun or sometimes a hunting rifle. I believe the SS grow restless. It's obvious that they do not share Heider's motivations, but their fear of him keeps them silent. Apparently, he has banned all BBC radio broadcasts and they are growing resentful at being kept in the dark. I am hoping for a mutiny. The longer this goes on, the more likely it seems the men will take matters into their own hands.

* * *

Near Kamindimbit, East Sepik Province, Papua New Guinea

'Chuck the stuck-up bitch over the side,' Boerman counselled. 'She'll be crocodile dung by morning.'

Sura watched Goki's face turn a shade darker.

'You forget Kaboro has promised he will take her as far as the border. And if Nash or the girl get off this boat, they become witnesses, not to mention the villagers and missionaries in Timbunke who will testify that *we* picked Carter up.'

'So, she went missing anyway.' Boerman grinned. 'Happens all the time.'

Goki flicked his fingers in exasperation. 'She's an American citizen, all right? The American State Department could make life very difficult for the boss if they lean on PNG, and we don't even know who Mia Carter is yet.'

'So, let's find out.' Sura was still seething from the confrontation. She had been publicly shamed, and the pain would not be excised until those responsible were made to pay.

Goki stared at her. 'What do you propose?'

Opening her attaché case, Sura pulled out a folder.

'Just because Kaboro has burdened us with an uninvited guest, it doesn't mean he can ignore protocol.'

After telling Jaap to stay put and keep out of trouble, she led Goki below decks and rapped three times on the cabin door.

'Doctor Carter, I need a brief word.'

The American's blue eyes were cold when she opened the door. 'What can I do for you?'

Sura held out a document. 'You need to sign this.'

Mia made no move to take it. 'What is it?'

'It's a waiver, from any claim that you might make against Shangri-La Productions during your passage to the Indonesian border.'

'*Shangri-La*? How ironic. No, I don't want to sign it.'

Sura marvelled at the American's incredible sense of entitlement. It was so ingrained that she had absolutely no concept of the danger she was in.

'Lieutenant Kaboro has already signed.' Sura pointed helpfully to the fake signature at bottom of the document. 'Are you really going to be so ungrateful that you will not pay us this simple courtesy?'

Mia read the document with a studied air of disdain.

'Indemnity from injury and accidental death?' She gave Sura a small smile. 'Very well. If it makes you feel better.'

Crouching down beside her bag, Mia unzipped a side pocket and took out her passport. Watching her copy out the number, paperwork resting on those long, brown athletic legs, Sura couldn't help but envy the woman her freedom, even if it was taken for granted. The contrast with her own circumscribed life was acute. Another reminder of why her plan must succeed.

'It's very brave of you to go and work in such a remote place, Doctor Carter. Have you no husband or boyfriend to worry about you?'

Mia handed her the document with a tight smile.

'Will that be all?'

Sura nodded. 'I'm sorry we got off to a bad start. Perhaps I'll see you at dinner? I would love to learn more about the good work you are doing in my country.'

'Sure you would.'

Back in the main cabin, Goki sat on the floor and relayed Mia Carter's name, passport number and description to TNI Headquarters over satellite phone.

'Top priority. And get me the general. Shangri-La out.'

Sura sat on the bed, massaging her calves with coconut oil.

'You don't really think she's an agent, do you?'

'No, but what are the odds of her getting on this stinking boat?' Goki paused to regard her legs. 'Smart move with the waiver, by the way. Can I ask why a girl of your class hangs around with such a fucking moron, though?'

Sura wondered if Jaap could hear them outside. Or what her father would think of Goki's increasing familiarity.

'A man who can't control himself is not a real man.'

Maybe so, thought Sura, staring into his bloodshot eyes. *But Jaap is my weapon and when he takes your life, you will know it.*

Goki's phone rang, and by the way he sat upright she knew it was her father. Military men only ever respected their own kind. It was their weakness. Listening intently, the commando nodded.

'Yes, sir.' Extinguishing his clove cigarette in her water glass, he stood up. 'Sir Julius will call Kaboro.'

'And the American?'

'Her ID checks out.' Goki smiled grimly. 'If Doctor Carter thought she was clever forcing her way onto this tub, she will soon regret it. Once we get to the border, I'm going to enjoy holding her pretty blonde head underwater.'

Kaboro found safe anchorage in a wide bend off the main channel, where a flock of white storks patrolled the shore. The sunset was intensely beautiful, smudges of mauve and burnt orange contrasting with the cumulonimbus clouds, which shrouded the peaks of the distant mountain ranges, all reflected in the lake like a gigantic mirror. It was the kind of beauty which made Nash think how wonderful the natural world was, a feeling tinged with sorrow for what was being lost.

After taking some photos, he went and found Douglas, who was sitting on the edge of the helicopter pad, working his way through a second six-pack of beer. They had not spoken since that afternoon, and Douglas seemed content for it to stay that way. Sitting down beside him, Nash sighed.

'I know you're pissed I told Mia we're here, but no one is going to beat us to the scoop now, are they?'

Taking a long pull of beer, Douglas took his time answering.

'The point is, it ain't your show. So, could you just humble yourself a little? At the rate you're burning bridges, they'll pull the fucking plug on us.'

'Frank, something stinks here, and it has done ever since they got on the boat. Forget about intimidating Saworno and undermining Kaboro, look at this incredible sunset ... Why isn't Boerman getting it in the can? I spent hours last night talking film with Sura and I swear she has no interest whatsoever.

If you ask me, they're behaving like a gang of thugs with something to hide.'

Douglas grunted. 'They're rough around the edges – so what? That's kind of how it is out here.'

'You think I'm too First World sensitive?'

'I was going to say precious.'

'Frank, there are principles here.'

'Which are fine when you can afford them. When was the last time you earned 250K for a month's work?'

'You're telling me I should have left Mia to that mob today?'

'No.' Douglas shook his head irritably. 'I backed you up, didn't I? Even if it was her bloody fault.'

Nash frowned. 'So, I should just shut up and stop asking questions so you can make a buck? I'm sorry, Frank, you might be relaxed with dodgy business arrangements, but it's not the way I operate.'

Douglas thumped a fist on the deck. 'Goddamn it, Robbie, *you* control the diving. No one can fucking make you do anything you don't want to do.'

Nash became aware Douglas was drunker than he'd thought, and held his tongue. Douglas flung his bottle angrily into the water.

'I'm not a fucking mind-reader. But it's like you're doing everything possible to fuck this deal up.'

Nash stared into the black water. Legitimate reservations notwithstanding, was he manufacturing excuses? The Hoosenbeck had been looming larger in his imagination, and he'd had another nightmare about Natalie. Had Frank heard him crying out? Singkepe certainly had, for he had asked him about it.

Douglas chuckled humourlessly. 'This gig was like winning the quinella with your last hundred bucks. A way of getting back to Aussie, chucking in a line, and putting my feet up for the last chapter. Ah well, I suppose it was too good to last.'

Nash thought of Jacquie, his parents, and the mortgage. About the disappointment of returning home empty-handed with doubt in his heart. Putting an arm around Douglas, he patted him on the shoulder.

'Now you're laying it on with a trowel. Don't worry, Uncle Frank, I'll pull my head in. Believe me, I need this as much as you do. Maybe even more.'

Nash was making his way back along the starboard side of the *Albany* when he heard Boerman's unpleasant booming laugh coming from the other side of the ship.

'Hey, stop that, leave me alone!'

It was Mia, and she sounded scared. Nash ran around the port side to find Boerman had backed her up near the ladder to the quarterdeck. The Afrikaner was shining a flashlight in her face.

'What are you sneaking around in the dark for, hey? Come on, answer me.'

'What's going on?' Nash demanded.

The powerful beam of light swung in his direction.

'Nash, this is none of your business.'

Nash shielded his eyes. 'Get that out of my face. Mia, come here.'

As she squeezed past the big man, Nash could feel his skin crawling. He didn't like her proximity to Boerman, or the dark water below.

'Go below,' he told her. 'I'll join you in a minute.'

'No. I think you should come with me.' Mia placed a warning hand on his arm.

'Looks like she doesn't need a hero after all,' Boerman sneered. 'Smart move, Doctor Carter. You might get to live a little longer.'

'Come on, Rob,' urged Mia. 'He's just an asshole.'

'You're right.'

As Nash turned to go, the big man seized his left forearm in a crushing pincer grip and pulled his face close.

'You didn't fool me today,' he hissed. 'You're gutless. And when we dive that cave, everybody will find out, too.'

Nash had to concede that Boerman had an uncanny instinct for sniffing out fear, for such an insensitive turd.

'Let go, Boerman. I won't ask you again.'

'Do it. Give me a reason to fucking *erase* you.'

The Afrikaner had a grip like an industrial vice. Nash took the man's offending wrist with his free hand and began to apply pressure. Boerman was massively strong, but his bulky gym muscles lacked lateral movement, whereas years of ocean training had strengthened every sinew and tendon in Nash's arms. He used that flexibility to break free and twist Boerman's forearm around the ladder, where the added leverage let him even the score.

'What's going on down there?' It was Sura on the quarterdeck. 'Jaap?'

Nash released the big man with a grin.

'Hadn't you better be running along?'

'Do you have to go?' Mia stood at her cabin door, rubbing the skin of her upper right arm. 'I could use some company.'

Her thick hair was tied back in a ponytail, exposing a slender neck which made her seem more vulnerable. Nash did not want to be alone with her, but seeing she was shaken up, he followed her into the cabin. Despite the heat, she closed the door.

'Why isn't there a lock?' She shook the handle in frustration.

'It's a military thing. Do you want to tell me what happened?'

Leaning against the door, Mia nodded. 'I was getting some fresh air when he got in my face with that bullshit about sneaking around.' She frowned as she examined the bruise forming on her bicep. 'Back in the States we call it assault.'

'I'll talk to Kaboro. You can press charges.'

'No.' She shook her head quickly. 'I need to get upriver.' Defensively crossing her arms, she shivered before looking at him closely. 'Rob, what *are* you doing with these people?'

The question caught him by surprise.

'Shooting a doco. Like I told you.'

'But it doesn't make sense. These Indonesians are paranoid as hell, and what about all these soldiers – doesn't it strike you as overkill they're armed to the teeth?'

Nash thought of his last expedition to PNG. They'd had a police liaison officer, and a couple of private security guys in case of trouble from the locals, but that was all.

'I suppose so, but aren't we heading into a war zone?'

'Is that what they told you?' Mia sounded doubtful. 'OPM are not that much of a threat. And why would armed PNG troops be *allowed* into Papua? Shouldn't the Indonesians be running security up there?'

He explained what he knew of the joint expedition – that the PNGDF were being provided as private security – but, given

165

his own reservations, he quickly ran out of steam and found himself staring into those mesmerising eyes. She blinked slowly, and then perhaps because of the sudden intimacy, smiled shyly.

'Why does Jaap keep going on about you being a hero?'

The question threw him. And he realised it was because he didn't *want* her to know about Natalie. Of course, that was stupid, because she would likely find out soon enough, but at that moment he didn't want to lose face in her eyes.

'An inferiority complex?' he ventured awkwardly. 'I don't know, isn't that what usually motivates bullies?'

'And he's your dive buddy in this cave?' She was looking worried again.

'Unfortunately, yes. And there's too much riding on this to turn back.'

He told her about Jacquie. Mia, being a doctor, was able to clarify things he didn't quite understand, like her chemo regime. Then he told her about his parents and Margaret River. The longer they talked, the more fraudulent it felt leaving Natalie and the accident out, but Nash was in too deep now, and when he sensed Mia was about to ask him whether he had a partner, he turned the spotlight back on to her.

Mia Carter was a high achiever, sporty like Jac, but driven to public service, which had led her into what sounded like a completely immersive and exhausting career.

'And you really plan to stay on in Papua?' Nash was feeling slightly embarrassed by the contrast with his singularly self-serving life.

'You sound like you think I'm entering a nunnery.'

He gave a sheepish grin and Mia laughed.

'People think that because they don't understand what a vocation is.' Her face grew intense and he saw the great strength in her. 'For me, the mission is nothing to do with religion. It's about helping people who really *need* help. It makes me feel like there is a point to what I do.'

'And you've never wanted a more conventional life?'

'You mean a hubby and kids?' Her laugh suggested this was never on the cards, and he shrugged. 'Maybe, one day. My parents would love me to stick around and take over their clinic in Connecticut. I love them dearly, but the whole idea bores me senseless.'

'I can imagine it's pretty tame compared to out here.'

She smiled. 'The mission's in the last great wilderness of Papua – no loggers, no mines, no roads. The first time I went for a hike I thought I'd travelled back in time. The forest is full of these incredibly ancient towering giants which humble you, and the tree kangaroos and dwarf cassowaries just stand their ground when you pass.'

'What about birds of paradise?'

Her eyes lit up. 'My favourites are short-tailed paradigalla, they carry on like tiny bossy penguins, but the King of Saxony and splendid astrapia . . . wow, don't they just take your breath away?'

Nash smiled in agreement. 'They remind me of vivid oil paintings.'

'Yes, like a Rousseau! Those vibrant flashes of colour magnified against the dark canvas of the canopy.'

Watching her come alive, Nash had the strange sense of looking into a mirror. This woman was obviously one hell of a doctor, but what he was seeing was an adventurous free spirit.

Perhaps aware she had revealed too much, she looked shyly at him.

'It's getting late. Will you stay with me tonight?'

At the surprised look on his face, she gasped and covered her mouth.

'I meant on the top bunk!' she added with a laugh. 'It would make me feel safer.'

'Surely after my exploits today I deserve the bottom bunk.' Nash chuckled.

Mia's white teeth gleamed wickedly. 'You can take your pick. Just promise not to snore.'

Nash stretched out on the top bunk, his feet hanging over the edge. With the fan languidly moving the hot air, he was painfully aware of Mia's proximity.

Stop it, he told himself. *The fact you're even thinking about her is wrong.*

He turned his mind to the expedition. What had his father said? *Use your instincts and make smart choices.* Today, he'd dived into a crocodile-infested river and fought a mob to save Mia. He was on the payroll of a dysfunctional and dodgy syndicate, heading for a war zone with a psychotic dive partner and – in the unlikely event he ever got to the bloody Hoosenbeck – a potentially life-threatening showdown with claustrophobia. Despite the sheer insanity of it, Nash was heartened by the sense something lost was returning. As if his DNA was trickling back into his cells. It went beyond the kick of danger. He fell asleep remembering Natalie had always said he hated backing down.

Chapter 17

Opening his eyes, Nash blinked when he realised he was in his old cabin. He became aware of the low vibration of the engines, then the anchor chain clattered in the hawse pipe. Checking his dive watch, he frowned. Why were they getting underway this early?

Mia was still asleep with one hand tucked under her dimpled chin when he dropped to the deck. Nash pulled on his shirt and tried not to stare.

Outside, the dense white mist was cool and damp, redolent of vegetation and the acrid tang of a nearby fruit bat colony. Although visibility was terrible, the *Albany* was nosing upriver. Even as he stood there, she put on more power, and birdsong erupted on the invisible banks. Nash spotted the morning watch by the stern, obviously confused, too.

When he reached the bridge, Nash was shocked to see the squat form of Goki at the helm. Jaap Boerman was sitting beside him, one huge bare foot resting on the control panel as he drank from a mug of coffee. Behind them, Ricki Hartono was relaxing with his feet up in the navigator's chair. They looked like a bunch of amateur fishermen on a weekend charter.

'Where's Kaboro?' demanded Nash.

'He's been relieved.' Boerman did not turn around.

'*What?* By whom?'

'Do I look like his fucking secretary, Nash? Go ask him yourself.'

Through the windscreen, the long bow of the *Albany* was groping through the mist. The sight reminded Nash of circling a foggy runway in a jet, and he appealed to Hartono.

'You're a pilot. Can't you see this is nuts?'

'We have radar.' He insolently flicked the screen beside him. 'This is what it's for.'

Radar provided no protection in a river full of submerged hazards. Realising his warnings were futile, Nash took the stairs three at a time and found Kaboro slumped in the mess, before a coffee he did not appear to be drinking.

'Sir Julius called last night,' he explained woodenly. 'I've been relieved of command.'

'For God's sake, why?'

'Obstructing progress and exceeding my authority.'

'That's insane.'

Through the porthole, tendrils of mist were spiralling past. That the defence minister of a sovereign nation could place a foreign national in command of his own personnel was extraordinary. Equally horrifying was Kaboro's passive acceptance of the situation. The man seemed to have given up.

'You are responsible for our safety,' Nash told him harshly. 'Surely you can see the Indonesians are dangerously inept. You must take back control of the ship.'

Kaboro shook his head firmly. 'As a military officer, I am obliged to obey orders. PNGDF personnel remain under my command, but Goki has the ship.'

Nash stabbed his finger at the porthole.

'Take another look out there, Kaboro. How many men will you command if we hit a log and sink?'

Daniel Yanos stepped nimbly into his new canoe and let momentum glide them out into the mist. For the past month, he and his brothers had laboriously carved the dugout canoe from an eight-metre-long, dead-straight kwila log, purchased upriver where the great trees fought for the light. Towing it home, they'd hauled it out of the water and made a huge fire. The red-hot coals scorched the wood and aided the hollowing-out process, done by hand with sharp steel adzes.

Daniel took his first stroke with the long paddle. A fishing canoe is prone to capsize while hauling in loaded nets, thus symmetry was vital. The other essential was an even hull thickness to ensure no bias, which could prove disastrous in the squalls and waves encountered on the wide river. To achieve this, Daniel and his brothers had used notched strings stretched along each side of the canoe to mirror curvature and thickness. After several stokes, Daniel knew the canoe was perfectly balanced. He felt a glow of satisfaction and hope for the future. A well-made canoe would last half a lifetime and feed many children.

In the forward seat, his son, Nathan, beamed back at him. This maiden fishing trip was his reward for helping to cut and carry tons of firewood. Looking at the smooth skin on Nathan's back, Daniel was reminded that his son would soon undergo the ritual of scarification. The agonising process involved slitting the skin with shards of razor-sharp bamboo, then packing the wound with tree resin to create a raised lump. When the multiple cuts healed, the scars became the scales of the crocodile, like those adorning his own flesh, and those carved on the canoe's exquisite crocodile-head prow.

171

Over a metre long, it was the canoe's crowning glory. The crocodile was not just a symbol of great power. It represented shared ancestry, a direct lineage between his people and the great reptile. Daniel had carefully repainted the prow with natural pigments, instead of cheaper house paint. The eyes of his crocodile were white and staring, to guide him through the mists that so often shrouded the great river. Between triangular carved teeth, the mouth was cerulean blue, so that the canoe would drink deep of the waters and feast on its bounty of fish.

Instinctively knowing they had reached the middle of the river, Daniel stowed his paddle and gathered up his lightweight net. In the old days, they wove them from rattan, but now they bought synthetic nets from the traders, which were stronger and easier to use. Daniel skilfully cast the net into the silken water. It was an auspicious start, for he immediately drew in six struggling bass, the best single catch he had ever made. Nathan helped position the wriggling fish, so they could be dispatched by a blow from Daniel's stout club. They stored the fish under a cover of broad taro leaves to protect them from the sun, which would soon appear once it had burned away the enveloping shroud of fog.

Soon, the canoe rode deep with its bounty of fish. Daniel was overjoyed, for he and his brothers would feast well tonight. They would buy beer off the trader man, as well as *tabac brus* and other useful items. But there was room for just one more cast.

As he drew in the net, Daniel thrilled to the huge weight of fish struggling inside. With a powerful heave, he landed the haul. In the bottom of the canoe, a huge circular disc thrashed among the silver and his blood ran cold.

'Look out!' he shouted. 'It's a pacu!'

Nathan immediately lifted his feet up. The pacu, also known as 'the ball-cutter', was an exotic species related to the piranha which had killed several men on the Sepik, fishing naked in waist-deep water. In its native South America, pacu grew to twenty-five kilograms on a diet of nuts and berries. But these transplanted fish had eaten all the Sepik's vegetation and been forced to expand their diet. Inside their massive jaws was a set of disturbingly human teeth, capable of removing large chunks of flesh, and the pacu had developed a taste for it.

This pacu was by far the biggest Daniel had ever seen. Already, it had taken several huge scoops out of the bass as it snapped furiously. It was an ugly, brutal-looking fish, about sixty centimetres long, extremely thick, with an undershot jaw. Many suspected the pacu were the malevolent spirits of murdered people seeking revenge. With a cry of disgust, Daniel raised the club and began to beat the evil creature to a pulp. So intent was he on making sure it was dead, that he didn't hear the rumble growing louder in the mist.

'Father!' Nathan called urgently. 'Listen!'

Just as Daniel looked up, a huge grey ship materialised. Twin arcs of spray flew high from its knife-like bow. The sound of its engines was the same noise that pigs made when transfixed by an arrow – deep and high-pitched at the same time. Daniel couldn't understand how something so big could move so fast. Seizing his paddle, he began to thrust through the water with all his might.

The *Albany* was travelling at her maximum flank speed of twenty-eight knots. She would need several hundred metres to stop and, at this point, the Sepik was not much wider than that, leaving little room for error. Nash wasted precious seconds pounding futilely on Sura's locked cabin door, because he figured it was the quickest way of stopping the madness. When she failed to answer, he decided the only option left was to take command by force.

Entering the bridge, he was astounded to find Sura sitting with Hartono, oblivious to the crisis unfolding.

'We're going too fast!' Nash bellowed at her. 'Make him stop!'

Goki looked round and snarled in perfectly good English, 'Will you shut the fuck up?'

Nash was registering this when, through the swirling mist, he saw a low shape dead ahead.

'Look out!'

Too late, Goki yanked the helm over. The *Albany* had barely begun adjusting to the new bearing when the canoe disappeared beneath her bow. The prow struck like a block splitter, exploding the canoe with an almighty bang, which they heard and felt through the soles of their feet.

Time telescoped. Goki was still hard aport, and 235 tonnes of ship, passengers, chopper, fuel and material were headed towards the left riverbank at fifty kilometres an hour. Diving across Boerman's lap, Nash yanked the throttle levers to full reverse.

Had he not done so, the *Albany* might well have been torn open when she hit the submerged mudflat five seconds later – a sickening blow which shook every weld and rivet in her body. In the eruption of water and mud, momentum carried her, bucking and slithering, until finally she buried her bow in a raised bank that was almost as tall as she was.

Daniel surfaced with desperation in his heart. Diving deep had saved his life, but what of his son? There was no sign of Nathan, or the canoe.

In the chopped-up water, Daniel cried out in panic, 'Where are you, boy?'

He swam blindly underwater with arms outstretched, hoping to blunder into him. He dived and dived again, and just when he had given up hope, there was Nathan! His boy was just a few canoe lengths away, one arm weakly raised. Blood was streaming from his head, and he looked as if he could go under again at any moment.

'Dad!'

'I'm coming!' Daniel screamed.

Suddenly, the water churned white, and a large fish broke the surface in a flurry of thrashing fins. Daniel's heart seemed to pump in slow motion.

Pacu.

Nathan began screaming. He disappeared for a moment, and when he came up again, two of the huge fish were attached to his face. They wriggled demoniacally and there was the terrible sound of flesh tearing as the pacu fell back into the water.

Daniel powered through the water like his ancestors, but, when he got there, Nathan was nowhere to be found.

After an hour of fruitless searching, an exhausted Daniel begged the gods to take him, too, but the crocodiles would not oblige with one of their own. Slowly, he drifted to shore and dragged himself up the grassy bank.

It was then he saw the stranded grey ship on the other side of the river. Rage spread through him like an infection, and he set off in a mad feverish sprint through the tall kunai grass. Oblivious to the cuts opening up all over his flesh, he sang to the spirits to welcome his son home.

Here, on this earth, it was time to gather his *wantoks* and exact revenge.

The impact had flung Nash all the way back to the bridge door. Thankfully, it had slammed shut, for he could easily have hit a stanchion or gone over the side. Getting to his feet, he saw the bridge was a shambles. Jaap Boerman lay sprawled in his chair, shaking his head like a heavyweight shrugging off a scoring punch. Between his feet, Goki wasn't moving. Through the now-cracked windscreen in front of him, the elongated branch of a giant fig tree reached out like a warning hand. Meanwhile, Hartono and Sura were trying to extricate themselves from a tangle of limbs. Everything was blurry and incredibly loud, and Nash became aware that the *Albany* was still on full power reverse, trying to wrench herself out of the mud. She was shaking so violently that it felt as if she was going to tear herself apart.

'Turn the fucking engines off!' he yelled at Boerman. 'The big red button!'

In the silence that followed, the sound of the aggrieved forest outside became apparent. Birds of all kinds were honking, squawking and shrilling at the insult. High branches could be heard shaking and snapping, and leaves were drifting down in a light rain.

Nash pulled Sura to her feet. She was pale, too unsteady to speak. Grabbing the first aid kit from the back wall, he shoved it into her hands.

'Help Goki!' With a dismissive nod at Boerman he added, 'And don't let that fucking idiot anywhere near the controls.'

Kaboro had reached the quarterdeck when Nash got outside. The front of his white uniform was stained with coffee, and he was staring in dismay at the ship's prow, embedded in the long grass of the sloping riverbank. Beneath their feet, the deck was slanted fifteen degrees to stern with a tilt to starboard.

'Goki hit a canoe,' Nash explained. 'Two people, I think . . . before he lost control. Tell me, Lieutenant, do you have the ship *now*?'

It was a cruel thrust, but Nash was angry; the expedition was over before it had even begun, and he wanted to provoke some resolve in Kaboro because they still had to get out of there.

Kaboro's expression was sombre.

'Yes. And I give you my word that I will see to your safety, but first I must organise a search for survivors and check the ship and crew.'

Down on the main deck, Nash spotted Mia with Douglas. She was examining his forehead while the old pilot buttoned up yesterday's shirt.

'It was Singkepe . . . I woke up with him sitting on my bloody head.'

'It's a bump, Frank.' Mia's face was scrunched at the stench of sweat and stale alcohol. 'You'll be fine.'

The old pilot's face fell as Nash explained the cause of the grounding.

'Robbie, I'm sorry,' he said miserably. 'I've stuffed up, haven't I?'

'Forget it. You couldn't have seen this coming. I can't believe it myself. What the hell were they thinking?' He glanced at Mia, who had the good grace not to say *I told you so*. 'I'm glad you're OK.'

Her beautiful eyes assessed him. 'Is anyone else hurt?'

'Captain Goki seems to have knocked himself out on the bridge.'

'On my way, then.'

'Hold on a sec.'

Nash turned and called out to Sergeant Singkepe, who was mustering his squad on the foredeck.

'Can you send an escort to the bridge with Dr Carter?'

'Moses, get up there!' Singkepe barked. 'The rest of you fan out – port, stern and starboard. Keep your eyes peeled, you hear? Stay sharp.'

'You were right,' Nash said quietly to Mia. 'There's something dodgy going on. Don't be alone with them, OK?'

'Sure.'

She smiled and touched his hand lightly before leaving.

Ensign Mohli and an armed sailor arrived to mount the search for survivors. Nash and Douglas helped them climb into the aluminium tender and cranked it down, a job made awkward by the off-centre davits. After firing up the outboard, the tender motored out into the river.

'Think they'll find anyone?' Nash asked Singkepe, who had just joined them.

'We'd better hope not.' The sergeant's eyes were troubled. 'If they get back to their village, we'll have a war on our hands.'

Payback was the muscle that underpinned the *wantok* system in PNG. It was why people didn't stop after road accidents;

trying to negotiate reparations with a machete-wielding avenger was a good way to lose your head.

It was only now that Nash thought to check his mobile phone. No satellite. How appropriate for such a fuck-up that they were in a black spot. He went down to the stern to check the status of their most obvious means of escape, and found Ricki Hartono had beaten him to it.

On the angled landing pad, the tail rotor of the multi-million-dollar Jet Ranger was now just centimetres above the water. That the straps had held, and the machine had not budged, crumpled or cracked under the impact, was something of a miracle.

'Looks OK,' said the pilot, flexing the drooping rotors, as if the circumstances of the situation were unrelated to his negligence.

'No thanks to you,' Nash told him bluntly. 'Be ready to fly. We may need to evacuate.'

Hartono looked surly behind his Ray-Bans, but held his tongue.

Kaboro returned from his survey.

'No sign of a hull breach,' he reported. 'Saworno says the engines are OK. A lot of the gear has been flung around, though.' He led Nash away from Hartono and dropped his voice to a murmur. 'The nearest police are in Pagwi. But there's only three of them, and they don't have a boat.'

'And the military?'

'Our closest troops are in Wewak. Currently, there is no air support.'

'So, what you're saying is . . .'

Kaboro nodded apologetically.

'We are on our own.'

Chapter 18

The first thing Mia saw on entering the bridge was Jaap Boerman crouching over Goki's prostrate form. The Afrikaner's huge hands were clamped to either side of the smaller man's head, and his startled expression reminded her of a little boy caught in the act of some wrongdoing.

'What do *you* want?' Sura was looking flushed, although the heat was yet to bite.

'What do *I* want?' Mia's eyes narrowed. 'Give me that first aid kit.'

'He's bleeding,' reported Boerman helpfully, lightly jumping to his bare feet.

'I can see that. Give me some space to examine him.'

Sura and Boerman sullenly pushed past, and Mia was grateful for the comforting presence of Moses and his assault rifle.

The livid contusion on Goki's forehead appeared to have been caused by striking the windscreen, but the blood pooling thickly on the deck was from a nasty laceration on the back of his close-cropped head. Moses got Mia a fresh tea towel from the sink which she used to stem the flow, pressing as firmly as she dared because she suspected he had a fractured occiput.

'I need to get him to a proper bed,' she told Moses. 'Do you think you could get some help to carry him down to my cabin?'

'No problem, miss. Shall I ask Mr Boerman?'

She glanced outside to the quarterdeck, where the big man was making no attempt to conceal his interest.

'I think one of your own men is best.'

Moses called down to Singkepe. Together they lifted Goki up while Mia supported his sagging head. In the process, something clattered to the floor and Singkepe frowned. Reaching down, he grabbed the vicious-looking combat knife and slid it into his boot. They carried the unconscious man past Boerman, and Mia felt her skin crawl as his eyes tried to meet hers. Down in the cabin, the soldiers carefully placed Goki on his side on the bottom bunk before Mia took Singkepe aside.

'Sergeant, I'm not sure this man's injuries are from the collision.'

'What do you mean?' He frowned.

She pointed to the back of her skull, then mimed slamming something down with two hands. Singkepe's eyes widened and Mia suddenly felt uneasy. Had she *really* seen Boerman assaulting him? It was a serious accusation. One that would be hard to prove and impossible to retract.

'I don't have definite proof, but I'm worried all the same.'

Singkepe observed her closely before nodding.

'Moses, wait outside the door. No one is to enter.' He nodded at Mia. 'Let him know if you need anything. I will pass on your concerns to Lieutenant Kaboro.'

Closing the door, Mia leaned against it for a moment and took several deep breaths to compose herself.

Has it really been just two days since I left Jayapura? What have I got myself tangled up in?

This alternative reality was fast becoming a waking nightmare, and she was nowhere near the border.

Mia did the best she could to clean up Goki's wounds using bottled water and antiseptic. Clipping away the hair with surgical scissors, she closed the ugly split on the back of his head with adhesive strips, then wrapped his head in a bandage as gently as she could.

Goki groaned softly as she finished the taping up.

'Can you hear me?' Mia asked in ragged Indonesian. 'You've been in an accident. Shall I get Sura to translate?'

On hearing that name, Goki flinched. He groped clumsily behind his back for a moment, then the effort overwhelmed him and he slid back into unconsciousness.

Mia realised he'd been looking for his knife.

One quarter of the stricken *Albany* was fully aground, and the several metres of exposed red waterline at her bow indicated the challenge they faced trying to get her off.

'What do you think?' Nash asked Kaboro, who was gauging their depth amidships to stern with a lead line. 'Is the channel deep enough?'

'Perhaps,' he frowned. 'Our draught is 1.75 metres. If we unload the cargo, we might get her off tomorrow on the last vestiges of the high tide. But if the propellers or their shafts are damaged, we're going nowhere.'

Nash nodded. Going nowhere was not an option. Not with God only knew what trouble brewing. While the chopper was an escape route, it could only take four at a time, and he was not keen on abandoning 175,000 dollars' worth of high-tech dive

183

gear. Kaboro had said the boat would be picked clean within twenty-four hours once the locals found it.

He looked down at the murky water and tried not to dwell on what it contained.

'I guess there's only one way to find out.'

Thanks to Kaboro's lashings, Nash's gear was mostly secure, but the Indonesian's scattered, jumbled equipment was blocking access to his rack of scuba tanks. Working together, Nash, Kaboro and Douglas began refilling spilled crates and stacking them out of the way.

'What do you need pumps in a cave for?' Nash stopped to ask, as they heaved the second of two high-pressure models to one side.

'Not to mention a couple of hundred metres of heavy-duty PVC pipe.' Douglas indicated the heavy rolls, still wedged in the angled bow cavity. 'Are they planning on pumping the bloody Hoosenbeck out?'

There was a trunk holding heavy 1500-watt portable lights; another contained truck batteries, two generators and a plastic barrel full of cables. When they uncovered the oxyacetylene kit, the growing doubt in Nash's stomach ballooned into a fully fledged conviction.

'They've been having us on. This was no film shoot.'

Douglas wiped the sweat from his eyes. 'What do you mean?'

'High-def cameras they'd keep in the cabins, but why aren't we seeing stuff like tripods, sound booms, underwater lighting rigs and camera housings?'

'What's all this shit for, then?'

'My guess is salvage.' With the bitter taste of disappointment in his mouth, Nash turned to Kaboro. 'You want to explain what the hell is going on here, Lieutenant?'

'Mr Nash, honestly I have no idea.' Kaboro sounded as aggrieved as he looked. 'My orders were only to take you to the mouth of the Hoosenbeck.'

'That's it?'

Kaboro thought for a moment. 'Yes, aside from awaiting further instructions from Sir Julius.'

Nash picked up the welding mask. 'Then I suggest we see what Sura has got to say for herself.'

They found her in animated discussion with Boerman on the sloping main deck, utterly oblivious to the tender sweeping the river for the victims of their stupidity. Such arrogant indifference summed up everything wrong about them, and Nash felt a surge of rage balling up in his throat as he marched up, holding the welding mask.

'What the fuck is this?'

Sura flinched as if he'd slapped her.

'What are you talking about?'

'There's no film equipment in the hold, just a shitload of salvage gear. I guess it explains the lack of a script.'

Sura took a step back, the pink end of her tongue darting out.

'Mr Nash, you are jumping to conclusions. Why don't you calm down so we can discuss this?'

'Stop lying!' Nash exploded. 'You lured us here under false pretences and it's just cost two people their lives.'

'You're way out of line, Nash,' the big man growled, but the threat rang hollow, and his eyes kept darting between Nash, Douglas and Kaboro.

'I'll bet you didn't even bring a camera.' In the ensuing silence, Nash gave them both a knowing smile. 'The expedition is over. You might as well spit it out. Why are we here?'

'I do not answer to you.' Sura's voice was thick with hatred.

It has to be money, thought Nash, keeping his eyes fixed on hers.

But if their purpose was salvage, what did they need him for? Perhaps what they were looking for was in the Hoosenbeck after all.

He turned to Kaboro. 'Lieutenant Kaboro, are you back in command?'

'Affirmative,' he boomed authoritatively. 'From now on I will make all operational decisions.'

Sura's lips drew back, reminding Nash of a cornered snake.

'My company *owns* this ship.'

'But you don't own us.' He smiled grimly. 'And until you come clean on what your real purpose is here, you're going nowhere except the closest police station to make a statement.'

'Fuck you, Nash!'

Unable to contain himself, Boerman muscled forwards.

'Stop right there!' barked a loud command.

Singkepe was on the quarterdeck, aiming the FN machine gun at the big man's head. Nash hoped to Christ it wasn't on full auto.

Sura clamped a hand on Boerman's tree-trunk arm and hissed, 'No, Jaap!'

Tense seconds passed before Nash nodded.

'Whatever you're up to, I'd put money down that it's something illegal. What say you, Lieutenant?'

Kaboro cleared his throat. 'Ms Suyanto, there are serious matters regarding the nature of your business that may require further investigation. Our priority, though, is securing and recovering this ship. Mr Nash will conduct an underwater survey to see if it is possible to refloat her, and I will then decide on an appropriate course of action. Until then, you will kindly restrict yourself to your cabins and the mess, and follow my orders.'

'You overreach yourself,' said Sura icily. 'Your role was made abundantly clear to you yesterday evening.'

Pursing his lips, Kaboro hooked his thumbs over his military belt.

'I am sure Sir Julius will understand that circumstances on the ground have changed.'

Balanced on the edge of the sloping helipad, Nash strapped the scuba tank to his bare back. It was going to be a shallow, muddy dive, which is why he was wearing a pair of shorts and a weight belt. Clipped to his forearm was a sheath knife – not that it would be much use against crocodiles and bull sharks. For these, Kaboro had posted sharpshooters around the ship, while Singkepe covered the bow with his machine gun in case of *wantok* attack.

'Watch your back down there, laddie.' Douglas was staring down at the murky water.

Nash hesitated before pulling on his mask. 'Is Mia OK?'

In the haste to get underwater, he hadn't had time to check.

'Honouring her Hippocratic oath with that stupid arse-hole, Goki. And don't worry about Sura and Boerman – would you believe they've confined *themselves* to quarters?' Douglas snorted derisively. 'Two of Singkepe's finest have been posted outside their door to make sure it stays that way.'

Nash grinned and stuck the regulator between his teeth. Taking firm hold of the mask, he took a big step and splashed into the tepid water. A moment later he landed on the muddy river bottom, to be instantly enveloped in a dense cloud of silt.

Feet buried in the mud, he reached up and located the square bulk of the stern. Its steel plate was covered in rough anti-fouling paint, and the sensation was eerily like searching for an exit in a silted-out cave.

By increasing the volume of air in his lungs, Nash floated free of the bottom. The silt soon dispersed in the current, leaving visibility at around an arm's length. Rolling on his back, he found purchase on the thin welded ridges between the hull plates and manoeuvred his way around the twin rudders. Although still locked at forty-five degrees, they were undamaged. Behind the rudders were the twin propellers. Running his hands over the big bronze blades, Nash hoped Douglas was right and Boerman was nowhere near the start button.

What Kaboro had feared most was damage to the vulnerable propeller shafts. These ran exposed for three and a half metres before entering the hull and, if snapped or bent, meant a dry dock repair. Nash did his best to sight along the shafts and feel for distortion. It seemed the *Albany* had been lucky. Her stern had not connected heavily with the bottom during the collision, because her flat semi-displacement hull, which gave her speed, had helped her skip like a stone. Nash began to feel heartened; maybe they could get out of here under their own steam.

The close inspection work helped keep his mind off potential wildlife, and soon he reached the stabilisers. These rudder-like blades projected at a forty-five-degree angle, just below the waterline, to provide control when the boat was up and planing. Here, he discovered the leading edge of the port stabiliser had been dented for about half its length. While the damage was not catastrophic, Nash guessed it would create drag and affect handling, and he duly fired away with the GoPro.

Amidships, there was only superficial hull damage – dents, scratches and gouges. Nash continued until his tank bumped the mud below. As the silt billowed up, he was reminded of 'gardening' the dirt-filled tunnels under the limestone of Mount Gambier, South Australia – excavating spoil to access new routes. Get too enthusiastic and you could end up digging your own grave.

In the zero visibility, the edge of anxiety he'd been suppressing began to assert itself. A feeling of breathlessness came over him, and he was filled with a nagging sense of dread. It was time to call the dive. Exiting on the port side, Nash prayed no one up top mistook him for an inquisitive croc.

It felt bloody wonderful to reach the surface and feel the expanse of sky overhead.

'How is she?' Kaboro was leaning over the rail, having tracked his bubbles.

Sitting in the mud, Nash gave him a thumbs up. 'No significant damage. But the leading edge of the port stabiliser is slightly bent.' He held up his hands to demonstrate.

'Seems we've been lucky, then.'

Nash nodded. The submerged mudflat in the river had been a blessing in disguise, slowing the ship down without tearing out her bottom. After sliding across it, they'd reached a deeper channel before running aground. The problem now was the viscosity of the mud in which the bow of the *Albany* was embedded. Kaboro explained the friction was too much for her engines to overcome.

'Can we loosen the mud's grip?' asked Nash. 'Dig it away from the sides?'

'Yes,' said Kaboro. 'And lighten the ship.'

Suddenly, there was a cry of alarm.

'*Crocodile!*'

Nash frantically scanned the brown river. He spotted a ripple by the stern. Was it a gust of wind, or the bow wave of an approaching two-tonne reptile? The steep bank behind him, with its impenetrable kunai grass, was ten metres away, but in the sticky ooze it might as well have been a mile. With difficulty, Nash broke the suction and stood up. The tank on his back seemed to weigh more than a man.

'Take my hand, Nash!'

Kaboro had dropped to his stomach, was reaching down. But no one alive had the strength or grip in the muddy slop to haul Nash out. He was on his own.

Another shout of 'CROCODILE!'

Christ, it's coming for me.

As shots rang out, Nash fought to be free of the heavy tank, with muddy hands slipping on the buckles. He swore in frustration. Stuck like this, he wouldn't even be able to shove the damn thing into its mouth . . .

Idiot, use your knife!

Nash whipped it out of the forearm sheath and in two quick slashes severed the infernal straps.

Now he had a fighting chance!

The roar of the tender's outboard filled him with hope as it swept around the stern. The bug-eyed sailor crouching in the bow reached out his arms for the grab. Nash flung his upper body forward to meet him. His knees crashed painfully into the sides of the tender as the sailor found a grip on his weight belt. With one powerful heave, he manhandled Nash on board, where they both collapsed in a muddy embrace.

Ensign Mohli was trying to restart the outboard, which had stalled in the mud, when there was another shout.

'Belay that – false alarm!'

'What do you mean?' bellowed Kaboro indignantly. 'Report!'

There was a pause. 'Sir . . . it's a floating log!'

Nash and his two rescuers stared at one another. Then they began to roar with helpless laughter.

Chapter 19

Under the protective gaze of Singkepe and his two best sharp-shooters, Nash organised port and starboard teams equipped with all the tools they could muster. Ladders were lashed to the sides of the ship so they could clamber down to the slop. There weren't enough shovels, so they used oars, buckets, bowls, even bare hands, to scoop the mud away from the hull. Soon they were covered in the sticky stuff, scraping, hacking and hurling the clods behind them. It was back-breaking work and Douglas declared his hangover to be the worst in six decades of excess. Watching the old pilot staggering about with mud smeared all over him, Nash took pity and told him to take a break.

'Penance, Robbie, once it's sweated out I'll be fine.'

'Remember to hydrate, Mr Douglas.' Kaboro offered a canteen.

'Stuff that. You got a ciggie, Saworno? Left mine up top.'

The old engineer pulled out a crumpled pack and shook one loose. Nash had insisted Kaboro keep him apart from the Indonesian contingent. Saworno could shed no light on Shangri-La's true intentions, and Nash believed him when he said that he had been hired simply to keep the engines going.

Pushing carefully through the long spiky grass, Nash made his way around the bow to check progress on the port side. As much as he didn't trust the Indonesians, it would have been stupid not to accept Sura's offer of help. He noted Hartono was already flagging, looking hard done by and stopping too often, whereas Sura was working with a will in a Gucci jumpsuit that would never look the same. Again, Nash found himself wondering what was driving her, for her output was only exceeded by Boerman, who was a human excavator, chopping out great clumps of mud with a mattock, flinging them carelessly towards Faiwalati and the other PNGDF men, who kept having to duck.

As the sun exerted its authority, morale began to waver. In near total humidity, fighting the muck sticking tenaciously to tools and feet was exhausting. After four gruelling hours, Nash realised it would take days to make a serious impression on the mud gripping the ship's sides. They required a mechanical solution.

'We need some kind of power jet,' he announced, over Faiwalati's lunch of stir-fried leftovers.

Boerman spat over the side. 'You see an equipment hire around here, Nash?'

'No, but you have pumps, don't you?'

Hacking away the kunai grass, they dug two level pads at the waterline and manhandled the two massive 100 mm pumps into position. The rolls of PVC pipe became malleable in the blazing sun and, under the watchful eye of Singkepe's sharpshooters, they swam them out to create intakes in deeper water, using rocks and plastic floats to prevent them blocking with mud or drawing air. Nash fashioned jet nozzles using spacers and reducers to concentrate each pump's powerful flow rate into a high-velocity water jet, and incorporated a ball valve to regulate the force.

'So, what were you planning to do with all this shit?' he asked Boerman casually while tightening a fitting. 'Pump out a sunken vessel? Locate a black box?'

The Afrikaner made no reply, but the flexing of his mighty jaw made it clear he loathed being questioned.

Nash had already suggested to Kaboro he should search Shangri-La's cabins as a matter of urgency, but the lieutenant was getting cold feet. Although he agreed the Indonesians had engaged in deception, there was no proof of a crime. If they refloated the ship, Kaboro suggested they make for the nearest major port of Wewak, a couple of hours north of the Sepik's mouth. Otherwise, they would use the helicopter to ferry all personnel to Pagwi and call headquarters. At this point Nash had laughed. If not under arrest, the Indonesians would simply fly out when it suited them, leaving two dead fishermen – and accountability for their actions – behind. But as he was learning, out here a different set of rules, or lack thereof, applied.

'OK.' He nodded at Boerman. 'Let's give it a test.'

The big man fired up the left-side pump as Nash backed into the murk. Within a few seconds the flexible fire hose on the outlet went rigid. As Nash turned on the valve, the hose reared back like a giant snake, trying to flail and lash. The powerful water jet sliced through the mud with ease.

'Works a treat!' he yelled to Boerman, who was watching with hands on hips. 'But point it the wrong way and it'll take out your eyes.'

Nash didn't want Boerman anywhere near him underwater, but he couldn't do too much damage on the other side of the ship, so he equipped them both with umbilical dive hoses running to his air compressor on the foredeck. Noting Ricki Hartono taking an interest, Nash had a quiet word with Kaboro, who posted a guard to watch over him.

They began work in chest-deep water. Sinking to his knees, Nash turned on the powerful jet and began excavating the face of the bank. The dislodged mud rolled downhill to disperse in the deeper water. The full-face mask with a built-in demand valve helped distance him from the viscous soup. Time soon became meaningless, and in a sensory environment dominated by touch, the quickest way to check progress was by sliding a hand along the newly exposed hull. It took them two hours to carve trenches right up to the bow – each a metre deep and half as wide.

'It won't be enough,' Boerman observed as they rehydrated on the bank. 'We have to get right underneath to break the suction.'

Nash suspected he was right. However, the idea of tunnelling beneath the flat-bottomed hull in a muddy coffin-sized cavity was appalling.

Boerman's big teeth gleamed whitely. 'What's the matter, Nash? Scared of a little mud?'

Nash was damned if he was going to let the Afrikaner get under his skin.

'OK, we'll try it. But we work from the keel to the outside only. Got that? From the keel to the outside.'

'*Ja*, I heard you the first time.'

They reconvened under the midline of the *Albany*, in zero visibility, a tactile meeting of shoulders. Nash constantly checked his orientation so as not to sweep in Boerman's direction. It was difficult, dangerous work, but by maintaining a generous excavation, Nash kept the claustrophobia at bay.

They carved away for perhaps an hour, and then Nash began to wonder just how much friction the remaining mud was exerting on the mass of the ship. He had already burrowed a good two body lengths into the bank; at some point the law of gravity would have to take over, and anyone caught underneath when the *Albany* slid into deeper water would become a smear of red paste.

Nash backed up to their starting point. Here, a narrow wall of mud demarcated their twin excavations. To his dismay, he discovered Boerman's was barely forty centimetres deep, and as a result, the crazy Afrikaner had burrowed in much further towards the bow. Gritting his teeth, Nash slithered inside and felt around for Boerman's oversized feet. There was no sign of him, just the hissing roar of his jet.

Damn the man.

He would have to go further inside.

Nash proceeded forwards on his belly, and as the excavation grew shallower, he wondered how on earth Boerman had even managed to fit in here. Then, with the hull hard against his back, the claustrophobia pounced.

The sense he was moments from suffocating was overpowering. In the full-face mask, he heard a voice keening in fear and was horrified to realise it was his.

'Idiot!' he chastised himself.

What he needed to do was kill the pumps. That would drive the bastard out.

Before he could act, a blow like a kick from a carthorse propelled him into the cavity and slammed him into the far end.

His first thought was a crocodile, but then a stinging blast across his back told him it was Boerman's water jet.

In the ensuing tumult, his fins were blown off his feet. Nash clamped his hands over his full-face mask as he began to rotate horizontally. In mounting terror, he realised each revolution was driving him deeper into the packed mud. The power of the jet was impossible to resist. He felt his air hose coiling around him, locking his arms against his chest. When it snapped, his next breath was liquid mud.

Abruptly the jet stopped. The yammering of the pumps was gone.

The overwhelming sensation was of tremendous compression, and it took him a few seconds to understand the full horror of his predicament. He was wedged beneath the hull of the *Albany* like a doorstop, unable to use his arms, hands or legs for leverage. Only his feet could move, and they were uselessly treading slop.

The old Nash would have methodically tried to untangle himself, conserving every drop of oxygen in his tissues. Now he reacted like a wild animal in a snare, thrashing and twisting as panic consumed him. The fury of his struggles intensified with each passing second.

But somehow a hand, then an arm, came free. Grabbing the coils of air hose, he ripped them down his torso and freed his other arm.

With hands like talons, he dragged his trapped legs behind him, blindly groping for what he hoped was the way out. The only point of reference was the back of his head bouncing on the hull. He thought he saw a lighter shade of brown and made for it. The pain in his diaphragm was indescribable . . . a prelude to blacking out.

When Nash exploded from the gloop, he looked like a possessed creature from another world. In a gout of vomit and mud, he dimly heard himself screaming – a terrible wail that sent the birds in the forest chattering.

'Put him down here, quickly!' cried Singkepe, as many hands picked Nash up and deposited him on the deck. He could feel a rough finger inside his mouth, another scraping mud from his nostrils. For a moment, it was like drowning again, and he began to protest.

'Let me through!' He heard Mia's voice. 'Move!' Her hands held the sides of his face. Then he was rolled on to his side. Something was put under his head. 'It's OK, it's OK,' she soothed him. 'I've just got to make sure your airways are clear.'

He tried to open his eyes. The pain was excruciating, as if his eyeballs were set in cement.

'I can't see,' he gasped.

She sluiced the debris out from under his eyelids with a bottle of water. The world was a murky soup of indistinct colour and light.

'Listen to me, Rob. I know it hurts like hell, but I want you to open your eyes as wide as you can. I need to see what's going on.' He complied for as long as he could. 'That's good,' she said, 'keep blinking. The tears will wash it out.'

Eyes burning and stinging, he began to regain partial focus.

'I think you'll be OK,' she reassured him. 'Some abrasions, but no visible damage. The iris looks fine. Keep blinking.'

Someone was sluicing him down with water. He realised he was surrounded by a sea of legs. Frank Douglas's worried face came into view.

'Are you all right, Robbie? Jesus, I thought we'd lost you there.'

Then Boerman squatted down, covered from head to toe in a thick coating of mud. The whites of his eyes glowed preternaturally with some kind of inner satisfaction.

'What the fuck were you doing, Nash? I had no idea you were under there until the pumps stopped and you came out of the water like a stuck pig.' His grin widened. 'I never heard any man squeal like that before – but more than a few women, hey?'

With a wink at Mia, he gave Nash a hearty slap on the shoulder which sent tentacles of pain radiating through his body.

'Leave him alone,' snarled Douglas. 'Can't you see he's in a bad way?'

Kaboro and two of his men carried Nash down to his former cabin. With Goki occupying the lower bunk, they threw the top mattress on the floor. When they placed Nash down upon it, he cried out. Every part of his body was on fire.

'Lieutenant, wouldn't it be prudent to arrest Jaap at once?' Mia sounded angry.

'Doctor Carter, I am sure this was an unfortunate accident.'

'How many more "accidents" are you prepared to accept?'

'Please, Doctor Carter, my men *are* in control, and everything will be investigated. How is Goki now?'

'I believe he has a fractured skull, and he needs to be evacuated as soon as possible.'

'I will arrange it at once,' replied Kaboro. 'We can get word out, too.'

'I'd say that's not a moment too soon.' Mia dropped her voice. 'Please don't underestimate these people, Lieutenant. I believe we are in great danger.

Nash must have fallen unconscious, because almost immediately there was a knock at the door. Muted talk. Nash heard them lift Goki up. The man groaned and cried something out in Indonesian. He sounded scared. Mia gently touched Nash's shoulder.

'They're flying him back to Angoram. A hospital plane can land there. Now, let's see to you properly.'

Gently she dabbed the grazes on his nose and forehead with an alcohol swab.

'You have multiple cuts and abrasions. No broken bones, but tomorrow you'll be black and blue.' She worked silently for a time before asking, 'What happened under there?' She ran a hand tenderly through his wet hair. 'Rob, can you hear me?'

Nash could understand every word, but he was mute. The terror had not only overtaken him – it had *owned* him so comprehensively that he no longer recognised himself. Dimly he heard the chopper firing up. Then he succumbed to oblivion.

Chapter 20

Hurtling above the Sepik at more than 150 kilometres per hour, the deafening roar of the turbine was vibrating the plates of Goki's shattered skull. His vision was blurring and spotting, and the metallic taste in his mouth was leaking cerebrospinal fluid, from where Boerman had pounded the back of his head against the steel deck. Goki had begged the stupid apes not to load him on to the chopper, but the fools had not listened. When the big *bule* had climbed in and slammed the door, he'd known his fate was sealed.

The helicopter's shadow flitted across the surface of the river like a dragonfly. Suddenly, it vanished in a stomach-churning descent. Framed in the side window, ominous shapes could be seen in the water below. Goki moaned as the *g*-forces added a new dimension to the pain.

Boerman leaned around and fixed him with a stare.

'You should really try minding your own fucking business.'

Without warning, he stabbed a giant forefinger into Goki's forehead. It felt like a nail being driven through his skull, and Goki screamed. Everything went black.

The habitat of the saltwater crocodile stretches from Northern Australia to South East Asia. Equally at home in a muddy billabong or fifty kilometres out to sea, it is by far the biggest reptile in the world. Old bulls are capable of growing to seven metres, and can weigh in at one and a half tonnes. They will attack anything, including adult water buffalo, and make their cousin, the alligator, look like a rubber bath toy. Few salties are left on the middle Sepik. An abundance of protein-starved hunters with guns had seen their numbers plummet, and the pacu were devouring the floating islands they preferred to nest in. But away from villages and towns, big crocodiles could still be found.

Dangling upside down above a pool of hungry crocodiles, Goki thought he was in a nightmare. One huge beast launched itself out of the water, and the cavernous pink gullet seemed close enough to touch. As the great jaws snapped together, Goki realised this was no dream. Now he became aware of the fury of the helicopter's prop wash. Craning his head up in agony, he saw his left foot was caught in a fully extended seat belt. In the maelstrom, Boerman was stepping carefully on to the chopper's skids.

'Help me!' Goki screamed desperately. 'Help me!'

Boerman inched his way along the skid until he was directly above him. As he took hold of the seat belt, Goki felt an irrational rush of hope. If anyone had the strength to haul him aboard, it was the Afrikaner. The big man's biceps swelled and Goki felt himself rising.

'Just like feeding time at the zoo!' Boerman roared, shaking the commando loose.

'No, *No!*'

Goki landed on his back with an almighty slap that knocked the wind right out of him. Before he could sink, the biggest crocodile – a six-metre veteran with one eye missing – snatched hold of his lower legs. Not to be outdone, the largest of the three smaller ones grabbed him around the chest.

As crocodiles possess no carnassial teeth to shear through flesh, larger prey items are usually drowned and stored in a lair to decompose and soften before being ingested. However, when two crocodiles tussle over the same prey, a prehistoric tug of war ensues. As the beasts fought each other, Goki knew pain that few ever would. Every joint in his body was popping. His chest was in a vice. Something tore inside his groin. The teeth embedded in his shins were puncturing bone, and he could feel them grinding, twisting and cracking.

The Jet Ranger hovered overhead for the finale. With a massive double beat of its saurian tail, the big crocodile reared backwards. With the smaller beast refusing to relinquish its prize, something had to give. With a sickening splintering of bone and sinew, Goki's legs tore away from his body in a massive jet of arterial blood. The bigger crocodile threw its head back and swallowed the legs whole, gulping them down like breadsticks, while the other fled the scene with its juicer prize.

'Christ almighty!' exclaimed Boerman, temporarily forgetting his conversion. 'Did you see that?'

Looking sick, Hartono banked away. Boerman leaned out for a last view of the crocs, but only a blood slick marked the site of the carnage.

Choking with despair, he swims Natalie to the shore, tenderly picks her up, and carries her into the garden. Here he digs a grave under the peppermint gums which she so loved. But it's been raining for weeks and the sides keep caving in, no matter how frantically he digs. The grave is barely deep enough, but Brendan and Jonathan are coming over for the funeral, so he

lays her down and pushes and pushes until she is gone. He is
placing the sprig of karri flower on top of the mounded soil,
when two hands erupt from the earth like claws and grab him
by the throat.

Liquid mud surges up his nose as he's yanked down into the
grave . . . He's drowning, choking in despair . . .

Breathe, why don't you!

BREATHE!

Alarmed by Nash's cries, Mia sat down on the edge of the mattress beside him.

'It's OK,' she soothed. 'Rob, you're safe now.'

He jerked violently, then cried out, 'No, Nat, no!'

Nightmares were unusual in non-REM sleep; was this some
kind of fit? Taking his hand, she placed her fingers on his wrist
to find his pulse surging in waves. Mia frowned. The edge of terror in Nash's dreadful screams after the incident with Boerman
had appalled her. Such primal fear, at odds with his profession
and the incredible courage he had already demonstrated, was
probably PTSD.

She kept hold of Nash's hand while she studied his battered
face close up. The strong jaw and sandy brown hair made him
seem earnest and trustworthy, while those slightly flared nostrils and sea-green eyes added a sensual, dangerous element to
the mix.

Unable to look away, Mia felt slightly guilty. As soon as she'd
set eyes on Rob Nash, she'd been surprised by the depth of
her attraction to him. It was visceral and instinctive. Stronger
than any she'd ever known. She'd been intellectualising it as a

response to her rescue – a knight in shining armour fantasy, which was frankly embarrassing – but seeing him now, so broken and vulnerable, she wasn't so sure. If anything, the attraction was getting stronger.

There was a knock on the door, and Mia relinquished Nash's hand as Frank Douglas stuck his head inside.

'How's he doing, doc?'

'Hard to know for certain. He didn't aspirate water or mud. Aside from the lacerations and bruising, I think it's mostly shock.'

Douglas crouched down stiffly beside the bunk, looking yellow and gaunt.

Probably his liver, she thought. *Too much booze and years of malaria.*

'He's been calling out for Nat,' she told him. 'Do you know who he's talking about?'

'Natalie was his wife.'

Mia was confused. Rob hadn't mentioned her last night.

'She died a year ago.' Douglas was staring at Nash with concern on his grizzled face. 'Losing her really messed him up.'

'How did it happen?'

Douglas glanced briefly at her. 'An accident.'

Mia understood he wasn't going to talk about it. *He's protecting him*, she thought, and wondered why. But there were more immediate concerns.

'Frank, what do you know about Shangri-La? Because I believe Boerman just tried to kill Rob – and I *know* he tried to kill Goki, too, because I caught him in the act.'

He stared at her in alarm. 'You're *serious*?'

She told him about Nash's altercation with Boerman the night before, and explained what she'd seen on the bridge after the grounding – perhaps thieves falling out.

'I don't believe Kaboro recognises the threat he's facing here. What do you think they're up to, Frank?'

He looked dazed. 'The job seemed genuine enough. Sura's a TV star in Indonesia, Robbie's the cave-diving legend, and they don't get any bigger than the Hoosenbeck Cavern.'

Mia's own theory was robbery. Big mining conglomerates were shaving whole mountain tops off in Papua, dumping hundreds of thousands of tonnes of spoil into the rivers, shipping out millions of dollars in precious metals.

Scratching his bristly chin, Douglas frowned as he listened.

'I just don't know, but it's obviously a front. The money *was* too good to be true.' He stared at her with haunted eyes. 'Shit, isn't it always? Oh fuck, what have I done?'

Mia thought quickly. 'What about Kaboro?'

'You think *he's* in on it, too?' Douglas was aghast.

'No, I think he's stumbling around in the dark like we are, but if he won't act and put them under arrest, then I don't think we're safe, not so long as we stay on this boat.'

Douglas anxiously rubbed his face with both hands.

'There's no easy way out of here, Mia. We can't just go wandering through the bush, not after what happened to that canoe.' Pensively, he sucked air between his teeth. 'Look, their hands might be tied, but Kaboro and Singkepe are firmly in our camp. Once we refloat the ship tomorrow, we'll head to the nearest town with an airstrip and a radio and get off there.'

'And if we don't refloat the ship?' Mia stared at him.

'Then I'll take that fucking chopper and fly us out myself.' Douglas pulled himself to his feet. 'I'm going to go and talk to Kaboro, see if I can persuade him to lock them up before they get back.'

'What do you mean, *they*?'

'Boerman took the evac flight with Hartono.' Even as he said it, Douglas registered the obvious with a groan of dismay.

'Kaboro let him go, too?' Mia shook her head. 'This keeps getting better.'

Mia looked up sharply as the rhythmic beat of the chopper reverberated outside. Checking her watch, she frowned.

'What's wrong?' asked Douglas.

'The return flight to Angoram should have taken at least another twenty minutes. They're back too soon.'

Chapter 21

As the ghostly form of the giant fig took shape in the cracked windscreen, Lieutenant Kaboro rubbed his smarting eyes. It had been a long and sleepless night, his strained senses alert to lurking threats outside in the jungle, and now within. Without comms, Hartono's dubious claim that they had dropped Goki at Ambunti after making radio contact with the medical services could not be verified, and Kaboro had been sorely tempted to arrest them on the spot. Staying his hand was the spectre of Sir Julius. The defence minister was a powerful and vindictive man who obviously had a financial stake in the expedition, whatever its true purpose was.

Muted conversation on the bow drew Kaboro's attention. Singkepe and his corporal were sharing a cigarette. The other sentries were scanning the riverbanks. It had been unnaturally quiet since the accident. That no locals had been sighted suggested trouble was indeed brewing, and Kaboro was counting down the hours to high tide.

A door banged loudly and Kaboro flinched. Ensign Faiwalati came into view, carrying a tray of steaming coffees. The genial young cook distributed them to the grateful soldiers and Frank Douglas. Kaboro was still smarting from their exchange last night. Douglas had accused him of gross incompetence, demanded he physically restrain the Indonesians, then wanted to take their helicopter. While Kaboro understood the man's concerns, there was no point inflaming the situation.

Kaboro chuckled as the irascible Australian took a sip of the too-hot coffee and spat it out with an oath.

At that moment, the tray of coffee abruptly crashed to the deck and Faiwalati fell to his knees. At first, Kaboro was outraged. Douglas must have struck him, for the cook was rasping like an asthmatic trying to breathe. Then Kaboro saw the long, thin stick protruding from his throat.

It was the opening drop of a monsoonal cloudburst of arrows. The deluge fell upon the *Albany,* salvos shattering or ricocheting off steel decks and superstructure. One ripped through the open bridge window and thudded into the captain's seat beside Kaboro. The long arrow was made of fire-hardened cane grass with duck feather flights. Sporadic gunshots boomed like accompanying thunder. A porthole on the lower deck exploded in a shower of glass. Sparks flew as a slug caromed off the windscreen frame.

'We're under attack!' Kaboro screamed at the men below.

By the time he reached the deck, Faiwalati was dead, an expression of hurt surprise frozen on his genial face. Kaboro was horrified to see most of the much-vaunted Long-Range Reconnaissance Group were huddling behind any cover they could find.

'Regroup!' he yelled. 'Find a target!'

Ululating screams and whistles immediately brought an accurate volley of arrows down on his head. At least two spotters were directing fire. On the bow, Singkepe was directing short bursts into likely-looking branches and thickets of kunai grass, in the hope of flushing them out.

The PNGDF was one of the few services in the world which faced attack from primitive weapons. Kaboro recalled the advice of a wizened highland instructor, a survivor of tribal conflicts from a time when it was acceptable to build a skull pile outside your hut, who had said, '*The arrow you see won't hit you, the one you can't, will.*' To reinforce this, he'd shot blunt arrows at them as they dodged and weaved. It had been a painful lesson. Unfortunately, with the volume of projectiles arcing through the mist, it wasn't much help.

Kaboro headed aft in a low crouch along the port side of the ship to rally the defence. Two of Singkepe's soldiers were mindlessly hosing the grassy bank with their M16s.

'Pick your targets!' he roared. 'Conserve ammo!'

Near the stern, he encountered the body of Singkepe's signaller. An arrow had severed his jugular and a huge blood slick covered the deck. Sidestepping the treacherous mess, Kaboro grabbed the dead man's M16.

Under the edge of the helicopter pad, the Indonesians were taking cover.

'Get below!' Kaboro yelled at Sura. 'It's not safe up here!'

Without waiting for a response, he pressed on to the starboard side. Here, the arrows scattered across the deck were so thick that he lost his footing and almost fell.

'Space yourselves,' he barked at two of his sailors huddling behind a vent peppered with bullet holes. 'Find a firing position and defend the ship.'

Catching sight of an arrow winging its way towards him, Kaboro ducked to let it bounce off the steel bulkhead above. When he stood up again, a blast of hot buckshot tugged his shirtsleeve.

Kaboro spotted the shooter – an old tribesman crouched down by the water's edge, grinning gleefully while he reloaded

213

a home-made shotgun. Kaboro shouldered the M16 and fired a three-round burst. The old man was still smiling when the high velocity 5.56 mm bullets tore his head apart.

Crouched behind the thick wall of Boerman's body, Sura clung tightly to his belt while he scanned the scene with a practised eye.

'There's no more than twenty of them,' he told her.

'How do you know?'

'Rate of fire.'

'Shouldn't we get below?' Hartono's eyes were wide and staring, and his breath was foul with fear. During prayers, one of the first arrows had missed him by centimetres and thudded into the tail of the Jet Ranger.

Ignoring him, Boerman turned to Sura. 'The mist will soon clear. You have to let me do something.'

Sura chewed on her lower lip before shaking her head.

'We can't risk exposure until the ship is free ...' Extended firing made her pause. 'Let Kaboro do the fighting, it will whittle down his forces.'

Boerman snorted in contempt. 'Listen to their fire control. These idiots haven't got a clue. We'll be picked off one by one.'

As if emphasising his point, a bullet smacked through the helicopter's skid, leaving a puckered hole. Sura suddenly saw the Avenue Montaigne slipping away.

'What do you propose, then?'

Boerman's face took on an evangelical cast. 'Regain the upper hand and flush them out into the open. To do that, we need height.' He nodded at the helicopter.

'Do it, Jaap.'

Boerman reached out and seized hold of Hartono's shirt front.

'Have the chopper ready to go in three minutes. You hear me?'

He took off in a fast, crouching run and Sura watched him go with pride. Jaap was a firebrand, often a fool, but when it came to the business of killing, he was in his element.

On the other side of the high riverbank, a natural berm provided a protected firing platform for the archers, who did not even flinch as bullets cut the air above their heads. Instead, they nocked another arrow in their black palm bows and awaited instruction on further targets. The men directing them with whistles and clicks were almost invisible in the long grass and trees. However, they were still vulnerable to a lucky shot.

Daniel was proud to have these men as *wantoks*. That they would risk their lives for his son made his heart swell with blood obligation. But he was worried about his father, who had gone to take potshots at the ship with his twelve-gauge. He'd heard its characteristic loud boom once, but since then nothing, and his father was not responding to their secret bower bird trill. Daniel hoped his father's gun had simply misfired; home-made guns of galvanised water pipe were not only unreliable – they occasionally burst, with catastrophic results.

A sudden burst of high-pitched whistles and coded calls alerted Daniel to a prime target at the front of the ship. A white man. No doubt this would be the captain responsible for killing Nathan.

Daniel took the enchanted arrow from his quiver and nocked. Calmly he drew back the bamboo bowstring with two leathery fingers. Visualising the trajectory, he released, and the black arrow surged skywards through the mist, feathered flights spinning like fireflies. At its apex, it turned slowly, and then plummeted out of sight. Blessed by the shaman, guided by the spirits of his ancestors, Daniel knew it could not miss. An immense weight lifted from his soul. His beloved Nathan was avenged.

Waking to the loud rattle of an automatic weapon, Nash sat bolt upright and gasped. Just about every part of his body was throbbing, searing or smarting. Somewhere, someone screamed an order. Running feet thrummed on the steel deck above.

'What's happening?' he cried out. 'I can't see!'

'It's payback.' Mia's voice was close to his ear. 'Wait a moment, your eyelids are stuck together.'

With a damp cloth she removed the dried pus from his eyes, and when he could open them, he saw his body was covered in plasters and antiseptic ointment where she must have tended to him.

Someone pounded on the cabin door and a voice cried, 'Faiwalati is hurt! *Doktor, plis, plis* can you come?'

'*Mi kamap.*' Mia got to her feet. '*Kwiktaim!*'

Nash reached for his shorts on the end of the bunk.

'Don't bother arguing,' he growled at her disapproving expression. 'I'm not an invalid.'

On the first rung of the ladder, he began to question his bravado. The skin across his back felt as if it had been flayed.

216

The gunshots grew louder, more percussive, as they reached the deck. Cautiously they stuck their heads outside the forecastle door. Poor Faiwalati was obviously beyond help, but another transfixed body lay under the crane in a sea of broken arrows.

'Oh Jesus, it's Frank.'

Douglas lay splayed on his right side with one arm stretched out. The other hand was clutching feebly at a long arrow embedded in his chest.

'Don't pull it out –'

Mia broke off as a bullet struck the top of the doorway and whined away. Nash was bracing himself to run the gauntlet when Mia clamped a hand on his shoulder.

'You can hardly walk.'

Before he could argue, she dashed across the open deck to crouch beside the stricken Douglas. Loud whistles were followed by a volley of arrows which crashed down around her, snapping and skipping away. How they missed, Nash would never know.

'Get out of there!' he yelled, appalled by her exposure.

When she ignored him, he limped as fast as he could across the exposed deck and seized hold of Douglas's ankles.

'No!' she shouted as he began to pull. 'There's risk of internal bleeding.'

The raw skin on Nash's naked back cringed as another arrow thrummed past.

'Too bad!' he shouted back. 'We're getting out of here!'

Grunting with the pain, he dragged the stricken Douglas along the deck, while Mia did her best to cradle the embedded arrow and stop his head banging on the steel.

When they reached the relative shelter of the forecastle door, Nash collapsed in a panting heap while Mia took Douglas's pulse. As she concentrated, two fingers pressed into his carotid, a curl of lustrous blonde hair fell down over her bumpy nose. Nash noticed that her eyelashes were incredibly long, dark and thick. It struck him that Mia was one of those women whose beauty kept revealing itself in new ways.

She looked up at him with a worried expression.

'I need somewhere to work on him, Rob.'

He thought for a moment. 'The mess?'

'Good. But first I need to remove this shaft before it jags on something and rips him open. Can you find me a hacksaw?'

'Seriously?'

'Do I look like I'm joking?' Her blue eyes blazed. 'And get me the first aid kit, too.'

With M60 in hand and a thousand rounds of ammunition draped across his shoulders, Boerman stormed back under heavy fire to find the helicopter cold and still. Studded in arrows, it resembled a novelty pin cushion.

'God damn it, man!' he shouted at Hartono, who was still cowering under the landing deck. 'What the fuck are you doing?'

'He won't budge,' said Sura bitterly. 'He's a pathetic coward.'

'I can't do it,' Hartono sobbed. 'Please don't make me go out there.'

Extending a long arm, Boerman reached in and dragged Hartono out before lifting him up like a bag of garbage.

'Get that *bleddy* chopper fired up or I'll kill you myself.'

With a powerful heave, he flung the smaller man onto the pad.

Kaboro had organised four sharpshooters on the bridge super-structure, but the attackers refused to expose themselves. On the bow, Singkepe was calmly reloading the FN. His corporal, Moses, lay flat on his back, a long stream of blood flowing from a nasty hole in the side of his head. Kaboro's mouth was dry. At this rate they would soon be annihilated.

'I've got one, definite!' Singkepe shouted up at him. 'But I can't see anything in this damned grass.'

The damned grass . . .

Fumbling with his keys, Kaboro opened the captain's cupboard and raked the contents out onto the floor. Snapping open the brass flare gun, he inserted a fat cartridge into the breech. If only he'd thought of this before.

Two years in Orlando Emergency had taught Mia much about penetrating trauma. While the long black arrow buried in Douglas's flesh looked horrific, it was a plug for torn veins and arteries. Best practice was to secure the object and have the patient transferred to a hospital, where scans and an ER surgery team would give them the best chance of survival. But there was no ER, and Douglas wouldn't survive an evac unless she could stabilise him. Not with blood pressure at around 50 over 120, weak and fluttering.

Nash returned with a toolbox and first aid kit. While he braced the arrow, she took the hacksaw and began cutting a handspan above the puncture wound. The fire-hardened cane

219

was incredibly tough, and its silica-rich fibres kept clogging the teeth of the saw. She made fast and light strokes, stopping every so often to clear the teeth. Then she secured the stump with gaffer tape.

'Will he make it?' Nash leaned over anxiously.

How many times had she been asked that question? As usual, there were no easy answers.

'He needs a hospital, Rob. All we can do now is make him comfortable. Let's get him to the mess.'

Ricki Hartono was terrified, but in the familiar surroundings of the Jet Ranger's cockpit he saw his opportunity to get the hell out of there, and worked the controls like a man possessed.

'C'mon, c'mon, c'mon,' he chanted, as the turbine spun up with agonising slowness. Numerous arrows were already embedded in the Plexiglas, and he pressed himself against the seat in anticipation of more.

Bang!

An arrow punched through, right in front of his face. Hartono found himself eyeballing a vicious hand-beaten steel arrowhead.

'Damn you, Jaap!' he shrieked as another slammed into the passenger door.

With agonising clarity, he recalled all the stupid decisions that had led him to this moment. An idle rich boy with a red-carpet military career and secure postings which had never put him in the line of fire, he'd lived it up with wine, women and song until a gambling addiction exploded the fantasy and beggared his parents. That had led to dereliction of duty under the influence. About to be dishonourably discharged, an eleventh-hour covert offer from the Suyantos had been a lifeline too good to refuse. Hartono burst out into manic laughter as he recalled assuring Goki he was 'cool as a cucumber under fire'. Ten minutes was all it had taken for him to understand that Ricki 'Maverick' Hartono was a show pony – and a show pony he would happily stay, if he could just get away from these fucking maniacs.

The desirable safety margin for warming up a Jet Ranger was four minutes. Hartono's instinct told him three was enough, for already the accelerating rotor had been struck by several arrows. Taking hold of the cyclic, he lifted off. A scrambling Boerman barely had time to leap onto the skids before they veered out over the river.

The big man wrenched open the rearmost passenger door and thumped down on the back seat in a sea of ammunition belts.

'What the fuck was that?' he snarled, protectively cradling the M60 like a small child. 'Try that again and I'll fucking cut your yellow heart out.'

Avoiding eye contact, Hartono ascended rapidly to a height of 250 metres. From there, it looked as if the ship had merely stopped for a quiet nibble of the riverbank.

Boerman leaned through the seats and snapped off several shafts threatening to poke out Hartono's eyes. Then, he extended his seat belt and looped it around the back of his heavy canvas belt. Cocking the M60, he opened the rear door and placed his boots on the skids.

'Take me in from behind,' he ordered. 'Low and fast.'

Hartono was thinking about questioning the wisdom of this strategy, when a sudden white streak flashed from the *Albany*. The dense thickets of grass burst into flames which began to spread rapidly.

Boerman grinned. 'Now we'll flush them out.'

Hartono gritted his teeth and put the chopper into a dive.

Kunai grass may be green, but its phenolic compounds burn with the fury of petrol. Like lines of Chinese crackers, the stalks exploded, sending shards of burned and burning grass high into the air, trailing plumes of white choking smoke. A terrible crackling roar filled the air, growing louder and louder as the flames sucked in more air.

Someone began screaming in anguish. Daniel looked to the top of the bank where, surrounded by flames three times his height, a man was stumbling in a circle as he was roasted alive. The stench of it was being blown in his direction, and he knew he had to get away.

Daniel began to run in the direction of the dark forest behind. Over the popping and crackling, he could hear the thrash of others fleeing, too. Impeded by the thick stalks, Daniel ditched his bow so he could use his hands to claw a path. He knew there was no way his father could outrun such flames.

Singkepe spotted two men in traditional costume huddled by the water's edge. As the raging fire scorched their flesh, they threw away their home-made guns and ran in opposite directions. Loping through the muddy slop, pain and terror lent them superhuman speed. Singkepe opened fire. These bastards had killed Moses. Other long-suffering soldiers opened up, too, in a furious and sustained volley. The noise was deafening, and they howled with glee as the running men were literally dismembered in a flurry of mud, blood, bone and flesh. Singkepe only realised he was screaming, too, when his clip ran out.

The kunai grass was thinning, and Daniel's heart swelled with hope. Suddenly a shadow roared overhead, and the grass flattened. The machine soared up against the edge of the tall trees and spun around to face them. Daniel saw the big white man standing on the skids with a long gun. He stopped running and crouched down, but almost immediately the heat of the flames was on him. There was nowhere else to go but straight ahead. Daniel put his head down and started running as fast as he could.

Boerman smiled gleefully at the frantic men charging towards him. The racing fire devoured their trails as it nipped and singed their heels. They reminded him of a panicking herd of springbok, and he roared with laughter. There would be no escape for these vermin. Boerman opened up on the leading runner with short exploratory bursts, adjusting his aim with minimal expenditure of ammunition. The M60's percussive boom was like coming home to *moeder*. Great chunks of dirt flew up around the sprinting man, and then his head exploded like a shattered coconut.

Boerman shifted aim to the next man, and the next. The M60 bucked in his brawny arms, raining red-hot cartridges as it spat leaden death. Just as it had during his days with the Legion, it gave him a massive hard-on, and the slaughter became a private, sexual thing.

Nash and Mia had not long got Douglas onto a mess table when the roar of the helicopter drew them to the porthole. The sleek gold Jet Ranger darting to and fro above the pall of smoke was like a rogue sheepdog herding its flock into a corner before tearing out their throats.

'It's Boerman!' Nash exclaimed, as they caught sight of him on the skids.

'Where did he get a machine gun from?' Mia trembled.

'From his bloody cabin, God damn it.' Nash was furious with Kaboro, and himself, for not taking unilateral action.

'Don't let him land with that thing,' Mia muttered. 'Go tell Kaboro . . . I'll see to Frank.'

Up on deck, the soldiers, who were now drained of blood-lust, stood there passively watching a primitive enemy mown down by technology that they were helpless against. Kaboro was soaked in sweat; he seemed to be in a kind of dumbfounded trance as the acrid smoke billowed around him.

'Kaboro? *Kaboro*!' Nash had to seize him by the shoulder to make him turn around. 'Did you order this?'

'Good God . . . No, I did not!'

'Then *find* Sura. Make her call them off!'

They located Sura on the helicopter pad, casually watching the carnage like a spectator sport, with a walkie-talkie in her hand.

'Get him to cease fire,' Kaboro snarled, pointing the M16 at her face. 'Do it, now!'

Hiding behind the thick bole of an old casuarina, Daniel listened to the last of his *wantoks* being cut down. The fire had almost burned itself out. Through the dissipating clouds of smoke, he could see the top of the grey ship above the exposed, scorched riverbank.

Daniel kept the bole between himself and the circling predator above. But eventually his shredded nerves betrayed him. Breaking cover, he sprinted across the charred ground towards the line of trees. The helicopter filled the sky behind him as it swooped.

Stumbling on a rock, Daniel fell heavily and rolled over in a heap. Face down, he played dead and prayed for the spirits to protect him. For a moment it seemed to work. The furious wind of the machine's blades beat steadily on his naked back, but there were no bullets; perhaps they could not see him? Then he realised they were playing with him, waiting for him to make a move.

Eventually, he could take the shame no more. Slowly getting to his feet, Daniel found himself staring into the blue eyes of a white-haired devil. He was so close that Daniel could almost touch him. Spreading his arms wide, he waited to join his father and son.

The devil smiled and pulled the trigger.

The battered Jet Ranger settled awkwardly on the sloping pad. It was surrounded by the six remaining PNGDF personnel, who had their weapons trained on the cockpit, while Kaboro stood with Sura and Nash. The rotor came to a halt and a sweaty Boerman stepped from the cockpit, smeared with ash.

'Don't thank me all at once,' he grinned happily, M60 dangling in one hand.

'Put down your weapon,' Kaboro ordered. 'You are under arrest.'

'Arrest?' Boerman scoffed. 'I just saved your life.'

Sura looked up and flashed her best media anchor smile.

'Lieutenant, why don't we all calm down and discuss this amicably? After all, we're on the same side.'

'The same side?' Nash said incredulously. 'This is a massacre.'

'Try and be reasonable. You can't expect us to just sit around while armed terrorists try to kill us. This is legitimate self-defence.'

Kaboro stared at her with the unblinking gaze of one long inured to the injustices of realpolitik.

'We might seem like savages to you, Miss Suyanto, but we have laws in Papua New Guinea. Now, get Mr Boerman to put his weapon down, or I will order my men to open fire.'

Chapter 22

Mia's expression was so full of apprehension that Nash felt a rush of protective concern.

'Kaboro has disarmed and arrested them,' he told her quickly. 'Sura, too. They're tied up and under guard on the quarterdeck.'

'Oh, thank God.' Mia's shoulders slumped momentarily in relief before she straightened up. 'Am I needed out there?'

'I don't think so.'

Her eyes narrowed in concern. 'Are you all right? You don't look well.'

With the immediate danger past, Nash was suddenly overwhelmed. Three young men had bled out on deck, and he had a feeling the blackened, twisted bodies scattered on the smoking riverbank would haunt him for the rest of his days.

'Boerman wouldn't stop,' he murmured, gripping the doorway as a wave of nausea struck. 'He just wouldn't stop.'

Mia stunned him by coming over and wrapping her arms around him. Despite the pain of his injuries, the slim perfection of her took his breath away.

'Thank you,' she whispered.

'For what?'

By way of answer she squeezed him tighter, and as they clung together, it struck Nash that this was no passing attraction. Something special was happening, something beyond his control, and it was only reluctantly that he released her when she pulled away to search his face.

'What happens now?'

Nash blinked, then felt like a fool when he realised Mia wasn't talking about them.

'Kaboro's gone out in the tender, looking for a signal to contact headquarters. At least we can evac Frank – Singkepe says he'll personally hold a gun to Hartono's head.' He stared for a moment at the unconscious Douglas. 'How is he doing?'

Mia's face fell. 'Rob, he's tachycardic, in shock. I really don't think he'd survive the flight, he's just not strong enough.' She put her hand on his arm. 'I'm going to try and improve his vitals, but the medical kit is rudimentary at best. They don't even have saline. I'm so sorry.'

Nash's face darkened as he remembered Shangri-La's claim they would provide first-rate medical backup.

'I've got a defibrillator in the hold,' he offered.

Mia's expression suggested it would make no difference, and Douglas's deathly pallor and ragged breathing told their own story. A cracked Formica table was a rotten place for a man's life to end.

Douglas's yellowing eyes suddenly snapped open.

'Get it out,' he growled in a low and hardly recognisable voice. 'Bastard hurts like hell.'

Nash managed to stop him from grabbing hold of the taped-up arrow stump.

'No, Frank, leave it!'

Mia helped to pin his arms. 'Listen to me, Frank. I haven't got the equipment to perform an extraction and there's no pain relief. Do you understand me?'

Douglas hissed in frustration. 'Jesus, what difference will it make now? Don't let me die with this mongrel thing inside me. It feels like a fucking hot coal. Get it out, or I'll do it by my-bloody-self.'

'Kaboro, are you still there? Can you hear me?' Sir Julius Michaels' voice matched his personality – high-pitched and histrionic; his sentences came in rapid-fire bursts.

'Yes, sir.'

In the wide shade of a mighty fig, the tender rocked gently on wavelets stirred up by the northerly wind. Clutching his phone, Kaboro smelled smoke and death in his clothes, and his mouth was stubbornly dry despite the canteen of water he had drunk.

'You say three of our men are dead. Is Miss Suyanto all right?'

'Yes, sir.'

Kaboro visualised the minister's plush office in Moresby, the framed photographs of armaments his dysfunctional defence force did not possess.

'Well, thank the dear Lord for that.'

'Mr Douglas is seriously injured, sir. Also, Mr Goki was evacuated by Shangri-La's helicopter yesterday, but I have grave concerns for his safety.'

There was a small pause in which Kaboro thought the minister would enquire as to what these concerns were, but instead his voice became cold.

'How could you have let this disaster happen, Lieutenant?'

Again, Kaboro reported the facts of the collision and subsequent grounding.

'Yes, yes, I know all that, but why weren't *you* on the bridge?'

'You relieved me, sir.'

'Go on, go on.'

'We were in the process of freeing the ship, when we were attacked by a large party of local men. It was a payback reprisal, sir.'

'That's illegal.'

'Yes, sir. Mr Boerman then deployed a heavy machine gun which he had smuggled on board. He killed all of them, sir. A total of nineteen men and boys.'

'But you were under fire at the time?'

Kaboro fought to stay calm. 'The villagers never had a chance to surrender. I have arrested Mr Boerman and the pilot, along with Miss Suyanto.'

'*Arrested* Miss Suyanto?' Michaels' voice rose to a shriek. 'Are you *insane*?'

Hurriedly, Kaboro reported their findings in the hold.

'Sir, I suspect this is a criminal group who have entered our country under false pretences. I have secured the crime scene and await further instructions.'

'For God's sake, man! Have you no shame? You should be thanking these men, not persecuting them for doing your job.'

Kaboro squeezed the phone so hard he thought it might shatter.

'Sir, with all due respect, I do not think the deaths of our citizens can be so easily dismissed.'

There was an ominous silence on the phone before Michaels spoke again.

'Now, listen to me very carefully. You will release our guests at once. Then you will apologise to Miss Suyanto for the inconvenience you have caused her.'

'But, sir –'

'You will then confine this stowaway, Doctor Carter, and the troublesome Mr Nash to quarters, while your men burn all the bodies. As soon as possible, you will refloat the ship and continue with the mission. Are we clear? The mission is paramount.'

Years of ingrained cynicism could not have prepared Kaboro for such an outrage. He realised it was the end of his seventeen-year military career.

'What you're asking me to do, sir, is illegal. I won't be party to it, and that is final. I will go on record and resign my commission.'

There was a long pause. Michaels' next words chilled him to the bone.

'Your son Toby is currently serving time in Goroka jail for a drug-related offence, is he not?'

Toby had run wild after his parents' bitter divorce, and joined a *raskol* gang before being arrested with a carload of ganja. Kaboro had spent his life savings on bribes to cut his son a deal: fourteen months of a five-year sentence in minimum security. A condition of early release was that Toby would enlist in the PNGDF on a degree programme. Kaboro had been counting the months down to the day his boy walked free.

Michaels' high-pitched voice snapped him back into the present.

'Lieutenant, if you refuse to obey my orders, I will contact the Attorney General and by this afternoon your son will be transferred to Bomana maximum security prison to serve out the rest of his sentence. Do I make myself clear?'

The arrow had punctured through the pectoral muscle into the pectoralis minor beneath, and possibly a rib. Mia figured the point probably hadn't penetrated or collapsed the lung, but it was impossible to be sure. What she really needed was an X-ray to determine the location of the arrowhead, its shape and composition, whether it had detached or fragmented – even better, an MRI to evaluate nerve damage.

Oh, for Gods sake, she chastised herself, *how about a fully equipped operating theatre, too?*

At least Douglas had passed out again. She could only hope he stayed that way, because there was no anaesthesia either.

Tentatively, she pulled the arrow stump with the pliers to assess its grip. She knew these kinds of penetrations were much harder to treat than bullet wounds. Arrowheads were usually attached with dried tendons or naturally derived glues, which became sources of infection. In contrast to the smooth track left by a bullet, the jagged edges of an arrowhead created wounds the body found difficult to wall off. Again, lethal infection was almost guaranteed. Without antibiotics, this fate almost certainly awaited Douglas.

Mia realised she was prevaricating. As a doctor, the dictum *first, do no harm* was weighing heavily on her mind, but without the possibility of getting Douglas to a hospital, was it any kinder doing nothing?

'OK, Rob. Hold him firmly in case he wakes up again.'

At the head of the table, Nash placed his hands on Douglas's shoulders. After dousing the utility knife and the wound site with a bottle of Kaboro's rum, Mia made two incisions above and below the shaft. As blood oozed out, she carefully pulled the incisions apart, the muscle fibres separating like strings of vermicelli. Just under the surface of the skin, she could see a thicker bulbous section which connected the shaft to the unseen arrowhead. Under her gloved finger, it had a scaly texture which felt like animal hide.

With the tip of the blade, she nipped away more of the clinging muscle. Then, she used the pliers again to check resistance. The arrow was embedded in the bone. She was going to have to cut deeper. Pushing her finger into the incision, she felt her way along the junction and cut through the next layer of muscle until she encountered the arrowhead itself. It was smooth, a little over a centimetre in diameter, possibly some kind of bone, but black in colour. She grasped hold of it with the pliers and began twisting.

Suddenly it came free, and Douglas came to with an ear-splitting scream.

Nash bore down as instructed.

'Hang in there, Frank,' he grunted, struggling to keep him still.

A hole was visible in the white of Douglas's rib, and before the wound refilled with blood, Mia caught sight of bright red lung tissue beneath. With her free hand, she placed a pad in the wound and applied pressure.

'Oh shit,' groaned Douglas.

'There is no frothing, Frank,' she encouraged him loudly. 'The lung is OK.'

Douglas mercifully passed out again, and Mia was able to examine the peculiar black arrowhead in the jaws of the pliers. Projecting from a scaly ball, it was as long as a man's finger, tapering to a sharp point with a distinct curve.

'What *is* that?' Rob was looking pale.

'It's a cassowary claw. The inner toe is used like a dagger for defence.'

The very idea of it – not to mention the bacterial load – was revolting. Mia proceeded to thoroughly clean the wound of detritus and bone fragments. Then she doused everything with generous glugs of rum, and stitched the lower pectoralis muscle closed with the light monofilament fishing line Nash had found on the bridge. For a drain, she used a small length of plastic tubing from the water filter. Finally, she stitched up the upper layers of the pectoral muscle and the epidermis and dressed it. By the time this was done, she was drenched in sweat.

'I've done what I can. What he urgently requires is antibiotics. I'll go and have a word with Kaboro about sending the chopper for some. That was the tender we heard a while ago, wasn't it?'

Nash frowned. 'Yeah, I thought he would have got down here by now.'

Suddenly, the tools on the tray rattled and sprang into life. A glass smashed on the deck, and the whole cabin began to shudder as the *Albany's* engines started up.

'High tide?' Mia stared at Nash.

'Yes, but we were going to stay put to preserve the crime scene –'

Nash broke off as an appalling smell filled their nostrils. Through the porthole, a huge column of oily black smoke could be seen climbing into the sky.

The PNGDF men had dug the pit in the soft and charred ground behind the riverbank. There had been little conversation, and resentment filled the air almost as thickly as the stench of charred flesh. Singkepe had dug with a vengeance. The men had a right to be angry. Kept in the dark over the purpose of the expedition, they'd been treated like shit from the start, and now they'd lost three good friends whom they were disposing of like rubbish.

Carefully, they'd placed the bodies of Faiwalati, Wirake and Moses in the bottom of the deep pit. Standing at attention, they'd sung the national anthem and wept tears of shame. Singkepe had led them in the Lord's Prayer, and then they got on with the gruesome task of collecting the mangled bodies of the villagers.

'That blond *faka* is a devil,' young Willy Makua had spat, holding the charred legs of a man whose upper body was indistinguishable from roadkill. He'd thrown the remains into the pit and wiped his hands on his combat fatigues.

'Is Kaboro really letting him go, sarge?'

'It's not his decision, Makua. He takes orders, just like you and me.'

'Yes, but –'

'Shut up, Makua!'

Singkepe had pretended not to notice the finger raised at his back. Getting shafted was part of service life. It was pointless to question it.

When every trace of the men and their primitive weapons was in the pit, he'd unscrewed the caps on a 200-litre drum of petrol and tipped it over. Petrol gushed over the macabre heap of legs, arms, bared teeth and staring eyes, distorting the air in a shimmering, fumey haze.

Lighting the match, Singkepe asked God to forgive him.

Chapter 23

'Kaboro, why are you burning the bodies?'

Nash stood in the doorway of the bridge, breathing shallowly through his mouth to block out the ghastly smell as the thick smoke filled the air.

'Please, I must concentrate on the ship.'

Kaboro's filthy uniform was now also stained with blood, and although he was focusing on the controls, his eyes were glazed, like those of a functioning alcoholic or a sleepwalker who'd ended up in the wrong bedroom.

'What are your orders? Where are we going?'

Kaboro increased power and the *Albany* began vibrating in protest. Nash could see Singkepe down on the bow, shaking his head to indicate no separation.

'Why won't you answer me?'

Kaboro thrust the throttles to maximum. The shaking increased to a frightening degree. A tin cup fell off the chart table and clattered to the floor. Pens danced up and down in their holder. The bridge windows blurred. Sweat was beading on Kaboro's brow. He loosened off the throttles, and then applied full power again.

'Damn it, Kaboro!' Nash roared over the din. 'How much are they paying you to sell out?'

Singkepe's arm shot into the air and Nash felt the deck lurch under his feet, as the ship slipped off the bank. Kaboro engaged forward thrust to arrest momentum. Then, he spun the helm and worked the throttle to hold her in the narrow channel. Easing her forward, he took her out to deeper water.

Footsteps sounded outside and Sura arrived with Boerman, grinning like a schoolyard bully let off with another warning. Nash felt physically ill. It was as if the *Albany* had just split her bottom in a wild swell, and a sea of chaos was about to rush in and swallow them whole.

He turned to Kaboro.

'Tell me this isn't some sick joke?'

Boerman chortled. 'The only sick joke around here is you, Nash.'

Sura looked radiantly triumphant. 'Lieutenant, kindly convey to Mr Nash the outcome of your communication with Sir Julius.'

Kaboro kept his eyes on the river.

'You are confined to quarters until your services are no longer required, Mr Nash. Then, at a suitable time and place, you will be escorted to the nearest international departure point and be required to leave Papua New Guinea.'

It was preposterous. Insane. Outrageous.

'So, I'm to be an indentured slave and you'll just sail on like nothing's happened?' Nash could hear the desperation in his voice. 'I can't believe this, Kaboro. I thought you were a man of honour.'

For the first time, Kaboro made eye contact. It was a look full of devastation.

'My personal judgement doesn't come into this, Mr Nash.'

'Bullshit it doesn't! We just watched this fucking maniac commit mass murder. Come on, man, stay the course. The men will follow you. I will follow you. We'll testify –'

'You keep talking,' Boerman jeered, 'but you don't seem to realise no one gives a shit!'

Bunching his fists, Nash stared at Sura.

'Shut your Jaap, or I'll shut him for you.'

When Boerman lunged as expected, Nash dropped to one knee and swung his right fist into the Afrikaner's groin. It was like hitting a bowl of jelly. In an explosion of breath, the big man crumpled to his hands and knees.

'That's for the poor sods you murdered today.'

He threw a savage knee at the Afrikaner's unprotected face, but the big man dropped his head to take the bone-jarring impact on his craggy forehead. With a gasp of pain, Nash tried again, but Boerman was too fast. With one giant hand he caught Nash's weight-bearing leg and upended him. Nash slammed down hard and flat on his back. In a flash, Boerman was on top of him, snarling like a pit bull. The enraged man's size and weight were irresistible. Pinning Nash with his knees, Boerman took him by the throat with his left hand and squeezed so hard that Nash thought his trachea was about to break. With a roar of triumph, Boerman raised his huge right fist like a piledriver.

It was Sura who saved his life. Before the Afrikaner could deliver the killing blow, she wrapped herself around his mighty arm like a pole dancer. Somehow her screams penetrated the red mist inside Boerman's skull. Abruptly, the killing rage left him, and he looked at her with a bewildered and disappointed expression on his bloody face.

'Go to the cabin, Jaap,' ordered Sura, 'and wait for me there.'

At the helm, Kaboro had not moved a muscle.

'Lieutenant, make your speed full ahead.' Sura looked down at Nash. 'The only reason you are alive is because you have a use to me. From now on, keep your mouth shut and do as you are told, and maybe it will stay that way.'

Sergeant Singkepe was waiting in the doorway. He gave Nash an apologetic nod, but the FN was still firmly pointed in his direction.

Boerman slammed his huge right fist into the metal wardrobe. Then his left. With a loud roar, he unleashed a flurry of blows, until the door was a crumpled mess hanging from one hinge.

'Feeling better?' Sura observed him dispassionately from the cabin doorway.

'Don't mock me!' he exploded, whirling around to face her.

'Get yourself under control, Jaap.'

'You should have let me kill that fucking devil. I could have pounded his smug face into pulp!'

'We need him. Just like we need the others to keep him working.'

'No – *You* need him.' He took a menacing step towards her. 'Ever since your meeting ... I've seen the way you look at him.'

She burst into a loud peal of laughter. 'Oh, you great big fool, where on earth did you get that idea?'

Disarmed, he suddenly looked like a sheepish teenager, and she reached up to ruffle his hair.

'The only white man I've ever been interested in is you. But, for sure, you're not so pretty.' She frowned at the bleeding split on his forehead. 'Especially now!'

With a growl he lifted her up, burying his face in her neck. She could still smell the battle on him – the blood, sweat and cordite. The rawness of it thrilled her, and for a moment she wanted him right there. But there was a more immediate need.

Placing her tiny hands on each side of Boerman's broad face, she stared into his china blue eyes.

'Do you trust me, Jaap?'

He blinked. 'With my life.'

'I want you by my side, but you need to know your place.'

'But –'

She placed her finger across his lips. 'No more buts. Whenever you take matters into your own hands you jeopardise my future. There cannot be any more mistakes. Do you understand?'

'You'd let me go?' His voice was a groan. 'Please, Sura . . .'

'Put me down, Jaap.'

On the verge of tears, he obeyed.

His eyes opened wide as she began undoing his belt. Pushing him down on the narrow bed, she worked the big man skilfully with both hands. Although temperamental, Jaap was a magnificent tactical weapon. And, as with any good weapon, he required regular servicing, something the daughter of a military man understood full well.

While Jaap bucked and moaned, Sura evaluated their chances. Despite all the setbacks and the unfortunate synchronicity of Doctor Carter ending up on this ship, the truth

was they were still on track. Thanks to Sir Julius Michaels'
insatiable greed, Kaboro and his goons were blundering about
in the dark, and with Goki out of the picture, her father was,
too, although for how long? Just thinking about that question
unconsciously tightened her grip, and Jaap came with a gasping shudder.

She was washing her hands in the small sink, when the chime
of an incoming Skype call jarred them both.

'It's my father,' she groaned, overcome with superstitious
dread at having inadvertently awakened his dark presence
merely by thinking of him. 'We must have signal.'

'Disable the vision,' Boerman hissed, doing up his pants.
'Quickly.'

'Sura, are you there? Sura?'

'Yes, Father.' She blamed the lack of picture on the quality of
the mobile hotspot.

'What on earth is going on out there?' The demand sounded
tinny through the small speaker. 'I've just had a disturbing call
from Sir Julius.'

Sura unconsciously bared her teeth. Of course, the greedy old
crook would have rung.

'We had a minor incident, Father. The boat ran aground. The
soldiers had to fight off an attack.'

'Stop lying,' he snarled. 'I told you this was a covert mission.
I told you to leave this to the experts.'

Sura met Boerman's eye.

'Father, I can explain.'

'Indeed, you have much to explain.' The disembodied voice
was silky. 'Start with why Goki is not answering my calls?'

'He was injured in the grounding, and I'm afraid he died of his wounds en route to hospital.'

There was a sharp intake of breath.

'Why wasn't I informed of this? Goddamn it, Sura. I know you're up to something.'

'Father, please stay calm and listen to me. Everything is now under control and we are back on track, proceeding with the plan.'

Seeing Jaap looking at his feet, Sura was bitterly reminded that she was another person whenever she dealt with her father. His blunt force was impossible to resist, and her voice took on a wheedling register that she truly despised.

'Father, can you hear me? You really need to trust me on this.'

'Trust *you*?' He spat the words with venom. 'How dare you lecture me. I should have put Tommy in charge. In fact, I think I will now.'

'Oh, really? By the time you get him sober, we will have already crossed the border.' Sura tried to stop herself there, but the rage bubbling up would not be contained. 'Fuck you and your empty threats, Father. There's nothing you can do, so why don't you just shut up for once in your life and put your faith in me?'

Sura's heart was pounding. She had only ever once raised her voice to him, and the beating he had administered with a crop had been so savage that she couldn't sit down for a week.

Abruptly General Suyanto hung up.

'Not good,' said Boerman grimly.

His pessimism seemed like a betrayal, but there was no time for second thoughts.

'My father is a pragmatist. For now, he will have no choice but to accept the fait accompli and seek retribution later. By then, of course, we'll be long gone.'

Boerman's slow nod suggested he knew that she was putting a brave face on it. From now on, they were on borrowed time.

Chapter 24

The ship was travelling upriver at near flank speed, despite the unpleasant vibration from the damaged stabiliser, which was creating drag. Mia Carter peered anxiously out of the port-hole at the green jungle passing by. There was no sign of life on deck, and Rob Nash had been gone for too long. Something was wrong.

'Frank, I need to leave you for a while.'

She paused to check the damp towel on his forehead and was puzzled to find it bone-dry. Douglas's skin felt like a paving stone in the hot sun. Mia frowned. It was much too early for infection to have set in. Rewetting the towel, she patted the still-unconscious man gently on the arm.

'Hang in there. I won't be long.'

When she opened the mess door, two spectres stared back at her. Mia cried out in alarm before she realised it was Singkepe's troopers, their uniforms covered in soot, reeking of petrol and crematorial smoke. The taller one's face was hatchet-grim.

'Go back inside.'

'But I need to see Lieutenant Kaboro.'

'It is not possible.'

'Excuse me, but my friend needs urgent medical attention. I must speak to the lieutenant.'

As Mia tried to push past, the tall guard stiff-armed her backwards, and slammed the steel door in her face.

'Hey!' she shouted angrily, trying the door again, but he was holding the handle on the other side. She banged on the door several times, tried it again, but fear soon tempered her anger. Somehow, the Indonesians must have got to Kaboro and regained control of the ship.

A sudden vision of Rob's lifeless body floating in the ship's wake chilled her until she shook herself out of it. They hadn't brought him all this way for nothing. But where did that leave her and Frank?

Two long hours passed. Too frightened to test the door again, Mia kept checking the portholes, but there was no activity on deck and, if anything, the jungle looked thicker and wilder. All she could do was monitor Frank Douglas, who continued to worsen.

There was no medical explanation for his condition. His thrashing convulsions reminded Mia of dengue fever, but his temperature had mysteriously returned to normal, and there was no vomiting. She could detect no whiff of corruption either; the wound site was draining freely, and the adjacent glands were not enlarged.

Mia was dribbling a little water down Douglas's throat when Singkepe arrived, firmly shutting the door behind him.

'Sergeant, please tell me what is going on.'

'No talking,' he said flatly. 'Orders.'

'Lieutenant Kaboro's orders?'

Singkepe went into the galley and began throwing chips, Coca-Cola, chocolate bars and cans of Spam into a cardboard box. Covered in stinking soot, the set of his wide shoulders suggested he was angry.

'There's juice under the cupboard,' she volunteered. 'And more bread in the freezer.'

His grunt of acknowledgement encouraged her.

'Look, Sergeant, I don't understand what is happening here, and maybe you and Lieutenant Kaboro don't know either. But you must know we've done nothing wrong. Please help us.'

Singkepe picked up his loaded box.

'Oh, come on, Sergeant,' she groaned. 'At least tell me if Rob is all right.'

The burly NCO hesitated. Mia knew Nash was popular with the men. When Singkepe inclined his head a fraction, she felt a rush of elation and relief.

She was about to ask another question when a series of violent convulsions began jolting Douglas as if he was hooked up to a power point. Mia went to his side as the comatose man fitted, making sure he was not vomiting or choking on his tongue. Singkepe appeared interested, despite himself, and came over for a closer look.

'Have you ever seen anything like this?' Mia listed Douglas's unusual symptoms.

Singkepe nodded thoughtfully. 'Traditional weapons are powerful. I've seen a slash from a pig jaw axe kill a big man in three days, while an old lady from my village got chopped up with a rusty machete and lived with 350 stitches.' His dense monobrow furled as he looked more closely at the trembling man. 'You got the arrow out of him, then?'

'Yes, would you like to see it?'

He put the box on the table, and Mia passed him the dish containing the grisly claw. It was as if she had just presented

247

him with his mother's decapitated head. Singkepe stepped back, shaking and pale with fear.

'Get it away from me!'

Mia had forgotten that superstition and belief in magic were common to many Papuans, and not just those in remote villages.

'I'm so sorry.'

'That's very bad medicine.' Singkepe made the sign of the Cross twice in quick succession. 'He gonna die for sure.'

'Why bad medicine?'

'Cassowary are female spirit ancestors. They are eating his manhood from the inside. They won't stop.' He shuddered. 'Not until nothing is left.'

Singkepe's fear of the claw was as real to him as her fear of his gun. Mia had seen with her own eyes how the awful power of 'pointing the bone' could kill healthy individuals within a week. But those afflicted believed they were cursed, so how did this apply to an old cynic like Douglas, who was surely immune to autosuggestion?

'You're saying there's nothing I can do, then?'

Singkepe paused. 'You could get the curse lifted, but this is very, very hard.'

'You mean . . . a witch doctor?'

He nodded reverently. 'A very, very powerful one.'

Mia had met a few witch doctors in her time. They appeared to be charlatans waving feathers and bones over hapless patients, who all too often died needlessly. What Douglas needed was a medical facility and powerful antibiotics. That was real magic.

'Sergeant. Will you please tell Lieutenant Kaboro we need to get Mr Douglas urgent help or he is going to die.' He nodded assent and Mia took the opportunity to make another appeal. 'We're not your enemy,' she whispered. 'If there is any way you can help us, *please* do it now before it is too late.'

He stiffened at the touch of her hand on his arm, and reluctantly she let go.

When the door closed, Mia allowed herself a moment to process the fear building inside her. The world of laws and known boundaries was slipping away, and without the tools to fight it she was like a spectator to her own demise, utterly powerless. A hot rush of longing filled her as she thought of her parents' love, and for a moment she surrendered to the warmth of its comforting embrace, but as the tears threatened, she understood giving in to the emotion would merely paralyse her, and so she pushed it back down and checked Douglas's pulse instead.

It was weak and fluttering, his breathing shallow. Examining the wound, Mia gasped. Impossibly, in just half an hour, a filament of angry red veins had sprung up to cover his entire chest.

It must *be a poison*, she decided, annoyed that Singkepe's superstitiousness was getting to her. *It has to be.*

At the mission, they sometimes encountered the consequences of such misguided belief – innocent women scarred for life or horrifically murdered. In a culture where someone must be blamed for every misfortune, those without support networks were most vulnerable. Resident sadists used heated irons inserted into orifices, or burned people alive in front of a baying mob, to atone for perceived evils. Mia was aware the PNG government had only recently repealed its barbaric Sorcery Act.

The legislation had sanctioned black magic as a plausible motive for self-defence, which meant it was essentially a get-out-of-jail-free card for murder.

Still shaking her head, Mia prepared a fresh dressing even though it was futile; poor Frank Douglas was going to die.

And yet Frank Douglas did not die, and after a night, and then another day of heat and discomfort, with the ship travelling further and further from help, the tracery of red lines tripled in area, spreading beyond his bandages, down his torso and up his neck. If Douglas was aware of what was happening, it was impossible to tell. Mia kept expecting to find him dead, whenever she woke from her broken sleeps. He was not getting sufficient liquids, but without a drip, it was only possible to trickle water carefully into his mouth. Meanwhile, there was no sign of Singkepe, and she sensed he was avoiding her, sending the scary tall guard in for supplies instead.

Early on the second day after the attack, Sura appeared with Boerman. She wore a stylish shoulder holster containing a small automatic pistol. Combined with the green jumpsuit, it made her look creepily fashionable – terrorist chic. Mia wondered if that was what indeed she was.

Sura peered down at Douglas and crinkled her nose.

'How disgusting.' She turned to Boerman. 'You know, I've just realised what he reminds me of. We did a story on a grotesque, noseless primate on the Mekong River in Myanmar, which has a passing resemblance to Elvis.' Sura indicated Douglas's deformed nose. 'Lacking a protective cover for its nostrils, the species frequently catches cold, and has to keep its head down during the constant rain.'

Boerman seemed to find this hilarious, and laughed loudly.

'Are you here to make jokes about a dying man, or do you have something useful to say?'

Sitting herself down on the opposite table, Sura gripped the edge and idly swung her legs back and forth.

'You worked with Doctor Paul Ford at the Ford Mission for three years, yes?'

Mia hadn't told anyone that specifically, which meant they'd been doing some digging.

'Yes.'

'And now you're going back. Why would anyone want to do that?'

'Sorry, I don't understand the question.'

Sura smiled faintly. 'You're a very attractive woman, Doctor Carter. Easy to see why the old man was keen to have you around. I wonder, though, what could he possibly have offered you to live in such a backwater?'

Mia was confused, both by the question, and by the fact Sura was talking in the past tense.

'Has something happened to Paul?'

'Answer the question.' Boerman came closer.

'Fuck off,' Mia snapped without thinking.

Boerman's cheeks flushed red as he showed her the back of his hand. Then Sura clicked her fingers at him, and he stepped back like an obedient dog.

Sura was staring in a way that made Mia feel cold, despite the stifling heat.

'Your situation is tenuous, Doctor Carter. While this may be unfamiliar to you, I strongly advise you to use your common sense and answer my questions.'

Mia barely heard her. 'Has something happened to Paul?'

Sura sighed and nodded at Boerman, who stepped up, engulfed Mia's right hand in a massive fist, and squeezed. The extreme pressure made her cry out. With his free hand he gave her a lazy slap across the face.

'Think about what it would be like to never operate again, Doctor Carter.' Twin bursts of scarlet had bloomed in Sura's cheeks, and Mia knew she was getting off on her pain. 'Now answer my question. *Why* are you returning to the Ford Mission?'

'To work . . . I want to help the people.' Mia was gasping with the pain. Boerman could crush the bones of her hand without even trying.

'The people?' Sura laughed mirthlessly. 'Oh, spare us another deluded Western bleeding heart. With every arms sale, your culture ruthlessly propagates its ideology, yet you have the gall to smugly pass judgement on my country's activities within its own territory.'

When Mia said nothing, Sura looked disappointed at her lack of rebuttal.

'Did Paul Ford ever give you any gifts? Cash, jewellery – gold, perhaps? I'm sure you're aware he was an extremely wealthy man.'

'You think this is about . . . *money*?' Mia grunted through the pain. 'Remote medicine is a vocation. Paul's only extravagance is good Scotch.'

'You mean, was,' Boerman corrected her.

The smug certainty in his eyes was like a knife to her heart as she understood *they* were behind the mission going silent. That it was the very reason they were here.

At her stunned reaction, Sura stood up.

'Let her go. She knows nothing.'

'What have you done?' Mia wasn't just thinking of Paul – it was the loving staff and their wide family of patients. 'Damn it, *answer me*, you evil fucking bitch.'

Sura stared at her for a long moment before answering.

'You know, Doctor Carter, I think seeing the look on your face when you find out the truth will be well worth the boredom of keeping your sanctimonious skin alive. Get your things packed up. We're dropping you and Elvis ashore.'

Chapter 25

Thrown, battered and bruised, into his old cabin, Rob Nash seethed. His heart wanted to keep swinging, bring on round two, but his head knew his body wasn't up to it. Not with two armed soldiers outside, who were highly agitated and probably as scared as he was.

Nash lay down on the lower bunk and stared unblinking at the grey steel bulkhead, which quivered as the throbbing engines drove the ship. He was frightened for Mia and Frank. And he wasn't buying the crap about eventual deportation. They were heading upriver, into the heart of fucking darkness, and the odds of coming back were diminishing with every nautical mile.

Two awful days passed, with no outside contact except for the delivery of bottled water, snacks and noodle cups, and the removal of a stinking toilet bucket. The stony-faced PNGDF guard refused to speak, and Nash had no idea if Frank was still alive, or what had happened to Mia.

The memory of how good her body had felt against his kept infiltrating his mind, setting up a churning turmoil of desire and guilt over Natalie. The familiar ache spread through his chest as he tried to conjure her being with his mind, but Nat was gone, and she was never coming back. Nash hung his head. It had only been a year . . . how could he be developing feelings for someone else?

With ample time to brood, his thoughts turned homewards. By now Jacquie would be wondering why he hadn't managed to get in touch. He could almost see her lower lip flapping up and down as she blew her fringe away in exasperation, then the forgiving shrug of her shoulders, because that was how it was with a brother who always turned up in his own sweet time. His parents would patiently accept this as the logical explanation while privately worrying themselves sick all the same.

Nash made himself a promise. If he ever got out of this, he would never put them through this shit again.

When at last the *Albany's* forward momentum ceased, Nash knew they must be close to the border. He listened to the loud rattling of chains as the anchors were deployed. A minute later, they were cranked up again. He realised the *Albany* was dragging her anchors in the current, and Kaboro needed several attempts to get them to bite.

Kaboro. Every time Nash thought of the man, he felt gutted. He had seen the good in him. It had to still be in there.

He heard the helicopter take off, then, soon after, it returned. A short time later heavy footsteps approached, the door was flung open, and Boerman filled the cabin with pent-up menace. Pointing a large automatic pistol at Nash's stomach, the Afrikaner's cold blue eyes assessed the likely threat. Nash was glad the big man's face bore the marks of their confrontation, because his larynx felt as if it would never function the same way again.

'Turn around, put your hands out.'

A cable tie was slid over his wrists and Boerman reefed it up tight.

'Where are Mia and Frank?'

Boerman pushed him roughly towards the door.

'Thought you wanted to dive the Hoosenbeck, Nash? About time you did some *bleddy* work for a change.'

Mia steadied Douglas as the Jet Ranger banked steeply over the gaggle of grass-thatched huts. Hufi was a place she'd visited a few times, a quiet hamlet, last stop on the river before the Indonesian border. Her heart went out to the terrified villagers below. Regular victims of border raids by poachers and Kopassus, they were taking no chances with the arrival of the Jet Ranger, and were weaving trails in a dense field of taro as they fled. But why had Sura dropped them here? Beyond being an inconvenience, Mia could only guess they were leverage.

Hartono carelessly set down too close to the huts, destroying several thatched roofs in the process. In the front passenger seat, Singkepe shot him a dark look. Opening the door, he helped Mia unload Douglas on the rough stretcher, followed by several boxes of supplies and the medical kit.

Once Hartono had departed, an unnatural quiet settled over the abandoned village. The chickens and pigs had also fled, and there were no birds in the trees. Mia cleaned the sweat from her sunglasses. Although early morning, there was a static feeling in the sticky air signalling the imminent arrival of the wet season.

'They're watching us.' Singkepe was scanning the line of trees through his binoculars.

'Can you blame them?'

Across forested hills, the mission lay no more than two days' march west, and Mia stared longingly across the ridgelines. Paul might be dead, but there was still a network of villagers up there who might be able to help. She glanced at Singkepe.

'You know dumping us here is the same as putting a bullet through Frank's head? What he needs is a hospital. I know of one not too far away. Couldn't we take him there? I would pay you well.'

Singkepe would not meet her eye. 'I think bush medicine his best chance now.'

They heard the chopper lift off from the *Albany,* invisible below the line of trees 600 metres away. When it turned upriver, Mia guessed it was headed for the Hoosenbeck. She wondered if Rob was on board, and whether she would ever see him again.

After a time, they heard voices, and a small group of villagers straggled in, mostly women in old Western clothes, some old men, and a string of naked children. Singkepe called over an old man with a knobbly stick, who flashed yellow tusks in a nervous smile.

'*Westap algeta man go?*' *Where are all your men?*

'*Sampela go wok awe, sompela pinis.*' He nodded mournfully at the forest. '*Indo nogut.*'

Between war, poverty and crime, Hufi was a dying hamlet. Singkepe gave the old man some cigarettes and asked if there was a witch doctor in the village.

The old man nodded excitedly. '*Ya, ya! Strongpele majik-dokta klostu hia.*'

Mia knew 'close to here' could mean anything from the next hut to fifty kilometres away.

'*Longwe wokabaut?*' she asked.

258

'*No tasol,*' the old man said, pointing west. '*Sikismail, sikismail!*'

He called over the oldest child, a skinny barefoot boy of about ten, clad in a pair of old football shorts. Receiving his instructions, the boy looked nervous. Ten kilometres through the jungle to fetch a terrifying sorcerer was a daunting proposition. Mia reached into her pocket, found half a roll of mints and handed them over. The boy beamed at her and, without another word, shot off with a trail of smaller children clamouring for a share.

She checked Douglas. Only the faintest movement could be seen in the rise and fall of his chest.

'We need to get him under cover,' she told Singkepe.

The old man led them to the *haus tamberan*, an ancestral worship house. The structure was a tetrahedron, looking something like a sail from the Sydney Opera House. The facade was dilapidated, the thatch in disarray. A faded motif of pointed ellipses edged with triangles, and a worn row of carved ancestral clan spirits, were further testament that the hamlet had fallen on hard times.

'*No misis kam in hia,*' the old man apologised at the doorway. *No woman allowed.*

Mia had always found it intriguing that a culture built on the primacy of male gender constructed its places of worship in the shape of a vulva. The symbolism was ideological. As a male-gendered space, women were forbidden to cross the threshold. It was a demonstration of power – of male possession of the womb, with ritualised combat against the evil spirits which existed in menstrual blood, so feared that women were banished during menstruation, for fear of contamination.

Singkepe brandished a few kina and the old man reluctantly let Mia enter. Inside, the atmosphere was dry and cool, and there was an ingrained odour of smoke from decades of ritual. They laid Douglas down on the beaten clay floor. It seemed a fitting space to meet your maker. The soaring ceiling functioned architecturally, like any place of worship – designed to cow the visitor and induce a feeling of reverence. It was made of a complex latticework of hundreds of flexible bamboo poles lashed together, covered in overlapping dense layers of sago spathe. Without maintenance, chinks of sunlight were breaking through, where rats or birds had stolen material for their nests.

Frank Douglas was now on the very edge of death. The poison had colonised his entire torso and neck, and advance parties were travelling down his extremities in thin red lines. There was nothing Mia could do beyond sponge him down.

Half an hour later, a burst of excited shouting heralded the return of the boy. Drenched in sweat, he announced the shaman's arrival. A ripple of trepidation swept through the village. Many of the older women picked up children and disappeared into their huts.

Covered in white and yellow ochre, the witch doctor entered the *haus tamberan* with suspicious eyes. His aggressive demeanour was augmented by an elaborate headdress of razor-sharp boar tusks and a huge cassowary claw speared through his septum. Around his neck were rows of cowrie shells, bird of paradise feathers, and strange nondescript tokens which looked like dried animal parts. He wore a traditional skirt of grass leaves, and carried a woven *bilum* or sacred bag, swollen with magic potions and herbs.

Noting his vicious-looking battle scars and missing finger, Mia realised a man of his age and experience might well know the chief of the local tribe near the mission.

The shaman came up to them and stared into their eyes. Singkepe flinched, while Mia averted her eyes respectfully. He gave her a disparaging sniff.

'*Woman in haus tamberan . . . nogut.*'

'We will go,' agreed Singkepe at once.

'Please, wait a minute.'

Haltingly, in the local dialect, Mia asked the witch doctor if he knew Kinsame. His dark eyes widened in surprise as she explained her connection, and that it was important that the soldier not know what she was saying, because she needed rescue.

The witch doctor glanced sidelong at Singkepe before nodding.

'*Orait, you stap. Nau lets fiksim dispela.*'

Together they crouched beside Douglas and Mia removed the bandage.

On seeing the wound, the witch doctor exhaled sharply.

'*Supsup bilong banara?*'

Mia nodded and took the cassowary arrowhead from her top pocket.

'*Dispela.*'

Frowning, he opened his *bilum*, and withdrew a large semi-dried plant leaf which he used to carefully pick up the claw. She asked why the one residing in his nose wasn't dangerous, too.

'*Hia muruk gutpela.*'

He was telling her that, in this region, the cassowary was not considered evil.

Taking a sliver of obsidian, the witch doctor proceeded to cut hair from Douglas's head, chest and pubic zone. Rolling it up in a small ball, he placed it on top of the folded leaf. After slicing a neat cut on his forearm, he drizzled on blood. Next, he placed a handful of dried herbs on top.

'*Wokim faia.*'

Singkepe threw across his lighter.

The flames flared with a crackle, giving off a foul odour of burning hair, cassowary skin and herbaceous oils. When they went out, the witch doctor rubbed the charred claw vigorously between his filthy hands, spitting repeatedly to work up a gluey paste. Mia had an inkling of what he was going to do with it, and every molecule of her Western medical training cringed.

The witch doctor began chanting a rhythmic drone, which set up a vibration between Mia's eyes. Poor Singkepe put his hands over his ears. Strangest of all was the effect on Douglas. For the first time in hours, he opened his eyes and seemed aware of his surroundings. Mia knew that imminent death could presage a brief return to consciousness. It was often the only chance families of the terminally ill got to say goodbye. She wished Rob were there.

Placing the ball of black putty on Douglas's open wound, the witch doctor forcefully massaged it inside the cavity. Mia felt sick. Yet Douglas showed no sign of pain. If anything, he seemed eager for it.

'*Mi wok pinis.*'

Standing up, the witch doctor wiped his filthy hands on his grass skirt. He stared at them expectantly. Mia quickly gave him the first thing to hand – a digital thermometer from her top pocket – and he winked.

'*Arrgghh!*'

At their feet, Douglas stiffened into a full body spasm as he bellowed a blood-curdling scream. Mia stared in horrified disbelief. The wound was pulsing before her eyes, the dilated veins writhing like sago grubs thrown on the coals for dinner. It was impossible, like a Hollywood special effect. She went to assist, but the witch doctor put his gnarled hand out and pulled her back.

'*His wok nau.* Let him fight the spirit.'

Chapter 26

Once they crossed the border and entered Indonesian airspace, the banter quickly dried up. Hartono kept low, hugging each bend of the river, while Sura scanned frequencies on the radio. Jammed into the rear seat beside Nash, Boerman trained his binoculars on the unfolding landscape. It was clear they feared detection by Indonesian forces; the question remained *why*.

They flew on, and the hazy ramparts of the looming central massif resolved into a wall of seemingly unbroken grey rock. Now close to its headwaters, the Sepik had changed from brown to milky green. On each side of the speeding helicopter rose thick walls of green rainforest, occasional super-trees erupting from the canopy like skyscrapers. On a tight bend, they surprised a colony of fruit bats, and several hundred cat-sized animals tumbled in their wake like a cloud from a giant explosion.

'*Tuhanku*,' breathed Sura, as the mouth of the Hoosenbeck Gorge came into view.

It was as if God had taken a knife and carved two perfectly vertical seams through the rock to create a gigantic gateway to a magical kingdom, half-hidden in the mist beyond. Erupting from this half-kilometre-wide mouth, the turquoise Hoosenbeck River ran deep and swift, colliding with the Sepik in a foamy broil.

As Hartono swooped into the gorge, Nash felt his pulse quicken. They really *were* going to the Hoosenbeck. Any boat

– he assumed it had to be a boat – which had made it up here must have one hell of a story to tell.

On either side of the gorge, dense rainforest clawed its way up the mighty cliffs – gravity-defying trees which had never felt the axe. Nash could only imagine the rainfall required to sustain such a precarious existence. It had carved dendritic side passages, insanely deep slot canyons snaking away into gloom where no vegetation could live, venting torrents of raging white water into the fast-flowing Hoosenbeck flashing below their skids.

After perhaps fifteen kilometres the gorge narrowed to no more than 200 metres, and Hartono gripped the cyclic more tightly. Bouncing off the rocky ramparts, the Jet Ranger's roar was an eerie ghost echo, which seemed to presage no good. Here, nature was losing her fight with stone. The dwindling trees crammed into two narrow strips had etiolated, their bereft crowns meeting above the water like hands clasped in prayer. They flew across a whole forest of huge skeleton trees – dead white trunks devoid of branches, suggesting a catastrophic die-back in the distant past. For a good kilometre, this continued until, dead ahead, the monolith dwarfed everything. It took Nash a moment to realise that this was the shadowy end of the gorge itself – a sheer black wall rising a thousand metres.

Forgetting his predicament, he eagerly craned his head down. Somewhere at its base, shrouded by tenacious trees, lay the mouth of the Hoosenbeck Cavern.

'There it is!' Sura pointed to the top of a wide arch and crescent; a hint of darkness beckoned within.

Hartono brought the Jet Ranger as close to the bastion as he dared, the tips of his carbon-fibre blades just metres from the rock. Gradually, he eased the chopper down, a few cautious metres at a time, but the downdraughts were playing havoc with his controls.

'I need more margin,' he told Sura. 'It's too fucking close.'

She leaned around to confer with Boerman. He put on a rucksack and picked up the coil of climbing rope.

'Give me ten minutes.'

'Make it five. We must conserve fuel.'

Hand on the door release, Boerman stared at Nash.

'I don't trust this *fok*.'

Sura took out a small pistol and pointed it at Nash's forehead.

'This is a low-velocity cartridge. Rest assured, if you try anything, it will not damage the helicopter when I shoot you.'

When Boerman opened the rear door, the volume was deafening. Chilled air rushed in, bearing the smell of wet rock and decaying vegetation. With boots planted on the skid, Boerman swiftly tied off one end of the rope and flung the remaining slack towards the ground. Then, gathering a loop, he connected it to the karabiner on his belt and attached a cammed descender above it. Reversing position, he gave Nash a grin and fell back, dropping for a couple of seconds before engaging the descender. Hartono swore as the chopper bucked and swayed under the impact. Within seconds, Boerman touched down, detached himself from the rope and was running for the nearest tree.

It was then that Nash noticed something very strange. What had become of the mighty Hoosenbeck they had just flown up? All he could see was a modest stream bubbling out of the cave and trickling down the wide and dry river bed in a pale imitation of the force that had carved it.

Suddenly, a series of concussions thumped against the bottom of the Jet Ranger, as loud as a foot pedal on a bass drum. The crowns of several trees swayed and crashed down in a cloud of leaves. Boerman was using plastic explosives. Hartono cleared the leaves and dust away as he descended. Most of the trees had fallen down the slope. He settled the chopper on a ledge close to the entrance.

'Kill it, Ricki,' instructed Sura. 'And stay here with the chopper.'

The mouth of the Hoosenbeck Cavern was a semicircular arch about the size of a three-storey building. That a mighty river had once flowed through here was beyond doubt. The rock had been carved by chemical processes and boulders ejected from inside the mountain. Enough light penetrated the interior for them to see that a couple of metres below the lip was an expanse of emerald-green water.

A vibration passed through Nash's body. He'd been dreaming of this for half a lifetime – ever since first reading about the Hoosenbeck while sitting on his parents' couch. But the moment was tinged with loss. It wasn't just the context of a gun pointed at his back. It was because he felt unfit to enter the element to which he had dedicated his life.

'Come on,' said Sura. 'We don't have time to waste.'

The vastness of the space was intimidating. The lake could not be encompassed by the light of their powerful torches, but what they could see was as long as a football field. According to the 1960s explorers, it reached twice as far again into the bowels of the mountain. Nash visualised its creation: the millennia of acidic snowmelt finding its way down some fault in the

Miocene limestone and steadily eroding this vast dome. He realised the Hoosenbeck both entered and exited the lake *below* the surface. At some point, around two hectares of unsupported roof would collapse, and the gorge would lengthen again.

Nash allowed himself to simply absorb the magnitude of the place. Analogies and allusions swam into his mind. Surely it was the hall of the mountain king which Tolkien had visualised in Middle-Earth? Or was it Dante's Ninth Circle of Hell?

Then the lines came to him unbidden:

In Xanadu did Kubla Khan
A stately pleasure-dome decree:
Where Alph, the sacred river, ran
Through caverns measureless to man
Down to a sunless sea.

The poetry conjured up his last journey with Natalie. En route to the Octopus, Nash had been musing on the final sentence in the foreword of his book: *For what we discover in caverns unknown to man is nothing less than the potential of human imagination itself.*

'It's almost there –' Natalie had her eyes on the undulating dirt road – 'but you need to drop the bastardised allusion.'

'You've got a problem with Samuel Taylor Coleridge?'

She punched him lightly on the arm and he grinned.

'No, Rob, I've got a problem with the fact your hero already used that line in the title of *his* book.'

'*Caverns Measureless to Man*,' Nash recited sonorously, 'by the late Sheck Exley, America's greatest cave diver. Tragically perished below 300 metres in a sinkhole at Zacatón, Mexico, 1991.'

Natalie frowned. 'I wish you wouldn't do that. Especially before a dive in the Octopus.'

Citing fatalities in the vocation he lived and breathed was Nash's way of acknowledging those who'd gone before and learning from their mistakes, but it was poor timing. He put his hand on Natalie's smooth brown thigh.

'You're right. I'm sorry.'

She blew him a kiss. 'I agree it is a perfect description for the lure of cave diving – especially if you happen to be a man! But I'm sure you're smart enough to come up with another.'

'OK.' He smiled at her. 'How about, "Because it's there?"'

'Idiot!'

Those seductive creases at the corners of Natalie's mouth, the delicious peal of her laughter . . . she *was* still there inside his head! For a moment Nash was overwhelmed. Then a prod from Boerman's pistol expunged the vision, and he was grateful for the darkness to hide his pain.

Their footsteps echoed mournfully, as Sura led them on a circumnavigation of the still lake. Mineral deposits on the walls indicated the ledge upon which they were walking would be a couple of metres underwater in the wet season. But it was another faint ring, a good five metres higher, which caught Nash's eye. Once the lake had been far deeper, but only for a short span of years, just long enough to leave the ghost of its presence.

Towards the back of the cave, the ledge sloped down into crystal-clear water. Sura gasped as she stepped into it. The shock of the icy snowmelt, not much more than nine degrees Celsius, was like wading through fire. For several minutes they proceeded at thigh-numbing height, until Boerman cried, 'Look up there!'

In the beams of their flashlights, a strange brown object drooped from the rock above. Like an oversized jungle vine or root, it was several metres long and as thick as a man's arm – a rusted steel hawser, grotesquely swollen as oxides cannibalised the integrity of the metal. The shackle was held in place by four heavily corroded bolt heads protruding from the limestone.

Boerman gave a triumphant whoop and the sound echoed brutally around the cavern. For Nash, it was heresy. Aside from the slow *plink* of dripping stalactites, and occasional shrieks of bats, these lost worlds were worlds of silence, demanding veneration.

'Look where the water level was when they drilled those bolts.' Boerman turned to Sura excitedly. 'It must be right here below us!'

Together they directed their flashlights at the water. It was gin-clear, the rocky sides of the cave clearly visible, tumbling down into unseen depths.

Nash cleared his throat. 'Isn't it time you told me what this is all about?'

WHUMP!

Nash's head snapped brutally back as Boerman's punch took him full in the face. Hands tied, head spinning, Nash staggered. Before he could fall, Boerman grabbed him by the shirt and shook him violently.

'So, Mr fucking know-it-all wants an explanation, does he?'

'That will do, Jaap.'

Sura sounded satisfied, and Nash knew it was payback for humiliating her on the ship. He spat out a mouthful of blood and ran his tongue around his throbbing lips. At least he still seemed to have his teeth.

'We're here for a submarine, Mr Nash.' Her exhilaration was eerily disembodied in the near darkness. 'A Japanese megasubmarine that moored in this cave more than seven decades ago and later sank. Somewhere down there is 200 million dollars' worth of gold bullion, and you're going to get every last bit of it out!'

'A submarine . . . *here*?'

Nash's astonishment turned to dread. If the Octopus had been a failed test . . . the flooded, rusted hulk of a submarine would be the ultimate examination of his shattered nerve.

Dont be a fool, he chastised himself, remembering the topography of the gorge outside. Sura was completely nuts. No submarine had ever reached this cave. It was physically impossible.

Sura's focus shifted to Boerman. 'Why would it sink after so many years on the surface?'

The Afrikaner played his torch over the severed hawser.

'When the water level in here dropped, the submarine must have tipped. With a stern hatch open, it would pour inside and fill her up fast.'

'And the cable snapped from the extra weight?'

'*Ja*, sent her straight to the bottom.' He paused to hopefully play his torch into the depths again. 'With a bit of luck, we'll be able to use the same hatch to swim straight inside.'

To Nash it sounded fantastical. While their confidence suggested they were in possession of compelling information, the physics simply didn't allow it. Water found its own level; thus, if you transposed that high-water mark outside the cave, a vast lake would have filled the whole gorge. And there was no way the fall to the Sepik allowed this. He figured the explanation was something to do with the cave mouth. Once, it must have been higher, possibly from a rockfall, which, of course, rendered the whole idea of sailing a submarine up that narrow steep gorge even more ridiculous. As for the hawser, the most likely explanation was that the Dutch had winched equipment into the cave.

Somehow Sura had swallowed a cock-and-bull story about sunken treasure. Nash exhaled softly. It was a common aberration. Because for an inert metal, gold had a corrosive effect on common sense. Nash recalled his second expedition to Mexico's Timoche Cenote – a giant freshwater sinkhole – while trying to complete a fifteen-kilometre connection to the Caribbean Sea. Navigating a maze of interconnecting tunnels, his team had come across a deposit of gold Mayan artefacts in a minor cenote. Nash had surrendered these to the Mexican authorities, but two American divers went to buy metal detectors. Nash had left them to it and made the breakthrough to the coast himself. Two weeks later, the Americans' bodies were found in a burned-out van by the side of the road. A local gang had tortured them. Later, someone had blown up the cenote while trying to remove a plug of ancient trees and debris, closing down that part of the system for good.

In the darkness, he could feel Sura staring at him.

'You said this lake is one to two hundred metres deep.'

'I'm a prisoner, not a consultant.'

Nash was risking another fist, but pushing back was the only way to get information which might lead to a way out. Sura shone her flashlight directly into his eyes, making him squint.

'Must I again remind you that your life, and those of your friends, depends solely on your value to me?'

'How do I know they're alive? I need proof.'

'You'll get it soon enough. Now, the depth, Mr Nash?'

'Put a line down and find out.'

'Did you bring enough rope?' she asked Boerman.

'We don't need it . . .'

'Very well,' she sighed. 'Let's get the gear.'

When Boerman dragged two rebreather units from the chopper's cargo cradle, Nash was incredulous. He'd assumed they were flying back to the *Albany* to equip themselves.

'You can't be serious. Without drysuits we'll freeze down there.'

Boerman glowered. 'It's a preliminary reconnoitre. Grow some balls, man.'

Sura's eyes narrowed. 'You have a better idea?'

'Yes. Properly equipped, we can survey safely and efficiently.' Nash explained that hypothermia was an insidious killer that crept up on you. 'In water this cold, our dexterity will be compromised in under five minutes. Within thirty to sixty minutes, we'll lose consciousness and drown.'

'It doesn't sound like an exact science to me,' Sura said doubtfully.

He explained the wide variable was reflective of individual physiology and size. Boerman would last longer because his huge bulk shed heat more slowly.

'Sura, I'm telling you this is a dangerous waste of time. You can see for yourself the size of the lake –'

'Says the master of wasting time,' Boerman scoffed. 'Let's do this.'

Sura nodded. 'Jaap, cut him free.'

In a last-ditch attempt to prevent Boerman killing them both, Nash hastily proposed a plan scratched out in the dirt of the cave mouth.

'The lake is around two hectares in area. In water this cold, we won't stand a long decompression, so let's avoid it by staying shallow and surveying what we can within the no-decompression limit.'

'But we need to get to the bottom,' complained Boerman.

Nash brushed the dirt aside and placed his stick on the rock.

'Limestone is white. It should easily contrast with something as large as a submarine.' He looked up at Sura. 'What's its length?'

'It's 120 metres,' replied Sura promptly.

Nash frowned. 'That's more than twice as long as a U-boat.'

'Stick with the task at hand,' she snapped irritably. 'What visibility will you have?'

'More than enough.'

That was a lie, because with these inadequate lights, the best they could hope for was 80 to 100 metres. Nash hesitated as something else occurred to him. Somewhere below them, the Hoosenbeck was finding its way out of this cave. It would be dangerously powerful, easily enough to suck in an unwary diver.

'You were about to say something, Mr Nash?' Her almond eyes were full of suspicion, and when he did not reply, she added balefully, 'If anything happens to Jaap, you have my word that I will fly straight back to Hufi and deal with Frank Douglas and Mia Carter. Do you understand?'

On a ledge below the cave mouth, Nash strapped on the rebreather and turned on his dive lights.

'Stay close, dickhe—'

Stepping into the water first, Boerman's voice died as cold shock sucked the air out of his lungs. Nash followed, and the nine-degree water was like a cleaver splitting his skull. For several seconds, his ear canals felt full of boiling water.

Descending to thirty metres, the only visual reference in the void was the blank wall of rock behind them, and the refracted glow of the cave mouth above. Their first pass was along the left-hand side. The water was crystal-clear, and the rock wall beside them plunged well over eighty metres until it vanished. There was no sign of the bottom, just a blue-green haze as the limits of visibility were reached.

Most so-called 'bottomless' lakes were rarely more than 100 metres deep, but there were exceptions. Boesmansgat, a bottle-shaped cavern in South Africa, was a shade under 300 metres. Zacatón, where Exley had died, was around 320 metres. The recently discovered Hranická Propast, located in the eastern Czech Republic, was reputed to be an awe-inspiring

400 metres deep. At such depths, even a minute of bottom time would require something like fifteen hours of decompression, not to mention managing HPNS – high-pressure neurological syndrome – with its associated tremors, dizziness and reduced acuity.

Already, Nash's fingers were wooden in the intense cold. Laboriously, he and Boerman finned back to the mouth, then returned to the far end again, each pass ticking off a 20-metre-wide swathe. After twelve minutes of immersion, Nash was shivering. Boerman was agitated and aggressively gesticulating towards the bottom, but Nash shook his head. Risking a long decompression for a non-existent submarine was insane. At least this way they could determine if the whole floor was beyond eighty metres and live to tell the tale.

At the end of the fourth pass, in the middle line of the cavern roughly forty metres below the cave mouth, Nash spotted what he believed to be the exit passage for the Hoosenbeck. The hole was a ragged trapezoid some fifteen metres across, which steadily narrowed as it drilled into the rock. At a guess, fifty to sixty cubic metres of water per second had to be flowing through this funnel – a force incomprehensible because it was invisible. Once, it would have tempted Nash to explore the hydrology of the system. Now, he just wanted to get the hell out of there.

Reluctantly, he turned to warn Boerman of the danger and was shocked to find the big man wasn't there. Thinking he must have baled, Nash looked up. By the time he looked down again, the Afrikaner was six metres below, blithely swimming into the hidden vortex.

With Sura's threats ringing in his ears, Nash went after him. Every extra metre descended meant more decompression, more time in the frigid cold. His calf muscles were tightening – a precursor to cramp. Fighting it off, he kicked harder. He was just two metres behind Boerman when the Afrikaner stopped swimming and tentatively stretched out his hands. Nash knew it was the periphery of the vortex. Then he felt its clutches, too.

Adrenaline pumped energy into his exhausted muscles, as he kicked savagely for the surface. Suddenly, he felt the big man grab his ankle.

They grappled in a desperate tandem, and then Boerman got hold of his weight belt. One look at the Afrikaner's terrorised eyes told Nash the man would never let go, so he stopped fighting and encouraged Boerman to swim with him. Doggedly, they swam up as the gaping mouth yawned. But, for every metre gained, the vortex gobbled two.

Too late, Nash felt the acceleration in the pit of his stomach.

Bang!

He grunted in shock as his rebreather slammed against the rock of the exit passage. They tumbled together for another three or four metres, until a ledge brought them up short with a bone-jarring thud.

It took Nash several moments to comprehend what had happened. He was pinned, upside down, with Boerman lying just below him. Like enemy soldiers in the same trench, their eyes met in a temporary truce. Above their heads was instant death. No bullets or shells hurtling past, just a subterranean torrent, ready to snatch them if they left this protective lee of rock. It was as if they were stuck in the throat of a sea monster, and beyond, cruelly framed by its jagged mouth, was the pale, inviting green of the cavernous lake.

Somehow, they had to get back there.

Nash made a climbing motion with his hands. When Boerman shook his head, Nash angrily drew a cutting motion across his throat. It was a simple equation: climb or you're dead.

Twisting himself around, Nash braced against the ledge and extended forwards, flattening himself against the rock. The vortex was buffeting his rebreather, transmitting force to his shaking knees. With his legs fully extended, he reached tentatively out with his right hand and found a handhold on the rock. Keeping his left leg flattened, he drew it up almost ninety degrees, until he located a ridge below his heel. It was the moment of truth. If he couldn't make the next step, all hope was lost.

The effort was like climbing a wall with a person strapped to your back. But fear lent Nash a desperate strength, and he fought his way upwards to secure the next handhold. With each metre gained, the mouth of the passage widened and the force of the water diminished. By the time he reached the mouth, he was able to see Boerman right behind him, and climbed around the lip to reach the haven of still water.

When he checked his watch, Nash felt even colder. Thanks to the Afrikaner's stupidity, their maximum depth had touched fifty metres, and their run time was almost half an hour. Now they were going to have to decompress for at least a quarter of an hour.

Nash was borderline hypothermic, but it was better than getting bent. With every added metre of depth, nitrogen became exponentially more dangerous under pressure. Coming up too fast was like shaking a bottle of Coke. Millions of tiny bubbles, tearing their way out of capillaries, was not only agonising; it could lead to permanent paralysis or death.

It was so bone-achingly cold that Nash's teeth felt brittle on the mouthpiece. In contrast, his numb extremities felt as if they belonged to somebody else. His body was shaking uncontrollably. After three miserable stops at twelve, nine and six metres, it was time for the last and longest: eight minutes at just three metres, with the surface tantalisingly close. Halfway through, Nash realised his violent shivering had stopped. A tired laziness crept over him as his central nervous system began shutting down. Signalling to Boerman, he called the dive. It was the lesser of two evils. They had to get out. Boerman was literally blue, and nodded assent.

Hartono and Sura had to drag them out of the water and take their gear off. They had lit a large fire inside the cave mouth, but additional heat worsened the impact of nitrogen diffusion, so Nash got into his clothes as fast as his unresponsive fingers would let him.

They had none of the milder signs of decompression sickness: skin tingling, joint pain or dizziness. Yet, they could not be complacent. Surviving a close call was no guarantee of getting away with it in the future.

Predictably, Boerman glossed over his own stupidity, and tried to take credit for their escape. At this, Nash simply burst out laughing. Sura frowned and checked her watch.

'Mr Nash, we take off in five minutes. Jaap will stay here while we ferry up your equipment.'

Nash shook his head. 'Threaten all you like, but I'm borderline bent, and I'm not adding altitude for half an hour.'

Sura conceded, and it was a significant moment: Boerman had proven himself to be a liability underwater, and she was smart enough to know it. Nash figured he had just bought himself time – at least until they discovered the submarine wasn't there.

Chapter 27

In just four hours, the terrifying spread of veins across Frank Douglas's body had retreated by a third. The witch doctor's strange poultice had cauterised the entry wound, allowing phagocytosis – the healing process whereby white blood cells engulf damaged cells, bacteria and pathogens – to begin. Having lost his deathly pallor, Douglas was breathing steadily in a deep, healing sleep.

Singkepe squatted beside Mia as she pulled the blanket back over Douglas.

'Powerful magic, eh?'

It was. But how could a filthy handful of charred organic matter mixed with human blood and saliva achieve this?

They heard the Jet Ranger returning to the *Albany*. Three quarters of an hour passed, and then they heard it again. She ran outside, hoping that Rob was on his way, but the Jet Ranger was headed back upriver, the machine gleaming like burnished copper in the rays of the setting sun. With a heavy heart, Mia went back inside and begged Singkepe to tell her what was happening.

'I'm sorry, doctor, but I really don't know.'

The obvious sympathy in his eyes was so frustrating.

'Well, do you *care*, then?'

Looking hurt, he went back to cleaning his machine gun.

'Soldiers must follow orders.'

'But what if those orders are wrong? I don't need to tell you these Indonesians are a bad business. Not after what they did on the river. And I don't think you like helping them.'

He paused to consider this. 'They are bad people,' he agreed. 'Very bad people.'

'Then *help* us,' she pleaded. 'We should report them to the police. They can investigate what is going on here. Surely that is the right thing to do?'

Singkepe looked uncomfortable. Eventually he gave a small shrug.

'Oh, come on,' Mia snapped in frustration. 'Why can't you –?'

He cut her off angrily. 'You don't understand, Doctor Carter. This is PNG. If you're a big man in this country, no one messes with you – not even the law. I got a family. Three kids and a wife. I know you want me to help you, and I feel sorry for you, but what's going to happen to them if I stick my neck out? Did you ever think of that?'

'No.' She swallowed and looked away. 'No, I didn't. And I'm sorry your country is such a fucking mess. But this is *wrong*.'

As night fell, two shy native women came bearing green banana-leaf plates loaded with chunks of fire-baked fish and *saksak* balls made from the pith of the sago palm. Knowing how many calories they were sacrificing to feed them, Mia smiled warmly.

'*Tenkyu*,' she told the women, patting her stomach. '*Namba wan!*'

Complete darkness fell with its usual speed. The inevitable presence of the ravenous mosquitoes was somewhat mitigated by the smoky fire, which tickled her throat. Mia lay down by Douglas, who was still cool to touch. With half an eye open, she watched Singkepe. Thick smoke trickled through his fingers as he quietly puffed on a cigarette. She hoped he would soon roll over and go to sleep. At any moment, help from Kinsame might arrive, and she dreaded being the cause of further violence.

She had fallen into a half-sleep when an urgent rustling sound at the rear of the *haus tamberan* startled her into consciousness. The fire was low, and she searched the gloom. There was no sign of Singkepe, and she figured he must be outside taking a piss. She had just got to her feet when a man wearing green football shorts stepped through the hole he'd just made with a gleaming machete. His sweaty torso seemed chiselled out of black marble, and his feet were bare.

'*Dokta* Mia?'

She felt a surge of joy. It was Kinsame's son!

'*Tenkyu, Paomente.*' She grasped his leathery hand. '*We must hariap, PNG soldia close!*'

He nodded and gave a low whistle. Three strong young men, also wielding machetes, clambered through the hole. Together they picked up Douglas on the stretcher. They'd hardly taken a step when Singkepe entered the hut. Seeing them, his brow shot up, and he levelled his FN machine gun at their stomachs.

'*Stopim nau!*'

Mia stepped between them, hands raised in the air.

'Please, don't shoot, Sergeant. These young men are my *wantoks*.'

The muscles in Singkepe's face were clenched. Beads of sweat appeared on his brow. Tense seconds passed and Mia prayed none of Paomente's men would try anything, then, unbelievably, Singkepe lowered his weapon and stepped aside.

'You're a good person, Doctor Carter. I will not stand in your way.'

She wanted to hug him, but made do with taking his hand.

'Bless you and your family, Sergeant. Please take care. And help Rob if you can.'

He nodded without conviction. 'I will try. God bless.'

Unblinking stars studded the firmament as they slipped through the village. There was little moon, and Mia marvelled at how Paomente and his men had reached Hufi in the dark. It was a reminder that, not so very long ago, men like these would have come as a raiding party to steal women and kill warriors for trophies and meat.

Tracking the river, they used faint pathways in the rustling kunai grass. Mia could hear the guttural throb of big salties on the hunt, and hoped there were none in their path. The men maintained an effortless jog which she soon struggled to keep up with.

Inside the rainforest, the darkness was absolute, yet the men slowed only slightly. How they navigated, she could not explain, for the only illumination was occasional fluorescent patches of fungi. Above them, possums called alarms, and bats crashed and swooped in showers of half-eaten fruit. When they took their first break, a ten-minute layover underneath a forest giant festooned in glowing green mushrooms, she heard a large snake gliding through the leaf litter.

'*Longwe*?' Mia asked, hoping he would contradict her.

Paomente's teeth gleamed, as if under black lights in a New York disco.

'*Ten pela, twenti!*'

Hours later, they came to another fungal nightspot, this time by a creek. Badly dehydrated, Mia had no choice but to drink deeply. The water was delicious and cold, with a hint of tannin from the leaves carpeting the bottom. She conveyed some water by hand to Douglas's lips, and to her surprise he drank greedily.

'Strewth, I must be dreaming.'

He was looking up at her with a bewildered child-like expression, and she realised the fluorescence was making her blonde hair appear as a dazzling halo.

'We're taking you to a hospital, Frank.'

He was silent for a moment. 'Where's Robbie?'

There was no point worrying him.

'He'll catch up with us later.'

They pushed on until the birds sang of the approaching dawn. A squawking and whistling spread into whoops, caws and shrieks. Light began to penetrate the chiaroscuro kaleidoscope of the canopy. Their feet plunged through the moist litter, leaving steaming footprints in the chill air. Signs of habitation appeared: tracks and axe holds on trees; a suspension bridge made of bamboo, timber and rattan.

In familiar territory, the men began to chat happily. They came to a glade, and Mia recognised the outskirts of the village. Chief Kinsame's house sat in the centre of thirty or so huts, interspersed and sheltered by trees, an elevated building made of rough-hewn timber-slab walls and a bark roof. It reminded Mia that they were deep in the foothills of the mountain range, with the swampy riverine flats far behind them.

Although life was short in Papua, Mia was shocked by how much Kinsame had aged. At forty-five, he was grey and emaciated, worn down by parasitic infections, especially malaria, which was rife.

He simply said, '*Yu bilong hia.*'

The words went straight to her heart.

'Thank you, Kinsame. I would talk longer with you, but I must go to the mission first and get medicine for my friend.'

'*Misin finis.*' His face was mournful. '*Soldia stil close.*'

'I understand. But I *must* go.'

He agreed that Paomente would take her once they had rested. She had known he would because, as *wantoks*, there was no other choice.

Chapter 28

A thin rectangle of amber sky revealed both the coming dawn and the extraordinary vertical narrowness of the Hoosenbeck Gorge. Viewed from below, it gave the impression of being trapped at the bottom of an immensely deep mineshaft, the sense of foreboding enhanced by a deep and oppressive silence.

Trussed up in a sleeping bag, Nash watched Hartono stiffly clamber out of the chopper and take a piss. Terrified of creepy-crawlies, he'd rejected a perfectly good swag, the structural integrity of which Sura and Boerman had confirmed around midnight. The lovebirds were still sleeping it off on the other side of the now-smouldering fire.

They kitted up after a breakfast of canned beef sausages, powdered eggs and Javanese coffee, ensuring time for ablutions, because once they were suited up there were no acceptable options.

Thankfully, Boerman was familiar with a membrane drysuit and needed no instruction. After squeezing his way into the insulated undersuit, the big man fought his way into the outer skin. Nash had to zip up the overstretched suit for him, because Sura didn't have the strength. Nash was wearing a more modern suit. Its semi-rigid matrix construction resisted compression, thus maintaining a thicker layer of warmer air between him and the outside membrane when under pressure. The closeness of the suit had never been a problem before, but now he felt smothered by what was essentially a high-tech plastic bag.

Weighed down with gear, they waddled into the cave and clambered down to the entry ledge, where Hartono had positioned the heavy-duty scooters.

The lithium-battery-powered tubes looked something like a stubby torpedo with a covered propeller. Capable of propelling a diver at speeds of 100 metres a minute for up to eight hours, they extended range and offset fatigue by a huge margin.

'Take it slow at first.' Nash made a point of warning his rookie offsider. 'These things will give you an embolism before you can blink.'

The Afrikaner waved him away. 'Stop trying to run the show. I know what I am doing.'

Nash glanced pointedly at Sura. If her bad boy screwed up, it would not be his fault.

They waited while Hartono jumped into a small grey inflatable and motored out to the centre of the lake. He threw in a coil of weighted line, which they would use as a guide and for decompression stops. Nash silently counted the seconds as the loops slipped into the water, and his bowels began to clench.

Christ, this thing is deep.

Eventually, Hartono yelled excitedly, 'It's down!'

'Shit, man, what is the *fokking* reading?' bellowed Boerman.

'It's at 203 metres,' echoed the reply.

Boerman grinned. 'We'll spot it easily.'

Sura looked less confident on her rocky perch.

'Mr Nash, repeat the plan.'

'We'll descend until we see the bottom and *no* further. That will be around 135 metres or so. We'll sweep using the same pattern as last time.' He looked meaningfully at Boerman. 'No spontaneous descents. Got it?'

'*Ja*, I heard you.'

Nash slid his legs into the loops of the scooter harness, pulled on his fins, and clipped himself to the machine. Easing off the ledge, they submerged slowly.

In contrast to the day before, Nash was warm and dry. Giving Boerman a thumbs up, he gently depressed the thumb speed control and cruised forward. Moments later, Boerman shot past like Wile E. Coyote on an Acme rocket, veering dramatically up and down, until he got it under control.

They steadily descended, switching from air to trimix, reducing the oxygen percentage to suit increasing partial pressure. At 100 metres they reached Hartono's line and hovered in the green void. No sign of the bottom, nor the dinghy at the surface. It felt like outer space – the sensation was enhanced by the fact that rebreathers shed no bubbles.

They'd reached 140 metres when slabs of calved-off limestone appeared out of the gloom like giant footsteps stacked haphazardly. Nash arrested their descent with the pale limestone floor visible fifty metres below. There was no time to waste. Every minute spent at this depth would cost them twenty-three minutes of decompression.

At maximum speed, they set off. With the floor of the cave unfolding in the glare of their brilliant lights, it was like flying through the world's biggest swimming pool, and Nash almost forgot the weight of water above him.

They were traversing the rear wall when a powerful down-draught of frigid pressure struck like an invisible hand and shunted them below 155 metres. Nash circled around to find the cause was a jagged fissure, no larger than a single-car garage, which marked the inlet of the Hoosenbeck. The immense power could only be explained by a charged passage, something like the intake for a hydroelectric generator on a giant dam. Nash realised the water column must extend for hundreds of metres above their heads, all the way to the top of the gorge and the mountain catchment. A secret vertical river, which, quite likely, was inexplorable.

Nash kept nervously rechecking his computer as he guided them towards the front of the cave. Seven minutes. Already, that was two and half hours of deco, and they had seen nothing for the whole 200-metre stretch.

Nine and a half minutes.

Traversing the front wall of the cave, all they found were giant heaps of boulders.

Eleven minutes.

The front left quadrant. As the distance unravelled, Nash knew that unless the submarine had sunk vertically, or had broken into two halves, it simply wasn't there, and thus his usefulness was about to come to an end.

Boerman was anxiously swinging his head from side to side. At any moment, the big man was going to come to the same inescapable conclusion. Against three, Nash knew he stood no chance, but against two, with the shadows of the cave at his disposal, he might yet find a way to escape and save Mia and Frank.

Boerman was far too strong for direct physical confrontation. Nash considered cutting the big man's rebreather hoses, but entanglement at this depth would probably kill them both. And should Boerman engage his buoyancy control device, his body would surface.

The back of the Afrikaner's unprotected head was the solution. Abruptly pulling into a steep climb, Nash gained height before angling back down. At full speed, the nose of his scooter would crack a human skull like a soft-boiled egg.

Nash was almost at maximum acceleration when something on the floor of the lake came into view – a cluster of streamlined tubes. At the last second, he aborted, sweeping around in a tight circle to rejoin the excited Boerman, who looked around and waved a triumphant fist.

It was a seaplane, lying upside down, and in such good condition that it might have been sunk last week. Twin floats stared mutely at the surface, and the red circles underneath each wing were unmistakably Japanese. Nash recalled they had developed a gigantic submarine which could carry several aircraft. How this one had got in here was a mystery. He could only assume someone had flown inside the mouth of the cave – an astonishing feat.

Ascending at nine metres a minute, they reached Hartono's line and stopped for just two minutes at a depth of 108 metres. It was the start of a complex five-hour-plus decompression sequence, to purge themselves of the dissolved nitrogen in their tissues.

Long deco stops were usually best treated as meditative spaces, but here every minute ticked past interminably as Nash tried to figure out his next move. A seaplane was all well and good, but finding the submarine that had launched it? It could be anywhere, including a thousand kilometres of muddy Sepik river bottom.

At long last, they surfaced next to Hartono, and cruised back across to the ledge where the midday sun streamed prettily into the cave mouth. Hartono helped lift the scooters out and hook them up to the generator to recharge, while Boerman went into a huddle with Sura.

Over a hot, sweet coffee, which stung his swollen mouth, Nash warmed himself up in a patch of sun while Sura and Boerman analysed the survey images on the laptop. Clearly, they were just as confused, and after a short, muted argument, Boerman swore loudly and walked a short distance away to begin throwing stones down the dry river bed.

'Mr Nash, would you come over here?' Sura indicated that he sit on a plastic crate and smoothed her shapely thighs. 'We have a conundrum. There is an Aichi Seiran torpedo bomber down there, which proves my submarine was once inside this cave. My question is – where on earth has it got to?'

Nash blinked at her expectant girlish stare. Did this entitled, self-obsessed maniac expect him to just pull a treasure map out of his arse?

'Sura, I'm a cave diver, not a psychic. All I can tell you is water runs downhill, so my guess is somewhere downstream.'

Her expression darkened. 'While you were down there today, I walked for nearly two kilometres along the dry river bed until I reached the resurgence of the river – a crystal-clear pool in which I saw brightly coloured fish swimming along the bottom. And I saw not a single shred of wreckage. Yet we have it on excellent authority the submarine *was* here.'

Nash stared at her curiously. 'How can you be so certain?'

'Because the mooring arrangement fits exactly, as does the seaplane left sitting on the catapult. You see, half the bullion was removed a few years after the war. But when they returned for the rest in the 1950s, the submarine was gone.'

Nash was growing interested despite himself.

'And you're *certain* it's the Hoosenbeck Cavern? You've seen for yourself the lay of the land – there could easily be other caves.'

'I can assure you we would not have come all this way otherwise.'

'Maybe you should reconfirm with your source?'

'No point.' Her eyes were flat. 'We don't make those kinds of mistakes.'

A nerve pulsed in Nash's jaw. He assumed that meant the source – whoever they were – was dead. Dry-mouthed, he licked his swollen lips and reminded himself that playing devil's advocate was not in his best interests.

'Is there anything else you can tell me?'

She nodded and reached into her bag. 'I have a fragment of a historical transcript which provides details on the submarine and its last voyage.'

Nash glanced at the title – *Being the truthful account of Dr Jürgen Fürth (George Ford)* – and began to read.

(Date unknown – Monday, 11ᵗʰ June?)

I have been locked up for days now in the stifling heat, and I fear I am losing my mind. The submarine has not moved for many hours

– possibly a whole day. I suspect we have reached the end of the navigable river. I have heard sounds of much activity – chains, boots, shouting – but for hours now, silence. I keep banging on the door, but no one has come. Perhaps they have left me to die?

I think we may be under attack! There have been several huge explosions. Thank God it must be over.

(Date unknown – Thursday, 14th June?)

Several days have passed, perhaps more, and we are moving again. I don't understand it. Are we going back downriver? I did not feel the submarine turn around. I am crushed. Beyond despair. This will be my final entry. I can go on no longer.

(Date unknown – Friday, 15th June?)

She came to me today! My darling. I heard a light knock and then I saw her fingers through the mesh of the door. Kissing them, I bathed them in my tears. 'Dearest Juju!' – she called me her pet name, and I cried even harder because I felt I was no longer a human being. She told me there is a plan to kill Heider. The SS suspect he will abandon them and steal the gold. He told me the submarine is hidden inside an enormous flooded cave. Ilse told me to be ready to move at the sound of gunfire. She will come for me when the mutiny starts. She does not trust anyone. We will escape together!

The moment Rob Nash read of the mysterious explosions and the lengthy delay, the fate of the *I-403* stood out as starkly as the cluster of dead trees he'd seen from the helicopter. More importantly, it suggested a plausible means of escape!

'That's one hell of a story,' he said, handing the document back to Sura. 'I'd love to know how it ends.'

She looked at him expectantly. 'Well?'

'If you're ready, let's go.'

'What on earth are you talking about?'

'If my hunch is right, your submarine is no more than a ten-minute walk away.'

Chapter 29

Where were the children swinging dizzyingly on the ropes beneath the generous shade of a massive fig? The happy families in brightly coloured clothing, chattering and laughing as they arrived for immunisations, treatments and prenatal checks? The mission had become a ghost of itself. The ropes dangled abjectly, the buildings were devoid of life, and Paul's plane lay marooned in long grass by the hangar, where even the windsock hung limply.

Mia was edging closer when Paomente froze.

'Stop,' he whispered. '*Bikpela snek!*'

She had just been about to step on a Papuan taipan with a girth the size of her calf.

The massive grey serpent reared and hissed, its black eyes intelligent and alert as it swayed within easy striking distance of her face. Paomente was holding a machete, but they both knew the snake was faster. Mia stood stock-still and hoped its innate aggression was tempered by the early hour. Thankfully, the taipan decided to save its venom, and slithered away towards the forest margin. As they watched it vanish into the thick grass, Paomente muttered that it was a bad omen.

'You can wait here if you like.'

'No, *Dokta* Mia.' He took her hand. '*Yumitupela go.*'

A sea of twinkling glass covered the wide veranda of the new clinic building. Bullet holes were punched through the weatherboards. An air conditioner had been blasted at point-blank range. Senseless.

'Hello!' she called out. 'Is anybody here?'

Inside the foyer they encountered the first of many large bloodstains, and Mia's spirits sank further. The reception was destroyed. Shot-up filing cabinets looked as if they'd been used for target practice; desks were overturned, and papers and files were strewn over the floor. A nurse's white shoe lay beside a clipboard. A blood trail led to the staff kitchen and a table covered in yet more blood. The fridges had been ransacked, food and drink thrown on the floor. The power was off; rotting food made the place stink like an abattoir, and the antibiotics she had come for were all spoiled.

Mia couldn't understand the devastation. Whatever Sura had thought Paul had of value, nothing could explain this level of hatred. In the ward area it continued. Beds were abandoned, sheets lying all over the floor. Bullet holes riddled the ceiling. The destruction was so wanton that she was surprised the place hadn't been torched.

The house had been ransacked, too. Paul's precious books, thrown into piles. His files, strewn and dumped. Paintings and photographs were torn out of frames, photo albums ripped to pieces. Even the carpets had been pulled up, loose boards jemmied.

Then Paomente tapped her on the shoulder.

'*Lookim.*'

Mia turned around to see a tiny elderly woman in a ragged green floral dress hugging herself with stick-thin arms. Mia stared, aghast. The old housekeeper's face was a criss-cross of ragged pink scars. Both nostrils had been slit, and her right ear appeared to be missing beneath a dirty bandage. Repairing the damage was going to take extensive reconstructive surgery.

'Millie? What have they done to you?'

The old woman wept as they embraced.

'You've come back. Oh, thank God, *Dokta* Mia, I've been waiting and praying someone would come.'

Millie led her outside, to a circle of massive European oak trees which Paul had told her were planted more than seventy years ago by his father. In the centre was a sandstone pillar with the name FORD carved in prominent Times Roman. At its base was a pile of raised red earth.

'My nephew laid him to rest.' Millie sniffed. 'He put Dokta Paul there, good and deep.'

Mia began crying. Funny how it took a grave to make it real. She put her hand on the stone and traced her fingers over the names chiselled in italics: *Elizabeth* and *George*. Curiously, there were no dates. Paul's mother's name was more eroded by the decades of rain. All Mia knew was that she had died when Paul was very young. He had told her it was too painful to talk about his parents, so she had let it be.

Who would carve Paul's name on the stone now? Mia wondered. Because the bereft and emaciated old woman beside her was like a living ghost among the death and destruction.

Mia put her arm around her. 'Paul loved you so much.'

'It's OK.' Millie's hand felt like a small bird's wing as it patted her forearm. 'God has answered my prayers. You've come back to run the mission for *Dokta* Paul!'

'Oh, Millie . . .'

A wave of conflicting emotions washed over Mia. She had planned to come back and work here for at least five years, open to the possibility that, with Paul's guidance, it might become her life, but what did she know about funding and hospital administration, let alone working under the Indonesian regime?

It reminded her of Sura's evil, and an icy resolve to get even filled her body.

'Tell me what happened here, Millie. Tell me everything.'

Haltingly, the old woman explained how two very bad Indonesian men had tortured Paul for gold, and something else he kept in the vault, before executing him.

'*Gold*, did you say?'

'Yes. They took a box, but they said there was much more hidden.'

Mia's head was spinning.

Why would Paul have kept gold out here? And where did he get it?

She listened in mounting dismay as Millie recounted how the Indonesians had gone on to get drunk and raped Nurse Jilly, before shooting everyone, except her, because they thought she was already dead.

It was so shocking and awful that Mia had to push the images away to concentrate on what needed to happen now.

'These men, Millie . . . would you know them if you saw them again?'

She nodded promptly. 'The one who cut me. Him short and very strong.'

Although she had anticipated it, Mia's heart skipped a beat.

'And the other?'

'The pilot was tall with . . .' Millie held up two circles over her eyes.

'Sunglasses?' Millie nodded, and then Mia pointed at her mouth. 'White teeth?'

'That's him!' Millie's excitement abruptly drained away. 'He's a very bad man, too.'

Mia thought for a moment. Goki might be dead, but Hartono was a link to Sura – maybe a way to make her pay for this horror. Taking the old woman firmly by the hands, Mia looked into her eyes.

'We're going to Kinsame's village. Then I will get you out of Papua. I will take you to my home in America, then you can tell the world what they did here and get justice for Doctor Paul.'

The old woman blinked several times.

'But *Dokta* Mia. We must fix the hospital.'

Mia bit her lip and tried not to cry.

'Millie, try to understand, it's not safe here anymore. I can't protect you.'

Paomente stiffened and cupped a hand to his ear.

'*Doktor Mia! Harim samting nogut.*'

It was the dull throb of an approaching helicopter. Not the clattering beat of the Jet Ranger – something much bigger and ominous.

'*Indonesian soldia!*' His eyes went wide with terror.

For a moment Mia wondered whether she should stay. Whatever Sura's designs, it was unlikely the whole Indonesian army was involved in a gold heist, otherwise why bother sneaking in via PNG? Perhaps these soldiers were looking for Sura, too?

Paomente was having none of it, and he almost wrenched her arm out of its socket.

'*Ronwe nau*! Go, go, go!'

Together they half-carried a terrified Millie to the orchard, where the safety of the forest lay just beyond the lines of mango trees. Halfway down a row, Mia thought they were going to make it until she glanced over her shoulder. The gigantic olive-green helicopter, with glinting Perspex cylinders at the nose and two domes for eyes, was bearing down upon them like a predatory insect. The noise drummed their flesh as it thundered across the top of them, almost blowing them off their feet in a stinky waft of avgas. At the end of the orchard, it lazily swung around.

'*Go hia*!' Paomente headed right.

Mia caught a blinding flash of orange.

Brrraaapppt!

Three mango trees in the row beside them disintegrated in flashes of wood chip and white smoke. A rain of stinging sap burned their eyes and skin. Paomente reversed direction, but this time two more trees on the other side were blown to pieces. The Indonesians were toying with them!

'Stop!' cried Mia, pulling them up. 'It's no good. They'll kill us.'

Paomente frantically shook his head. 'No, no! *I mas go*!'

'They always kill *blackpela*!' Millie shouted, her voice barely audible over the roar.

Mia knew she had to do something. Releasing them, she faced the killing machine and put her hands in the air.

'Here I am!' she shouted, slowly waving her arms back and forth. 'Come and get me!'

Paomente and Millie hesitated. Then, they headed in opposite directions, Millie hobbling back towards the mission, Paomente sprinting for home.

The monstrous helicopter immediately surged forward, its steel skids clipping the top of a mango tree.

'No, wait!' screamed Mia. *'Wait!'*

Brrrrrappt!

The fury of the weapon was terrifying. More trees exploded, and great clods of grass and earth were thrown up in the air as Paomente desperately zigzagged. He had almost reached the line of trees when he just broke apart in front of Mia's eyes. A cloud of red mist hovered over the area like smoke.

Mia had no time to process what had happened, for the helicopter turned its hateful snout towards Millie, still staggering along as fast as an injured septuagenarian was able. With Mia sprinting in its wake, and screaming *'Stop! Stop!'* at the top of her lungs, the helicopter bore down on the little old woman.

Brrrrapppt!

Clouds of dirt and debris kicked up by the massive rotors obscured the view. When it cleared, Millie was gone, hidden somewhere in the long grass. Mia kept running as the helicopter settled nearby like a bloated spider. Ignoring jabbering cries, she ran on until she spotted Millie's white hair and slid to a halt beside her.

The old woman was on her side, both legs shot away below the shins. Thick red blood pumped into the grass. Mia grabbed hold of the ragged, splintered stumps with her hands.

'Tourniquet!' she screamed at the man approaching. 'Get a tourniquet!'

The Kopassus officer was immaculately dressed in a neat camouflage uniform. He wore an incongruously bright red beret with a smart gold insignia at a rakish angle. On his chest was a name badge which read ALATAS. Calmly, he unbuckled a black holster on his belt as he walked the last few steps. Withdrawing a pistol, he cocked it, and before Mia could protest, emptied the whole magazine point-blank into Millie's head.

Covered in blood spray, Mia went into shock.

The officer reloaded his pistol. The bland look on his cheerful face incensed her.

'What have you done?' she screamed. 'What have you done?'

Without changing expression, he smacked her savagely across the face, then with a closed fist, which made her ears ring. When she tried to cover up, he punched her in the solar plexus. Grabbing her by the collar, he stuck the hot barrel of the pistol under her jaw. She was dimly aware that his breath smelled of peppermint.

'Call yourself a soldier?' Mia said angrily. 'You miserable little coward.'

She thought he was going to strike her again. Instead, he pushed her to the ground and lit a cigarette.

'No more childish games, Doctor Carter. Tell me where Frank Douglas is.'

They're working with Sura.

Mia's insides heaved and abruptly she threw up.

Oh God, what had she done? Because of her, Millie and Paomente were dead. And if these murderous bastards went to the village looking for Frank Douglas, they would surely kill them all, too.

Wiping her mouth, she looked Alatas in the eye.

'Frank Douglas died on the journey from Hufi. We left his body in the forest. I can show you where if you like.'

'*Bohong bitch*!' Wrenching her palm up, he ground his cigarette into her flesh. 'I can tell you are lying.'

Chapter 30

On the pale water-worn limestone, they moved fast under the dense canopy. On either side of the dry river bed, trees as thick as a man fought for the light. Interspersed among them, like ghosts among the living, were the limbless white trunks of long-dead gigantic ancestors. Nash began to think about what he was going to do if the submarine wasn't there, and his tension was mounting with every step.

'I'm beginning to wonder if this isn't some desperate fantasy.' Sura gave voice to her misgivings. 'Why don't you explain what this is all about?'

'Do you see all the dead trees? Something killed them at the same time.'

'No shit, genius,' Boerman snapped from the rear. 'The gorge flooded.'

'But what *caused* the flood?'

Nash directed their attention back up the river bed. From where they were standing, only the top of the cave arch was visible. They could make out the faint white line on the cliff face, and another glimpse through the trees on the walls of the gorge.

'Those mineral deposits prove that where we are standing was once more than twenty metres deep. Given the fall of the gorge, how is that possible? What could have contained that depth of water?'

'This isn't show-and-tell, Mr Nash.'

'In Fürth's account, he thought the submarine had reached the end of the river.'

Sura sighed. 'And then he heard explosions and they continued on –'

'But not for several days, quite possibly more, because he had no way of telling the time.'

'And your point is?' grumbled Boerman, slapping a mosquito feeding on his neck.

'When we flew in, just after the gorge narrows, I spotted an old collapse, a huge landslide now covered in trees. The Hoosenbeck resurgence appears downstream of it.'

Sura nodded. 'I walked right through it.'

'What if the SS fixed explosives to the walls of the gorge *behind* the submarine?'

Sura's eyes lit up. 'To create a dam. It makes sense!'

Nash nodded. 'And then they waited for the water to rise like a lock. That is how Heider was able to get the submarine into the cave.'

Boerman looked aggravated. 'So where did all the water go, huh?'

'We're almost there.'

Nash began walking again. Sura came up alongside him.

'Are you saying the dam collapsed and swept the submarine away?'

'No, the dam was eroded later over time.'

'Then I don't understand.'

'Cast your mind back to seventy-odd years ago, when this gorge was flooded for more than a kilometre. Can you imagine how much all of that weighed?' He did a quick calculation.

'Let's call it forty million tonnes, bearing down on this very rock.'

'Seems solid enough to me,' said Sura.

'Limestone is actually riddled with subterranean pockets. Existing voids would have expanded as the water forced its way in through cracks, and steadily dissolved the weakest stone. Years passed, until a critical mass was reached, when the weight of all that water became too much for a large cavity to support.'

Ahead, on his left, Nash saw the vegetation thinning out. He had spotted it on the way in and, with the lure of the cave, hadn't paid it much attention.

'And *then*?' Boerman demanded. 'Come on, man, finish it.'

Nash came to a halt and turned around. 'And then, in one catastrophic event, the roof of the cavity collapsed. As millions of tonnes of water poured into the void, the level of the dam dropped suddenly. The steel hawser tethering the submarine snapped like string, and it was swept out of the cave, down the gorge . . . into this!'

Boerman and Sura stared in amazement as Nash pointed through the trees. Adjacent to the main river channel was a sinkhole. Jammed with huge logs, shrouded in hanging vines, it was almost completely camouflaged. Making their way cautiously to the crumbling edge, they peered into the gloomy depths and Sura gave a small cry. For there, emerging vertically like some mythical sea monster from the depths, was the rusting bow of an enormous submarine.

With eight torpedo doors and a hull three storeys high, the huge scale reminded Nash of nuclear leviathans he'd seen at

Pearl Harbor, but the bizarreness of its last-century oriental curves in this exotic jungle location made it appear like a relic from a forgotten civilisation.

Boerman took Sura's hand and kissed it several times.

'You did it, *liefling*. I knew you were right all along!'

Sura was blushing like a bride. 'Of course, we must thank Mr Nash, too.'

Was the compliment his eulogy?

With his usefulness at an end, Nash braced himself for a surprise push in the back.

Instead, Boerman bent down and picked up a fist-sized chunk of limestone. He lobbed it into the jumble of logs and vegetation and they listened to it rebounding off timber and steel, until the sound of it shattering on the rocky floor echoed up. The Afrikaner whistled appreciatively.

'That's one deep hole.'

Sura looked quizzically at Nash. 'I don't understand. This sinkhole is not only deep, it is also dry. How can the Hoosenbeck possibly resurface just a few hundred metres downstream of this location if the two are connected?'

Nash gratefully seized the lifeline. 'You can't think in terms of straight lines of fall. Limestone gives rise to complex hydrological systems – multiple passages funnelling underground rivers which can flow intermittently, depending on rainfall. The discharge from the Hoosenbeck Cavern is currently bypassing this sinkhole.'

Sura's eyes narrowed. 'What do you mean, *currently*? Are you saying this sinkhole floods when it rains? That it is connected to the Hoosenbeck?'

He nodded quickly. 'The Dutch speleologists would have encountered this sinkhole when they explored the valley. It must have been full at the time, or they would have discovered this submarine.'

'They came in March, the end of the wet season,' Sura murmured.

Boerman glanced up at the sky, now studded with plump white clouds.

'And it's due any time.'

'Then we need to move quickly.' Sura put her hand on the Afrikaner's broad shoulder. 'Jaap, run back up, fetch rope and two harnesses.'

'Two?' The big man paused.

'Mr Nash is going to assess the situation with you.' Before Boerman could argue, she snapped her fingers. 'Hurry!'

The Afrikaner took off at a run and Nash breathed again. As long as the threat of inundation remained, his dive skills had currency.

Sura took out her pistol.

'Sit down there, Mr Nash – yes, right by the edge – and please, don't try anything stupid.'

She made herself comfortable on a fallen log and checked her phone for a signal. In the silence, he became aware of the faint sound of running water in the sinkhole far below. Yes, somewhere down there was his escape route.

Sura coughed and bared her little white teeth in a smile.

'You're an interesting man, Mr Nash. In many ways you remind me of myself.'

Nash raised his eyebrows.

This is going to be interesting.

'We're both dreamers who think big, and are prepared to take risks to achieve our goals.'

'We are nothing alike,' he promptly replied. 'I don't kill people for money.'

'Oh, really? How do you explain what happened to your wife? Wasn't her death a direct result of your ambition?' Sura looked like a cat focused on its next meal. 'It's what drives you, isn't it, Mr Nash? You deconstruct the mysteries of the earth *to be the first.*'

A white-hot rage ignited within him and Nash found himself bellowing, 'You don't know shit! You have no fucking idea about me or her, so shut your fucking mouth!'

Satisfied she'd drawn blood, Sura nodded calmly. 'There is one key difference between you and me. While I am true to myself, you have allowed conscience to distort who you are. Guilt has weakened the courage of your convictions. That is why *you* are afraid, and *I* am not.'

A thudding of boots saved Nash from replying. Boerman arrived, festooned with rope, his big chest heaving with exertion. Sensing something had just happened, he looked inquiringly at Sura, who said irritably, 'Well, what are you waiting for?'

Boerman petulantly flung a climbing harness at Nash's feet.

'Come on, hotshot, put it on!'

After fastening it to the nearest stout tree, the Afrikaner gave the rope a few tugs before launching outwards off the lip. In a hiss of hot nylon, he plummeted twenty-five metres in a single drop. Alighting smoothly on the topmost wedged log, he used it

314

as a runway to pick up speed in one great bound, soaring across the chasm to land on another dead tree near the submarine's bow. Here, he tested the integrity of the stack, jumping from log to log, with booming thuds that echoed around the sinkhole. Then he unhooked himself from the rope, barked a warning and, like a major league pitcher, flung the descender skywards to Nash, who snatched it painfully out of the air.

Sura watched on as he clipped himself to the rope.

'Watch your step, Mr Nash, and remember your friends.'

It took him four attempts to land the gut-wrenching swing to the log jam. Nash had made the mistake of looking through the latticework of slippery tree trunks to the rocky floor of the sinkhole, a dizzying 100 metres below.

'You're afraid of heights, too?' Boerman chortled delightedly. Standing unroped on a mossy log, he confidently thumped the hull of the submarine with a closed fist. 'We need to climb around to the other side to access the deck. It will be easier to get down that way.'

Sura called down a warning to be careful.

'*Ja, ja!*' he yelled up. 'I heard you the first time.'

The big man spotted a crack in the rusted steel plate. Wriggling his fingers inside, he used it to lunge up and grab hold of the bottommost torpedo door. Nash watched in ghoulish fascination as Boerman hauled himself bodily around the huge curvature of the hull. Without a safety rope, there was no room for error and, crazy as it was, there was something magnificent about it.

'I'm on the deck!' the Afrikaner eventually shouted down. 'Get your *bleddy* ass up here!'

Even with a rope, Nash took his time. With slippery surfaces and hard jagged edges, any kind of fall was potentially lethal. He was catching his breath, just above the topmost torpedo door, when Boerman's big arm looped down.

'You're like a fucking old woman!' he bellowed in frustration. 'Take my hand!'

'Thanks, but I'll pass.'

A few minutes later, he reached the big man, crouched on the nose of the pneumatic catapult track. It was a precarious perch. Nash's stomach contracted at another lethal drop to the circular waterproof hangar door.

'*Kom*, we use it for a ladder.'

The garish smudge of rust across the left side of Boerman's face made him look like an extra from a *Mad Max* movie. Unencumbered by rope or common sense, he climbed swiftly down through the remnants of the track mechanism, which had once flung five-tonne torpedo bombers into the air. The steel was treacherous. Sections which looked strong enough to support a car suddenly snapped in Nash's hand.

'What's happening?' Sura's voice floated down.

'Almost at the hangar!' Boerman roared. 'The door is closed!'

'Be careful –'

There was a sharp snapping sound. In a shower of debris, the Afrikaner plunged several metres, landing feet first on the nose of the conical hangar door. Its steeply sloping sides offered no purchase, and Boerman's boots slipped on the flaking rust. Slamming down hard on his side, he inexorably slid towards the edge, and Nash willed him to fall, but with a last desperate grab,

Boerman managed to grasp a handle near the edge of the door and swung wildly to and fro like a pendulum.

Biceps bulging, the Afrikaner slowly hauled himself up. Nash inwardly cursed. Boerman was one of those people fate would simply not take care of.

'Still here, Nash.' Boerman grinned up at him. 'I'm still fucking here!'

It took Nash ten minutes to negotiate the treacherous conical door on his backside, and his arms were shaking until he reached the secure handholds of a triple twenty-five mm anti-aircraft cannon mounted on the hangar roof.

A short distance below, Boerman was standing on the face of the offset conning tower.

'Hopefully, we can get in this way,' he said, before striding up to the top.

Something peculiar then struck Nash about his now-uninterrupted view to the stern. The entire deck was curved like a roller coaster track. He realised the submarine had bent like a giant banana from the tremendous force of crashing into the sinkhole floor, which must have cracked open the hull below.

He was heading over to Boerman when the rope abruptly pulled up taut. Nash realised he'd reached the end of the line.

'Unclip your ass,' jeered the big man. 'Or I'll come and get you myself.'

Tiptoeing along the horizontal conning tower, Nash lay down beside Boerman and craned his head over the parapet. A set of fixed pressure-proof binoculars stared back at them. It was easy to imagine the Japanese captain scanning the horizon for enemy ships, unaware the greater threat lay beneath his feet.

Stumps of periscopes, and the remains of radar cones, also projected from the deck. Boerman then performed another outrageous feat of free climbing, trying to get the hatch to open while hanging upside down.

When at last he conceded, puffing and panting, they went back along the conning tower and continued the terrifying climb down through the rusting steel framework. The rear section, which had spent more time underwater, was severely corroded. At times, they literally had to kick footholds in the rust until, at last, they were able to stand without danger of falling on the flattened, bulging stern.

Nash eagerly surveyed the carpet of young tree ferns growing strongly in the shallow silt of the sinkhole floor. There were no older plants except for plucky dwarf specimens clinging to the walls above, suggesting inundation was indeed a regular event. There were several promising overhangs in shadow, suggesting caves and passages, but it was the small stream bubbling its way down to the low point which pointed to the location of the main exit passage he was expecting.

'After you, Nash.'

With mounting excitement, Nash clambered down over the split-open pressure hulls and mangled propellers to reach solid ground.

It was only now they were able to appreciate the behemoth above their heads. Boerman whistled, for it was truly an astonishing sight. Foreshortened, the gigantic submarine looked like a tinplate toy lost down a drainpipe after a storm. Nash had to remind himself that the chaotic tangle of twigs wedged tightly around its bow were actually massive trees. It looked disturbingly like a giant set of Jenga. If one log went, several hundred tonnes of timber were poised to follow.

A gaping crack in the submarine's hull, forty-five metres above their heads, drew their eyes. Floor plating was spewing out, and severed pipes looked ready to fall. Chunks of broken metal dotting the floor of the sinkhole suggested this was a regular occurrence.

'Well, we have a way in,' said Boerman cheerfully.

While the big man took shots with the GoPro, Nash surreptitiously looked around for a likely weapon. If he could escape through the exit passage, double back and take Sura by surprise, he would have a pistol and a pilot. Frustratingly, the fragments of rusting steel were either too big or insubstantial. It would have to be a stone.

He looked up to find Boerman assessing him with a shrewd gaze which suggested he knew full well what Nash was thinking.

'OK, *Mister Expert*, let's check out the rest of this *bleddy* hole. I'll be right behind you.'

They traversed the crumbling limestone walls, with the Afrikaner carefully checking each shadowy overhang to make sure it offered no means of escape. The stream terminated in a large crescent basin of deep, wonderfully clear water, and Nash's hopes disintegrated. Somewhere, in the shadows of the sinkhole wall where it plunged out of sight, was the huge passage through which the water in the flooded gorge had escaped. Unfortunately, without dive gear, it was not an option.

Back at the crumpled stern, Boerman held up his massive hand like a traffic cop.

'Tomorrow we ferry in the gear. You'll be staying here.'

Now Nash understood the reason for their thoroughness.

'Don't look so pissed off.' Boerman grinned. 'I could have told you after you'd climbed back up to the rope.'

Testing a handhold on the buckled steel of the stern, Boerman pulled himself up and climbed at speed to the conning tower. Nash watched as he efficiently jumared his way out of sight to the surface. The rope was then pulled up. Some time later, he heard the helicopter taking off, before the sound gradually faded away.

Chapter 31

Being the truthful account of Dr Jürgen Fürth (George Ford), July _? 1945

It has been three weeks since we escaped the clutches of Martin Heider. Our escape is so miraculous no one would ever believe it. Fortunately, it is a tale that will never be told. When Ilse led me out of the submarine into the vast cave lake, I believed it was a hallucination. Electric lights strung over its superstructure made the I-403 look like an ocean liner, except it was crewed by dead men. The bodies of the Japanese collaborators lay where they had been gunned down. Ilse told me some of the SS had slipped away last night, but not before they had assembled two of the torpedo bombers.

The sleek seaplane faced the bright opening of the cave, which hurt my eyes to look upon. Climbing onto one of the floats, Ilse told me to hurry, for Heider was preparing to leave. She opened a flap in the belly of the plane, and I saw the cavity was stuffed full of gold bars. Ilse began throwing them into the water, and we did not stop until we figured we had removed enough to compensate for our combined body weights. Not a moment too soon, we sealed ourselves inside, for Heider and the sole surviving Japanese pilot clambered into the cockpit, and started the engine with a deafening roar.

The flight was terrifying. It seemed to take forever to get airborne and we bounced around in shocking turbulence. We were terrified the gold bars would shift and crush us in the cramped torpedo bay. Perhaps twenty minutes had passed when suddenly the gold shifted to the right, and the plane became unbalanced. I held Ilse in my arms as we descended with the engine roaring fit to burst. The impact was terrible, and I do not know how long we were unconscious, but I woke to the sounds of hammering.

Opening the torpedo bay, I realised the plane was lying on its side on a muddy riverbank. Ilse was still unconscious when I slithered out onto the ground, and the first thing I saw was a silver Luger sitting on top of the body of the pilot. I could hear Heider in the water, working on something. I could barely crawl around the wreckage, but then I saw him. He was sitting inside one of the detached aircraft floats and practising paddling with a palm tree seed pod. I had never fired a gun in anger before. But seeing the monster preparing to escape his crimes, I could not let him go. When Heider saw me pointing the gun, he simply laughed. Whether it was confidence that I would be unable to pull the trigger, or merely acknowledging the irony of fate, I will never know, but I shot him between the eyes and he slipped down into the float and I watched it drift away. A short time later a native man appeared. Thank God there was kindness in his heart.

* * *

The excitement of the gunship crew was perhaps the most sickening thing of all. Having flown back to Kinsame's village, they attacked without warning, the people below mere vermin to be eradicated, point scores in a giant video game. An image, which would haunt Mia forever, was a mother fleeing below with her baby pressed to her breast, both dismembered when a heavy-calibre round punched through her back. White phosphorus rockets turned panicking families into flaming torches. Only a handful of Kinsame's people escaped, mostly young men, fit and fast enough to avoid encirclement by the supporting Kopassus ground troops. While killings and torture in Papua were all part of a dirty war that had simmered for decades, this was a massacre without military purpose. Whatever crime they were helping Sura engage in, it was beyond belief or justification.

Numbly, Mia watched from the helicopter doorway as they brought Frank Douglas out of Kinsame's scorched hut on a stretcher. Already looking stronger, he was propped up on his forearms, eyes staring in disbelief at the carnage.

'You gutless arsehole!' he raged at Kapten Alatas, who was dispassionately smoking a cigarette while his men mopped up. 'Why'd you do it?'

When they loaded him into the gunship, Douglas's eyes widened.

'What happened to you, kid?'

The concern in his voice opened the floodgates and her face crumpled.

'Frank, I brought them here. It's all my fault!'

The faces of the dead swam accusingly in her mind – Paomente, Millie, Kinsame, the three young men whose names she'd forgotten. Hadn't Kinsame told her to stay away? Douglas put a comforting hand on her shoulder while she wept.

'You couldn't have anticipated this. Mia, you *didn't* know.' He blinked away his own tears. 'Come on, kid, let's hold it together now and find a way out of this.'

She took several deep breaths and wiped her face on her shirtsleeve.

Douglas lowered his voice. 'Did you manage to get a message out at the mission?'

She shook her head. 'The communications were destroyed. But at least I know what they're after.'

Douglas was stunned when she told him.

'In the *Hoosenbeck*?'

They broke off as Alatas clambered into the co-pilot's seat. It was a short hop to the mission, which was now a hive of activity. As they circled to land, a soldier was slashing the grounds with the mission tractor. Two green canvas tents were pitched in the shade of the big fig. Mia's empty stomach did a double flip when she sighted the familiar gold Jet Ranger beside the house; she dreaded seeing Sura, but at least she would see Rob.

'An advance base,' Douglas muttered as the engines wound down. 'Looks like Sura had it all planned.' His brow furrowed. 'Wonder where Kaboro fits in?'

'I think they're collateral, Frank.'

Alatas stepped into their compartment and prodded Mia's back painfully with his boot.

'Let's go.'

Two soldiers opened the gunship's door and dragged out Douglas's stretcher.

'Hey, take it easy,' he growled as they roughly bumped him against the skid. 'I'm not dead yet.'

They were taken to Paul's trashed office, given a can each of lukewarm orange soda, and a guard cut Mia's cable tie so she could drink.

'Where do you think Rob is?' she sighed, rubbing circulation back into her wrists.

'Probably still on the ship.' By the gleam in Douglas's eye, she realised her feelings were showing. 'Don't worry, kid.' He gave her a wink. 'He's tougher than you think.'

Under the watchful eye of a young guard, she checked Douglas's wound. Incredibly, there was a healthy scab with not a trace of infection.

'In *three days*?' She screwed her nose up. 'That's just not possible. How do you feel, Frank?'

'Like a blue steak and an icy cold beer.' While she chuckled, Douglas glanced casually over at the guard and, without changing tone, said, 'You ugly dog-fornicator. Your mother must be a real bitch.'

Mia tensed for an explosive reaction, but the guard simply continued to stare at a point above their heads.

'You'd have to be a monk not to react to that.' Douglas returned his attention to her. 'Listen, we may not have much time to talk. I'm getting stronger, but not enough to run. You have to take off at the first opportunity you get. Don't go back to Kinsame's village – it's the first place they'll look. Head north till you hit the river. Find a village. Beg, borrow or steal a way downriver, just get across the border –'

'But what about you and Rob?' She was trying to keep her voice light, but the thought of leaving them was abhorrent.

'We'll scoot as soon as we get the chance. Right now, you're our best shot at getting the word out.'

'But what good will *that* do? Someone high up in the PNG government is already involved, and I doubt our authorities will do anything more than make overtures. By then it will be too late for you.'

Douglas acknowledged this with a solemn stare. 'Mia, would you rather we all just conveniently disappeared? If you get word to the embassies, maybe it will put the pressure on the Suyantos, muck up whatever grubby scheme they've got going. We've got to find a way to push back or they win.'

'OK,' she nodded, thinking of the jungle trails she had walked to the river. 'I'll do it, Frank.'

'Good girl. We'll wait until dark. If necessary, I'll create a diversion.'

Sounding tired, Douglas lay back with one arm under his head and ran his eyes over the old world books and paintings scattered over the floor.

'Say, how the hell did you ever find this place?'

Mia smiled as she remembered her first visit. How bizarre it had been to find an archaic chunk of European culture transplanted to the tropics, for the mission website had given no indication she would be stepping back in time. Paul had welcomed her with a gin and tonic, invited her to sit down in a rattan chair on the wide veranda, then talked his head off while a cooling zephyr from the distant mountains blew the humidity away.

'Fate, I suppose. But none of this makes sense, Frank. Work was Paul's life, and he worked non-stop every day of the year. I can't believe he was interested in money.'

'Takes a lot of money to run a hospital, though.'

'Yes. And there are sister hospitals in Africa and South America, too. But who keeps gold under their bed in this day and age? Especially in a place as tumultuous as Papua?'

Douglas raised a shaggy eyebrow. 'Hate to say it, kid, but usually it's someone with something to hide.' He sucked on his mangled lower lip for a moment. 'What I don't get is how the Hoosenbeck fits in. No one in their right mind would stash gold up there, surely?'

They mulled over it for a time, and then Douglas asked her why she'd wanted to work here. She explained it was the people – the sense of purpose and energy she had found helping those with so little.

He looked puzzled. 'And you couldn't find that back home? Your health system doesn't do much for the poor, does it?'

Mia grinned self-consciously. 'You're absolutely right, Frank. But doling out antidepressants and blood pressure meds to overweight, indifferent people living off junk food is demoralising. Out here I get to vaccinate kids who would otherwise die. I get to keep people healthy so they can physically carve out a living. In Papua you don't have a choice about getting off the couch. And, I will admit to loving the adventure!'

Douglas smiled at her approvingly. 'I get it. After Vietnam, I couldn't hack civilisation. I needed the nitty-gritty of the frontier. No buggers strutting around telling you what to do, wide open spaces, and freedom to go where you bloody well choose. Course, that starts to pale when you get old. Then you start thinking about creature comforts. Pathetic, really.'

Mia thought of her parents' snug life in Connecticut. Its convenience, security and conformity were charms lost on her. When she'd announced she was returning to Papua, her father had put down his paper and sighed.

'Aw, Mee, we thought you'd got it out of your system.'

Her mom, always averse to emotional displays, had even cried.

'We thought you might take over the clinic one day. And stop telling me it's not dangerous.'

Then they had hugged her tightly and given her their blessing.

Wishing she could tell them how much she loved them, Mia looked over at Douglas, who still had a faraway look in his eyes. While her father was biologically young and healthy, the expat bore the scars of a long and tough existence.

'Just how long have you been out here, Frank?'

'Almost half a century.' He shook his head in wonder. 'I can't tell you how many times I was going to quit this shithole and try to get a job teaching snot-nosed grammar school kids how to fly. But something always drew me back.'

'Was it the people?'

Douglas frowned, but perhaps the last three days had changed him, because with a thoughtful nod he conceded, 'You know, kid, you might just be right.'

They heard laughter out in the hallway, and then Alatas and Sura came in. They were looking so exuberant that Mia was instantly outraged.

'Well, well, the intrepid Doctor Carter . . . didn't you turn out to be elusive?' Sura sat down on the leather couch, crossed her slim legs and looked around. 'You know, this place is like an adventure novel come to life – evil Nazis hiding out in the jungle, sitting on a stolen fortune for generations. If I hadn't found the evidence myself, I would never have believed it.'

Hate was an emotion Mia Carter had no experience of, but she could feel it coating her tongue and the words dripped out thickly.

'I have no idea what you are talking about. The only evil I've ever seen in this place is sitting right in front of me.'

'Oh, so Paul never spoke to you about his mysterious mother and father – how he came to be living in the middle of nowhere? Show her what he kept in the safe, Kapten.'

Alatas produced an exotic pistol finished in gold and silver. In one smooth motion, he cocked it and pointed it at Mia's face. She barely heard Douglas's cry as the smirking Alatas pulled the trigger. The loud click was followed by girlish giggles from Sura, and Mia had to hang on to the orange soda rumbling in her gut.

'That was a dog act,' said Douglas shakily.

Alatas reversed the pistol and held it up so Mia could see the details.

'It's a Luger 9 mm, handcrafted in Berlin in 1937 for Paul Ford's biological father. Observe the engraved initials on the barrel.'

'M. H.?' Mia glanced dully at Sura. 'I don't understand.'

'Paul's surrogate father, and the founder of your precious Ford Mission, was Jürgen Furth, a Nazi doctor travelling back to Europe on a Japanese submarine which deviated up the Sepik in 1945 – the only one out of several hundred Japanese sailors and a squad of brutal SS men to make it out alive. He found his way back to Germany, only to return a few years later as George Ford. It's not hard to understand why, Doctor Carter. Four tonnes of gold bullion is a compelling incentive.'

Whether this fantastic tale was true or not, Mia could only wonder what she had done to make this woman hate her so much.

'What exactly do you want from me?'

Sura raised an eyebrow. 'Clearly you don't have to be intelligent to gain a medical degree. What I want, Doctor Carter, is the gold, and an incentive for your new boyfriend to get it out for me.' She stared at Mia's hands, then looked at Alatas in annoyance. 'Why isn't she tied up? I want these two on location first thing in the morning.'

Chapter 32

Being the truthful account of Dr Jürgen Fürth (George Ford), Papua, October 1945

My darling Ilse is pregnant. The news should fill me with joy, but the dates do not lie: it is Heider's. Ilse is bereft; she calls it her abomination and wants me to end it, but I won't do it. Her fever is so bad I fear she will lose the child anyway. I am terrified of this because a stillbirth out here will surely kill her. I curse the lack of equipment, the heat and the insects. These simple villagers have done their best to help us with food and shelter, but the few medical supplies we fled with are almost gone and I think I must return to the submarine. This has been the darkest of days.

*   *   *

Perhaps a world-class free climber might have found a way up the sheer and crumbling sides of the sinkhole, but for Nash, without a rope and pitons, it was suicide. And had there been any likelihood of finding usable rope inside the submarine, it might have justified a daring traverse of the log jam to reach the cracked hull. Which left the crescent pool as the only possible way out.

Nash warily eyed the still water. Free diving caves was known as sump diving, and it was one of the most dangerously stupid things you could do. He had retrieved several bodies of those who'd tried – most of them cocky teenagers on a dare who'd panicked and drowned in terror. But he also knew the submerged exit passage could just as easily rise up to fresh air and freedom.

Thanks to years of training for big wave hold-downs, Nash could hold his breath for a full three minutes under exertion. But there were other factors to consider. Diving alone in darkness, without a light, his autonomic nervous system would flood his system with adrenaline, gobbling up precious oxygen. The lack of a mask, weight belt and fins would compromise his efficiency and duration, and, as ever, there was the lurking threat of claustrophobia. He decided on an initial foray of two minutes, setting the timer on his dive watch for a one-minute turnaround.

Nash involuntarily shivered. In diminishing light, any kind of free dive was exponentially more dangerous. After three minutes breathing up, he slid into the chilly water. The smooth rock bottom steadily dropped away, and he swam along the arm of the crescent, getting his bearings. Descending to nine metres, he sensed the exit passage looming in the shadows. Then, the alarm went off, and he ascended with half a minute to spare.

So far, so good.

Nash stretched out like a lizard on the warm stone by the middle of the pool. Skin tingling, he began the breathe-up cycle again.

This time, he picked up a basketball-sized rock before stepping off the shelf. The gravity assist preserved vital oxygen, and on the way down he pinched his nose to equalise the pressure in his ears. The light was a dull green when he landed on the bottom. He figured his depth to be around twenty metres. This was one hell of a passage.

Nash swam up at a forty-five-degree angle, looking to connect with the sloping wall of the sinkhole and stay orientated before the darkness closed in.

Doubt began interfering with his internal compass, and he stopped swimming and checked his illuminated watch. Just a few seconds to go before the alarm sounded. Gratefully, he turned back. By the time he cleared the underhang, his lungs were starting to burn. He forced himself to not race for the air, and broke the surface close to the two-minute mark.

The light was diminishing quickly, and he was cold. But he knew he hadn't explored as far as his lungs could take him. This time, he breathed up for a full ten minutes, and reset his turnaround for one and a half minutes.

Diving straight and true, he took a direct line to the top of the exit passage and swam inside. The greenish glow behind him steadily gave way to grey, and then finally, pitch black. Now, he had to trust his internal compass. He swam on and on, gaining confidence until suddenly his fingertips encountered rock. Fear drilled through him. He wanted to turn back, but he needed to establish whether the rock was sloping down, or he was drifting up.

Turning turtle, he pulled himself along arm over arm. The roof was sloping up! Then the alarm went off.

'Plan the dive, dive the plan', the saying went. Nash should have immediately returned to the pool. But the rock was climbing so steeply, and he sensed he was almost at the surface.

Another five seconds passed . . . *eight, nine, ten* . . . The realisation that he'd probably passed the point of no return fought with the desire to turn back. But he had to be close . . . surely . . . He'd been ascending for what seemed like ages.

Have I miscalculated?

His head banged painfully into rock. Nash felt around desperately, finding an unbroken wall beneath his scrabbling hands. It was a dead end!

His final alarm confirmed it. Three minutes had elapsed. There was no point going back. Nash had less than thirty seconds to live.

With nothing to lose, he groped sideways for several metres. With every handhold, flashes of his life popped up unbidden: his mother's hug when he graduated; his father's quiet hand on his shoulder at Natalie's funeral; Jacquie chasing him around the yard, aged four, with a water pistol. A great sadness filled him as he realised they would never know what had happened to him. And then his hand met nothing . . .

It was a ledge! Dragging himself around, Nash got his feet planted. Lungs on fire, he pushed off with all his might. One final hurrah, straight up like an arrow.

A scant second later his head broke the water.

Air, sweet, blessed air!

Nash sucked it in, deep draughts echoing in a perfect void of blackness, and by the volume of his echoes, he knew it was a large chamber. He swam for several metres, until he encountered a sloping rock surface. Jittery with cold and adrenaline, he clambered out.

His next moves were critical. He was reasonably certain that he could follow the mental route back and find the green glow of the entrance pool. But the longer he stayed here in the pitch black without any visual reference points, the faster that fragile mental map would degrade.

Nash had one precious source of light – his watch – but the battery would not last long. He activated it just long enough to absorb the topography within the illuminated five-metre radius and was heartened to see the slope continued up. Fortunately, there were loose rocks and branches, detritus from the last flood event, and without ever taking more than three steps from his position, he gathered these by feel, building a succession of small cairns. In this way, he laid a return trail, taking perhaps half an hour to travel fifty metres.

His heart sank as the rock began sloping down again. Sure enough, he soon hit water. Bitter disappointment coursed through him. How long did this next sump continue for? It might have been a few metres, but in absolute darkness, without any point of reference, it might as well have been twenty kilometres.

What he should have done next was to immediately head back while there was enough daylight to guide him to the entrance pool. But Nash was suddenly overcome by his predicament, and slumped down in exhausted despair. What was out there anyway? The whole ramshackle edifice of his life was one he no longer recognised – one he didn't know how to live. Perhaps being marooned on the shore of a netherworld beach was a fitting way for it to end?

'Sonofabitch!' he roared in the sightless grotto. 'It wasn't my fault, Nat! Do you hear me? It wasn't my fault!'

A wave of self-pity and frustration engulfed Nash. Everyone had been so quick to blame *him*. But Natalie was an experienced cave diver, and *she* had made the error coming into the squeeze, not him. The whole dive had been dissected by the coroner, who had ruled it an unfortunate accident. And yet, why didn't the formal exoneration give him any comfort? Why had saying sorry to Brendan and Jonathan felt so fucking hollow?

'What do you want me to do, then, Nat?' he said wearily. '*Join you?* Go on, then, give me a sign.'

His echoes rolled away into nothing, and it occurred to Nash that if he wanted to live, the only way was to retrace his footsteps . : .

Four sharp tugs on his safety line . . . Natalie – no doubt worrying about where he'd got to. Reluctantly, he had backed up. Halfway out of the narrow squeeze, the slight drag on his regulator told him the two-litre mini tank was running low; its 400 litres of compressed air was only good for six minutes at this depth, but Nash loved the freedom it gave him to check out promising leads.

Back at camp, he elaborated on his findings over a strong cup of coffee.

'I think it'll keep going all the way to Cocklebiddy. But it's tight, Nat. I'll need the six-litre bale-out cylinder. Pushing it ahead of me, I reckon I can just about wriggle through there.'

'Just how small is this squeeze?' Natalie asked, anxiously.

'Remember the last time you had constipation?' He began to chuckle, when suddenly she burst into tears. He looked at her in bewilderment. 'What's wrong?'

'I was scared.' Her shoulders shook. 'Why did you just take off and leave me there?'

'Babe, it's OK . . .' He tried to take her hand.

'No, it's not OK. You said three or four minutes, and you were gone for nearly seven. Do you know what it's like not knowing if you're ever coming back?'

'What's got into you? I was just around the corner. It was nothing. Come on, Nat, you're overreacting.'

She was pale and reserved the next morning.

'Did you sleep badly?' he asked.

'I think I might be coming down with something.'

He let her brush off his suggestion that she stay in camp. The connection to Cocklebiddy was there – he knew it – and someone might beat him to it.

Giving Natalie a cheery thumbs up, he swapped his rebreather for the smaller six-litre tank and entered the passage. Exley's rule of thirds meant he had six minutes of exploring before he needed to return, with a third of his gas intact for contingencies.

Retracing his route to the dog-leg he tied a new line to the existing one.

Man, did he love breaking new ground!

Squeezing after his small tank, he made his way down a gradual slope, heart beating faster as the squeeze widened out into kinder dimensions. But around the next bend, it abruptly terminated in a narrow, impassable slot.

Frustrated, Nash lay on his side and shone his light through. To his amazement, there was nothing on the other side but a dark blue void. A chamber, and a bloody big one at that! Perhaps he'd been too hasty in his judgement. Yes, the slot was narrow, but it was also a good metre wide, and barely half that long.

337

His wrist-mounted dive computer told him he was right on the edge of the threshold. By rights, he should turn around, now. But how long would it take to slip through and get a photograph? An advantage to this was that he could reverse direction to return.

Nash moulded himself to the contours of the rock, shimmying forwards on elbows and knees, pushing the tank ahead of him. Negotiating a super-narrow squeeze like this was something like birth. He had just pushed the tank through when he felt the single tug on the line. It meant stop, and Nash frowned. It was unusual for cave divers to pull on a line, because it could easily get stuck or break.

Confined in the squeeze, Nash gave her an awkward two-tug response: code for 'I'm OK'. Then, gripping the edge of the slot with his free hand, he pulled himself forwards and popped out into open water.

The chamber was a vast half-hemisphere, so huge that in the periphery of his dive lights the deep blue water became impenetrable black. Nash was ecstatic. It was the elusive connection to Cocklebiddy!

He fired off a few quick shots with the GoPro and was turning to go when, suddenly, there were more tugs on the line. These were jerky, disconnected. Was she signalling 'Come up' or 'Emergency'? Nash gave four quick tugs to signal he was returning. The responding tugs had no discernible pattern. And they seemed weaker. A chill came over him.

Nash found re-entering the slot much more difficult than he'd anticipated. After two abortive attempts, he literally drove himself inside with powerful beats of his fins. Powering up the slope towards the dog-leg, he was stunned by a shimmering ball of silver.

It was a massive pocket of gas trapped at the apex of the sloping roof. At first, he couldn't understand it. His open-circuit bubbles of trimix would have contributed nothing like this amount, and Natalie was on a rebreather, with no bubbles shed at all . . .

Her helmet lights were ominously still. Her floating arms were lifeless. When he got to her, she was unresponsive, mouth slack on her regulator mouthpiece. With agonising clarity, Nash knew instantly what had happened. Of much smaller build, Natalie had been able to enter the squeeze with her rebreather and it had caught in the dog-leg. While she struggled to get free, her breathing loop hoses had torn, venting the contents of her oxygen and diluent tanks in a catastrophic gush.

Reaching around, he retrieved her secondary mouthpiece and forced it into her mouth. Depressing the button, he expected a blast of trimix from the bale-out tank on her thigh, but there was nothing. She'd taken off the backup to fit inside the squeeze.

Quickly, he pushed his mouthpiece between her slack lips. Her cheeks expanded with gas, but her eyes stared sightlessly.

With just a light shove, Nash pushed her lifeless body back through to the first chamber. That moment would haunt him forever. Her entrapment had been a relatively minor affair, but, exacerbated by sheer terror, she had not been able to back out.

It took Nash ten minutes to put on his rebreather and drag Natalie back up the tunnel to the main chamber. Inflating his buoyancy vest, he sped her to the surface. Dragging her out of the water, he laid her on her side to clear her airway.

While he searched for her pulse, he felt an intense itching break out all over his body. He couldn't leave her to go and decompress. No fucking way.

There was no pulse.

'C'mon, baby, c'mon,' he urged, rolling her on to her back.

Although it had been more than fifteen minutes since Natalie had drawn her last breath, Nash performed a relentless, brutal CPR, shouting, begging, praying and willing her to breathe.

Why had she missed or misinterpreted his awkward first response on the line? Why had she foolishly come in to check he was all right?

Why?

Chapter 33

Jayawijaya Province, Papua, confluence of the Hoosenbeck and Sepik rivers

Sweeping in from the west, the now beaten-up Jet Ranger banked around the ship in a long, lazy circle. On the quarter-deck, Kaboro drained his morning coffee and braced himself for a day of further compromise. At least he now knew what he'd sold his soul for. Sir Julius had called to explain the expedition was, in fact, a covert salvage job, vitally needed to replenish department coffers.

'The deal with General Suyanto is fifty-fifty, Kaboro, and not an ingot less. I want every man on that vessel watching that cargo like his life depended on it.'

For a moment, Kaboro wondered where the bullion was destined for. Probably the Bahamas or some other offshore tax haven. But it was no longer any concern of his. All that mattered now was saving Toby from the horrors of Bomona jail.

The Jet Ranger settled on the pad, and Kaboro's bubble of unease grew as two armed Indonesian soldiers and an officer alighted with Sura. He noted their red berets with distaste. *Kopassus.* Sir Julius hadn't mentioned their involvement.

On deck, he exchanged looks with Singkepe, who had marshalled the men.

'I don't like this,' the NCO muttered.

'Probably just more fingers in the pie. Keep the men calm.'

Singkepe's cool stare made Kaboro feel ashamed. It summed up his loss of face since the massacre, especially with his own crew, who would no longer meet his eyes.

Sura came up with the Indonesian officer and flashed that repellent TV smile.

'Good to see you, Lieutenant. This is Kapten Alatas. He's the local authority.'

The Indonesian officer made no attempt at a greeting. Not missing a beat, Sura pressed on brightly.

'Once we've finished logging in your weapons, you'll fly up with me, so I can explain the salvage operation to you. Your men will then follow in the kapten's gunship. We expect it to take a day or two at most.'

'Log in our weapons?'

'Sir Julius didn't tell you? We have extremely strict firearms laws in Indonesia. Relax, Lieutenant, your weapons will be quite safe on board.'

Kaboro could feel Singkepe's tension as well as his own. And when he didn't respond, Sura irritably took out a satellite phone.

'Very well, call Sir Julius. Explain to him how your sergeant managed to let a woman and a sick man escape into the jungle and jeopardise our mission.'

Slowly, Kaboro unclipped his Browning and deposited it on the deck.

'Come on, men, let's get it over with.'

Looking at the growing pile of old FN FAL rifles and M16s, Kaboro couldn't help but contrast their firepower with that wielded by the Kopassus troops, who were carrying high-tech Brügger & Thomet MP9 machine pistols with 30-round transparent box magazines. A curious choice for Papua, he thought, where rain, mud and impacts took a heavy toll.

Singkepe was last to surrender his beloved machine gun, and the doubt was evident in his stooped shoulders. Again, Kaboro felt ashamed. Sergeant Singkepe was a real soldier.

'Thank you,' said Sura. 'You've been most co-operative.'

Two things struck Kaboro simultaneously: one, his unarmed men were all lined up conveniently on the port side; and two, at some point the Kopassus men had levelled their machine pistols at their stomachs. He was about to raise the alarm when Sura jumped back.

The Kopassus men opened fire point-blank.

Rat tat tat tat tat tat . . .

Kaboro saw flashes and felt thunderous impacts before he even heard the rapid crackle. Stumbling back, he felt himself falling over the stanchion. The world turned upside down.

Thump!

Water closed over him, a final wet embrace. As the current took Kaboro, he felt only the bitter ache of remorse. He'd betrayed the men, and still he'd failed Toby.

The deck was awash with bodies leaking blood, and Sura had to step up on a ventilator to avoid it. Only one figure was still moving. Although riddled with 9 mm Parabellum rounds, the big NCO was doggedly trying to drag himself towards his abandoned weapon. Legs paralysed, he was propelling himself on his elbows, grunting with the effort.

'Now what do we have here?' Alatas drew his pistol with a laugh. 'A rare black orang-utan. The forest is over there, monkey man!'

His men giggled. A nervy, jittery kind of hysteria. Sura recognised they were high on killing, excitement and revulsion filling them in equal measure.

'Get on with it,' she said. 'We haven't got time for games.'

Alatas made his way gingerly across the blood-soaked deck. Taking careful aim so as to avoid ricochet or blood spray, he put two bullets into the top of Singkepe's head. The big man sighed and lay still. Alatas holstered his pistol.

'Throw them over the side,' he barked at the soldiers. 'Quickly now.'

Only when the sound of the Jet Ranger had dwindled to nothing did Saworno timidly make his way up the ladder. With shaking hands and a bone-dry mouth, he peered through the hatch into the passageway. From down in the engine room, the sounds of gunfire and screams had chilled his blood. He had been waiting in terror for someone to come down and kill him, too, because, aside from the lieutenant, he had no friends left on this ship.

'Kaboro?' he called tentatively into the passageway. 'Is anyone here?'

They had used a hose, but there were still pools of diluted blood drying on the deck. Saworno walked the perimeter of the ship and checked the milky water below. There was no sign of anyone. The current had taken them all.

The little engineer felt completely adrift. When he'd been offered this job, it had been a godsend; his retirement pension was inadequate, and there was the joy of returning to a job he'd loved, with the bonus of escaping his wife's nagging tongue. Saworno anxiously checked the sky for the chopper. Had they forgotten he existed, or did they just see him as part of the engines? Either way, it was clear they would want no witnesses.

He scanned the banks of the river. The dense riverine jungle was like an alien world, and he knew he would not survive it either.

'Your time is over,' he said aloud. He would not see his beloved wife, Amirah, his son, Intan, or his three grandchildren again.

The thought of them gave him pause. Even if he was consumed by the jungle, what if they took retribution on his family? *Inshallah.*

He was too old to fight, too old to run – and that only left one option. He had to get word out about the evil happening here.

Old muscles a-quiver, he began lowering the tender.

Chapter 34

Only by the dim light of a dying watch did Rob Nash know it was dawn outside. Even so, it took him more than an hour to summon up the courage to make the long swim back out of the darkness. The jade glow of the entrance pool welcomed him in like an old friend, but its comfort was fleeting. His sleepless vigil had provided no answers, and the hollow pit in the centre of his chest had returned.

Huddled on a rock, trying to get warm, Nash was startled by a single thunderclap high above the escarpment. The wet was coming. Although it would buy him time, the thought of diving inside the flooded guts of the great submarine looming over-head made him feel even more chilled.

A short time later, a huge green military chopper lumbered overhead, its enormous blades threshing down a thick rain of leaves and insects. Nash was baffled. Why all the subterfuge and needless death if General Suyanto had intended flying up here in the first place? Soon, he heard the snarl of chainsaws and guessed they had lowered men to cut a landing pad. There was a break, and then the chainsaws started up again. One helicopter left, another arrived, then Sura's Jet Ranger flew overhead back up to the cave.

All the anger and frustration at being trapped down here like an animal in a pit erupted, and he roared 'Bitch!' at the top of his lungs. It echoed around the sinkhole, and he yelled it again for good measure. The release of anger ignited something in his belly – a ball of radiant heat. Instinctively he knew it would need to burn a whole lot brighter if he was to survive.

There was activity above, lots of swearing in Indonesian, and then eventually a rope and harness were sent down. Nash was hauled up by a team of soldiers in red berets, who roughly manhandled him at gunpoint. He was stunned to see they had already erected a camp next to a huge helicopter gunship. In a mess tent, he was given a bowl of spicy goreng. After twenty-four hours without food, he ate fast, cooling his traumatised throat afterwards with a bottle of iced tea.

A shock of blonde hair through the fly screen drew his eye. He was already on his feet when Mia Carter was pushed inside the tent. She was in a man's collared shirt, which was too big, and her hiking trousers were torn and bloodstained.

'Mia!'

Her eyes lit up and he pulled her to him.

'Oh my God, Rob.' They embraced, and then she pulled back to search his face. 'What happened? You look . . . different.'

'So do you.' One side of her face was swollen, and she had a nasty black eye. 'Who did this – Boerman?'

A tremor of rage passed through him, and all he could think of was tearing the Afrikaner apart.

Two sweating soldiers carried Douglas in on a grubby canvas stretcher and placed him on the ground. The old pilot was gaunt and ravaged, but undoubtedly alive. Delighted, Nash dropped to one knee to embrace him.

'Uncle Frank! I wasn't sure I'd see you again.'

'I have some fine fellows and this angel of mercy to thank for that.' Douglas smiled at them both. 'Jeez, it's good to see you, laddie.' The old pilot was choking up, something Nash had never seen before.

There was movement outside, and the two soldiers came to attention as Sura and a well-dressed Indonesian officer with a supercilious air came in. Seeing the rage in Mia's eyes, Nash knew he had a new enemy.

'*This* is your illustrious cave diver?' Alatas chuckled sceptically. 'He looks more like a drowned rat.'

'The rain is coming, Kapten,' Sura said curtly. 'Mr Nash, you have your friends as promised. I want you inside that submarine, planning your strategy should diving become necessary. Be ready in an hour.'

A distant roll of thunder underlined her instructions and, with a glance at Alatas, she led him out of the tent. The two soldiers took up position outside and another chopper flew overhead.

Nash stared at Frank and Mia. 'Why didn't they just fly us up here?'

Mia explained these were not Suyanto's men.

'You think Sura is double-crossing her father?'

'I wouldn't put it past her,' muttered Douglas.

With an hour to spare, they filled in the gaps. For Mia, the realisation that the Ford Missions were built on Axis gold was painful to reconcile with their purpose. Nash tried to put her at ease.

'From the transcripts I read, Paul Ford's father was no Nazi. So maybe it was about making amends?'

'But wouldn't it have been better to just come clean? I mean, is it really charity when it's someone else's money?' Her voice caught in her throat. 'They burned the mission when we left. What a tragic and *stupid* waste.'

Nash told them about finding the sub, and what he knew of the Hoosenbeck system.

'There's a flooded exit passage at the bottom of the sinkhole. Last night I went in there looking for answers, but I didn't find any.'

Mia took his hand. 'They're not going to let us go, are they?'

'Any ideas, Frank?'

The old pilot lowered his voice. 'The border is only ten klicks away. If we snatch one of these helicopters, I could fly us to Tabubil in less than half an hour.'

Nash cleared his throat. 'Are you really in a fit state to fly?'

'Help me up.'

Together they got Douglas into a sitting position and, after checking no one was watching outside, pulled him to his feet. He swayed, but stood on his own, before taking a tentative couple of steps and turning around.

'Reckon I can make ten klicks.' He chuckled at Mia's amazement. 'Maybe we should find that old witch doctor and cut a patent?'

Nash grinned. 'What's to stop them following us over the border, Frank?'

Douglas let Mia ease him down before answering.

'Tabulil is the site of the Ok Tedi mine, one of PNG's richest. I can't see them coming in after us with a few hundred foreign mining workers watching on, can you?'

It was a logical destination, but Nash had plenty of doubts. Douglas may have been able to stand up, but he looked like a living skeleton wobbling on his last legs, and there was still the question of how they were going to pull it off.

350

Mia gave Nash a worried look. 'Is there any other way?'

'The gorge is a dead end hemmed in by thousand-metre cliffs. Even if Frank was healthy, they'd catch up with us long before we reached the Sepik. But I don't know how we're going to steal a chopper without a firefight. You said these Kopassus soldiers are special forces.'

'Trained killers,' confirmed Douglas. 'I counted twelve troopers and the gunship pilot. Then we've got Boerman, Sura, and Hartono and that scumbag Alatas.'

'Seems like long odds.' Mia shivered, wrapping her arms around her knees.

'But a dark night will go a long way towards evening things up. What we need is a diversion. Look for explosives, a gun, even fuel to start a fire. I heard them say they think the salvage will take a couple of days, so keep your eyes open and take the opportunity when it presents itself. When the shit hits the fan, don't hesitate. And if we can't get a chopper, you run, and you *keep* running.' Douglas looked steadily at Nash. 'And don't bloody worry about me – agreed?'

Taken at gunpoint to the sinkhole edge, Nash was amazed to see they had already constructed a scaffold of clamped steel props, which jutted out to support a heavy-duty block and tackle. A thin cable led down through the jumbled log pile. Sura was waiting with one hand on her hip and a walkie-talkie in the other.

'You will assist Jaap with the survey,' she instructed, as he was fitted with a head torch and harness, 'and report to me on the logistics of removing the gold and the opium.'

He blinked at her. 'Opium?'

'According to the manifest, there were three tonnes bound for pharmaceutical plants in Germany.' Impatiently, Sura indicated the end of the gorge, where dark clouds were massing over the escarpment. 'Should you prefer working dry, I suggest you stop asking questions and get a move on.'

They lowered him through the precarious log pile where, swaying from side to side, he caught sight of a sweaty Boerman bulging out of too-tight shorts and a vest. The Afrikaner had been busy constructing a plywood gantry, stayed with half a dozen steel cables, which led like a gangway to the split in the submarine's belly.

The haphazard affair swayed underfoot as Nash tentatively detached from the cable. Typical Boerman! And it was a sickening straight drop of fifty metres to the floor of the sinkhole, with one lousy guide rope to hang on to. Nash hadn't planned on looking down, but halfway across, he couldn't resist checking the crescent pool. Its area had already increased by a third as it crept across the sinkhole floor, and Nash realised the lonely beach he had spent the night on must now be completely flooded. Had he stayed another hour . . . he'd be dead.

The gantry bowed and creaked ominously as Boerman joined him. Taking a secure hold of Nash's harness, he bared his big teeth in a grin.

'I go, you go. Now, tell me what is happening down there.'

'It's raining in the mountains and the run-off is entering the Hoosenbeck Cavern and finding its way into the sinkhole from below.'

'*Ja, ja*, Nash, I know that, but *how*?'

352

'This sinkhole must be on a side branch of the underground river. As its volume increases, it's backing up and filling the sinkhole from below.'

Boerman's frown betrayed his incomprehension, and Nash used his hands to demonstrate.

'The underground river runs from the exit passage you almost drowned us in, remember? To the resurgence, two kilometres downstream.'

He did not share with Boerman what was going to happen once the subterranean discharge reached full capacity. Then, the Hoosenbeck Cavern would quickly overflow and pour down the old river bed; a torrent of white water would plummet into the sinkhole, and that huge passage he had free-dived would become a raging rocky drainpipe, at least a kilometre long! Just the thought of it made him shudder. Thank God he was never going back in there again.

'Enough chit-chat.' Boerman propelled him towards the submarine. 'Now we work.'

Bracing himself on the swaying plywood, Nash stared into the cavernous belly of the *I-403*. Inside the twin fused inner pressure hulls, dark passageways ran near-vertically towards the bow-like elevator shafts. There was another deck above this one, but from this angle he could not see far inside. Looking aft, he saw the hull had split along a bulkhead dividing the offset control room on the port side. The huge double-height space incorporated the base of the conning tower. A periscope dangled down, its bronze handgrips seemingly awaiting a captain's guiding hand. Porcelain gauges gleamed whitely through their rusting cases. He could see levers and valves, the frames of rotted seats and an illegible sign on the wall.

'You first, Nash. We'll start with the bow.'

Nash craned his head up. The long narrow tube was unnerving. God only knew what it would be like underwater.

The big man gave him a shove. 'Move your yellow ass, man.'

Placing his right boot on a severed hull plate, Nash grabbed a broken steel beam and climbed inside. The experience was disconcerting, like being in a condemned apartment building that had frozen while toppling over. Nash tested every rusty handhold as he climbed. Many proved unsafe, and it was slow going. Resting on a horizontal door frame, he looked inside a small cabin scoured out by raging water. By the remains of a single bed frame, he guessed it had belonged to an officer.

'*God verdomp*,' Boerman growled behind him. 'Hurry up.'

After fifteen metres and twelve empty cabins, the vertiginous corridor terminated in a bulkhead hatch which Nash didn't like the look of. Assuming that it could be opened, it looked poised to slam down on their heads, and he looked back enquiringly at Boerman.

'Get out of the way,' he snapped impatiently.

Nash crouched on the wall of the adjacent cabin and watched the big man take a lump hammer from his belt. Like a blacksmith, he pounded the steel surface while Nash put his fingers in his ears to muffle the deafening clangs. The big man now grabbed on to the handle, swung his legs up and locked them into the sides of the passageway. Letting rip with a stream of unintelligible Afrikaans, he began to exert pressure. Hidden

354

muscles on his arms popped out under the strain. With a shriek of protesting metal, the handle suddenly gave. With a grunt of satisfaction, Boerman began winding the door open.

Nash could hardly stand it. At any moment, he figured the heavy door would drop down and bat Boerman into well-deserved oblivion. But he was to be disappointed. As an internal hatch, it was hinged to swing *away* from the control room – so as to protect it in the event of an emergency – and Boerman needed all of his brute strength to shove it up and over.

Abruptly, the dank smell of a rarely visited basement washed over them.

'Fucking unbelievable!' Boerman exclaimed. 'The water never got in here!'

They were stepping back in time. The cabins were exactly as they had been abandoned more than seven decades ago. Beds were still made, albeit dangling from the wall, their linen black with mould. Threadbare caps and uniforms hung askew from hooks. Mottled pictures of loved ones, bags and belongings lay scattered in corners. Traditional Japanese items evoked the land of the rising sun: tatami mats powdering in a pile; shattered saki bottles and tea sets; a katana samurai sword.

Nash felt like a grave robber disturbing a tomb. Boerman had no such qualms, and eagerly rifled through the artefacts. In the next cabin, they found a mouldy black uniform with death's head badges, and a sleek machine pistol still shining under a thick layer of grease. Boerman picked it up and cocked the mechanism.

'A fucking' MP40 he breathed. 'It's in mint condition! I could pop you with it right now, Nash.'

The Afrikaner had a worrying look in his eye that Nash recognised from the massacre.

The last cabin in the compartment was the only one fitted with a solid steel door.

'It must be a strongroom,' said Boerman eagerly.

Perhaps expecting it to be locked, he wrenched the handle and pulled. The heavy door swung down like an axe and slammed into the wall with a loud bang, missing Nash by millimetres. Boerman nonchalantly clambered inside.

'Get up here, Nash. I need more light.'

The tiny room was clearly a security store. Rows of empty lockable drawers lay in piles. The big man began tossing them out, and they clattered and banged eerily down the long passageway.

'Ha!'

Boerman reached into the far corner. There, in the middle of his wide hand, a golden ingot gleamed under their torch lights.

'One bar?' Nash tried not to sound too pleased.

'There will be more.'

It was much easier to open the next bulkhead door. On the other side they found a dry passageway of storerooms filled with jumbled piles of swollen tins of ancient food, and sacks of rancid rice flour hardened into bricks. Nash spotted an intact bottle of blue kerosene and a carving knife in a galley, but with Boerman watching his every move, he could do nothing beyond note them for future reference.

The final bulkhead door led into the torpedo room. Here, every possible thing that could be dislodged had been flung backwards when the submarine crashed down. Nine-metre torpedoes had slid back out of their cradles like a collapsing stack of lumber, and the crumpled propellers were blocking the bulkhead door like a portcullis. Surveying the tangle of lethal debris above his head, Nash was amazed it hadn't blown.

Boerman led them back down to the second section and located a side door, which gave them access to the port-side pressure hull without having to go all the way back to the split amidships. There was no corresponding strongroom on the lower port side, but they found a ladder accessing the top deck, which had also remained dry, and from here were able to double back around to the upper starboard side.

'You see,' Boerman said happily, standing before an identical strongroom door. 'What did I tell you?' Finding it locked, he beamed. 'Now we're in business.'

After a nerve-racking climb down, they returned to the gantry below the split hull and clambered into the ghostly control room. Here, even Boerman could make no impact on the bulkhead doors leading aft.

'No matter,' he reasoned, spitting on his inflamed palms. 'We'll cut our way in to the opium.'

Then he ran untethered to the end of the gantry. Victoriously holding up the ingot of gold and the MP40 he expanded his mighty chest and roared '*Banzai*!' at the top of his lungs.

Chapter 35

The Kopassus command post was a spacious TNI standard-issue twenty-man army tent with sealed floor and ridge poles. A desk and a computer had been set up, along with several folding chairs, a large whiteboard, two powerful fans and crates of assorted equipment. Outside, a generator purred quietly.

'You've done well at short notice,' Sura told Alatas, who was pouring them drinks at the small fridge. 'This is very civilised.'

It was strange how the man always looked like a well-pressed peacock, no matter the circumstances. She supposed it helped having a corporal as a personal valet.

'Your father doesn't do things by half. Neither do we.'

'Is that inter-service rivalry, or something more primitive?'

He passed her a glass of iced tea. 'You know, I can't get that night in Jayapura out of my mind.' His eyes gleamed over the rim of the glass. 'Perhaps I might find you in my tent this evening?'

Sura produced a wicked smile. 'Sounds tempting. But I won't be able to relax until we have what we came for. Perhaps we can celebrate then?'

Alatas drained his glass and banged it down on the table. 'Well, we'd best get this show on the road.'

The tent filled with his troops, who stood at the back while Rob Nash and Mia Carter were seated on chairs in the front row. Beside Alatas, Jaap towered over the whiteboard, his face grim. Sura knew he was getting jealous again, and that Alatas's familiarity was the cause.

Alatas cleared his throat. 'Rain is imminent, so listen carefully to Mba Suyanto because I want this matter expedited as a matter of extreme urgency.'

With a suggestive grin, he passed her the whiteboard marker, which she promptly tossed across to the glowering big man.

'Jaap, would you please take us through the plan of attack?'

Stooping down, Boerman drew a narrow bucket to represent the sinkhole, and then the outline of the curved submarine within. This elicited a few sniggers from the back row.

'Are you boys or men?' Sura stared them into silence.

Boerman added two vertical lines bisecting the submarine's outline.

'There are two decks inside each pressure hull.' Then he drew a cross on the upper starboard side, about halfway to the bow. 'The gold store is here, but it's a long way from the split in the hull, over here. So, we'll blow a hole in the side, right next to the gold store, to expedite access and retrieval.' With the back of the marker he tapped the lower half of the submarine. 'While we weren't able to access the stern, we know there are compartments full of opium. So, we will also cut a hole just aft of the rear deck gun.'

'Thank you, Jaap. Are there any questions?'

Nash promptly put his hand up. 'Are you seriously proposing to use explosives near the torpedo room? It's barely ten metres away.'

Jaap frowned. 'It will be a controlled demolition, Nash. Do you have a problem with that?'

Alatas raised an eyebrow. 'How many torpedoes are we talking about?'

Sura consulted her notes on the *Sentoku* weapon systems.

'Assuming none were fired, twenty half-tonne warheads, plus several tonnes of bombs, and in the hangar, there are light torpedoes for the seaplanes.'

'That's at least thirteen tonnes of high explosive!' Alatas turned to Jaap and shook his head. 'Are you barking mad? You will cut your way inside with the oxy – do you understand?'

Jaap flushed.

'That means no explosives! Acknowledge.'

'*Ja, ja*, I heard you the first time.'

Sura shot Jaap a warning look before checking her watch.

'It's already 1700 hours, which means we only have two hours of daylight left.'

In a loud voice, she issued their instructions. A small group would ferry the oxyacetylene kit into the submarine so Boerman could cut through before dark. Another would relieve Ricki up at the cave. The rest would continue building the winch to remove the opium. Sura abruptly broke off as she realised the entire Kopassus contingent of thirteen was present.

'Who, pray tell, is guarding Frank Douglas?'

Two soldiers at the rear stared at each other in alarm, then jumped to their feet and dashed out.

'This is unacceptable.' Sura glanced angrily at Alatas.

'More like fucking incompetent,' murmured Jaap cheerfully.

They heard yelling and then a moment later, one of the terrified guards burst back inside.

'*Dia tertidur! Dia tertidur!*'

'He's asleep?' Alatas guffawed. 'Well, no harm done.'

'I expect better, Kapten,' Sura seethed.

He gave an indifferent laugh. 'Shall I order a firing squad? Now, what say you and I partake of something stronger. I have some very nice Scotch whi—'

His words were drowned out by an almighty thunderclap that seemed to roll across the roof of the world. Heavy drops began thumping into the canvas, as if they wanted to punch right through it. Within seconds, the camp was enveloped in a deafening tropical downpour.

Sura silently cursed her luck. The wet had arrived.

Cursing, grunting and shouting, Nash and two soldiers hauled, pushed and fought the wet and slippery oxyacetylene kit up the long vertical passageway, using nothing but a short knotted rope and raw muscle power. It was exhausting, difficult and dangerous, not least because they had prudently positioned Nash below, but at least it cost them two crushed fingernails and a broken thumb when he slipped, leaving them no choice but to take the strain of the massive cylinder.

It took them almost an hour to manhandle it to the top deck, where Boerman impatiently waited. Free of the awful burden, Nash slumped against the inverted floor and tried to catch his breath.

'Maybe next time you'll keep your big mouth shut,' snapped Boerman, pulling on a welding helmet. 'Now fuck off and give me some space.'

Only too glad to escape the noxious fumes, Nash joined the soldiers on the gantry and waited in the driving rain, which was whipping across them in sheets. The reflected glow of the cutting torch could be seen in the top deck cavity, and the occasional spark made it all the way down to the flimsy platform, before sputtering out in the puddles.

The double hull was made of high-tensile steel, and Boerman was cutting for almost half an hour before a loud banging erupted inside the submarine.

What is he doing? thought Nash, before flinching at the horrific grinding sound of a heavy steel plate sliding down the outer skin of the submarine.

He realised Boerman had knocked the hull section outwards.

The man is completely insane.

In the near darkness, Nash caught a momentary glimpse of its bulk falling towards them. It seemed inevitable that it would smash the gantry to pieces and send them plummeting to their deaths, but with a juddering crash the sheet of curved steel bounced off the last jammed log, somehow missing the steel stays before plunging to the bottom of the sinkhole, where it landed with a gigantic splash.

Nash's ears pricked up at that.

'Keep it coming, you bastard,' he urged the rain clouds above.

While he had absolutely no intention of diving, the chaos of the rising water was going to help them escape.

'*What?* What did you say?'

Over the torrential rain hammering the tent, it was impossible to hear the jabbering voice of her Jakarta contact, so Sura pressed the satellite telephone to her ear and buried her head under a thick towel.

What she heard made her cringe.

Alatas looked up from his camp chair.

'News?'

'I've just received word that my father left for Papua an hour ago.'

The merriment in his eyes abruptly died and was replaced by an intense probing stare.

'You told me he was *under control.*' A ruthless undertone had crept into his silky voice, and for the first time she understood the reputation he had won in East Timor silencing the opposition.

Sura kept her face composed. She had made no mention of falling out with her father. Why risk spooking Alatas and his master?

'He must have got wind of something from Sir Julius. You know he's no fool.'

Alatas reluctantly tore his gaze away and swilled his whisky around before draining the glass. He brooded for a moment, then shrugged.

'Well, it's nothing we can't handle.'

Sura breathed out slowly. 'How so?'

'He won't reach Jayapura until later tonight, and I can assure you we won't be giving him a lift. If he has the balls to invade our turf, he will require helicopters from his base in Sorong, which will take six hours just to reach Jayapura and refuel.'

Oh, he has the balls, Kapten, thought Sura grimly. *In fact, they're probably waiting for him at Jayapura already.*

Alatas got to his feet and reached for the bottle of whisky.

'Worst-case scenario, I can't see him getting here for *at least* twenty-four hours. That's ample time to salvage the gold and some of the opium.' Refilling his glass, he gave her a smile. 'You don't even have to risk him interdicting your ship. I can fly you back to Jayapura with your share of the gold.'

'While you depart with three tonnes of opium worth at least thirty million US dollars? I'd hardly call that fair.'

Alatas shrugged. 'Assuming it's there.'

'Oh, it's there, Kapten. Doctor Ford was very clear they never touched it.'

'Sura, look around you. This operation has been awfully expensive. And don't forget, we are sacrificing a quarter tonne of our share to expose your father's dirty deal with Sir Julius.'

'Oh, Kapten –' she smiled mockingly – 'just how much does your boss think the presidency of Indonesia is worth? I think Kopassus is doing very nicely indeed.'

His mouth became a thin line. 'And I think you're greedy.'

Sura shook her head. To live the rest of her life without constantly looking over her shoulder meant bulletproof identities, American and European addresses, expensive round-the-clock security.

'Kapten, you do understand that there is no going back for me after this. My father will never stop seeking revenge, especially if he loses the presidency.'

Sura suddenly felt cold at the thought of his imminent arrival.

'I hate to see a beautiful creature afraid.' Alatas came over and put his hands around her slim waist. 'Why not stay with me, Sura? I have a remote villa in Brunei no one knows about – you could live there like a queen. Let *me* keep you safe.'

She let Alatas nuzzle her neck. As his big hand slid up between her thighs, she pushed back, eliciting a small groan from him.

Yes, you'd like that, wouldn't you – at least for a while? I'd be a campaign trophy, and then, when the shine wore off, you could put two neat bullets in my head, and no one would ever know.

Still, there was no harm in keeping Alatas keen. With her father on the warpath, only Kopassus had the muscle to delay him while she made her getaway.

Heavy squelching boots approached the tent, and Sura pulled away a split second before a rain-soaked Jaap appeared in the doorway.

'Don't you know how to knock?' Alatas snapped.

Boerman's eyes widened as he took in their body language.

'What is it, Jaap?' she asked quickly.

With a face like stone, he held out two gleaming ingots.

'We're inside the bullion store. And it's all there.'

Chapter 36

A drenched Nash crawled woodenly into the four-man tent and collapsed between Mia and Douglas, partially visible in the light thrown from the command post.

'They've f-found it,' he reported through chattering teeth. 'Upper d-deck.'

Mia felt his back. 'You're chilled to the bone!'

She helped him peel off his soaked clothes, wrapped him in a blanket, and vigorously rubbed warmth into his frozen limbs.

'Bet the bastards had no hot food for you, either,' Douglas growled. 'Here, laddie, get this into you.'

It was a precious bar of chocolate. Nash was too famished to ask where it had come from, and wolfed it down. Infused with ginger and chilli, its sweet heat helped revive him enough to explain that with the sinkhole floor awash, the Indonesians would not risk getting the gold out until first light.

'This may well be our last night, and I couldn't get hold of a diversion.'

'Is this diversion enough for you?'

Nash gasped as the cold steel of the MP40 was pressed into his hands.

'Jesus, Frank. How the hell did you get hold of this . . .?' He broke off as he realised Douglas must have got it during the briefing.

'It was under Boerman's cot,' Douglas chuckled. 'I couldn't manage the M60, but this thing is cleaned, loaded and ready to go.'

'What if he finds it gone?'

Nash had a vision of all hell breaking loose at any moment.

'Then we make our stand. But I suspect he's as buggered as you. So, I say we make our move first thing in the morning, when the main squad starts breakfast. I'll take down the two jokers outside, you two grab their weapons, and together we fill that mess tent full of lead.'

Nash bit his lip. The whole thing sounded like a fantasy.

'Wouldn't it be less risky to take them by surprise? Why not tonight, while they're sleeping?'

Douglas shook his head. 'They're spread out over four separate tents. By the time we deal with one, they'll be coming at us from three sides. No, we need them bunched. And it will be daylight, which will help me find my way around the cockpit.'

'Can you really fly that gunship?' asked Mia.

'Trust me, kid, I can fly anything.'

It was essential they be able to fire the Kopassus weapons, and Douglas painstakingly explained how to cock a Brügger & Thomet MP9 submachine gun, manage its crossbar safety, and go with short bursts at the body, no matter what setting the fire selector was on when they picked it up. Nash was amazed by his knowledge.

'How the hell do you know all this, Frank?'

He laughed briefly. 'Hanging around with mercenaries, there are only two topics of conversation.'

Mia had gone very quiet, and Nash asked her what was wrong.

'I'm sorry, but I'm not sure I can do this. And if I get it wrong, we're all dead.' Her voice was shaking.

'Do nothing and we're dead anyway.' Douglas delivered this gently. 'Look, kid, I know you're about saving lives, but this is kill or be killed. Personally, I'd rather be around to feel bad about it afterwards. How about you?'

'OK.'

'Robbie?'

'I'm in.'

Douglas placed his hands on their shoulders.

'Chin up. Our advantage is total surprise, because they don't see us as a threat. No second thoughts in the morning. When we go, we go.'

Nash lay there, trying to still his racing mind. It felt like madness to even think of taking on such highly trained troops, but he knew it was the fear talking. The Nazis had managed to kill a million innocent people at Treblinka with a tiny detachment of thugs, using fear and confusion to string people along who were desperately clinging to the belief that salvation might be just round the next corner. In contrast, they knew salvation wasn't coming, but knowing that didn't change the fact that killing people – even those who meant to kill you – was fundamentally abhorrent.

Mia reached out and took his hand.

'I'm too scared to sleep, Rob. Will you please hold me?'

She nestled in with her back against his stomach, and he placed his arm around her waist. They listened to the rain steadily drumming down, and then Douglas began to snore. The sensation of Mia's slim body in his arms was bittersweet. She was utterly delightful, a beautiful woman with brains and guts in equal measure. But he couldn't let himself dwell on hopes for a future.

'Have you ever anyone killed anyone?' she whispered. 'Sorry, I keep thinking there must be a way to just talk our way out of this.'

Jonathan's accusing stare came to his mind.

'That depends on who you talk to.'

She was silent for several moments, and then rolled over to face him.

'Rob, Frank told me Natalie's death was an accident. So why are you still blaming yourself? I've felt this . . . *torment* . . . in you since the day we met.'

Had they been anywhere else, he might have – no, *would* have – opened up to her, because after last night in the cave, the doubt eroding him from within had returned with a vengeance. But he couldn't dwell on Natalie, not now . . .

Suddenly, Mia kissed him hard on the lips. Then she placed his hand on her right breast. The shock of its firm weight, and especially her desire, ignited something primal in him. Devouring her succulent mouth, and running his hand down her flat stomach, Nash wanted to spread her wide and drive into her – for it was probably their last night on earth – but then Douglas began making that awful choking sound which heralded a new cycle of snoring.

'Do you ever feel like you can't catch a break?' she whispered.

Grudgingly glad of a circuit breaker, Nash chuckled softly.

'I don't know how he does it.'

'Sleep at a time like this . . . or ruin ours?'

He kissed her lips tenderly. 'I want to know you, Mia.'

'You will.' She stroked his face, ran her hands through his hair. 'You will.'

Nash was still hearing those sweet words when he was woken at two thirty with savage kicks to the soles of his feet.

'You come now!' barked the panicking soldier, his torch flashing around the inside of the tent as he stamped his feet in the mud. 'Get dressed. Hurry!'

Douglas reached for the MP40, but Nash stayed his arm. 'Wait.'

Shielding his eyes from the dazzling torch beam, he asked the soldier what was wrong.

'Mba Suyanto says you come now . . . too much water!'

The rain was falling in solid curtains. Continuous thunder and pulsing flashes of reflected lightning told of the maelstrom in the mountains above. As they squelched up to the command tent, Nash could see Sura in animated discussion with the murderous Indonesian officer who had beaten Mia up.

'I will fly the first load down tomorrow and send Ricki back for the second –'

She broke off as Nash stepped inside. The overhead lantern light accentuated the fatigue on her face, and for the first time he saw her real age.

'Mr Nash, the water has already reached the stern of the submarine. How much time do we have until the sinkhole fills?'

'It will depend on how much rain falls.'

'Jaap?'

In the corner of the tent, Boerman sat like a statue in a collapsing chair.

'We've had 175 millimetres in the last three hours.'

Nash pointed skywards. 'It's the mountain catchment you need to worry about. The sinkhole is filling due to back pressure in the subterranean system. Which means the level of the Hoosenbeck Cavern will be rising, too.'

'And if it overflows the cave?' Alatas asked this archly.

'You mean *when* it overflows the cave? Then it's going to barrel down this river bed in a raging torrent, and then you'll have it coming from above *and* below.'

As the Indonesians glanced at each other, an opportunistic gambit popped into Nash's mind.

'You can't stop it,' he emphasised. 'It's just a matter of time, and I reckon sooner rather than later.'

'There's still three hours until dawn.' Sura gave Alatas a worried frown.

'I'd monitor the cave,' advised Nash casually. 'Get a sense of how fast it is rising, then plan how much time you have left.'

Boerman looked immediately suspicious, and Nash thought he'd overdone it, but then Alatas nodded.

'Yes . . . that sounds logical. How would you do that?'

'Construct a depth marker in the cave. It will let you estimate time and volume on the overflow.'

Nash briefly explained what materials he would need.

'Jaap, take him up there now,' Sura commanded. 'Get it done.'

'And take these men with you, too.' Alatas nodded at the bedraggled guards outside. 'Leave one with a radio to report on the water level in the cave.'

Clamping a paw on Nash's shoulder, Boerman propelled him outside to a supply tent to collect the materials he had listed: timber, tools, synthetic cord, gaffer tape and a measure. Finding these under flashlight was not easy in the chaos of plastic crates, and Boerman grew increasingly irate at the Indonesians' lack of organisation.

'Call yourselves professional soldiers? It's a fucking disgrace.'

At the rear of the tent was the weapons rack Nash had been hoping for. But the proximity of the guards made it impossible to investigate. Then Boerman came to his rescue.

'Are you two going to just fucking stand there?' he bellowed. '*Membantu kita menemukan gaffer tape!*'

As the guards began opening crates, Nash slipped to the back of the tent. His plan required a concealed weapon – a pistol or a knife with which to ambush these three en route to the cave. With the deafening thunder and the rain bucketing down, no one would hear the shots or screams. He could improve their odds and sneak back down here before dawn.

His heart soon sank. While three automatic rifles and a pump-action shotgun were perfect for their dawn attack, there was nothing remotely concealable here.

Nash glanced out at Sura's illuminated command tent. What if he dropped Boerman and the guards fast . . . would that give him time to take out the leadership? Frank could then help take out converging guards in the chaos . . .

Nash ran a hand down the smooth barrel of the shotgun.

Pick it up and there's no turning back. It might not even be loaded . . .

373

On the other hand, a better chance might not present itself. He was poised to commit himself when his fingers encountered the thin security cable running through the trigger guard. He'd almost blown it!

He was easing away when his foot encountered a low wooden box. With Boerman and the Indonesians still cursing among the crates, Nash reached in.

Jackpot!

Beneath his fingertips lay a cluster of heavy steel balls. Casually, he transferred a hand grenade to the deep pocket of his hiking pants.

He was reaching for a second when Boerman growled, 'Come here, Nash.'

Heart in mouth, he approached, blinking in the light of the big man's head torch. Then Boerman shoved a bag of materials and a three-metre length of timber into his arms.

'Let's go, genius.'

They trudged up the gorge in the rain and darkness, and the grenade seemed to grow heavier with every step. The big man led them alongside the river bed, now knee-deep in storm water run-off, with the guards bringing up the rear, but what Nash needed was a tight grouping. And what then? After pulling the pin, would he have three or five seconds? And how exactly did you even pull the pin? Wasn't there a safety catch? He considered taking the grenade back to Douglas – it would be perfect for taking out the crowded mess tent – but the bulge looked like a baseball in the pocket of his soaking pants, and they always searched him before letting him get back inside the tent.

As they clambered up to the ledge to the cave mouth, the rain-streaked Jet Ranger appeared mournfully out of the gloom. What had Sura said just before he came in? *I will fly the first load down tomorrow and send Ricki back for the second.*

Nash's mouth went dry as he understood what he needed to do.

After the driving rain, it was eerily silent inside the Hoosenbeck Cavern. A silence loaded with threat. Nash fancied he could feel the vibration in the rock beneath his boots, of all those hidden tonnes of water flowing through the exit passage.

While Boerman shone his torch on the ledge they'd used as the entry point, Nash removed the roll of cord from the bag and transferred it to his pocket. The knowledge of what he was about to do made every movement feel artificial, and he was sure the guards would read his intent like a book.

'It's come up at least a metre.' Boerman sounded worried. 'What now?'

'Carve depth marks on the timber,' replied Nash. 'Then stack rocks around it, so it doesn't float away.'

Boerman stared at him incredulously. 'We came all the way up here for *that*? Why the fuck would you bother, when one of these dickheads can simply stand here and watch?'

It was completely unnecessary. But Nash had guessed rightly that Sura would go for any semblance of control, and take comfort in measured increments.

He shrugged. 'You want to go back down there and tell her, then?'

Angrily, Boerman picked up the length of timber from the ground and pulled out his combat knife. As Nash turned to go, he snarled, 'Where the fuck do you think you're going?'

'We need rocks and they're outside.'

'*Tinggal bersamanya*,' Boerman snapped. *Stay with him.*

It was clear the Kopassus troopers didn't take kindly to receiving orders from a foreign mercenary who referred to them as dickheads, nor did they fancy another drenching in the pouring rain. While they sheltered in the mouth of the cave, Nash located a large rock and carried it back inside to dump beside Boerman. After his third load, the guards lit up cigarettes and Nash seized his chance.

Scurrying over to the Jet Ranger, he rolled underneath. With trembling fingers, he pulled out a length of the synthetic cord, tied one end to the grenade's ring pull, and experimentally tugged. It wouldn't budge until he removed the safety clip preventing accidental removal, which took another ten seconds to figure out by feel.

Nash glanced anxiously over his shoulder. The glowing cigarette ends in the cave mouth were still stationary, but for how much longer? It was tempting to just wrap the cord a few times around a skid, but he could not risk his handiwork being discovered in daylight. At last he found a convenient niche to secrete the grenade, in a bracket weld where the landing skid braces intersected.

He had just unravelled the remaining cord when a guard yelled, '*Di mana dia?*'

Flashlights swept back and forth in the rain. Rolling on to his stomach, Nash wrapped the free end of the cord several times around a large flat rock, before tying it off with a hasty half hitch. They were almost on him now. Keeping the helicopter between them, he crawled a few metres, undid his trousers, and squatted a split second before the flashlight beams found him.

'*Jangan bergerak!*' an angry voice challenged.

'Sorry, had to go!'

There was a pause before they averted their beams.

'*Cepat* . . . hurry up!'

Nash waited a few moments, then he stood up and buckled his trousers.

'What the fuck took you so long?' Boerman challenged when they returned to the cave.

'Call of nature.' Nash dropped two more rocks down with a thud. 'You want some more?'

The big man had finished carving increments on the timber staff and had positioned it on the ledge. Even as Nash watched him add the rocks to the pile, the water was visibly creeping higher.

'Enough of this bullshit.' Boerman wiped his hands on his trousers. 'If it floats away, one of these dickheads can go for a swim and fetch it.'

Chapter 37

'Poetic justice,' Douglas murmured in the gloom of the tent. 'I like it. And if our attack goes to plan, we can always disarm your party trick and fly the Jet Ranger out of here. Would be less explaining to do on the other side of the border, too.'

Douglas was right. Not only did they have to escape from Indonesian Papua; they ran the very real risk of retribution in PNG, and could not count themselves safe until they were off the island completely.

Nash looked down at the shadowy form of Mia, fast asleep under the coarse blanket, and felt like crawling in beside her. Then he thought of all those crazy night surfs, how he had wished for death to take away the pain. Now death was staring him in the face, he realised how much he wanted to live again.

Douglas seemed to divine this in the darkness.

'You'll do fine tomorrow, laddie.'

'You think so?'

'I know so – you're a chip off the old block.'

'Did you two see much action, Frank?' Nash was curious, because his father had never spoken of the war.

'Hell yeah. We got strafed and bombed, mostly from trigger-happy Yanks, but your dad never flinched. I used to call him the Party-Pooper, because when the bullets were flying, he was pretty much the same as when we were docked in port.' Douglas grunted to himself. 'The thing about your dad is he never took short cuts, and he always planned meticulously. Sound familiar? Of course, I was the exact opposite. A hothead, good for a bar fight, not so good when it came to strategy.' Douglas chuckled nostalgically. 'Hard to believe we were such good mates.'

'I always wondered why you two drifted apart.'

'Peter grew up and I didn't. That's why I stayed in the navy. But then I pushed it too far. Flew drunk and crashed. An airman died. Dishonourable discharge.' In the near darkness, Douglas looked away. 'No one in the service gave me the time of day after that. Your mum and dad, though, they kept a seat at the table . . . I just hope it wasn't charity.'

'It wasn't, Frank.'

There was a long pause with just the rain drumming down.

'Robbie, I'm so sorry I got you into this. I really am.'

'Crazy as it sounds, Frank, I'd rather be here. When you came, I was in a very dark place. I'm not out of it yet, but I can see a chink of light. Enough to make me believe there is an end to it – and maybe a beginning, too.'

Douglas surprised him by ruffling his hair. 'Robbie, lad, if I've learned one thing in this life, you've got to forgive yourself before you can move on. No one else can do it for you.'

Work had begun before dawn, with shouted orders and the rumble of generators powering up. Portable tower lights cast a strange yellow glow over the scene, making it look like some bleak pit mining operation from the nineteenth century.

And all the while, the rain kept tumbling down under black skies.

'Well, that's torn it,' muttered Douglas, peering through the tent flap at the bustle of activity.

'Plan B, then.' Nash was dry-mouthed with fear and anticipation.

Douglas turned to them. 'When Sura's chopper blows, I'll come out firing. So, take your chance wherever you are, because you won't get another.'

Mia looked at each of them in dismay.

'This is not a plan. It's going out in a blaze of glory.' Her eyes searched Nash's. 'There *must* be another way.'

'If there is, you've got about fifteen seconds to think of it.' Douglas cocked the MP40. 'Our friends are coming.'

He lay back down on his stretcher and pulled the blanket over the weapon.

Nash put his hand on Mia's arm. 'We're out of options.'

Mia flung her arms around him, then Douglas.

'Goodbye, Frank.'

Nash embraced him, too.

'Don't look back,' Douglas whispered. 'Fight, run ... it doesn't matter – just fucking survive, you hear me?'

In two gleaming yellow piles, the gold bullion was stacked on a blue tarpaulin. It was a production line: Boerman was down inside the submarine, jemmying open the stubborn drawers, passing the precious bars out to a soldier, who placed them in a steel bucket. This was carefully hauled up, ten kilos at a time, through the hole cut in the submarine's hull, to the sinkhole edge. From there the bars were passed, one by one, along a line of soaking wet soldiers, with Sura and Alatas there to ensure none found their way down a pocket.

Kitted up in his drysuit, Nash watched on with Mia. He sensed their moment was passing. The end of the gorge was invisible in thick grey cloud, and he feared Sura would be unable to fly out.

Making matters worse, she was about to put them to work.

Clutching a walkie-talkie, Sura squelched across in an oversized poncho.

'The Hoosenbeck has risen a metre in the last fifteen minutes and is close to the lip. You two will be roped down to help salvage the opium.'

Nash exchanged glances with Mia. This was a disaster. Frank would be left fighting on his own, and they would be trapped like rats in a bucket.

'Take your gear for when it becomes necessary to dive, Mr Nash. Should you attempt an escape, your girlfriend will be shot.' Sura smirked briefly at Mia. 'Are we clear? Your fate is in your own hands.'

It was a pantomime; they all knew this woman intended to kill them. Staring into Sura's disingenuous eyes, Nash realised he was glad that she was going to die. A flicker of something entered her expression – some flash of intuition – and he quickly got back in character and looked down.

'Yes, perfectly.'

With fingers clumsy from cold and nerves, Nash strapped on his preferred rebreather. Clipping mask and fins to his weight belt, he also decided to take a small pony tank of emergency compressed air. The size of a large vacuum flask, it contained just 540 litres, good for about nine minutes at shallow depth. Its purpose was to allow Mia to hide underwater, because if Sura's numbers were correct, around sixteen Olympic-sized swimming pools were pouring into the Hoosenbeck Cavern every half an hour, and they were going to be inundated at any moment.

A powered winch had been set up to access the stern of the submarine. There was no harness; they were simply shoved into a cargo net which creakingly lifted them up.

'The overflow will hit us very soon,' Nash told Mia as they were lowered into the vine-shrouded overhang. 'Whether Sura flies or not, all we can do now is buy time –' He broke off as frigid run-off from the sinkhole edge coursed over them and made her gasp. 'Use this pony tank and get underwater. Stay shallow and use the submarine as cover. Use the sinkhole walls, too, find underhangs to stay out of sight.'

'I can't stop thinking about Frank.' He could feel her trembling against him.

'He'll know what to do.'

Nash felt terrible leaving the old man, too. He figured Douglas would take as many as he could to give them a chance. But would it be anything like enough?

They passed through the log pile and between their dangling feet the flattened stern of the *I-403* came into view, a rusty peninsula surrounded by jade-green water. A soldier was squatting by a square hole cut aft of the deck gun with the oxy. Dense mist rose up as the water met the warmer air.

'See how turbid it is?' Nash said, as they swayed back and forth. 'They won't be able to see you underwater.'

'But how are we ever going to get out of here?'

Mia was staring, wide-eyed, at the vertical walls and the impossible spectacle of the inverted submarine. Her fear was mounting with good reason, but he needed her not to panic.

'It's going to fill fast, remember?' He kissed her cheek quickly and tried not to think of water temperature and all the other variables ranged against them. 'Just focus on staying alive, and we'll float to the top.'

A young NCO with darting eyes helped free them from the tangles of the cargo net – no easy task at a twenty-five-degree angle. Rapping Nash's equipment with the barrel of his pistol, he yelled, 'No room! No room!'

Nash quickly hooked the rebreather over the breech of the deck gun and wedged his fins into a raised edge of broken plate. With a nod to Mia, he clipped the pony tank on, too.

'You go, you go!' The NCO waggled his pistol at the rough-cut hole. It looked mean, dark and dangerous. 'You go, you go!'

The NCO's voice rose in pitch. For a moment Nash seriously contemplated trying to seize the weapon, but then he saw the upturned face of another armed soldier waiting inside the submarine.

The hole was less than a metre square, and Nash had to squeeze his broad shoulders through before dropping into thigh-deep, freezing water. LED lights illuminated a steep and dangerously corroded passageway which ran on through another bulkhead. Then Mia's shapely legs appeared. After helping her down, Nash took her by the hand, and they followed the soldier, sloshing through the water until they stepped through a bulkhead door into a vast engine bay stinking of grease which, thankfully, was still dry.

The twin engines contained within the double-height compartment were primitive-looking beasts, each the size of a medium truck, and Nash was astounded to see a second pair in the adjoining hull through the interconnecting hatch. No wonder this leviathan had been able to power its way around the world.

They stepped aside to let two troopers carrying plywood tea chests pass by. The opium within gave off a thick cloying smell that was resinous and earthy, reminiscent of hashish, although more bittersweet. Through the bulkhead door ahead, they saw another soldier hoisting a tea chest to his shoulder.

'*Ayolah!*' he yelled at his comrade who was escorting them. '*Percepat!*' *Hurry up!*

The twin compartments were stacked from floor to ceiling with hundreds of tea chests. One had broken open, and spilling from its hessian liner were black five-kilo balls of raw gummy opium. After seven decades curing in airtight storage, it had intensified in strength. Already light-headed in the pungent fumes, Mia warned Nash to avoid the gooey mess, lest the opiate-laden oil be absorbed by his skin.

'What was this used for?' Nash asked Mia as they lugged their loads back.

'Morphine,' she grunted. 'It must be worth a fortune.'

Rain was falling heavily through the ragged square of daylight when they reached the stern. The water was now lapping their waists, and in the press of slippery bodies passing up tea chests, Nash's claustrophobia felt like thick treacle slowly filling him up inside.

They went back for another load, and when they returned, the water was noticeably higher. A nervy trooper tried to argue his way out, but the NCO angrily ordered him back. Nash knew the stern would be underwater in ten minutes. What worried him more was the overflow. When that hit, anyone stuck down here without air or lights was doomed.

'We've got to get out of here,' he told their guard, rapping on the curved steel above.

'*Lebih dalam*! *Lebih dalam*!' added Mia for emphasis. *Deeper! Deeper*!

This time she could barely keep her head above the frigid black water. The Indonesians, who were of even shorter stature, were panicking.

'*Biarkan kami keluar bajingan*!' they screamed in unison. *Let us out, motherfucker!*

The NCO yelled at them to be quiet so he could hear the walkie-talkie. At last, he nodded, then kneeled to pull the first man out. When it was their turn, Nash pushed Mia up, and then she helped pull him out.

They stood upslope of the shivering troopers while the cargo net, laden with tea chests, ascended in the driving rain. Nash's eyes were fixed on the jade-green water creeping swiftly towards the hole in the deck.

He was giving Mia further instructions on the pony tank when there was a sudden disturbance in the sinkhole. A great gout of water and air belched up from the submerged exit passage, driving powerful waves in every direction. The soldiers cried out in alarm as a waist-high wall of white water bore down on them and washed right over the stern. The last man in line was swept, howling, into the green water and never reappeared.

'It's coming,' Nash told Mia grimly. 'Be ready.'

By now the cargo net was almost down, and the NCO had his pistol out. He gesticulated at Nash to come forward and take the walkie-talkie.

'It's overflowing the cave!' Sura sounded shrill. 'If you want your friends to live, keep salvaging the opium.' She broke off to shout at someone. 'No, no, take it up to the helicopter. I'll be right behind you. Tell Ricki we're going as soon as I get there.' There was a squawk as she returned her mouth to the receiver. 'Do you understand me, Mr Nash?'

'Yeah, I heard you the first time. Have a safe flight.'

Nash grinned manically at Mia. The parting shot was gratuitous, but he figured they deserved it.

When the cargo net hit the flooding deck, the terrified soldiers fought each other to get inside. Nash turned to retrieve the pony tank when Mia screamed.

'*Rob!*'

The NCO had an arm wrapped around her throat, and was dragging her backwards into the cargo net. His pistol was aimed at Nash's face.

'You stay! You stay!'

Mia reached out in silent dismay through the web of ropes as the net tightened.

Nash watched helplessly as the heavily laden net was hoisted into the air.

Chapter 38

Like a sluice gate opening on a dam, the lake in the Hoosenbeck Cavern overflowed and instantly transformed the river bed into a white-water rapid. Within minutes it had reached the Kopassus camp, almost sweeping away a slow-moving gunship pilot, before recklessly charging on until it smashed headlong into the rocky remains of Martin Heider's dam. Here it slowed, backing up, growing ever deeper as it relentlessly funnelled through to rejoin its underground twin at the resurgence pool and become whole again. But there was one more twist in the Hoosenbeck's annual transmogrification. As volumes increased, and the subterranean system reached maximum capacity, the river rose even further, and just above the Kopassus camp, an offshoot broke free of the riverbanks, racing along a scoured channel to plunge more than a hundred metres into the sinkhole with a bone-shaking roar.

Ignoring the chaos unfolding outside, Boerman worked like a machine, jemmying and hauling the solid, massively heavy lock boxes out of their inverted frames, smashing open their infuriating mechanisms, shaking out their precious contents, then loading the steel bucket with gold bars.

A hand thumped him on the back.

'Fuck off!' he roared. 'Can't you see I'm busy?'

'*Air juga semakin bertambah!*' his terrified assistant screamed. *The water is rising!*

When Boerman got up and stuck his head out of the hole in the hull, he was stunned to see the once-fatal drop had become a pool of white water swirling just ten metres below the gantry.

'Mba Suyanto says you talk now!' the soldier babbled. 'You talk now!'

'OK, OK!' Boerman flung down the crowbar. 'I heard you the first time!' Snatching up the walkie-talkie, he depressed the talk button. 'Sura, where are you?'

'Where do you think?' The radio squawk made her voice sound even more enraged. 'We're about to take off for the *Albany*. Why aren't you doing what I told you? The sinkhole is flooding.'

'But there's thirty kilos to go, *liefie*.'

'Damn it, Jaap, there are 200 kilos sitting up there unattended! Do you want Alatas making off with it?'

Boerman's jaw clenched. 'I'm heading up now.'

'Good. Once Alatas is gone, *kill* Carter and Douglas. Then *stay* with the gold until Ricki returns. *Understood*?'

'And Nash?' Boerman's eyes narrowed. 'Don't forget, you promised me.'

'Two chests of opium is the same as a Maserati. I want Nash loading tea chests into that cargo net until the very last minute, do you hear me? You can kill him just before you leave.'

Jaap beamed with delight. He would start by throwing down Mia Carter's head to him.

'Thank you, *liefie*.'

'Shut up and listen carefully. Once we reach the ship, I will have Saworno head downriver at flank speed. You and Ricki will rendezvous with us on the move, before returning for the remaining opium. When next you reach us, we should be across the border, safe from my father's clutches. Understand?'

'No problem, *liefie*.'

'Don't fuck it up. Out.'

Boerman decided to give Sura a wave from the gantry before he climbed the rope. Sure enough, the Jet Ranger rose over the line of trees and headed his way.

The explosion was savage – a blinding orange fireball which simply blew the chopper apart. One second it was there, the next it was flying chunks of smoking debris. The sound boom rolled over a second later, followed by a hot wave of stinking avgas.

'*Menyelamatkan kita, Allah*,' breathed the soldier beside him.

'*No!*' screamed Boerman. '*No!*' The animal howl of despair came from the deepest depths of his soul. Without Sura, life had no meaning, no value. She was his anchor, his purpose, his future. And she was gone. *Gone!*

The wave of all-encompassing pain gave way to a slow hammer pounding inside his brain. His blood ran cold as capillaries, veins and arteries turned to ice. How could it have happened? The blast . . . it wasn't a petrol explosion. The viciousness of it . . . it had to be a super-fast accelerant. Something like C-4. Or a grenade . . .

Boerman looked down to where Nash was crouching above the deck gun, and then he *knew*.

'Satan strike me dead! Last night at the cave!'

The only thing that could have stopped Jaap Boerman then was a heavy-calibre bullet between the eyes, perhaps two. With a strangled shriek of hate, the Afrikaner charged along the wildly swaying gantry towards the Kopassus trooper. Ripping the man's gun free, he swatted him aside with a backhand that would have stunned a horse. With a howl of terror, the soldier tumbled through the air, legs and arms whaling.

Boerman raised the MP9 to his shoulder and emptied the entire magazine. Bullets sparked off steel, but the infernal Nash was too quick and dived into the milky green water.

'Damn you!'

And then Boerman realised there was a much better way to make Nash pay.

'Come on, move your ass!' Kapten Alatas shouted at his soaked and exhausted men.

Already they had loaded a thousand kilos of gold into the crew compartment of the Mi-24 Hind, and there was still room for more.

'Yes, yes, take it, take it!' he yelled, pointing at what was left of Sura's pile.

If she was stupid enough to leave twelve million US dollars lying about, he had no qualms about relieving her of it, but they needed to expedite before she flew overhead and called up her massive *bule*. Disturbed by the thought, Alatas signalled to the pilot to gun the twin Isotov turbines.

Wedged on a narrow isthmus between the sinkhole and the raging Hoosenbeck, the Hind's enormous rotors quickly whipped up a hurricane, flinging tents and utensils into the sky. Alatas grinned at the sight of the big-titted doctor cowering in the lee of her guard. If not for her weight, which was worth around three million dollars, he would have happily got better acquainted with those beauties, but no matter, delayed gratification in the fleshpots of Bangkok would certainly suffice.

'Come on!' Alatas roared, anxious to be gone.

Battered by the downdraught and spray, his men fought to stow the last of the bullion.

One foot inside the gunship, his gut clenched when Sura's Jet Ranger popped into view overhead. Then it exploded.

Blood drained from the kapten's face. General Suyanto must have launched an attack!

'*Pergi, pergi, pergi!*' Go, go, go! he screamed at the pilot to take off.

They were barely off the ground when rounds starred the ballistic-resistant windscreen. Flinching, Alatas craned around in his seat. He was amazed to see it was old Frank Douglas, staggering in the massive prop wash, an archaic machine gun in his hands.

The kapten was not unduly worried, for the Hind's cockpit was essentially a titanium tub. But then, at point-blank range, Douglas took aim at the stubby underwing pod containing the thirty-two rockets, that were so effective at turning native huts into bark splinters.

'Take off, damn you –'

The huge explosion neatly flipped the Hind onto its back. The mighty rotors fragmented into great scythes, dismembering most of the watching Kopassus troopers in an eye-blink. Then the fuel tank ignited, turning the stricken aerial battle tank into a furious pyre.

A groggy Alatas awoke to find himself paralysed and ablaze. He began to shriek as the flames engulfed his flesh, hissing and spitting. The last thing he saw was an exquisite slender tongue of liquid gold running along the upturned cabin roof before, mercifully, the rest of the Hind's munitions went up in an almighty roar.

Swimming virtually blind beneath the choppy white water, Nash had just exhaled when his rebreather cut out. It was rotten timing, for against the deep rumble of the cataract plunging into the sinkhole, it was impossible to know whether the maddened Afrikaner was still shooting, or awaiting his opportunity. With teeth clenched, Nash cautiously stuck his head above the surface, just in time to see a massive fireball ripping right across the top of the sinkhole. He flinched as a smoking chunk of wreckage spun crazily through the air, before realising it was the remains of the gunship.

'Go, Frank!'

The heady rush of savage ecstasy ended just as abruptly. Frank and Mia were still up there. If they were still alive, how was he going to reach them?

Movement on the sinkhole wall drew his eye. It was Boerman. Climbing up the line of the block and tackle, faster than humanly possible, he looked like an albino gorilla fired up on crystal meth, driven by the much more addictive need for revenge.

With the gantry out of reach, Nash looked around frantically for another way up. The sinkhole lip was still a good fifty metres above him, and there were no ropes reaching down to the water. That only left the submarine.

Swimming hard on the surface against the drag of his gear, he hauled himself up on the rearmost anti-aircraft gun, now just above the waterline. Unharnessing the rebreather, he realised a bullet had shattered the oxygen sensor, and flung it aside.

Above him, the submarine rose at its crazy angle. At least atop the long hangar section there were plenty of handholds.

He had climbed perhaps a dozen metres when an insane roaring, audible even over the crashing waterfall, made him stop and look up.

'*Nash! Nash! Nash!*'

On the crumbling sinkhole edge, mighty arms raised like twin columns, Boerman held Mia's supine body high above his head. At least Nash *thought* it was her body, for when Boerman shook her in his fury, he saw her legs kick as she fought for balance. Nash lurched from desolation to despair. The madman was going to fling her down and dash her to pieces on the logjam, and there was not a single thing he could do beyond reach out in supplication.

But the crazed Afrikaner had other ideas.

'Stay there, you fuck!' he bellowed. 'Stay right where you fucking are!'

Slinging Mia over his shoulders, the big man hooked onto the line, and launched off the lip. Nash prayed Mia wouldn't fall as Boerman braked his descent in a white mist of smoking rope. When they slammed down on the gantry, Nash thought it would break, but it bounced them into the air like a springboard, before swaying violently back and forth.

Boerman untethered from the cable and began dragging a terrified Mia along the gantry. She fought with all her might, but her blows and kicks were like a child's to a raging bull. Then they vanished from sight.

Boerman was taking Mia inside the submarine. But why?

Nash knew Boerman's oxy-cut hole was just twenty metres further along on the starboard side, but there were precious few handholds he could use to reach it. The quickest way in was via the gantry. Climbing fast, Nash had just reached amidships when a furious banging of metal on metal inside the hull stopped him dead. What the fuck was Boerman doing?

Stepping around the remains of the inverted safety rail, Nash used fingers and toes to grip a join in the steel plate, barely clinging on to the near seventy-degree incline as he inched around the curvature of the hull. Somehow, he had to get far enough around to drop down to the gantry, without breaking his legs in the fall. Gritting his teeth, he was close to the point of no return, when he craned his neck down and saw Boerman perhaps five metres below, staring up at him.

'Where is she?' he yelled down.

'I'm going to give you a chance, Nash, which is more than you gave Sura.' The big man was shaking, trying to get a grip on his emotions.

'Let Mia go! You know this has nothing to do with her.'

Boerman's face was grey-white, his blue eyes strangely washed-out like chips of mica.

'You won't admit you're a coward. So, I've set you a challenge to prove it.'

'No games, Jaap . . .'

'I've locked your woman in the forward compartment.'

'You've *what*?'

Boerman gestured at the churning water, which had almost reached the gantry.

'In about ten minutes, she'll be stuck in there for the rest of the wet season.'

'Damn you, Boerman. That's inhuman.'

'Save your energy, Nash. You'll need it.' Boerman turned to go, and then he paused. 'Oh, and just in case you're thinking of hiding down there with that pony tank and waiting for all of this to go away . . . I'll be up here, wiring this old sub to blow.'

Pony tank?

Flushed with adrenaline, Nash had completely forgotten it was hooked to his belt.

'Boerman, wait!'

The Afrikaner gave him a two-fingered salute.

'See you in Hell, Nash.'

Returning to the cable, he hooked on and swiftly began to climb.

Chapter 39

Nash coiled himself and leaped as far as he could, landing right beside the gantry in the churning water. Surfacing with a gasp, he slithered onto the plywood, which was already beginning to float, then made his way to the split in the hull.

Inside, the passage stretched up and away like a dark tube.

'Mia!' he shouted, at the top of his lungs. 'Mia!'

There was no answer.

Nash hesitated. The tube was about to become a deathtrap, full of jagged steel edges and dark corners to trap and pin him. It was as if a switch had been thrown, and abruptly the strength drained from his limbs. His feet felt glued to the platform, which wobbled from side to side.

Only self-loathing propelled him inside. And the water followed like a malevolent presence as he woodenly climbed the passageway. The light dimmed to a flickering green glow as the water pulsed and surged at his heels. The confines of the tube seemed to shrink. His chest began to constrict. All he wanted to do was escape to the light and air . . .

And then he froze.

Clinging to a door frame in abject terror, Nash was tormented by his failure. How could something that was once so easy be so desperately hard? A profound grief choked him. The old Rob Nash wouldn't have hesitated. Where had he lost him?

Of course, he knew. He'd known all along. He'd lost him in the Octopus the day Natalie died.

In that moment of complete despair, Nash finally confronted the obvious truth he had steadfastly *refused* to face through all the soul-searching, the inquest, the trial by media, and the damning look in Jonathan's eye. The awful, shameful and ugly truth that his obsession had cost him everything, because if he had just gone back at the first sign of trouble, his beautiful Natalie and their precious unborn child would still be alive today.

It was his fault.

A great racking sob erupted from the very centre of his being, echoing stark and lonely in the shrinking void of air.

'I'm so sorry, Nat. Forgive me.'

The purging of denial left him momentarily empty, unable to think, respond or act until the super-chilled water cresting the collar of his drysuit made him gasp. The shock of it seemed to galvanise his will and free his paralysed limbs. Turning on his helmet dive lights, Nash realised he was just five metres below the closed bulkhead door. Was he going to let another woman die?

'Mia!' he roared, 'Hold on!'

He climbed with a will, desperate to atone, only to be confronted by the horror of Boerman's vengeance. Where once there was a door handle, only a raw stump of metal remained. The Afrikaner must have pounded it off with a lump hammer.

Again, Nash roared, this time in frustrated anguish. The bulkhead door was totally impossible to open from this side.

Incredibly, there was a muffled return cry.

'Rob, are you there?'

Its source was a small, ragged hole in the bulkhead near floor level. Boerman had also severed a gate valve, designed to give crew trapped underwater a chance of escape under pressure by flooding the compartment. It had been done so Mia would slowly drown.

'Mia,' he called though the hole.

'Rob, where *are* you?'

He directed his dive light carefully through the hole.

'I see you!' she shouted. 'Oh God, help me!'

'Mia, listen – can you open the door?'

'I'm tied to something! I'm trying to get free, but these cable ties are cutting me to pieces.'

Nash pressed his forehead to the cold steel. Even if he found a way to plug the hole and slow the water down, the door would soon be impossible to open. Mia's only hope was to escape via the top bulkhead door, but in order to reach it, she needed to be able to climb.

'Rob? Are you still there?'

Somehow he had to reach the top bulkhead door from the other side and climb down to free her. The only access was via the hole Boerman had cut in the hull, which was twenty metres above their heads, but the Afrikaner knew full well it was his only option, and would simply pick him off.

'Rob, I'm scared. *Don't leave me!*'

'Mia, listen to me. I'm coming to get you from the other side, but you *have* to find a way to get free.'

'I'm fucking tied up,' she sobbed angrily. 'Didn't you hear me?'

'When the water comes in, stay with the air, all the way to the top. Breathe to the very last lungful, do you hear me? And then hold your breath for as long as you can. Because I might have to let the pressure equalise before I can open the door.'

Nash's ears popped as air was squeezed into the end of the compartment by the rising water. It was close now, gurgling and hissing, finding its way into every crack and crevice.

'Rob, I can't get free!' she shrieked. 'Just shut up and say goodbye!'

The insistent water was sloshing around Nash's neck. He was choking with grief and impotent rage, but he knew that if she was to have any chance, he had to stay calm, right to the very end.

'Mia, you're going to get free and I will see you at the top. One more thing . . . Do *Not* try and open this door or the water will crush you – do you understand? You have to go up. You can do it. I know you can.'

'Rob –'

With a glug, the hole went under. Nash thought he heard a shout of terror as the first spout of water jetted into her compartment. The thought of Mia trapped in there by a couple of cheap fucking cable ties was driving him mad, and an involuntary sob racked him as he cut off the sleeve of his drysuit and wedged it into the hole to try and buy her a few more minutes.

He reassured himself the pony tank was still attached to his weight belt. Its miserable 540 litres of compressed air would have to save both their lives now.

With water now swirling about his ears, Nash pressed his pursed lips against the rough bulkhead to suck in every last precious lungful of air. Then, with a silent goodbye to Mia, he flipped over and pushed back down the flooded passageway. Hand over hand, he dragged himself down, kicking his feet in a steady swimmer's beat.

Swimming clear of the submarine, he encountered a milky green fizz which blocked any clear indication of the surface. But it no longer mattered, for Rob Nash was not going there.

His plan was not really a plan – rather, speculative ambition. In fact, the only thing that exonerated it from the realm of the suicidal was the belief that survival was theoretically possible, as opposed to certain death at the hands of a professional killer above.

Unclipping the pony tank, Nash slid its regulator into his mouth. At his current depth of fifty-four metres, one cautious breath consumed ninety litres, or one-sixth of his air supply. Instantly, his lungs began to burn, and he had to clamp down on a coughing fit. While the compressed air he was breathing was proportionally identical to its surface composition, its partial pressure had increased, meaning the percentage of gas he was absorbing had increased to dangerous levels. Not only was the nitrogen hit on his nervous system equivalent to consuming seven full-strength beers; the concentrated oxygen searing his alveoli was a precursor to a convulsion. His precious air supply was now a toxic soup.

It was now that he caught his first blurry sight of the exit passage – a black maw, swallowing driftwood and other debris. He had a scant second to register that the ledge from which he'd free-dived had been swept clean of rocks before the incredible power of the Hoosenbeck swallowed him, too.

It was a giant water slide – a moment of negative *g*, followed by sickening acceleration. Nash clutched the pony tank to his chest and curled into the tiniest ball he was capable of forming. Such was the velocity of his descent, he thought he was about to be dashed into the floor of the passage. A second later, he was hurled upwards, in an out-of-control fun park ride, somersaulting end over end.

Teeth clamped around the regulator, he breathed again. The stubborn drag told him the pony was nearly spent. He almost lost it when a violent surge sent him spinning sideways. For a moment, his legs were extended, and he snatched them back in as the wall of the passage grazed his foot.

He knew the passage had widened into a great chamber, for his speed and rate of spin decreased. Nash tentatively opened his eyes to a black nothing. His head torch was gone. So, too, his mask. Tumbling slowly end over end, he felt like an astronaut, untethered from his spaceship, drifting deeper into space. Somehow the Beatles' 'Tomorrow Never Knows' began playing on some synaptic sitar. Oxygen toxicity? In the icy water, he could only surrender to the void like an embryo floating in a vast stone womb.

He began to accelerate again, and a sudden series of S-bends flung him all out of shape. Legs akimbo, desperately clutching the cylinder, he sucked in a last puff of air and the pony was dead. Releasing it, he heard a savage clank as it impacted the invisible rocks hurtling past. The incredible speed was unrelenting, a limestone sleigh ride from Hell which went on and on . . .

He was becoming hypoxic. Lungs burning, his diaphragm went into involuntary contractions as the carbon dioxide build-up demanded autonomic respiration. His whole body, every last cell, was ablaze . . .

And then, suddenly, the pain vanished. Was replaced by pure elation. And, in its thrall, Natalie came to share the penultimate moment with him. His Natalie, with that mysterious smile, her peach-curve chin, her beautiful smell of frangipani and coconut cream. He felt her soft hands stroking his face, and in that loving embrace, he understood she now forgave him everything, and he was so joyful, because now at last he could surrender. Now he could let go and just *breathe* . . .

'Robert . . . Robert . . . *Robert!*'

He froze, as she shook him violently.

Nash blinked in surprise. Natalie was demanding that he live. She was turning away, ascending into the light, and all he could do was follow . . .

Where once he had erupted from the Sepik like a creature spawned in Hell, this time he was reborn. Risen to the surface of the Hoosenbeck in a boil of green-white water.

Oh God, how that first breath hurt. Exquisite agony. And then, the deep sucking gasps, the sounds of air, of white water, of rain and birds calling.

Nash slowly side-crabbed towards the bank. Weak and exhausted, he grasped hold of some reeds and pulled himself out. It took him a moment to recognise where he was, for the water levels had changed so dramatically. It was the resurgence pool, two kilometres downstream of the sinkhole.

And then he remembered Mia.

Tearing off his drysuit, he began to run.

405

Chapter 40

Nash was half-drowned, half-naked and barefoot, but he ran the bank of the flooding Hoosenbeck as if in training for an Olympic 1500 metres on a rubberised track. He vaulted rotting logs and ankle-breaking boulders, scrambled over slippery ledges, ploughed unthinkingly through thick kunai grass. A large green python barely had time to rear, as he sailed over it. When his T-shirt snagged a vicious hooked vine it ripped it open, leaving three bloody lines down his chest.

With the roar of the waterfall plunging into the sinkhole growing louder, Nash forced himself to slow down as he pushed through fringing vegetation. He was desperate to get to Mia, but somewhere Jaap Boerman was waiting.

Creeping through a thicket of waist-high ferns, Nash's eyes widened at the sight of the tattered remnants of the Kopassus camp, now wedged on a tongue of land between the sinkhole – now three quarters full – and the fast-running Hoosenbeck. The wreckage of the burned-out gunship lay like the crumpled remains of a cremated whale amid a carnage of charred and scattered bodies.

It was impossible to tell which one was Frank Douglas.

Nash forced his grief back down, determined that his sacrifice would not be in vain.

Cautiously he made his way through the camp, eyes peeled for movement. Not a tent was left standing, but Sura's whiteboard and chairs were bizarrely standing intact, and the generator was still powering the arc lights, which had fallen into the mud. It was then that Nash trod on something in the mud. It was a small mattock the soldiers had been using to chop rough storm-water channels away from the waterlogged camp. Not much of a weapon, but better than nothing.

Near the block and tackle, Nash spotted a bright yellow roll of detonator cord, suspended on a tent pole spool lashed between two chair legs driven into the ground. A line of det cord snaked along the ground before plunging over the sink-hole edge.

A chill passed through him. True to his word, Boerman was wiring the sub.

Nash cautiously approached the edge and peered down through the tattered foliage. He was horrified to see the water had almost reached the access hole in the submarine. Once it poured inside, the section above Mia's compartment would rapidly fill, and any chance of rescue would be dashed. The line of yellow det cord also ran down through the hole. Nash placed a hand on the block and tackle. It was quivering, the thin cable under immense strain.

Partially obscured by the overhang, swaying twenty metres above the jumbled log pile, Boerman was using a jumar to haul himself up. The big man was moving slowly. Perhaps fatigue had finally set in, or maybe he thought the fight was over.

Some instinct made him look up, and his blue eyes widened in shocked disbelief. It was obvious what the Afrikaner's next move had to be. The det cord was in front of his face, and one shot at close range from his pistol would blow them all to Hell!

With a cry of rage, Nash slammed the mattock down hard on the cable where it lay taut on the steel frame.

Boerman had just freed his pistol when the cable severed. Nash was staring into his eyes when the big man plunged. Fear, dismay and regret, perhaps for thwarted revenge, crossed his face in that split second. For one dreadful moment, it seemed the Afrikaner's obscene luck would not desert him, for he fell neatly through the tightly packed log jam. But then, right on the waterline, he struck a partially submerged log with an awful *thwack*. Perhaps fate was determined to make sure of it, for a remnant branch punched up through his chest to transfix him like a vampire.

There was no time to organise a rope. Still clutching the mattock, Nash sprinted back around the sinkhole towards the cargo net winch, which offered the fastest route to the water.

Without hesitation, he launched over the edge. Plummeting thirty sickening metres through the log pile, he slammed into the water with a great stinging crack which numbed both feet. Regaining the surface, he swam through the chop, negotiating the additional hazard of shifting logs as the lower parts of the jam became buoyant.

Water was pouring over the edge of the access hole. Sliding over the jagged lip, Nash reversed position to drop into the churning pool below. In a couple of strokes, he crossed the inverted passageway, and climbed up to the floor hatch, which appeared as a darkened window. The infernal line of yellow det cord marked Boerman's route to the torpedo room. Had he also found time to sabotage the forward bulkhead door on the lower deck?

Hauling himself inside the inverted floor hatch, Nash clung on to the horizontal ladder and lowered himself down. His feet didn't quite reach the bulkhead, so he dropped the last half metre.

The bulkhead door was closed, but its circular handle was intact!

'Mia!' he bellowed, desperately hoping she was alive to hear him. 'Hang on!'

Dropping to his knees, he tried shifting the handle. Boerman had opened this door and later closed it, but try as Nash might, it would not budge.

Nash tried loosening the friction by banging around the handle with the head of the mattock. There was no time to listen for an answering sound. At any moment, the water following the route he had just taken was going to pour in from above.

Locking his hands on either side of the handle, Nash centred his entire being on turning it. He drew upon every reserve of strength left in his body, and the flesh of his palms burned and tore as, shouting out to God, the universe, even Natalie, from somewhere the power came . . .

It gave!

Frantically, Nash spun the stubborn wheel.

He barely had time to whip his head back as the massive bulkhead door flew up in his face, its steel edge missing him by inches, as a belch of tightly compressed air blasted up through the hole, dragging a column of churning white water and Mia Carter in its wake.

In the near-darkness he only just managed to grab hold of her before she fell back through with the gout of expelled water.

Mia was a dead weight and, clutching her limp body, he feared that he was too late, but then she jerked in his arms.

'Hang in there!' he yelled, turning her on her side to let her vomit.

She had just begun to suck in air when water began pouring down upon their heads. The top compartment was overflowing!

'We gotta go!'

Hauling Mia upright, Nash leaned her against the wall, which was really the floor. Then he jumped up to grab the horizontal ladder, locked his legs under her arms and, with a roar, lifted her up.

'Grab the ledge!' he screamed. 'Come on, Mia!'

With a sob, she flung out an arm, and then another, and hung there by her armpits. Dropping down, he seized her lower legs and pushed her up and over with a splash into the top compartment. Here she waited for him, half-drowned, and half-blinded by the light streaming in through the upper third of the access hole.

'Almost there.'

Taking her under the shoulders, he pulled her through the hull and out to freedom.

Holding Mia in open water with the sky overhead and the rain at last abating, Nash could have been forgiven for thinking the worst was over. But escaping the dark clutches of the submarine was only a momentary respite.

'Rob, I'm hypothermic,' she slurred, barely audible over the din of the waterfall. 'I've got to get warm.'

She was indeed desperately cold, with pale skin and a worrying bluish tinge to her lips. It would take at least a couple of hours for the sinkhole to fill to the brim, and there were no ropes, even had they the strength to climb them.

Swimming Mia around the hull, Nash dragged her up on the nose of the hangar door. It was here that he discovered the state of Mia's wrists. Deep cuts and lacerations showed where she had rubbed away cable ties and flesh on the rusting metal.

He hugged her close to share his body heat, and tore strips off the sleeves of her shirt to bind the wounds on her wrists. Clinging together, they watched the waterfall tumble into the sinkhole.

Mia put her chilled lips against his.

'I thought I was dead.' She stared into his eyes. 'When you grabbed me, I was gone.'

He kissed her several times. 'I've got you now and I'm not letting go.'

He felt her stiffen. 'Boerman . . .?'

'Will never hurt you again.'

She nestled in more tightly before looking up at him again.

'I'm sorry about Frank.' Nash listened to her account of his final moments. Seeing the pain in his eyes, she pushed her frozen cheek against his. 'He really loved you.'

'I know.'

The water was now lapping their feet, and Nash pulled Mia to her feet.

'We've got to keep moving.'

For the next hour they kept ahead of the fast-rising water, making their way along the steeply sloping catapult ramp, until they were standing on the very nose of the I-403. Although the exertion had temporarily warmed Mia, it would still be a long while until the sinkhole filled, and now there was a greater threat. In the swirling water, the log jam had become a deadly unstable mass of shifting tonnage.

'What are we going to do?' Mia asked fearfully, as one of the massive logs thudded against the hull, rolled over and slid under another. 'We'll be crushed.'

A voice echoing down made them flinch.

'*You mekim wanem*?' What are you doing?

Above them, a young Papuan man was clinging onto the edge of the block and tackle. He was dressed in old khaki trousers, a grubby blue T-shirt and a bandana, and his expression was somewhere between fear and curiosity.

'*Indonesian soldia putim hia*!' Mia yelled, miming the act of shooting. She then interlaced her fingers and held her hands up. '*Plis helpim*!'

The Papuan was joined by an older bearded man in a Free Papua T-shirt, with an AK-47 slung over his shoulder. They conferred for a moment before the older man bellowed '*Husat*?'

'*Dokta Mia Carter, America.*' Mia put her hand on Nash's shoulder. '*Dispela hia Rob Nash, Aussie.*'

'*Yu wok Ford Misin*?'

'Yes!'

Another giant log crashed against the submarine and rolled in the grinding chop. Mia pointed to the suspended cargo net on the other side of the sinkhole.

'*Plis move hia and pullim ap*!'

As the men fanned out along the sinkhole edge, Nash counted at least ten of them, armed with a hotch-potch of rifles and shotguns.

413

'They're OPM,' Mia confirmed.

'By the time they set it up over here, we'll be paste,' he told her.

'What are we going to do?'

'Run!'

Taking Mia by the hand, Nash stepped onto a log facing that direction, a twenty-metre giant with a remnant canopy still locking it to the western edge of the pile. Although a good metre wide, it was slippery as hell and they ran in awkward baby steps to maintain balance.

'Keep going!' roared Nash as he saw the next route opening in the shifting pile.

Without hesitating, they leapt across a rapidly closing pocket of water to another log, a scant moment before the great lengths of timber came together with a jarring shudder, driving the first under and rolling theirs. Nash's bare feet skidded, and for a heart-stopping moment it seemed as if they would fall into the giant mangle, until Mia's counterweight brought them back from the brink.

The men above were rapidly lowering the cargo net, and it was almost down.

'We're out of options!' Nash yelled as they approached the end of the log.

Before them lay an open patch of water, not much larger than a suburban swimming pool.

In one motion he used their momentum to propel Mia forwards, one hand in the small of her back, and then dived in after her.

By the time they'd swum half a dozen strokes, the net was down, and they swam inside.

'Go, go, go!' yelled Nash, as two great logs began swinging back like oversized clappers.

The net had just cleared the surface when the behemoths came together. Nash felt the enormous mass of the impact miss his dangling right foot by inches. Mia cried out and he thought the worst, but it was just the net pinching the flesh of her thighs.

They rose swiftly, swaying from side to side, and Nash prayed they wouldn't drop back into the blender below. Then strong arms swung the net over the lip, and they were pulled to their feet and given hearty handshakes and back-slaps by the mob of excited men.

Their leader was the bearded man they had seen from below. With intense bulging eyes, and an impressive pink scar down the side of his face, he introduced himself as Donte Babo, an independent OPM commander operating in the areas around the mission. He explained that Indonesian air activity and the need for payback had drawn them up the Hoosenbeck Gorge, a place they usually avoided.

'Why is that?' Nash asked.

'*Nogut magik hia. Dewel bilong men I dai.*'

Mia translated. 'He's says it's bad magic, that the ghosts of dead men live here.'

And now Douglas had joined them. But there was no time to bury him, even if they were able to identify his corpse among the many.

'Tell Babo we need to get out of here before more soldiers come,' said Nash. 'By now they will know something is wrong.'

Babo was distracted by an excited jabber of raised voices. It seemed the OPM men had just discovered the golden Hind.

Nash and Mia stood by watching while they celebrated. About a third of the bullion had pooled in the fury of the immolation, but many bars were available to pick up, and the men were beside themselves. A delighted Babo explained that now they would be able to buy powerful weapons to fight the Indonesians.

Mia clasped her hands together. '*Plis helpim sik tu. Ol needim.*'

'*Of kos!*' Babo agreed. '*Plis, yu bringim tu.*'

Magnanimously, he offered them several bars with a wide gap-toothed grin.

But Nash's sharp eyes were on two fast-moving dots coming up the gorge.

'*Helikoptas,*' he barked. '*Hide!*'

With the Hoosenbeck raging at their backs, the closest available cover was the belt of living trees in the lee of the southern wall of the gorge. A giant fig at the very base of the cliff seemed to offer the best protection and, along with most of the OPM men, Nash and Mia made a dash for it through a waist-high carpet of ferns. The fig's huge and twisted trunk was like a four-storey building, supporting a scaffold of massive grey branches which spread the majestic green canopy above them. Throwing themselves down between thick buttress roots, they cautiously looked back.

The lead machine was a large olive-green Bell 412 transport, with a red and white insignia on its nose. As it banked in a tight curve over the sinkhole, Nash felt his skin crawl, for stencilled on its flank in prominent white letters was the name *General W. Suyanto*. The second helicopter was another Mil-24 Hind gunship, and it opened fire immediately.

The violence of its Gatling gun was tremendous. Several OPM men weighed down with too much booty were cut to pieces. From the other side of the fig tree, Babo bravely stood up and opened fire with his AK-47, but the Hind was indifferent to the rounds sparking off its flanks. Meanwhile, General Suyanto's Bell hovered just above the old camp, apparently enjoying the show.

'Evil bastard,' growled Nash, wishing they had the weapons to fight back.

The Hind targeted a small group of OPM men crouched behind a sizeable tree further downslope. Unable to puncture the trunk, the pilot unleashed a salvo of hissing rockets, which brought the whole tree crashing down in an orange ball of flame.

As the shrill screams of the dying filled the air, Nash knew they would be next. And while the thick buttressed roots of the fig might offer some protection from bullets, it would not protect them from high explosive.

High explosive – but didn't they have their own?

Crouched beside them was the teenager who had first spotted them, shivering in fear, his old Lee–Enfield forgotten. Nash snatched it up and worked the bolt.

'Get down!' he screamed at the top of his lungs. 'Everybody, get down!'

Unceremoniously, he rested his knee in the small of Mia's back to keep her there.

It was Uncle Frank who'd taught Nash how to shoot – out on the Douglas family's station near Mukinbudin – with an old .303 Lee–Enfield that left his shoulder black and blue, knocking out bottles, cans and, once, a feral piglet, which he'd felt bad about.

Nash took a bead on the bright yellow roll of det cord. He knew pentaerythritol tetranitrate exploded, rather than burned, at unbelievable speeds of more than 6500 metres per second.

'This one's for you, Frank.'

As the Hind turned towards them, Nash squeezed the trigger.

The detonation was instantaneous – a ball of brilliant light, followed a millisecond later by an all-encompassing deep *whump* that sucked the air right out of his lungs. The ground seemed to contract, then expand. Above them, giant branches flexed like sap wood and snapped. Nash pulled Mia to him as the debris began to fall, a maelstrom of steel and rock, and half a million cubic metres of displaced water. Huge weights of ragged steel whizzed through the air like a meteor shower. Rocks the size of basketballs peppered the ground like hail. Bludgeoned and severed branches began to crash down on top of them. A half-tonne lump of stone shook the ground five metres away. A branch the size of a tree fell directly across them, but the mighty buttress roots took the impact.

When things finally stopped falling, a thin, high-pitched whine continued to drill inside Nash's head. Mia clasped her hands around the side of his face and yelled 'Are you all right?'

To his great relief, he could still hear her.

Crawling on hands and knees, they extricated themselves from the shattered remains of the fig and emerged into an alien landscape. For half a kilometre, not a tree or shrub remained unscathed. It had been – in Boerman's parlance – erased.

What was left of the *I-403* now dotted the landscape for as far as the eye could see. Most were fragments, no bigger than a toaster,

418

although embedded above their heads in the severed trunk of the mighty fig was the mangled remains of an anti-aircraft cannon.

Nash was stunned to see the force of the explosion had ejected three quarters of the water in the sinkhole, and enlarged it by a third as the sides caved in.

'Do you see how fast it's filling back up?' Nash marvelled at the Hoosenbeck overflow pouring unabated into the expanded sinkhole. 'The explosion must have sealed off the exit passage.'

One by one, the surviving OPM men appeared, looking shocked, stunned and relieved. Babo came over to Nash and embraced him.

'*Tenkyu*,' he said gravely. '*Man bilong pait.*'

'He says you belong in a fight.'

'*Tenkyu.*' Nash smiled. 'Please tell him I would like to try and find my friend.'

They searched for half an hour, and although they checked numerous body parts, there was no sign of Douglas. The only object relatively unscathed was the melted mass of gold bullion, flung several metres from its original position. Nash was about to give up, when he spotted something small and white, gleaming in the mud.

'Don't tell me that's his teeth!'

Mia screwed up her face as Nash slid them into her top pocket.

'They're not going on the mantelpiece,' he chided her. 'There's this place in North Queensland called Wonga Beach – white sand, fishing shacks and long lazy days. I think it's just the place to buy Uncle Frank his last beer.'

Epilogue

Four Seasons Hotel, Singapore

Even though the night air was soft and sultry, Mia Carter still hadn't quite thawed out. Safe and sound, feet up on the balcony rail of their suite, it was hard to believe that a week ago she'd been drowning in a steel tomb – that her life might have ended there, instead of beginning anew with this man, Rob Nash, whose strong hand rested intimately on her thigh.

Helped by OPM, they had walked for a week, evading Indonesian patrols and aircraft, before making it across the PNG border where, to their amazement, a party of Australian journalists had found them. It seemed Saworno had got out by boat and raised the alarm. This had expedited their immediate evacuation from PNG, with no backlash from Sir Julius Michaels, who was destined for Bomona jail. It also meant the 9.8-kilogram chunk of melted gold bullion, their farewell present from Donte Babo, was safely being accommodated in the hotel safe.

Of course, her joy at being alive was tempered by loss. So many good people had died, and although there were other hospital missions in Papua, the US ambassador was adamant that Mia should never set foot on Indonesian soil again.

At the thought of that lonely stone marker among the oak trees, she felt a lump in her throat. Rest in peace, Paul.

Whatever the truth really was, I will always remember the good you did and the kindness you showed me.

Sitting beside Mia, Nash sensed she was re-evaluating where she was in the world.

So was he.

Rob Nash was not a religious or superstitious man, but no one would ever persuade him that Natalie had not come and saved his life that day under the Hoosenbeck. She had forgiven him. Now he was going to write a true account of the accident and publish it in the national cave diving journal. He was going to ring Brendan and explain. And he was going to take Jacquie and his parents on a holiday to Wonga Beach, and properly bury what was left of old Frank Douglas.

And he was going to go cave diving again.

Staring out at the glittering skyscrapers, Nash felt a moment of regret. That vast hidden passage, blocked by countless tons of rock, was gone, and with it the mysteries of the Hoosenbeck system. But who was he to begrudge anything? In its stone innards, he had been made whole again. He had found himself, and he had found Mia.

Nash brought her hand to his lips and kissed it.

'What now?'

Acknowledgements

I am indebted to John Vanderleest of the Australian Cave Diving Association for his invaluable technical advice and generous feedback. Any errors and omissions are mine. Thanks also to big wave surfer, Damon Eastaugh, for his insights on the Cow Bombie. I would also like to thank Simon Mann, Tor Larsen, Geoff Martin, Michael Potts and Tom Davies for their unstinting belief and support on the journey, and of course my family, in particular my wife, Cathy, my father, Ian, and my sister-in-law, Pip Austin.

I would also like to acknowledge and thank *The Wilbur and Niso Smith Foundation* for the opportunity it afforded me, David Llewellyn for his incisive manuscript development, my editor, Claire Johnson-Creek for her perceptive insights, my agent, Charlotte Colwill, for her care and guidance, and last but not least, the people of the island of New Guinea, who I hope will forgive any liberties taken in my imaginings.

THE WILBUR &
NISO SMITH
FOUNDATION

The Wilbur Smith Adventure Writing Prize supports and celebrates the best aspiring and established adventure writers today. Writers are recognised in three distinct categories with awards for published, unpublished and young writers.

Cave Diver by Jake Avila won the Wilbur Smith Adventure Writing Prize, Best Unpublished Manuscript award in 2020.

Launched in 2016, the Prize is administered by The Wilbur & Niso Smith Foundation, a charitable organisation dedicated to empowering writers, promoting literacy and advancing adventure writing.

Find out more at www.wilbur-niso-smithfoundation.org.